The

Gathering

Storm

John Righten

My thanks to Kate, Jules, and Jacky for translating my scribblings into the Queen's English.
To the Rogues we lost along the way.
Tom, 'The Colonel'
1935 to 2014
To my son, Logan, born to my wife, Kate, who has made my life complete.

This is a work of fiction. Any resemblance to actual events or persons, living or dead, is entirely coincidental.

This book contains strong adult content.

The 1930s epic: The Rogues Trilogy

Churchill's Rogue, The Gathering Storm & *The Darkest Hour*

The 1960s thriller: The Lochran Trilogy

Churchill's Assassin, The Last Rogue & *The Alpha Wolves*

The 1990s odyssey: The Lenka Trilogy

Heartbreak, Resilience & *Reflection*
&
The Benevolence of Rogues & *The 'Pane' of Rejection*

For the latest updates on all my novels go to
https://www.rightensrogues.co.uk
 facebook.com/theroguestrilogy
Instagram rightensrogues

John Righten, real name John Enright, has delivered medical aid to orphanages and hospitals across the globe, including Romania during the revolution, South America and Bosnia during the war. His Rogues novels are based on the characters he encountered during his many dangerous missions, when he enlisted unlikely support from those he terms 'benevolent rogues'. John has worked in over forty occupations, ranging from a gravedigger, a cocktail barman, and a tree-surgeon, to a professional poker player, and government "Transactor". He has ridden a British Army motorbike across India to support several children's charities and worked in a mental health facility in Manhattan. He is married to Kate and has two sons, Logan and James.

Along with his autobiography and a play, John has written three trilogies: The 1930s based epic adventures, The Rogues Trilogy; the 1960s thrillers, The Lochran Trilogy; and the 1990s odyssey, The Lenka Trilogy.

Churchill's Rogue was shortlisted for the inaugural Wilbur Smith Adventure Writing awards. *Heartbreak* won the Page Turner Audio Award.

Prologue

The first novel in The Rogues Trilogy, *Churchill's Rogue,* begins in December 1937 in Chartwell, Winston Churchill's country home. Sean Ryan, an ex-Irish Republican fighter, but one of those present when the Irish Treaty was signed – bringing the war for him to a close – has been summoned by Winston Churchill. Churchill is fighting a lone battle with enemies on all sides in Parliament, due to his passionate speeches warning of the Nazis threat. The Irishman's recent clashes with Italian fascists in Ethiopia brought him to the attention of Churchill's sources. Churchill asks for his help in rescuing a woman and her son who have escaped their Nazi interrogators. Though distrustful of his former adversary, Sean agrees to help. The same day, Churchill asks Lieutenant Amelia Brett, from Naval Intelligence, if she would 'volunteer' to be the liaison between the men. She agrees. Later, Lord Sloane, a rich and powerful British aristocrat and junior minister in the Admiralty, meets Churchill and makes it clear that the government opposes his plan.

In the Black Forest, Major Klaus Krak, known to his enemies - he has no friends – as Cerberus, and his bodyguard, Grossmann, execute General Vaux of the Wehrmacht. This is the beginning of The Night of the Long Knives, as the Nazis ruthlessly purge all opposition.

Sean is given a contact in Hungary, an anxious young man called Paul Budakov. He tells Sean that the family he has been sent to help, Magdalena and her son, Tóth, are at Budapest's main station. The SS lie in wait, but Sean helps the family escape. On their journey, he learns that the woman lost her sight when she was tortured by the SS. This adds to Sean's suspicions. Why would a great statesman like Churchill ask for help from a former enemy? Why does he want to help a young woman and her son who he claims he has never met? How did the woman, now blind, and her son escape so easily from their interrogators? And why did the Nazis go to the trouble of having snipers positioned to assassinate such an easy target at the train station?

At the same time, an international band of men and women are fighting for the Republic in the Spanish Civil War. The unofficial leader of the unit, known as the 'Rogues', is Lenka, a young Polish Jewish woman. Her best friend, Jewel, a terribly scarred Australian nurse, is hailed in the international press as an 'angel on the battlefield' for her courage in treating the wounded from both sides. As a result, she has unwittingly become a symbol of the Republican cause, and Lenka learns that a unit of Moroccan mercenaries has been sent to kill her. Lenka orders her two best fighters, Vodanski, an exile from the Red Army, and Jake, an American adventurer, to bury their mutual hostility and join forces to protect Jewel. Chris, a young man from Edinburgh, arrives in Madrid to find his sister who has volunteered as a nurse and he joins the Rogues while he continues his search. He and Jewel fall in love. By late 1938, the Rogues are targeted by the Moscow controlled communist army and, along with their former Socialist and Anarchist allies, are denounced as fascist collaborators. Knowing the war is lost as the Republic has turned on itself, Lenka leaves Madrid and escorts an exodus of children fleeing Spain. Jake and Vodanski join her, but Jewel and Chris decide to stay to treat those in her makeshift hospital. After leading the caravan of children over the Pyrénées to safety in France, the three Rogues decide it is time to return to their homes. All know that war is not far away.

In Moscow, Vodanski discovers his wife and child have been sent to a gulag as punishment for his 'crimes against the State'. Lenka returns to the orphanage where she was raised in Krakow, to learn that German raiders have taken the staff as prisoners. Jake heads back to America, to help secure entry for refugees into the States. He is a marked man in the eyes of J. Edgar Hoover for fighting for the Republic.

Lenka contacts London to warn them of the Nazis' incursions into Poland. Her pleas for help to get her children to safety reach Churchill – one of the many great and good she has written to since she was a child. Amelia sends a message to Lenka to inform her that an Irishman who may be able to help has arrived in Vienna.

In Vienna, Sean hands over Marianna and Tóth to a contact from the British Embassy to take them on the next stage of their journey to England. Lenka arrives, and he agrees to help her transport the children, who are mentally and physically disabled, from the orphanage through Germany and then to England. When they arrive in Krakow, Sean armour plates the orphanage's dilapidated bus, and they set off over the mountains to cross into Germany. After various encounters with the SS, on motorbikes and on skis, and traversing 'Snipers' alley', they cross the border and finally reach Berlin. There, they arrange for the children to be transported by train to the Hook of Holland to a waiting ferry organised by Churchill to get them to England. In Berlin, in an illegal underground bier keller, they are united with Jake, Vodanski, and Chris and Jewel now that the Nationalists control Spain. Amelia arrives with Jocky, a 'technical expert' from Glasgow. For the first time, all the Rogues gather together. But they are betrayed. The Gestapo enter the bar and there is only one way out. The Rogues escape, but Jewel is killed. This is only the beginning of their battles against Cerberus' Alpha Wolves, his newly established army of elite torturers and executioners.

Having made their way to the station and with the children on board the train, Sean learns that Magdalena and Tóth have been captured. They are now captive on Cerberus' train on the other side of the city and about to depart for Himmler's 'specially adapted' Fortress. Sean races across Berlin to save them. After boarding Cerberus' moving train, Sean has a fierce fight with Grossmann, and they topple from the train. Though severely injured, Sean crawls through the forest and reaches a ridge to see that the train has already entered the Fortress. Plumes of smoke begin to rise from the castle's retrofitted chimney. The book closes with Sean's grey-green eyes having turned glacial blue – an anomaly that results when he is consumed by rage – fixed on the Swastika flag flying proudly in the night sky, unfurled by the plume from the furnace.

As the trilogy unfolds, we learn of the origins of the Rogues and why they became the men and women who defied even their own governments to protect those who would fall victim to the Nazis. In *Churchill's Rogue*, we read of the stories of Sean, Jewel and Vodanski and what made them who they are. We see for the first time the young Sean's eyes turn glacial blue, when he is forced to watch his family murdered in front of him by the British. We learn too, of the tensions between the Rogues - the Russian and the American, and Sean and Jocky – that reflect the different ideologies and cultures of their countries, but also of that between Lenka and Amelia, which is strictly personal.

'You see these dictators on their pedestals, surrounded by the bayonets of their soldiers and the truncheons of their police. On all sides they are guarded by masses of armed men, cannons, aeroplanes, fortifications, and the like – they boast and vaunt themselves before the world, yet in their hearts there is an unspoken fear. They are afraid of words and thoughts; words spoken abroad, thoughts stirring at home – all the more powerful because forbidden – terrify them.'

Winston Churchill, British & US radio broadcast

16th October 1938

Chapter 1: The Lady

July 1938, New York

New York was unbearably hot in July, so the breeze from the river and the cool surface of the plastered walls of the newly constructed building provided a welcome respite to the tall, blonde, wounded American. Jake wiped the sweat from his forehead and looked at his bloodied palm. There had been three attempts on his life in as many days. His hair, face and clothes were caked in so much blood that it was hard to discern which wound it had come from, or whether it was his or from those sent to kill him.

Eighty metres down the slope, in the undergrowth, sat Samuel Clark. Until that day he had peace, having made the farthest corner of Fort Tryon Park his sanctuary for nearly twenty years. From here, the war veteran could look down on the Manhattan skyline and gaze at 'The Lady' in the moonlight. She was beautiful; looks deceive, as he had learnt too many times, but not her.

Ten minutes earlier, when he had first heard the men in the distance cocking their submachine guns, he had moved to the densest part of the wood. He remained undetected as the silhouettes of men and machine guns passed metres in front of him. Samuel knew they were stalking the tall, powerfully built, but injured man who had broken into the building at the top of the hill the night before.

Jake's forehead was bleeding from the first assassination attempt at Grand Central Station. Blood seeped from the wound on his thigh, left by the bullet he had removed after the second attempt to kill him as he slept in Central Park. The clattering of submachine gun fire and exploding windows had partially deafened him, but that was yesterday. Though he could not see them, he heard the snapping of sun-dried twigs beneath the assassins' boots as they made their approach through the undergrowth. This would be the fourth attempt on his life in as many days.

Last night he made his way to the north side of Upper Manhattan. If his luck was finally to run out today, at least no more innocent New Yorkers would die. One elderly woman and a police officer were caught in the submachine gun fire that sprayed the plate-glass windows of the East River deli as he sat drinking his tenth coffee.

He remembered this place from his childhood. It was the only place on the island of Manhattan that he could think of that might be deserted. But to his surprise he discovered that a museum had been built, the Cloisters, which, according to the wooden sign by the entrance, would house rare medieval artefacts from New York's Grand Metropolitan Museum. The building was in a transitional phase; the edifice had been erected and secured, but it was empty of contents and there were neither tourists nor security guards. Jake stared out into the surrounding forest. The only ones to die tonight would be those who deserved it – and in those, he included himself.

Earlier, Jake had carried out a reconnaissance of the perimeter. This time he had picked the ground for the next encounter. A ring of sturdy metal fencing encircled the construction site. The only way for a vehicle to enter was through the galvanised iron gates. There had been two access roads, each a temporary construction, comprising of eight forty-foot-long steel sheets bolted together. But with the building complete, one of the roads was being dismantled. All that remained of it was one precariously balanced metal sheet, its base resting on temporary earthworks weighed down by sandbags while the other end extended over a twenty-foot drop into a ravine.

The American met the first intruder who reached the highest point of the scaffolding with a US marine Smith & Wesson knuckle-duster knife to the jugular. This was an extra the 'Chinaman' in Brooklyn had thrown in with the arsenal of weapons that Jake had requested. He did not appreciate how rare a gift it was, as it would not be distributed to the US Army for another year. The big American had smiled, as the man in the cramped basement in Chinatown reminded him of Jocky – if his friend wore a purple and yellow satin robe and grew a ponytail, he could easily be a distant relative.

Captain Calvera, formerly a lieutenant in Mussolini's fascist militia, the Blackshirts, made his way gingerly along the path around the recently constructed fortress. Scanning the terrain, he rotated his Thompson submachine gun in a semi-circular motion as he made his way forward. He disliked the *crudity* of submachine guns, as any fool could kill with one. In the victorious Second Italo–Abyssinian War of 1935, and more recently in the murders he had carried out in Italy, Switzerland and France, he had used the Beretta and the Modello rifle, *subtle* weapons which suited his fastidious style. But the order to use the weapon came from his commander; and not even he dared to disobey Cerberus.

The year before, he had been chosen on the personal recommendation of Rodolfo Graziani, the Viceroy of Italian East Africa, known as the 'The Butcher of Ethiopia', to join a new international unit, the Alpha Wolves. This followed a request from the SS to Benito Mussolini's National Fascist Government. Calvera had come to Graziani's attention for instigating an attack on a Swedish Red Cross hospital to erase evidence that patients were the victims of Italian bombers using mustard gas.

This mission, his sixteenth leading an Alpha Wolves' execution squad, was on the personal orders of his commander, Major Klaus Krak, the man more infamously known as Cerberus. The mission was of extreme importance. It would be the first execution by the unit on United States' soil, though it was not the first time that their target was American. So far, all attempts to eliminate the target had failed. He knew that if the man escaped tonight, he would take his own life rather than face the penalty for

4

failure. A few weeks earlier, he and other leaders of the Alpha Wolves' execution squads had watched as a half-dead Ukrainian was paraded in front of them. He was the leader of the only other known failed Alpha Wolves' assassination attempt; the target being the Russian Rogue who had been tracked to a Siberian labour camp.

Calvera and the others stood in a circle around the man, whose wrists were bound behind his back. Cerberus' gargantuan bodyguard, Rerck, chosen to replace the recently slain Grossmann, slung a steel chain up and over a beam and tied the other end to the Ukrainian's ankles. The bodyguard winched the man up towards the ceiling without exhibiting the slightest effort. Cerberus sat expressionless on an upholstered armchair as he watched the proceedings. When the man's head was four feet from the ground and parallel with Rerck's waist, Cerberus raised his hand to bring a halt to his elevation. He spoke only one word: 'Begin'. The goliath lit the blowtorch that lay next to the bone china tea-set on the only table in the room. He turned the blazing flame on the man suspended from the beam. For over an hour, he slowly and systemically seared the skin off the man's body, continuing well after his victim was dead. He stopped only when his commander ordered him to do so.

The Italian was unimpressed by the crude method of reducing the man to blackened bone, and he found his screams irritating. His key concern was not to get blood on his immaculate uniform or polished boots. However, he did not stand too far back in case his superior mistook this for squeamishness; he had no wish to one day be the cause of a smirk on his commander's face.

The Italian dismissed the possibility. Over the years he had killed eight men in hand-to-hand combat, been instrumental to and survived every battle during the Abyssinian campaign, and he had assassinated nearly twenty men and women since the Alpha Wolves had begun operations. To the men of his Italian unit he was *Il Invincibile*. He believed he was indestructible and that no one could kill him, not even the most brutal of the Alpha Wolves, Rerck.

Jake had made his way down two levels of the wooden structure to the lowest level of the scaffold platform. He crouched in the darkness and waited. The American could not see the assassin as he approached below, but he could hear the rattle of cartridges in the drum of the submachine gun – a design fault in the 1920 model. A regular user of such a weapon would be experienced enough to carry it with respect in such a situation, so that its bullets remained as still as possible before ignition. The man was just about to walk directly below him, when the American swung down from one of the horizontal wooden supports. The Italian leader of the assassins heard the swoosh through the air and attempted to swing his weapon to point at whatever was moving above him and unload his crude weapon.

The American smashed his boots into Calvera's weapon, wedging the tip of the barrel under his chin. The Thompson submachine gun could release over 600 rounds per minute, but whatever the exact number of bullets that entered Calvera's skull, they were enough to obliterate most of his head.

Jake knelt on the torso of the man once known as *Il*

6

Invincibile when he heard the eruption of metal crunching against metal. Jake looked to his left to see a truck bursting through one of the access gates of the compound. The American aimed his pistol at the Mack truck as it drove up the metal drive at full speed with both reinforced gates buckled and dangling from its sides. Before he could identify a target, thunderous gunfire cracked from his right and to his surprise it was directed at the truck. Why the other assassins were firing on the vehicle made no sense. He had no allies here; the Rogues he had fought beside in Spain and Germany were either dead or fighting their own battles in Europe.

But he had more immediate concerns as he was the target of fire from men running along the wooden platform above. Jake stood up on *Il Invincibile*'s corpse to provide height and leverage, so he could reach the wooden beam and swung himself back up onto the raised wooden platform. He lifted the Remington rifle that he had left on the ledge of the stone arch, one of many of the Chinaman's weapons he had stashed around the complex in readiness for the next attack. Jake tried to shut out the noise of the bullets whizzing around him as he focused on sounds that would betray his assassins' locations. The first of the intruders to abseil down the guiding ropes from the wooden scaffold controlled his descent, while expertly releasing a spiral of fire from his submachine gun.

Jake glimpsed the man, but it was enough. His shot hit the abseiling assassin in the left hip, turning his body into a leaden weight before it landed on the wooden planks. The American spun around and hit another man who had already opened fire as he abseiled down onto the other end of the platform. Jake's aim was better than the man's rapid-fire 'grapeshot' approach and his bullet hit the second man in the chest, propelling him backwards off the wooden tower into the surrounding undergrowth.

The Mack truck was hurtling up the steel road with submachine gun fire ricocheting off its thick metal frame. From the cabin of the speeding vehicle, Sean Ryan aimed his Winchester rifle at an assassin running through the undergrowth, hitting him in the shoulder. The impact launched the man backwards to be swallowed up by the darkness of the forest.

'Ahead,' shouted Vodanski.

The Irishman fired a second round off at the man standing in the middle of the road ten metres in front of them, who was about to open fire with the Thompson submachine gun. The bullet hit him in the neck, spinning him towards the gravel. The wounded man's rigorous training kicked in. He threw one hand up to his open wound to reduce the blood loss, while stretching out the other to secure his weapon. As the truck hurtled towards him, the assassin rolled out of the way before it crushed him under its wheels.

'Whoever trained them, trained them well,' observed Vodanski.

'Our American friend's a popular guy; he's attracting the best from all over the world to greet him,' said Ryan, as he swapped the empty rifle for a Smith & Wesson Model 19 .357 Magnum.

'I did not understand their eagerness to meet the blonde idiot, until I saw they were armed,' said the Russian.

Ryan's smile did not distract him from hitting another assassin rushing out of the darkness in the right eye with a single shot. The 'Tommy-gun,' otherwise known as the 'Chicago piano' for its popularity with The Mob, slipped from the dead man's fingers.

'We need to level the playing field,' shouted the Irishman.

The Russian swung the truck, which they had stolen fully laden with boulders, around at a right angle with the ease that a child would turn his tricycle.

Using the truck as a shield, Ryan dived out of the vehicle.

'Bollocks!' he roared, bouncing heavily along the metal road.

The Irishman was furious with himself for announcing his position to the men making their way through the undergrowth to his left. However, the pain in his right leg – held together by a dozen metal pins that would not be out of place on a tank – tore at every nerve in his battered frame. Three streams of submachine gun fire ricocheted all around him. Ryan scrambled off the road, while retaining his cane, which was a present from Jocky, as well as his gun.

Ryan regulated his breathing. A spray of bullets arrived to his left, forcing him to roll further away from the road into a ditch. He landed face down on the man he had just shot in the throat. Both men seized each other's throats, as bullets exploded the bark off the trees above them. The Irishman stabbed the fingers of his right hand into the man's open wound; the shock killing him instantly.

The Irishman drew the Thompson from the man's limp fingers, while he frisked the dead assassin's jacket with his other hand for spare cartridges. He found two fully loaded cylindrical drum magazines hanging from his belt. Ryan examined the weapon. It was the first time he had held one since the last months of the Irish Civil War.

One of the three Italian assassins, who had trained his fire at the man who had tumbled from the truck, was making his way along the edge of the trench by the side of the road. The assassin heard a noise below him and aimed his Thompson into the darkness of the ditch. Crouching down as he scurried along, he glimpsed a penetrating pair of glacial blue eyes looking up at him. Before he could train his weapon on them, he heard a click, then a silver tongue flashed from a cane, glistening in the moonlight. Before he could depress the trigger, a thin rapier blade shot up into his groin. The tip of the blade returned to slash his throat before a scream could pass his lips. As the assassin dropped into the ditch. His killer smothered his mouth with one hand, while launching successive rabbit-punches to his windpipe until he could breathe no more.

To his left in the distance, Ryan saw a pair of darting eyes observing everything in the darkness. It could not be Jake as he could hear gunshots from the building up on the hill. It was not Vodanski, as he could hear the familiar recoil of the Winchester from the direction of the truck up on the road. If it was another assassin, why were they sitting back and watching? Friend or foe, he had to discover which.

Samuel clasped his trembling fingers tightly across his chest as he rocked back and forth. The sounds of gunfire around him dragged him back twenty years to the battle in the French woods. He was caught once more in the carnage that followed, the initial whizzing sound of the bullets and the dull thuds as they imploded into the bodies of the men falling around him.

Samuel was eighteen years old when he enlisted in the Harlem Hellfighters, to fight in the Great War. Within a month, the only African American unit in the United States Army was in France, fighting as part of the French 16th Division. The Battle of Belleau Wood was fierce. They fought their way through the woods, repelling several German attacks, often using only bayonets and fists. Friends fell all around him, showered by the metal rain of enemy submachine guns.

Despite having a leg amputated after his wound had gone gangrenous – as US medical staff had orders to prioritise injuries to white soldiers above that of their black comrades – he was proud when his unit was awarded the Croix de Guerre. Their commander Captain Lloyd W. Williams epitomised their bravery, when he was ordered to withdraw, he declared, 'Retreat? Hell, we only just got here.'

The French called them 'The Men in Bronze' and to Samuel and his comrades' surprise, they fought beside them on the battlefield. But when those who survived the war returned home, they were met by the blind rage of prejudice. Politicians, horrified by reports of black and white soldiers fighting alongside each other, reinforced the laws that divided American society.

Shortly afterwards he sought sanctuary in the park, only emerging to collect his war pension, to buy food and tobacco, and, occasionally, treat himself to a Hershey Bar, when he could afford it. The taste of the milk chocolate revived memories of his childhood growing up in Harlem and that special morning when his daddy had walked him down the Upper West side of Manhattan and he saw The Lady for the first time. His father told him that she symbolised one of the fundamental tenets of their country; welcoming all to its shores, irrespective of race, creed or colour.

'There are those who don't share the lady's ideals,' he told the young Samuel, 'but even fucked-up sons of bitches are entitled to their opinion.'

Hours earlier, Samuel knew that the man in the Cloisters had lost a lot of blood, as he had followed the coppery red trail to the huge oak entrance doors where a large pool of blood had collected. From there the trail continued to the base of the scaffold. Though his silhouette suggested an athletic build, with such a loss of blood and the number of armed men after him, he could not evade his pursuers for long now they had breached the walls of the Cloisters.

Now, he lay in the darkness, having had lost sight of the man who leapt from the truck and rolled into the ditch. He had disappeared into the forest, probably to die. Even the driver of the truck who, by his reckoning, had killed four, maybe five men with the Winchester who had advanced up the incomplete metal road towards him, was pinned down. The invaders had learnt from the futility of their frontal attack and were directing all their firepower at the truck; trying to hit the fuel tank. The remnants of the assault force of twenty men that had invaded the little hillside were massing together behind the sandbags. Samuel watched as two men on the metal rampart by the main gates lugged an enormous machine gun into view. They positioned it so that for the first time they could hit both the new construction and the truck without exposing themselves.

The enormous weapon was the latest in United States Army weaponry, a recoil operated Browning M2 HB, the '50 calibre'. Samuel shook when it launched its first spray of gunfire and gigantic clumps of stone and sandstone shot out from the newly constructed walls, as if kicked from within by a raging giant. The war veteran had not seen anything as powerful since he first saw a German tank powering its way arrogantly across a French battlefield.

Under the covering fire of such a weapon, he watched as the first of the grenades were lobbed towards the Mack truck. One landed to its left. Another bounced along the metal road before exploding, sending shrapnel in all directions. The man in the Cloisters and the two men who crashed through the gates in the truck, whoever they were, would be dead within a matter of minutes. The assault force had control of the exit point and they could remain behind the sandbags at the base of the last remaining piece of road until the entire complex, including the truck, was blown to pieces. He could hear sirens in the distance, but even if the police arrived in time, it would only add to the fatalities as they would not be prepared for this kind of firepower.

Samuel had time to think, as no one could ever creep up on him here – not like the German who had plunged a bayonet into his femur twenty years ago. He knew that he must do something, even if it was only to distract gunfire from the police when they arrived. A hand clasped his mouth, forcing his head against the chest of the man behind him. His assailant bent down and whispered in his ear. 'I mean you no harm, friend; I just need a little information.'

A grenade landed metres inside the perimeter wall, and Jake could hear men above him scrambling to jump off the scaffolding. He leapt down into the main courtyard, in the centre of the museum. The tremendous explosions were punching the massive building blocks that were loaded into place by cranes, out of the perimeter walls. The intruders inside the building were viewed by their colleagues manning the huge gun as expendable. If he was going to die, he was going to make sure that those trapped inside the museum would die along with him. He collected the second of his M901s, which he had stored under a builder's hod-carrier. He held one of the semi-automatic pistols in each hand as he surveyed the terracotta roof and the windows below.

Jake positioned himself so that the moonlight exposed the courtyard and the whole of the roof apart from the one section directly above him. To his right, he saw a man leaping down to a level below. He swung his pistols around and fired. The bullets hit their target and the limp body bounced off two lower gables before landing in the courtyard. Out of the corner of his eye, Jake saw bats fly out of the turret in the far right of the courtyard – he had located the others.

Under the cover of the columns surrounding the courtyard, the American made his way to a toolbox he had placed next to the newly installed fountain. He ignored the ammunition he had stored inside it and picked up the Mills 'pineapple' grenade, another small, though this time expensive, extra from the Chinaman. Jake zig-zagged towards the turret and lobbed the device in through an open window at its base. He threw himself behind a stone column and waited with his pistols drawn. Before the grenade went off, four men leapt from the tower as Jake expected, and the cries of the M901's greeted each of them before their lifeless bodies landed with a volley of thuds in the courtyard.

An explosion erupted just behind the Mack truck, shredding its four back tyres. Just before the blast, Vodanski had thrown himself to the ground, only to lift his head afterwards to discover the Irishman flat on the ground a few feet away from him.

'How did you get up here?'

'Every new building has to have a main sewage system, and I just crawled along it. I wouldn't have lasted long if I had tried to make it up here across open ground.'

'You were lucky to find it.'

'Every museum has a local tour guide, and he kindly showed me the way.'

The Russian was puzzled by the comment but focused on survival. 'I hope you have come up with a plan as their grenades are getting closer.'

A grenade landed a few feet in front of the Mack truck and blew the windscreen into the cabin.

'They seem contented enough parked on the ramp behind the sandbags, and blowing us and the fort to shit,' said Ryan, massaging his right leg.

'That's why the assault party have made their way back from the woods to join them,' noted Vodanski. 'Focusing all one's men and firepower in one place would usually be a fatal error, but we have nothing to hit them with.'

'We have the Mack. I need you to cover me as I crawl into the driver's seat,' said Ryan, as his leg moved easier.

'Then what?'

'I will drive it off the hillside, land on the ramp and drive towards the bastards.'

Vodanski did not look impressed. 'Your plan is to drive a ten-tonne truck with punctured tyres, fully loaded with stone, leap a gap of three metres to clear a fifteen-foot drop, land on the ramp below and drive towards the most powerful automatic weapon I have ever seen?'

'Do you have a problem with the plan?'

'You driving the truck?'

'Yes.'

'No – I don't have a problem with the plan.'

'If I drive fast enough, I might bridge the gap and even if I lose control of the vehicle when I land, there is a good chance the boulders will fly out and bounce down the ramp towards them.'

'Are there any Irishman older than forty-years of age?'

'If you have a better idea, I'm not precious about this one,' said Ryan.

'It's your life, or what little is left of it.'

'Look, even the truck doesn't reach them I'll cause chaos down there. When I do, I have no doubt that you and Jake will pick them off.'

The Russian bridled at the mention of the American's name, raising his head and clenching his teeth. When Ryan first met Jake and Vodanski, he thought their clashes resulted from when men with similar characters are forced

16

to work together. But the Russian's animosity towards the American had been palpable when he mentioned Jake during the flight to America. Upon landing that morning, they were met by a telegram from Jocky. *Third attempt to kill Jake yesterday*. Stop. *Resulted in the dead policeman and bystander.* Stop. *US sources believed Mob have doubled their resources for further attack.* Stop. *Jake believed wounded.* Stop. *Extent of injuries unknown.* Stop'. The Russian remained indifferent to the last piece of news.

Ryan stared down at the enormous gun in the distance. He understood now that the men hunting Jake were not gangsters; these were trained soldiers fighting on American soil.

Another blast of gunfire took out both the Mack's side windows. Ryan dragged himself up into the truck's cabin. Vodanski stood up and with the Thompson that Ryan had thrown to him, directed covering fire towards the base of the ramp. Ryan turned the key, and the powerful engine shuddered angrily into life. The Russian reloaded. Gunfire erupted from the ramp once more. Ryan released the handbrake. A bullet ricocheted off the empty frame and grazed his neck. The truck crawled forward. Another grenade exploded where the truck had been standing. The sound of another whizzing through the air sent Vodanski running for cover towards the stone arch of the building's main entrance.

With his foot flat on the accelerator, Ryan drove the fully laden truck towards the edge of the hillside as fast as it could go. But a Browning shell landed in front, blowing the radiator into the engine, reducing the truck to a crawl. Meandering towards the edge, it slowly tipped over and plunged into the ravine.

As Vodanski watched the truck disappear over the edge, he heard his friend exclaim a very familiar cry: 'Bollocks!'

To the Russian's surprise – and he was a man who had seen much and was by nature difficult to startle – he saw several of the enemy, the wall of sandbags and a now-unmanned automatic weapon, flying upwards into the night. Like a hunter jerked into action by a flock of birds taking flight, Vodanski stood up and emptied the drum of the Thompson into the screaming men as they shot above the skyline. Gunfire erupted from the main building as Jake took advantage of the now-exposed targets. Between the merciless gunfire of the two men, most of the assassins were dead before they hit the ground. Two more were killed when they did. Two others were writhing around on the ground in agony until the roars of Jake's pistols silenced them.

'You fucking brainless cowboy! I came to this shithole of a country to find out why they are trying to kill us. We needed some alive,' yelled Vodanski towards Jake, perched up on the scaffold.

'Fuck you, Stalin. Like you, they are fucking robots and know shit!' shouted Jake.

Both had their fingers on the triggers of their weapons until they heard shouting and the shattering of glass from the gorge.

Jake made his way down the guide rope dangling from each wooden platform, but with all the explosions and smoke, he still had no idea who was inside the truck.

Vodanski ran to the edge of the hill. The Russian

understood what had happened. The combined weight of truck and boulders had clipped the tip of the unsupported end of the metal ramp. This turned the metal sheet of the temporary road into a catapult, flipping the other end upwards. This launched the men on the end of it, along with the wall of sandbags they were crouching behind, into the air like circus acrobats.

The Russian slid down the grassy slope until he reached the cabin of the vertical truck. He had to admire the American design, not because it was one of the first heavy-duty diesel engines to be built, but because the framework of the vehicle, including the chassis, were still intact. He could not see Ryan as boulders were piled high around the driver's cab. A bloodied fist smashed through the cracked back window of the burning vehicle and tried to push one boulder aside. The Russian knew that even if he added his own strength to Ryan's it would not be enough to lift the gigantic boulders to free him. Vodanski worked his way round to the side of the truck and grabbed hold of the crumpled roof riveted to the chassis and began to wrench it. After three attempts, it came away. As Vodanski lifted Ryan out of the cabin, he was once again surprised, this time by the sight of a black man with only one leg slipping down the slope, crutch in hand.

Vodanski dragged Ryan up the slope away from the heat and black smoke with Samuel doing his best to help. They covered their heads as the fuel tank exploded with the intense heat. The Russian grabbed both men and threw his body on top of them to protect them from the flames and the fragments of metal falling around them. He released the men and looked at the bloodied, but familiar stoical look on the Irishman's face.

'Your plan worked perfectly, Irishman, until you put it into action.'

'With that kind of humour, I bet you're often mistaken for a German.'

The Russian tore a piece from his shirt and pressed it onto the wound in Ryan's throat. Jake slid down the grass verge. He ignored Vodanski, 'Good to see you Irishman, welcome to America, the land of the *free*,' nodding towards the Russian?'

With his torn hands, Ryan checked his body and was pleased that he appeared not to have broken any more bones, and that the injury to his neck was only a flesh would.

'Good to see you too; not sure about your friends though,' he said, wiping the blood and diesel from his face and neck with his hand.

'When you see that American idiot tell him his country is full of little men with big guns trying to be Russian,' said Vodanski

They could hear the wail of sirens growing louder as police cars stormed the park.

'When you two have stopped baring your arses at each other, any fear of taking me to a fucking bar?' exclaimed Ryan.

Jake smiled, 'Rumour had it you were dead, Sean.'

'It's a lot more difficult to do than people imagine. Can I introduce you to my new friend,' turning to the man who directed him to the sewer inlet pipe. 'Sorry my friend, I was so busy getting shot I forgot to ask you your name.'

'Samuel, Samuel Clark,' replied the breathless man, as

Jake and Vodanski shook his hand.

As the fire in the gorge took hold, the three men dragged Sean further up the slope, laying him down only when they had reached the metal road.

The American sat down and retrieved what was left of a half-litre bottle of Old Kentucky Bourbon from the inside of the sheep-skin lining of his long, brown leather jacket and handed it to Sean. The night before, he had used a little to cleanse his knife before digging the bullet from the latest assassination attempt out of his thigh. He had emptied half the bottle to numb the pain. Sean took a long swig and passed it to Samuel, who politely drew only one mouthful. The veteran grimaced as if he had received a punch to his chest, as it had been a long time since he had drunk something that matched the label on the bottle. Samuel pressed the cane into Sean's hands. He looked determinedly at the three men. 'If we are being invaded, I want to sign up.'

Jake slapped Samuel on the shoulder and smiled. Samuel passed the bottle to Vodanski, who raised it to him in a gesture of welcome. Jake held his hand out for his bottle, as he was next in line for a drink, but the Russian drained its contents in three large gulps. Jake refused to express his annoyance, as that would mean having to acknowledge the Russian's existence.

He shouted to Sean to make himself heard above the crescendo of sirens, 'So what happened after Berlin?'

'It's a bitter story, Yank.' But when Jake and Vodanski hoisted him up, he added, 'but once I have a drink in my hand, it's one that must be told.'

Chapter 2: The Gathering of the Wolves

September 1938, Munich

'I am sure that to your countrymen and women you would be what they call a good man; indeed, I have heard you called a courageous, even a noble man.'

A stream of bloody spittle hung from the mouth of the man sitting opposite. But he could do nothing, as each wrist was bound, palm upwards, by heavy leather straps to the arms of the purpose-built steel chair. The prisoner was wearing only his blood-soaked underpants. He raised his bruised and battered face to look at Major Klaus Krak, the commander of the Alpha Wolves – the man his enemies, he had no friends, called Cerberus.

The major was an expert practitioner of both physical and psychological torture. With the naked blade, he had exposed the main muscles in the man's limbs to the limit of what he assessed he could endure and remain conscious. Rerck would press his hands on any open wound when his commander signalled that the flow of blood might lead to a heart seizure. Once the blood loss was stemmed to what the major judged to be an acceptable level, he would order the seven-foot-tall bodyguard to bind the wounds with narrow leather straps. The bindings, along with the other devices in the room, had been manufactured to Cerberus' exact specifications.

'Yet, I have not heard you referred to as a devoted husband or loving father,' the major lied. 'One cannot be both. You see, to be both a courageous man and a family man is incompatible.' The major grinned, as he did at such moments. Cerberus particularly enjoyed practising his techniques on those who were immensely powerful and mentally strong, as it allowed him more time to experiment. After four hours of applying the cut-throat razor with his gloved hand, his victim was still conscious – it was indeed a rare pleasure for the major. The prisoner's eyes were submerged under cushions of dark blue skin, but despite this, the look on the face of the major's latest victim was one of resolute defiance.

Cerberus wondered if he had applied himself to his task with his usual vigour, but after looking at the amount of blood and exposed muscle tissue before him he felt reassured. His smile broadened.

'To be truly courageous in the face of such a formidable force,' he nodded in the direction of the Führer's portrait on the wood panelled wall, 'you must be prepared to sacrifice not just your life, but those you love.'

It was these words rather than the blade that finally broke Xavier Merck.

'I'll sign . . .,' he whispered. 'I'll sign any confession.'

'Confession! Oh no, I intend to take from you far more than that.'

Cerberus noted with satisfaction the tremble he had been eagerly waiting to hear in the man's voice. He pressed on with the zeal of a cat that has just discovered that the bird under its paw has a broken wing.

'In front of me, I do not see a brave man. Instead, I

see a self-serving creature who would abandon those he proclaims to love to enhance his standing with his fellow anarchists and terrorists.' Cerberus could have resorted to psychological terror earlier, the proven and most effective method to extract information, but as he was not pressed for time, he indulged himself. His smile disappeared behind his thin lips and his eyebrows dropped as he leaned towards his victim. 'What kind of animal are you? Have you no interest in what will happen to your family?' Cerberus gestured to the door for his bodyguard to fetch refreshment; Rerck did so immediately. The major shook his head. 'Your martyrdom may be of some interest to those who hardly know you. However, will they – indeed can they – protect your wife, your mother (indicating that he knew Merck's father was dead) and your three children?'

The leader of the anti-fascist opposition in Bratislava was again trying to cough up the blood building in his throat. He spat another large glob of blood, saliva and fragments of broken teeth onto his naked chest and tried to hide the terror in his voice.

'They know nothing and are of no interest to you.'

He raised his bloodshot eyes, desperate for is torturer to ask him about his comrades rather than his family.

'Do not be so presumptuous as to tell me what I should think. Now, tell me your compatriots' names and where they live?'

'I cannot–'

'Do not add stupidity to your litany of failings. You know of my reputation, and you know what I am capable of,' releasing a smile bereft of warmth.

Xavier launched a stream of obscenities at the major.

Cerberus slowly drew the well-oiled razor even deeper into the man's sliced wrists, while the blue wormlike veins in his temples agitated beneath his translucent skin. The sudden massive loss of blood triggered the expected shock to the man's heart. Blood streamed down the chair's steel legs, expanding the dark red circle on the bare wooden floor.

'I do not tolerate profanity and in normal circumstances I would have you silenced. However, I am a professional and I never act on emotion, even when I am insulted. You try to goad me into killing you, but death will not liberate you – we still have much to do.'

Cerberus reclined, and removed his black leather gloves by their bloodied fingertips, as Rerck returned with a silver tray laden with a china tea-set. A unit of his Alpha Wolves had stolen it from the house of a retired banker, Siegfried Wallenberg, in Stockholm. His intelligence unit had extracted information from the thousands of radio messages they intercepted each day, and one of these had led them to Sweden. The retired banker was using his fortune to help finance medical convoys to institutions for the mentally ill in Czechoslovakia. His late wife was Czech, and her brother was still a patient in one of the facilities.

Though Wallenberg refused to expose his network despite undergoing torture in his home, Cerberus' men discovered Xavier's name as his contact in Bratislava. Once Cerberus had what he came for, he ordered Rerck to end the interrogation. He did so with one short punch from his granite-like fist to the old man's face, reducing the man's frontal lobe to mush. The major observed the banker slumped in front of him in the steel chair as he sipped his tea. He was fascinated by the fragility of the human body.

Meanwhile, his men were silently and methodically moving from room to room, executing the three generations of the banker's family that resided in the four-storey mansion.

Cerberus smirked when he saw the tea-set, not for its beauty, but because it symbolised the effectiveness of his methods. The institution in Prague was closed due to an outbreak of diphtheria: not surprising given that the flow of medicines had been severed. The murder of one man by the Alpha Wolves had led to the destitution of over two hundred 'sub-humans' and placed a leading opponent of fascism at his mercy.

It was typical of Cerberus' plan for the brute force of his Alpha Wolves to have far greater consequences, way beyond the elimination of their immediate target. Over the last two years, with Reichsführer Heinrich Himmler's resources and the support of his commanding officer, SS-Obergruppenführer Reinhard Heydrich, the success of the Alpha Wolves had exceeded their expectations, though not his own. He placed the blood-smeared, ivory-handled razor gently down on the red cloth. He smiled, keeping his eyes fixed on the blade as if it were a family heirloom – it was, but not his.

Xavier made one last attempt to save those who shared in his goal of protecting the independence of his beloved homeland.

In a low, unsteady voice he pleaded, 'I brought together those who oppose you in the region. With my death, the anti-fascist movement will disperse. You need not waste your time on them.'

Cerberus leaned forward on the reupholstered mahogany chair, holding a cup and saucer delicately in his hands.

'Your arrogance knows no bounds. Not only do you once again tell me what I should think, but you declare that your compatriots have no ideals of their own. They fight only because of you and not to keep their country free of us terrible Nazis? You are a liar, a coward, a vain, self-important man, and now you add disloyalty to your vices.' Cerberus sipped his Earl Grey tea, as he tapped his skeletal fingers on the armrest. 'Perhaps you wish to distract me from the part of our discussion that interests me most . . . your family.'

Xavier tried to speak, despite the well of blood building in his throat. 'They . . . have nothing to do with this . . . I–'

'Of course they have. They are your family, the family of one who opposes us. For that, they will pay the price . . . unless?'

'Please . . . I . . .' mumbled the man, dubbed by the Gestapo as the Carpathian Lion for his opposition to the growing fascist paramilitary presence in Central Europe, before he broke down in tears.

'If you refuse to take responsibility for your actions, then you leave me no choice but to caste sentence on your family.' He took a sip from his china cup. 'For your family to live you must tell me in the little time that you have left, the names and addresses of all your political contacts.'

'I can't, I . . .' his voice was so weak that his pleas were barely audible to his torturer.

'Your words are those of a man who loves his so-called honour, cause, whatever you term it, above his duties as a son, a husband and as a father. You disgust me.' This time Cerberus was telling the truth as he despised Czechs, as much as he hated Slavs and Russians. He edged forward. 'Life is full of difficult decisions. Now you leave me with no option but to make yours for you.' Cerberus turned to issue an order to his bodyguard, who was standing in the far corner of the room obscuring the door behind him. 'Bring the women and the children up from the cells and put them next door. Move my equipment in there too. I will begin at once.'

The weeping man in the chair opposite reeled off a list of names and addresses of every man and woman who he knew would defend the country's liberty.

Cerberus methodically entered the information onto a ledger marked out with rows and columns, using an elegant fountain-pen that was engraved *'TO MY WIFE, GRETA. MY ETERNAL LOVE. SIEGFREUD X'*. When a page was completed, he carefully blotted the ink, before turning to the next. When he had recorded all the names and addresses surrendered by his prisoner, he inserted four full pages into a bulging file marked CZECHOSLOVAKIA: RESISTANCE GROUPS/ NATIONAL & LOCAL. The major closed the ledger and placed it into the matt black leather briefcase by his side. He turned to Rerck and instructed him to lift the dying man's head up by his hair, so he could hear their conversation.

'Do you still want me to put his family next door?' asked Rerck.

Xavier looked at the Gestapo officer and spoke his final words. 'Please . . . I . . . beg . . . you–'

The major took another sip from his bone china cup, 'No.' He lifted his head. 'You see, unlike you. I am a man of integrity and I keep my word.' Rerck released his hold and Xavier's chin rested onto the mixture of vomit, blood and sweat on his chest – until he heard the major's next words. 'Bring them here, instead.'

'And the prisoner, major?' asked Rerck.

'He wants to be a martyr; crucify him up against the wall in front of his family,' commanded Cerberus, nodding towards the wall opposite the door.

Xavier frantically struggled at his bindings. He screamed until his heart seized. He relaxed only when his body fell silent.

'Leave my instruments here,' said Cerberus, calmly. He delicately lifted the brittle sea-shell thin cup to his thin lips, as if he were lifting a butterfly to kiss its wing. He smiled at the horrified frozen face of the man in the chair in front of him. 'Justice will be done.'

Three days later, on a drizzly morning in Munich, Major Klaus Krak entered the large dining room of the Bürgerbräukeller beer hall. It was here that Hitler, Rudolf Hess, his deputy, Hermann Göring, and around three thousand other Nazi followers had launched their abortive putsch in 1923. One hundred of the four hundred-strong Alpha Wolves – all those not currently involved in active operations outside Germany – had been standing to attention in the hall for four hours. The unit's international operations, one hundred and twenty-six so far, were responsible for over seven hundred executions and twenty-four disappearances - those currently undergoing interrogation. They were also instigators of numerous scandals, manufactured or otherwise, that had forced several high-ranking politicians and army officers to resign or commit suicide. Their victims included prominent Jews, leaders of the Roma community, those suspected of being homosexuals, supposed detractors within the Wehrmacht, and those known or thought to be political opponents. When they received the order to go to Munich, the new recruits believed it was to receive praise for their ruthless execution of the major's orders. Those who had met the major knew otherwise.

The major could sense their excitement as he stepped up onto the barren stage – he felt none himself. He also knew, and welcomed the fact, that there would be some who would be unsettled to be in the presence of the tall, cadaverous-looking creature known as Cerberus.

He gave the customary salute of a superior German officer, but he did so without enthusiasm, as if he were acknowledging a lowly clerk in a corridor. He dropped his arm. The silence within the hall was shattered as his legion saluted and roared a deafening: 'Heil Hitler!'

Cerberus had been present for many of Adolf Hitler's speeches as the Nazis rose to power. The Führer would begin almost casually, his hands clasped in front of him as if he were chatting freely amongst close friends. Gradually, his voice grew louder, as his gesticulations intensified until in the throes of his speech, he was throwing his fists in all directions in what appeared to be abject fury. It was a well-rehearsed performance, which whipped his audience into a frenzy of hysteria – apart from Lieutenant Krak.

Cerberus recognised that the Führer, and the Reichführers, sought not only unquestioning obedience but adoration. However, the major had no interest in giving speeches to win hearts; his only interest was seizing control of minds. It was his commander, Obergruppenführer Reinhard Heydrich, who had ordered him to assemble the Alpha Wolves. Heydrich needed to test their loyalty, in the expectation that they might be ordered back to Germany to suppress all opposition to the Jewish pogroms.

Cerberus scanned the largest ever gathering of the Alpha Wolves like a predator searching for the weakest in a herd. They were an intimidating sight in the sinister black Gestapo uniform manufactured by a company owned by Hugo Boss, long-term member of the Nazi Party. Two additional items had recently been added to their livery. On the top right-hand jacket pocket was a silver-plated wolf's head and hanging from their leather belts was a thick black metal plate to be attached to their SS helmet in battle, protecting the face by obscuring all but the eyes.

The major began his address. Those waiting in the icy-cold hall with the expectation of being lauded with praise were quickly disappointed. 'In a matter of weeks, we will test the loyalty of the *Herrenvolk*,' those regarded as being of pure Aryan blood, 'to the Führer as we escalate our programme to rid us of the *Untermensch*,' those regarded as sub-human. 'When we act, we expect every German man and woman to join us in our attacks or stand aside. Those Germans who actively oppose us will be treated as if they were *Untermensch*.' Deafening applause erupted throughout the hall.

'Save your applause as our work is only just beginning.' His voice registered neither pleasure nor anger, nor did he raise it to be heard. Rerck stood in front of the wooden stage to his commander's left, scanning the floor for a reaction. The room was silent. The major glowered with distrain at those before him. He despised acts of spontaneity.

'Each of you were selected to join the ranks of the Alpha Wolves because of your proven devotion to the Führer and your heroism in battle. Your goal is to deliver the Führer's vision: a world dominated by a new purified Germanic master race. Your service to the Reich takes precedence over your duty to your family and outweighs the importance of your life.' He paused, not for effect as his superiors would have done at this point but, as did Rerck, to monitor the faces before him. 'Your immediate task is that every execution must be carried out without thought or question. Thinking will lead to consideration, to doubt and finally compassion. Our enemies will rightly interpret this as weakness.'

Rerck walked through the ranks of men and women searching for signs of uneasiness, even fear, betrayed by the rapid movement of the iris or sweat on the temple – usually both.

'Your long-term objective is of no lesser importance. To create a master race in our image, we must purify society. Your targets are only the visible sores; the virus lies dormant beneath the Jew; the Slav; the homosexual; and the liberal who confuses the German people by offering them choice. However, the infection is so advanced, that we cannot eradicate it with one incision. But before we reach the farthest strains of the disease, we will weaken its ability to fight back. That is why, when you torture and kill your victims, you will do so without mercy, without pity and always with the utmost brutality.'

For the first time, he released a thin smile. 'As for their followers, you will appropriate their homes; confiscate their possessions; strip them of their clothes. Through acts of terrorism and sabotage you will cut off their supplies of food, heat and water. By dehumanising our opponents, you will remove their self-respect along with the will to live, let alone to fight. Shame is the confederate of fear, and under the combined weight of both our victims will be brought to their knees. Then when we march through their streets, rather than build barricades they will slink off into the shadows.'

Chests inflated and jaws rose through the hall.

'Some of you have been personally selected from the Gestapo, whose black uniform and *Totenkopf* (silver death skull insignia) we wear, while others of you have been selected from the ranks of the SS. You are the elite: the vanguard of Germany's advance. By your merciless acts, the world will know and fear the Alpha Wolves for the next ten thousand years of the Reich.

Rerck stood at the back of the room, as his commander surveyed the unyielding faces of the men and women before him.

'If you do not do so already: fear me. If I discover that any of you show compassion, forgiveness or tolerance, I will order those standing beside you today to butcher your family in front of you.' Cerberus paused to study the one hundred faces locked on him. 'Only then I will deal with you personally.' Without any change in tone, he closed his speech. 'Let the others, who are at this very moment eradicating our enemies, know that I will personally erase any stain that any of you threatens to leave on the swastika.'

Cerberus surveyed the room one last time. The reaction of the audience was, as he expected, one of pride.

Now that their commander had finished, the Alpha Wolves responded with the fascist salute. The major nonchalantly raised his arm and uttered the words 'Heil Hitler,' as he turned to leave the hall.

His audience continued to roar, even louder than before, while keeping their straightened arm and flattened hand fixed in position in the air. If anyone in the hall was disappointed to be threatened with execution, rather than receiving lavish praise, there was no evidence of it. Cerberus could still hear the deafening mantra coming from inside the beer hall as he stepped out into the pounding rain. Rerck opened the door to the red and black Mercedes. He noted his commander's insouciance as he slithered inside and disappeared behind the darkened windows.

Chapter 3: The Path of Greatest Resistance

August 1938, London

Churchill hated hospitals. There was always some idiot trying to put his cigar out. Seven years earlier he had been knocked over by a car in New York. It was his own damn fault. The medics were very kind, but it was a perpetual battle of wills to keep a good Havana lit. There was another thing he hated about hospitals – injections. But he smiled as he remembered embarrassing one young nurse when she asked where he would like her to administer it.

'Use my fingers or the lobes of my ears, and of course I have an almost infinite expanse of arse.' His doctor, an excellent fellow, prescribed 'the use of alcoholic spirits at mealtimes the minimum requirement to be 250cc.' The good doctor had not set an end date for the course of treatment, so his patient was of the opinion that it was indefinite.

Despite his aversion to hospitals, it took every ounce of willpower for Churchill not to march straight over to St Bartholomew's Hospital in search of Sean Ryan, and again when the patient was transferred to the Chelsea Hospital. The Statesman was desperate to secure answers to the questions that had troubled him since he had arranged for the Irishman to be brought back to England for treatment following the severe injuries he suffered falling from the train in Berlin.

It was two weeks after Sean Ryan was transferred to Chelsea Hospital, when the driver opened the door of the black Daimler LQ 2-20 and his passenger emerged. With the aid of his silver-tipped cane, Churchill and the driver made their way up the steps, strode past the sentries guarding the entrance and hurried along a corridor until they reached the room bearing a sign that read:

QUARANTINE
STRICTLY NO ADMITTANCE

One of the two guards posted outside the room opened the door to admit the Statesman, who raised his left hand to signal to his driver to remain outside.

Churchill looked at the man lying comfortably in the bed, as if posing for a painting of Bacchus. The patient was drinking readily from a bottle labelled 'Aunt Bessie's Tonic Water'. However, Churchill recognised the odour of a good quality malt.

'Jocky, how have you been? It has been a while.'

'I'm fine *yer* honour.'

'You go by the moniker of Sean Ryan these days, I see.'

'That's the name on my medical chart, so as long as I keep *me* mouth shut, so my dulcet tones don't betray me, no one is the wiser.'

'There is always a tell that unveils a disguise. I can no longer go under the pseudonym of Gypsy Rose Lee, as sadly, my figure is not what it used to be.'

'I think *yer* slapped me once,' said Jocky, laughing. The Scotsman was delighted to once again meet the man whom his father had been proud to serve in two wars. 'Ah well, it was a good ruse while it lasted. The nurses are wonderful, but it has been a challenge I can tell *yer* to stand in for a Fenian.'

'How so?'

'I've had to convince everyone I'm as thick as a brick.'

'A Herculean endeavour, requiring immeasurable skills in the art of subterfuge. I will ask the King to have a special medal pressed in recognition of your supreme sacrifice. In the meantime, I should be happy to relieve you of some of your burden in exchange for a good cigar. The odour invading my nostrils is unmistakable. Hibernian . . . an Islay single malt whisky . . . Lagavulin?'

'Aye *yer* honour, sixteen-years-old, distilled for five days and then again for a further nine. It smoothly caresses the throat like a *who'ers* tongue.'

'Your knowledge of such matters is far greater than my own; perhaps you should go into advertising.'

'Well, many have commented that I have the body of a god.'

'I was referring to your lyrical nature, rather than securing a modelling assignment,' said Churchill.

He smiled as the only image of a God that came to mind was a rotund, laughing Buddha. However, he politely kept the thought to himself.

Jocky poured two fingers of whisky into a couple of medicine glasses by the side of the bed.

'Sorry, but these places have *nay* call for the fine crystal I expect *yer* are used to and the only other container is under me bed *yer* honour.'

'Please don't trouble yourself any further; I adapt where necessity demands.'

The Scotsman handed a beaker to the man he had met on a few occasions since coming to London to find work. The men lit their cigars and relaxed with their drinks, savouring the blended burnt leaf and peaty aroma. Churchill reclined into the plain, wooden chair opposite the healthy patient in the bed opposite.

'If you're here, where is Ryan?'

'Ah, *yer* know the Irish powder keg?'

'We have met twice, each time under different circumstances.'

'Well, then *yer* know how to find him, just walk towards the explosion.' Churchill lifted the medicine glass to his nose to savour its delicious fragrance, before taking a sip, leaving the other man to continue. 'That a great man like yourself would share a drink with a working-class scumbag . . . sorry forgive my language . . . like me, explains why *yer* were once loved by the people.'

'You are, like your namesake, an impertinent fellow. You say "once", so no longer? How so?'

'Well, *yer* honour, *yer* talk of war with the Germans and people don't want to hear it. Too many lost fathers in the last one,' he added, clearly pained at the thought of the loss of his own.

'This, in your opinion, is the view of the British people?'

'Aye, and not just in God's country,' referring to Scotland, 'but also in that wasteland to the south,' referencing England. 'And when the Nazis attack, don't think the Yanks will jump in; I've met a few, and they are not going to be dragged into another European war. As for the French making a stand, don't hold *yer* breath. The last German occupation knocked the *shite* out of them. When the Nazis march into Paris they will surrender quicker than a *who'ers* drawers in a naval dockyard.'

'Ah, if only I could conjure such delightful imagery in my speeches in the House.'

'And don't forget that the Nazis have allies of their own. The Italians and the Japanese will align themselves with the bastards quicker than I would break a vow of alcohol and sexual abstinence.'

'My word, would they really form an alliance with such haste!'

'The man in the street is more worried about the Soviets and a Communist world revolution. He does *nee* care about a jumped-up clown with one bollock, a black penny stamp under his nose and tackle so wee he needs braces to hold up a pair of shorts . . . if *yer* forgive my French *yer* honour.'

'After that lightning tour of global foreign policy, and your very vivid description of the German Chancellor, I will in my defence declare that I am not the warmonger I am portrayed to be by my opponents. I do not ask the men and women of Britain to throw themselves in the path of the Nazi juggernaut.'

'But forgive me your honour, isn't that what *yer* are doing?'

'No, I am warning them that they are already in its path and that the vehicle is heading towards us at such speed that we cannot avoid it. The only way to survive is to try to bring it to a halt before we find ourselves under it.'

'I *nay* need convincing. I saw the *bastads* in action on the streets of Berlin.' Jocky paused. 'Can I ask *yer* one question *yer* honour?'

'Speak freely.'

'Why would an important man such as *yerself* devote time and money to help a few refugees flee Europe?'

Churchill's remembered the Irishman asking him a similar question. His amiable demeanour disappeared.

'Are we as a nation to stand back while innocent families are banging on our door, pleading for help as the hounds of fascism tear at their flesh? If we possess any decency, we must not only open the door, we must do all we can to help them enter. That Western governments avert their gaze as the enemy stands on the horizon rattling its weapons is bad enough, but to stand idly by while they blatantly unleash their rabid dogs on women and children is intolerable.'

Never had Jocky felt such emotion stirring in him – an overwhelming sense of pride in hearing these words, but also shame that he needed the danger faced by so many explained to him.

The Statesman's was not finished, and his voice rose as he leaned forward.

'If Herr Hitler thinks he can commit such vile abuses and be left unfettered, then he does not understand the sense of justice that is ingrained in the heart of every British man and woman.'

Jocky remembered his late father telling him how as a boy he had served under Churchill when he was a second lieutenant in the Fourth Queen's Own Hussars. The man who was happily sipping whisky with him was the only Englishman he had ever heard his father say a good word about. Now he understood why. This was not a politician trying to win over an audience in a hall, but one man speaking to another, honestly and with conviction.

'By a misfortune of birth *yer* are an Englishman, *yer* have a heart as large as any Scotsman.'

Churchill released a broad, cherubic grin. 'Perhaps my salvation lies in the fact that my mother was American.'

This was not the first time Jocky had spoken freely in the presence of what his boss in Admiralty House, 'The Commander', would call 'the upper echelons'. However, this time, he felt that his usual candour would not result in the police being called to lead him away in handcuffs. The man opposite was neither haughty nor wary, indeed he appeared to revel in the presence of such an 'undesirable reprobate'.

Jocky recalled the Right Honourable Justice Barking using that description following the incident with 'Lady' Susanna 'Suze' Carstairs, in the Owners and Trainers enclosure at Royal Ascot two years earlier. Conducting his own defence at his trial, Jocky explained to the judge that he had a right to be angry, after he "edged his hand up past Suze's suspender-belt and discovered that she was hung like the winner of the 2.30". This did not help his defence and explained why his sentence was more than the usual thirty-pound fine for common assault. This, despite the fact that he was the one hospitalised after being knocked out by Suze who had a "right-hook worthy of the Glaswegian flyweight boxer Benny Lynch." Jockey spent the following week at

His Majesty's pleasure in Wandsworth prison.

'But *yer* stand alone, *yer* honour,' continued Jocky.

'Nonsense, I have the love of my family, and the son of my old friend to provide me with an excellent malt, even if he is using a nom de plume.'

Jocky glanced at the undisturbed fruit in the bowl on the table next to his bed. 'Quite right. I'm a true Scotsman and *yer'll* never catch me eating anything as healthy as a plum.'

Churchill enjoyed the company of those who refused to take themselves too seriously, and released a hearty laugh, before adding, 'So you see, I have no need for your sympathy, as I am far from alone.'

The Scotsman was struck by the thought of how isolated the great man had become. Just a few years earlier Churchill had been vilified in Parliament when he stood up to argue the case that Edward VIII did not have to abdicate after marrying the American divorcee, Mrs Simpson. It was a measure of the man's loyalty, but also his impetuousness, as it was widely known that the King was already resigned to vacating the throne. As a result, Churchill was shouted down by both sides of the House – an action that was unheard of in modern British politics.

Thirty minutes later, Churchill emerged from the hospital room. His driver quickened his step to keep up. 'Is everything all right, Sir?'

'Always good to get out and about and meet the uncommon man.' Before he stepped into the car, he turned to the driver. 'Remind me to send Mr Ryan a bottle of Pol

Roger from my supply when we return to the House.'

Ten hours earlier, in his chambers in the Houses of Parliament, Churchill looked at the injured man sitting in the mahogany chair precariously close to the freshly lit fire. Churchill got up from his desk and walked to the window to look upon the black abyss of the simmering night waters of the Thames. He examined his sombre reflection in the dark glass.

'Do you have any proof of the terrible events you say are taking place in Himmler's Fortress?'

'No,' replied the real Sean Ryan.

Four hours later, the Irishman had rowed a small boat across the Thames, mooring the vessel by Middlesex bank beside the gothic building known throughout the world as "The Mother of Parliaments". The boat had not drawn attention as it was but one of many that traversed the river at night; part of a twenty-year project to rebuild the building's crumbling limestone exterior walls. Wobbling unsteadily, Sean clamped onto a drainpipe with his right arm as the other was in a sling. Slowly, and with great deliberation, he adopted a rhythm of throwing his arm up to reach a higher section of the pipe, winching himself up and locking himself into position with his knees. He repeated the technique until eventually he found an open window. Entering the bastion of British democracy, he found himself sitting in a ladies' lavatory.

Sean stepped into the oak-panelled corridor and manoeuvred his way through the building unchallenged by adopting the nonchalant appearance of one who belonged there. Following directions from a cleaning lady, he found and entered Churchill's chambers.

The Irishman's walking stick and slight limp did not adequately convey how severe his injuries had been. But Churchill knew. He had been given a transcript of a German telephone exchange between the Reichstag and Berlin's Police Headquarters. In the exchange, three references were made to 'The Anschluss Incidents in Berlin: 12 March 1938'. It detailed the results of an inquiry led by the Chief Inspector of the Berlin Police covering a fire in an underground beer keller, a violent altercation that occurred hours later in a Berlin alleyway, and finally an incident involving a train departing the city. The report concluded that the two incidents in the city were an attempt by rogue elements of the Sturmabteilung (SA) to reassert their authority over the Schutzstaffel (SS). However, the incident involving the train came under the jurisdiction of the Reichsführer Heinrich Himmler, as it involved a mode of transport assigned to a special external operations force, which due to state security could not be named. As such, it was deemed a national, rather than a local security matter, and was no longer part of the inquiry.

Two days later, a radio message sent to the German High Command was also intercepted by British Intelligence. It stated that the file on the man known as 'The Englander' had been sent to the archive department of the Gestapo on Prinz-Albrecht-Strasse. The file had been closed following the conclusion of several extensive searches, which uncovered human remains in a forest clearing thirty miles to the north of Berlin. Items of clothing were later discovered a few hundred metres away in a den inhabited by a pack of wolves. According to forensic records, these belonged to Sean Ryan, an Irishman known to German security services as "The Englander", and an unnamed SS bodyguard. Churchill grinned broadly at the repeated references to The Englander, a term often used in correspondence by various hostile security services to describe the Irishman – a misconception that he knew from his dealings with the man irritated him immensely.

When Sean entered his chambers, Churchill did not stir. The Statesman made no attempt to hide the draft of the speech he was to give to the Commons the next day. It was another attempt to urge the Government to immediately launch a major rearmament of its navy. Neither did the Irishman say anything, as he limped towards the small table positioned between the main desk and the fireplace. With his good arm, he helped himself to one of the brandy glasses and filled it to the top from the crystal glass decanter. Without being invited, he sat down in the armchair nearest the fire that was starting to build. Only when Churchill placed his fountain pen down on his desk to look up at him, did Sean begin his story.

For twenty minutes Churchill sat quietly as the Irishman recounted the events that had taken place after he had left the other Rogues at Lehrter Bahnhof. He skipped over the aftermath of his battle on the train and described the details of the attack in New York and what Vodanski had divulged about events in Siberia. The Statesman did not move as he quietly pondered the enormity of the horrifying events described. He rose from his chair, walked to the mantelpiece and stared into the flames below.

Finally, he spoke. 'You say you cannot substantiate your story, but what have you learnt of the men killed in the New York attacks?'

'Nothing was discovered on any of the bodies that implicates Berlin. The New York Police Department believe that the New York attack was a local gang war. It's too fantastical for them to believe anything else, even with the discovery of a fifty-calibre Browning. As for the attack in Siberia, we know little. If a trail were found that led to Germany, would that information have reached Moscow? Even if it had, would Stalin contemplate that the Nazis would be so brazen as to carry out an operation within the Soviet Union? But, as always with the Russians, who is to know what they are really thinking?'

'Are you of the view that these assassination squads were formed with the aim to hunt down you and your friends?'

'Though I'd love to believe that I and the others are the cause of using up so much of the Nazi's resources. But we are but one target of some master plan, which I believe is coordinated by a shadowy character who prowls behind the Nazi High Command.'

'This subterraneous beast, is this the same one who brushed you with the tips of its talons in Budapest?'

'Yes.'

'If the *Narzees* are behind all this, then Herr Hitler is taking an incredible risk if his covert operations are discovered.'

'Every operation is superbly planned and executed. As I said, so far there is nothing that incriminates Berlin. The makeup of each assassination squad matches that of some local, usually criminal, element. The boarding passes, and the papers found on the bodies in New York, are for return flights within America rather than to Europe. Even the immigration stamps on the dead men's passports cover every major country in Europe – except one.'

'Nothing could be more incriminating,' said Churchill, nodding. 'You say local, so the assassins were recruited from the country of the intended target?'

'Local is perhaps a misnomer. I should have said a native of the region. Those I encountered in New York looked like they had just come off a film set. Everything was what you would expect of 'The Mob', but the clothes were immaculate. There was no sign of wear, even on the heels of their spats.'

'Do bullet holes count as wear?' asked Churchill without a hint of a smile. 'My intelligence sources in the US State Department support your conclusions. The descriptions of the Italian corpses washed up in the Hudson River match those of recent arrivals from Italy. Not one of them had any known criminal connections to the United States. The Americans have discovered that the tattoos on the corpse of a man whom they believe was the leader of one gang, match that of a particularly infamous lieutenant in the Italian Army known as *Il Invincibile*. However, it is difficult to authenticate this as his face was shot off. Once again, not exactly the typical background of a New York gangster. Though harder to confirm, our Russian contacts say that the unit sent to kill your friend, Vodanski, were all Latvian.'

Churchill slumped back into his armchair with such force that his polka-dot bow tie slipped at an angle like a large exotic butterfly that had been rudely disturbed.

'My Polish contacts say that these units are part of an international Nazi operation under the personal orders of Himmler. It is called 'The Wolves', an elite squadron comprised of members drawn from the SS and the Gestapo whose mission is to murder key opponents of the Nazi regime in foreign countries, to weaken them in advance of invasion.'

'Your informers are nearly right. I've heard,' Sean said, without naming Paul, his Hungarian contact, as the source, 'that they call themselves 'The Alpha Wolves'.'

'Dear God, another reason we cannot let the *Narzees* win. The subtleties of language will be subsumed under their desperate attempt to manufacture some over-inflated quasi-mythological Aryan symbolism.' The Statesman shook his head. 'More brandy?'

Sean had already stretched forward and with his good arm lifted the glass decanter up from the smaller, oak table to his immediate left and topped up both glasses.

As he spoke, he dropped the glass stopper back with a clatter into the neck of the container, 'There's a brain behind this; a sharp but psychotic one who makes contingency plans in the event of failure. In my experience, that is rare for the Nazis; whether through arrogance or a lack of imagination, they do not seem to contemplate failure and therefore make no preparation for it.'

'Himmler replaced that blundering idiot Göring as head of the SS some years ago. Perhaps his scheming is only now coming to the fore?'

'Perhaps. On the surface, they are as different as night and day. Göring was a pilot in the Great War, while

Himmler is more comfortable behind a desk. But in all other respects they are the same: both fanatics driven by all this Aryan master race supremacy shit. No, I believe this is someone who sits behind Himmler.'

'His deputy Reinhard Heydrich?'

'Vicious and brutal enough, but a reptile who likes to bathe in the limelight. No, this is a far more shadowy creature.'

'Where do you expect to find your answer?'

'The woman's husband is my only lead, so I must return to the Continent.'

Churchill hauled himself from the leather armchair and returned to the mahogany desk by the window. The river offered one of his many favourite views, but this time he raised himself up on tiptoes to peer out the window to discover where the man had tied up his little rowing boat. He could see it, about thirty feet to his left. Churchill smiled. It was incredible; not only that, the man had rowed it there, but that he had scaled the building up the iron overflow pipe above it with the use of only one hand. He made a mental note to have a quiet word with the Serjeant at Arms, the head of security for The Palace of Westminster. Churchill collected what he came for from the desk and slid the drawer back into its recess. Returning to his armchair, he handed the folded note that he had only received an hour ago to the Irishman. Sean looked at the address scribbled on the paper.

'Amsterdam is your destination,' said the Statesman as the Irishman emptied his glass of its contents and stretched his hand out towards the decanter. 'You appear to have a terrible thirst tonight?'

Sean said nothing, opting instead to empty his refilled glass as he needed the alcohol to deaden the pain. He had been reliant on a walking stick for nearly six months and added a sling following the leap from the truck in New York. However, he had resolved to throw the sling away after tonight, despite his doctor's insistence that he should wear it for another month.

The Irishman poured two more fingers of brandy into a glass, but the Statesman had barely touched his. As the warm glow emitted by the fireplace illuminated his visitor, Churchill assessed the man. He was a different man to the one he had met in their two previous meetings.

When Churchill first encountered Sean Ryan, he judged the teenager to be the most adept of Michael Collins' bodyguards, even though he was by far the youngest. He had a stern, resolute, though reserved demeanour, as he continually scanned the windows and, unlike the two 'carthorses' as Churchill remembered the other bodyguards, he was not in the slightest bit overawed by his genteel surroundings. He might as well have been on patrol behind enemy lines rather than in the dining room of the Prime Minister's residence at 10 Downing Street. He was professional in his approach, far beyond his years. Even when the Anglo–Irish Treaty was signed that day in 1921, he had not exhibited the same elation as all the others: including Collins. Perhaps at that poignant moment the young man already knew that the agreement would drag his country into a bloody civil war or knew that it signed the death warrants of his boss 'The Big Fellah'.

At their second meeting, sixteen years later at

Churchill's country home, Chartwell, the sombre teenager was now a man – a man who had an irreverent attitude to life and authority. The dossier presented to Churchill before their meeting provided details of the man's history in the intervening years. Even in these turbulent times, he had experienced more than most. Ryan had fought in the Irish Civil War in support of the newly declared Irish Free State, had survived several attempts on his life by the Irish Republican Army (IRA) and numerous dangerous encounters with fascist paramilitaries as he travelled the world. The Sean Ryan who sat in his study at Chartwell often crossed that finest of lines that separates confidence from arrogance. Churchill knew many such men, who as he termed it 'had the confidence of privilege' in his elite circle. But this was a man without wealth or connections who revelled in being an outsider. A man who stood alone; no one to decide where he would go and what he would do; he was beholden to no one.

Six months had passed. Despite his injuries, the man sitting in the leather burgundy armchair in front of him possessed the arrogance of the older Ryan but the single-mindedness of the younger. Churchill had read the Polish woman's report. He knew of the loss of those the Irishman treated as friends, first in Hungary, later in Poland and finally in Germany. However, strange as it seemed, if anything, this, combined with his physical injuries, made him appear an even more formidable presence. It was not simply the outcome of his battles, and the time that had elapsed that had changed him, but as Churchill knew well – it was the result of that cruel partnership between terrible loss and absolute failure.

The Statesman was pleased to see that the man still possessed the reserved insolence coupled with that same laconic menace. Having heard his story and assessed the man, there was only one question for which Churchill required an answer – did they still share the same objective?

As he extracted a sip from his balloon-shaped glass, the elder man embarked on finding his answer. 'What do you intend to do once you find the woman's husband?'

'I need to know why the Nazis sought the death of his family. An answer that I know you seek too.'

Churchill was heartened to receive such a clear and unequivocal response.

'True, but to seek the answer is an indulgence when there are other families that at this moment risk a similar fate. Time is short, and my resources are not inexhaustible.' Churchill edged forward, as he always did when he was about to issue a challenge. 'When we met, we agreed to set aside our differences as we shared one purpose; to save the innocent who are hunted by the *Narzees*. It remains my objective; does it remain yours?'

'It does, but I believe that if we can discover why the woman and her son were murdered, it will help us save many more innocent families.'

'I am a politician, so I know when I am being manipulated. There is no reason to believe that discovering the answer you seek will save other lives.' Churchill took a sip from his brandy glass. 'Perhaps you are fooling yourself and are seeking to make sense of the *Narzees*' actions, where logic does not play a part.' Churchill reclined back into his seat, but his question was direct and its intention clear. 'Is it knowledge or revenge you seek? If you take the path of vengeance, then we must go our separate ways. I can have no part of some private vendetta.'

'If vengeance is what drove me, I would still be fighting you,' replied Sean, taking not the slightest pause to consider his answer.

'Good. I'm sure you understand that I will not be embroiled in any act that betrays my oath as a loyal servant of the King and my allegiance to Parliament. Neither will I sanction any action that provides Herr Hitler with an excuse to bring war nearer to our shores sooner than he has planned.'

'I killed in self-defence or to protect those we were trying to rescue; not because I'm waging some covert war against the Nazis. The last time we met, I told you that I would not be manipulated into fighting for the British Empire. You convinced me that you wanted my help to save a woman and a child and nothing more. In that task I failed, but if you wish to save other families, as I do, then we shall remain allies.' Sean raised his glass to the man opposite, 'As uncomfortable as that is at times for both of us.'

Churchill returned the toast. 'After looking at the reports of your actions, I do believe that you killed only to defend those you tried to protect.' Churchill stretched towards the half-full decanter and refreshed the man's glass, but not his own. He returned to the comforting embrace of the armchair. 'Therefore, we continue to share the same objective.'

The Statesman slumped into his chair. 'When you entered here, you told me an extraordinary story revolving around Himmler's Fortress and of your belief that the woman, Magdalena Ilona, and her son, Tóth, have been executed by the *Narzees*.'

It was the first time the Irishman had heard their names spoken since Berlin. It pained him far more than any of his injuries, but he merely gave a brief nod of his head.

'Everything tells me that you are as resilient as before, but appearances can be deceptive. At our last meeting I also asked you whether, when the day arrives that you experience failure, will you return to the fight? You are still a young man and you will recover from your injuries, but are you still mentally strong enough for the task ahead of you?'

'Your assessment of me six months ago was wrong. Failure is well known to me. My most recent cost Magdalena and Tóth their lives, and before them, many others died did so because of me. The only difference is that six months later, I am the one sitting in front of you and asking for your help to save those hunted by the Nazis.'

Churchill knew when an ally or foe was beaten. This man – who accumulated fresh wounds as easily as a schoolboy collects grazes to his knees on a gravel playground – was not.

'Failure is nothing new to either of us. When you venture out into the world and take risks as we have both done, then we must bear our failures. Later, in a time of peace, we can dwell on our mistakes. The ultimate failure is to let failure itself beat you into submission. As for the woman and her boy, if your fears are correct – and let's be clear, you have no evidence of this, nor have you witnessed that this was indeed their fate – then this is truly terrible.

But I know no more than you as to why this poor family were hunted down and killed by the *Narzees*.'

'You believe what I have told you?'

'Yes, but my faith in humanity rejects it and without firm proof of these atrocities the British Government will not listen. Doors are slammed in my face. As our Scottish friend implied, I'm not viewed as a messenger of reason. But I have heard of the persecutions of the Jewish people and with deep regret I share your fear that death was indeed the fate of the young woman and her son.'

Churchill rotated his brandy glass in his hand and looked downcast into the dark whirlpool. 'I have made many speeches on the terrible violence being inflicted on the Jewish citizens in Germany and Austria. I cannot comprehend the sense in condemning anyone simply because of where they were born, their race or religion.' He continued to whirl the contents of his glass but did not touch its contents. 'I first spoke on the floor of the House to warn of the persecution of the Jews when the *Narzees* came to power five years ago. I was ignored then, as I am now.'

He glanced up at Sean, who was clearly in discomfort. The man was in a constant struggle to retain a rigid posture in the pliant upholstered armchair that withdrew its support wherever he rested against it. Churchill had read the Irishman's litany of injuries when he had him flown back from Germany and driven to St Bartholomew's Hospital for further treatment.

The Irishman's doctors produced an eight-page report. When the Statesman read it, he noted the fanciful remark that the 'patient's fractured rib-cage was comparable to a vandalised glockenspiel'. However, overall the medical assessment was positive. The patient would be able to walk again, despite the breaks in his right leg, due to the twelve steel pins inserted from his hip down to his tibia. Two more were fixed to his broken left collar bone. The doctor recorded that the patient refused to say where he had undergone surgery and who had implanted the pins. The multiple stab wounds had healed, to the extent that he was not losing fluids anymore. Churchill circled two additional remarks with his fountainpen: "the man had refused to take any painkillers" and that "whoever had operated on him previously had produced the finest surgery that the attending physicians had ever seen".

'Your Scottish doppelgänger said he stepped into your shoes, or should I say gown, two weeks ago. The same time you were supposedly transferred from St Bart's to Chelsea Hospital,' he paused. 'St Bart's were glad to see the back of you, by the way.'

'One of the patients remembered me from the days of the Irish rebellion. He believed he had a score to settle.'

'Did you not have scores yourself?'

'No, but I'm not what you would call a pacifist.'

'It explains why you put the man in hospital, or should I say back in his bed,' replied the Statesman, shaking his head. 'May I ask why you decided to forgo the excellent treatment I had gone to all the trouble to arrange for you in Chelsea Hospital? Including the considerable expense of a private room, I may add.'

'The day before my transfer from St Bart's our Scottish friend came to visit me. He informed me that there had been several assassination attempts on two friends of ours, the Russian and the Yank.'

'At least you had one friend prepared to visit you.'

'I don't think that I or the Scotsman see each other as friends.'

'That so few become close to you is beneficial in your line of work. Such anonymity is useful when you switch identities, particularly when your impersonator is half your height and has an extra ten inches to accommodate around his waistband.'

Now that Churchill finally had his answers, he mischievously decided to test the man to see what he knew of his role in recent events. It could be of importance if the man was ever captured alive. 'Time to lay our cards on the table,' which to Sean meant that the man had far more hidden up his sleeve than he thought. 'Do you know who financed the operation to help you and the Russian fly to New York?'

'Why ask a question to which you already know the answer?'

Churchill's stern look did not betray him. 'The income from my books and newspaper articles is meagre and two tickets to the United States would place a strain on my personal finances' – which it had.

Sean was not daunted by the man's denial. 'Despite what Jocky told us, I can't see his bosses at the Admiralty stumping up the funding. However, as you wish.'

'Talking of which, the matron of the nursing staff of the Chelsea Hospital will be glad to see the back of your accomplice. Our friend has an eye for the ladies and she's was not best pleased with his behaviour.' Sean grinned on hearing that the man who had adopted his identity had reverted to his base nature. 'Sister Thekla has a fearsome reputation,' continued Churchill, 'I hear she is six feet, three inches tall with a moustache more pronounced than Otto von Bismarck. She is infamous throughout the hospital for terrorising the doctors as well as nurses. An hour ago, I had to deal with a complaint made on her behalf from the hospital's Board of Governors.'

'I take it that Jocky made an improper advance'?'

'His intentions were entirely honourable, it appears. He approached her with flowers and chocolates. However, when she rebuffed him by saying it would take a lot more than that to have dinner with him, he replied that he was happy to partake in, what he called, 'a business arrangement' and produced a five-pound note. His flirtation landed him back in bed, but not from reaching an accommodation, but rather from receiving a knee to his groin. I hear the cause of much mirth amongst the nursing staff.' Churchill spoke with an exaggerated seriousness in his tone, 'In light of his bravery on manoeuvres, I have told him that I will lobby the King to have a special medal struck in his honour; perhaps with something engraved in Latin. You know the Lothario better than I, any suggestions?'

'Never mix romance and commerce!' said Sean. For the first and only time, the men laughed freely together. Sean noted, 'We all have our little weaknesses.'

'Indeed, we do, but let us move on to our strengths,' as Churchill reached once more towards the decanter on the table beside him. The Statesman looked at the man's cane. 'Will it be a permanent fixture?'

'Only until I have made my way safely past the

Unionists in the lobby.'

Churchill was aware of the instrument's secondary purpose. 'You would put my colleagues to the sword? Yet, you say that the war between us has passed?'

'It has, but as with the man in the hospital there will always be those who will never forgive,' he said and raised his glass to toast his host, 'on both sides.'

'True, there are many on my side that will never accept the treaty signed by The Big Fellah. As indeed, there are many on your side who will never accept swearing an oath to the King. But what of you?'

'The Treaty was the best we could have attained. With the Great War over, we knew that unless we agreed you could finally turn the full firepower of the British Army on our people.'

'You shared Collins' pragmatism.'

'I'd swear allegiance to the devil – which is what we did – if it meant we could finally have self-determination for the twenty-six counties.' Sean looked at the cane, 'You know I have brought a weapon into this room, yet you haven't tried to call security?'

'I believe I am a good judge of horseflesh.'

'You trust me?'

'As you say, "we all have our little weaknesses", but if my trust in you is found wanting, I have my trusted Mauser in my coat pocket. Despite its intricate mechanism, it has served me well in the past.' He patted the right-hand side pocket of his black coat. 'After all, some of your ancestors may have been part of the Irish conspiracy to blow up the Lords as well as the Commons, two hundred years after Guy Fawkes. Sadly, as a servant of this House I am forbidden to take it into the Chamber, though on many an occasion I would have had good reason to use it.'

Sean knew he was lying about the gun, for despite popular crime novels, to carry a gun did not necessarily lead to the obvious bulge on a person, but it did affect how a man's suit hung. Churchill's black pin-striped blazer appeared perfectly symmetrical when he had raised himself up from behind his desk. Sean knew of only three men who had their suits cut to accommodate the additional weight, and they were all professional killers.

Despite his sixty-five years, the Statesman continued with his ruse, as he still possessed a young man's craving to taunt danger.

'With your injuries slowing you down, I have not the slightest doubt that I would shoot you before you reached me.' He could see that the man opposite was not perturbed, but he enjoyed the game. 'More of this?' he asked, as he lifted the decanter and was impressed to see how much of its contents the Irishman had already consumed.

'Yes, a double of whatever it is.'

'Courvoisier, the Cognac of Napoleon, though I prefer Hine myself. However, it is an excellent substitute. Before I address the House in the morning, I must endure speeches from the backbenches on how we can reach a gentlemanly compromise with Chancellor Hitler. I am tempted to smuggle this into the Chamber as fortification may be required.' Sean raised the decanter to top up his glass. 'Providing, I am left with any.' From what Sean knew of the man, he was playing to his reputation, as no man had a greater respect for the laws and traditions of Parliament than he. 'After the Treaty was signed, Collins and I corresponded. Did you know that?'

This did not surprise Sean, as he knew that both men had developed a respect for the other. He reflected that if Collins were still alive, the Irish Government would be on less friendly terms with Germany.

'Collins was a man reared in fierce conditions who lived in ferocious times,' acknowledged Churchill. 'He supplied those qualities of action and personality without which the foundation of Irish nationhood would not have been re-established.'

'The IRA assassinated him for it.'

'By signing the Treaty, unbeknown to him, he signed your death warrant too. To our knowledge there have been four attempts on your life, and I must tell you that I received a report earlier this month that the IRA has raised the price for any information leading to your whereabouts.'

'It's always nice to be wanted.'

'Clearly, given the choice, you will choose the quickest path even if it offers the greatest resistance. I take it that your Scottish doppelgänger was useful in evading your enemies?'

'I guessed that once I had been treated for my injuries, I would to be sent to a military hospital and kept under twenty-four-hour armed guard. Therefore, any assassins waiting to kill me would be left scratching their arses outside the hospital, having to wait until I was discharged. Any Nazis on my tail, would also have to postpone any thoughts of making an attempt on my life. So with my enemies left twiddling their trigger fingers thinking I was inside the hospital I could join the others and surprise the Alpha Wolves unit in New York. And talking of surprises, you didn't raise an eyebrow when I entered the room.'

'At my time of life, it would take more than you breaking into my chambers to surprise me.' He adopted a serious tone. 'This is Parliament after all – it's full of criminal activity.' His congenial manner disappeared. 'Why come here at such a late hour? You could easily have made your way here after dusk?'

'I was in no rush to breathe in your cigar smoke. It's bad for my health. But as I said, I need resources.'

'Four men were found in the wreckage of a Bugatti parked outside Chelsea Hospital a few hours ago. Would this explain the lateness of your visit this evening?'

Sean remained impassive.

'Scotland Yard believe it was an Irish terrorist cell that accidentally blew itself up. Fragments of forged Irish passports were discovered amongst the wreckage.'

The Irishman said nothing, but the information about the passports was another new and dangerous development.

Churchill had learnt to read men, and the Irishman was as canny at hiding his emotions as any worthy opponent in the House.

It was Sean's turn to lean forward. 'If we are washing the dirtiest of linen, and you don't know already, the Nazis knew I was coming to Budapest.'

'Do you know who the informer is?'

'A number of people were involved in the arrangements in Budapest, Vienna and Berlin,' and looking directly at Churchill, 'but London links them all.' He scanned the Statesman's face for a reaction and was met by a frown. Sean pressed on, 'I think I know who betrayed us and if I'm right, through them I will find the man behind the deaths of Magdalena Ilona and her son, Tóth.'

'The shadowy creature you mentioned?'

Churchill did not respond to the mention of a traitor, but though he was disappointed to hear that there was a spy amongst them, he was not surprised. He was perfectly aware that when governments speak of peace negotiations – it means that their secret services are at their busiest, desperate to discover the ploys and weaknesses of friends and foes alike. Indeed, much of the information he received was privileged and came from the few remaining friends he had in the War Ministry and across the Atlantic.

'Keep your friends close and your enemies closer,' continued the Statesman. 'But I never saw the sense in that myself; I prefer to keep them at a discrete distance but in view. In the meantime, as I have said, I pray vengeance does not consume you and erase the path that leads to the puppet master.' Sean remained silent. Churchill continued, 'I will not bother to ask you again who you believe the traitor is, for if you wanted me to know you would have told me.'

'As I say, I'm not certain.'

'What news of the Polish woman Lenka, the lynchpin that holds you all together. I have not heard from her for days.'

Days, thought Sean. He had not heard from her since Berlin. He said nothing but was grateful that so far, she was not a target for the Alpha Wolves. Perhaps this was because the Nazis knew she was the beacon that drew them all together, and through her they could always find the Rogues – of course, there could be another reason.

Now that both men had said as much as they felt the

other should know, they drained their brandy glasses. Sean leant forward and perched precariously on the lip of his leather chair. He rubbed his empty glass between his hands and stared into it, as though it were an oracle that would provide him with answers. Churchill watched the troubled fighter. 'Do you have accommodation for tonight?'

'A bar.'

'Come to my club.'

'Best I keep a low profile.'

'I'll cover the drinks bill.'

'Then it hurts even more to decline your offer.'

'Why not?' asked Churchill, aggrieved.

'Because you are notoriously reckless; you know I have two targets on my back and you would walk alongside me. You are a risk to my reputation.'

'Pray, how could I besmirch your good name?'

'Because, you are starting to make me look sensible.'

'Are you concerned for my life?'

'Not overly. But, in Parliament, you are a lone voice in opposing the Nazis. No one is listening now, but soon they will have need of your leadership.'

Churchill huffed as he would have enjoyed introducing such a disreputable character into such an establishment and ruffling the feathers of other members when they heard of his late-night guest, especially Lord Sloane and his ilk.

'I will have further arrangements made for when you reach Amsterdam, but it may take a day or so.' Sean nodded. 'Then farewell, but this time can you leave by the main gates.'

'I have no pass; will this not raise questions about how I got in?'

'Of course, but questions are what we do here. It is only when we are met by an honest answer, that our suspicions are aroused. However, I'm sure you will furnish them with an acceptable falsehood if challenged.'

'I'll leave the rowing boat moored below your window. Who knows, you might need to make a quick escape yourself one day.'

'Abandon Parliament! I never dreamt of such a thing even during one of Baldwin's – the former Prime Minister – 'interminable speeches. On your way out go to the police box by the main gates and ask for an envelope. Inside is an undated, pre-paid reservation granting you stay in a nearby establishment. It also contains one hundred pounds to help you on your journey.' Churchill smiled, letting the pain of recent times fall from his face. 'But, the results of my journalistic endeavours are not to be spent on pursuits such as those of our Scottish friend.'

'Actually, that's not for me. I'm quite old-fashioned when it comes to women.'

'I am surprised considering the life you lead. However, I too have never paid for a lady's services, even when I was single and fighting at the front.'

Sean looked at the man he once considered to be his enemy and was again pleasantly surprised to hear that they shared similar values that transcended their backgrounds. He also wondered how long ago the Statesman had prepared the letter and deposited it at the police box by the main gates with the expectation that Sean would break into the Palace of Westminster in search of him.

'What name is it under?'

Churchill told him just as the largest of the five bells,

known as Big Ben, in The Elizabeth Tower rang the hour twelve times. Before the final chime, Sean had made his way to the oak door and closed it behind him without either man offering a handshake or saying goodbye.

In the hall, Sean caught a glimpse of a young red-haired woman who was standing in a doorway at the end of the passage. She abruptly turned away and disappeared down the main staircase. With the aid of his cane Sean made his way down the stairs and quickly mingled with staff emerging at the end of their day. Ahead of him, the woman was moving as briskly as her tight skirt would alone and glancing back in his direction. Sean was pleased to see that she was not a professional, so he decided it was not worth following her to see who was keeping an eye on the Statesman.

But when he reached the gate, two policemen were blocking the woman's path.

'You're far too pretty to be running anywhere,' said the gaunt-faced constable.

The Irishman slammed his cane down on the window hatch of the police box.

'Leave that lady alone and get over here now!' he yelled.

The officers were uncertain how to react, when the angry man with the stick barked at them once more. 'You have an envelope for me marked Mr P. Anther. I want it now!' The stouter of the two constables stepped aside, allowing the woman to run across Parliament Square to catch a bus. Only when she was seated did Sean notice her take a sly glance towards the main gates as the omnibus pulled away.

As the officers walked back to the guard box, the thinnest one attempted to challenge the arrogant man with the cane. But the man bellowed once more. 'Get a bloody move on or I will wake Neville,' Chamberlain, 'from his sleep and together we will search your office for the document. Then, he can deal with you two imbeciles!'

The officers quickly began to root through the documents in their office. The tubbier officer remembered the fine Basildon Bond envelope, because to his amazement it had been handed to him by a Member of Parliament – one of the most famous politicians at that. He breathed a sigh of relief, as he passed the document through the open hatch to the rough-looking but clearly well-connected gentleman. The man snatched it from his clammy hand and deposited his sling on the ledge of the window. 'Share this between you. It may restrain you from greeting the Nazis too enthusiastically if they ever come knocking on these gates.'

Sean limped out the gates making no attempt to conceal his smile.

Two hours later, Churchill was in the middle of redrafting his speech when he received a telephone call from the Admiralty.

'Lord Sloane here. Winston, it has been brought to my attention that you were paid a visit by the Irishman tonight.'

'As always, you are exceptionally well-informed.'

'You have friends who are concerned for your welfare. As it happened one spotted your visitor. Your thick Irish Johnny even helped her on her way to catch her last bus home.'

The aristocrat's laugh reverberated loudly down the telephone, before line fell silent.

'Ogilvy are you still there?' pressed Churchill, 'I'll too old for a crank,' selecting his words with the utmost deliberation, 'call.'

It got, as intended, a response.

'What news of the woman and boy that you sent the Paddy to help?'

'The Irishman believes that they are dead.' Again, the line fell silent. 'Ogilvy are you there?' asked a disgruntled Churchill, but the man on the other end had already replaced the receiver.

Chapter 4: The Gulag

January 1938, Vorkuta

'My God, you're Vodanski Bulgakov! You were in all the papers. The Hero of Kiev they called you. But that was before you were denounced by the NKVD,' Stalin's secret police. Vodanski continued to watch the three guards by the door at the far end of the dormitory, as the slight man sitting on the bare bed opposite babbled on. 'Your wife and daughter were prisoners here. I heard the guards say that you would come here one day to find them, but they are too stupid to recognise you now that you are under their big red noses.'

Vodanski turned to look at the excitable prisoner sitting on the urine-stained blanket.

"Were?"

'The Commandant here, The Butcher, selects female prisoners and keeps them chained to his couch. He picked your wife, which was unusual as he always picks younger girls. She was very beautiful, your wife.' Gevork grinned as if he were paying the big man a compliment. 'I believe he chose her because of you. I think The Butcher got a kick from violating your woman.'

Vodanski's throat was dry, and he had to swallow hard what spittle he had in his mouth before he could speak. 'What of my daughter?'

'The guards say that The Butcher told your wife that her daughter was safe, as long as she willingly submitted to him. I overheard the guards say that when they she would look through The Butcher as if he were transparent when he took her. One night, this riled the Butcher's fury, and he choked her to death and as he did, so he told her he had already murdered her, sorry your child. He . . .'

Vodanski struggled to suppress the overwhelming urge to silence the man with one blow to his face, but he managed to whisper, 'Leave me.'

'Big man, there is a way out.' Vodanski had no interest in escape, not yet, but he looked again into the bulging, dark, deep-set eyes of the man opposite. 'You are strong and big enough to break through the barbed wire, and I'm sure you can run fast enough to sprint across the killing zone and evade the bullets from the guards in the towers.'

The animated man looked towards the three guards at the end of the large room littered with broken bunks and broken men and gave a furtive nod.

Vodanski leaned into the man's face, 'And when you warn the guards of my escape, how much is your reward?'

Gevork straightened up, as he gripped the frame of his bunk, 'I'm taking a hell of a risk in talking to help you, and in return you accuse me of being an informer. You are new here, but I have learnt that our survival depends on us helping each other.'

Vodanski studied the emaciated prisoners around him. The fifty or more other inmates were curled up under stained, grey blankets, many still wearing the threadbare clothes they were arrested in. A further ten were walking around aimlessly. The wooden hut contained little furniture beyond a few bunk beds, and an overflowing communal bucket emitting an overwhelming odour that the prisoners no longer seemed to notice. In the middle of the room was a stove which, despite the sub-zero temperatures, remained unlit.

Vodanski glowered at the little man, 'Not once have you asked if I brought any food with me. That must be because you look remarkable healthy, despite your clothing, amongst these poor emaciated bastards. You have managed to secure extra rations, which explains why you have sidled up to me.'

'No, you're wrong. I'm a Communist and I believe that the people of the world will rise up as one and we–'

'You sound like an academic, but you know that what you say is bollocks as you live under the system.' Vodanski surprising himself for though they were talking in Russian, not only had he cursed in English, but had used Sean's favourite word. Vodanski trained his eyes on the soldiers. 'But let's see if I'm right.' He seized the opposite by his throat and began to choke him. If his assessment was right, the guards would react instantly to try to protect their informer – if he was wrong, the guards might amble over to watch. He also knew that to carry out his plan, it would have to be done quickly before sleep deprivation and hunger eroded what strength he possessed.

The two guards on either side of the corporal lifted their standard Mosin-Nagant M91 rifles to aim at the gigantic man throttling the informer in the centre of the room. The corporal ordered Vodanski to release Gevork, who was futilely struggling to free himself. Some prisoners glanced over, but most just tightened their blankets around themselves.

Vodanski released the little man, letting him drop to the floor and writhe around grasping his throat trying to breathe. The meek, submissive man who the guards had thrown on the floor at the other end of the dormitory less than an hour ago, straightened up. The colossus stood six feet three inches in height. No longer were his shoulders hunched and his head bowed as he strode towards the three guards.

With the rifles of the men beside him trained on the man, the corporal, either through bravery or a false sense of his own invulnerability, goaded the advancing giant.

'Svyatogor,' the giant-warrior from Russian mythology, meaning "scared mountain", 'let us talk about your wife and your daughter, we have much to tell you,' he sneered, seemingly oblivious of the approaching danger. 'I discovered things that a man should never know about his wife and daughter, but The Butcher liked to–'

Vodanski lunged at him, parrying the rifles either side of him away with his arms before smashing his head into the corporal's jaw. He seized the corporal by his genitals with his left hand. The guards, taken by surprise at the speed of the attack, pounded their rifle butts repeated into Vodanski's head. It did not stop the corporal's attacker from crushing his testicles until they burst in his vice-like grip. Vodanski remained motionless until the man choked his last breath as blood vessels burst throughout his groin and his heart gave out. Only then did Vodanski close his eyes and control his fall to the ground.

Three weeks earlier, Vodanski had walked up the stone

steps of The People's Commissariat of Internal Affairs, in Moscow's Lubyanka Square, the headquarters of Lavrentiy Beria, the new 'Executive' of the NKVD. Following a polite request, he refused to accept the familiar standard official response of *NYET* on each floor of the vast building. He worked his way up each floor until he reached the offices of the Minister for Information on the top floor. He found the office he sought with DEPUTY MINISTER FOR INFORMATION COMMISSAR MIKHAILOVICH BLOKHIN painted in fresh gold-leaf letters on the glass-frosted panel of the door. Vodanski made his way into the room, leaving the two guards who tried to bar his way with their Tokarev SVT-40 rifles lying unconscious on the floor.

'What the . . .' shouted the Deputy Minister for Information. His superior, who had recently drunkenly boasted to a confidant that he had 'fucked one of Stalin's mistresses,' had been arrested the day before for reasons that, due to the hasty arrest, had not been formalised yet.

'I am Vodanski Bulgakov. Tell me where my wife and daughter are, or I will use your kidneys to paint these walls with your blood.'

The officer, though a small, slight man, was a tenacious type, not easily cowed, and he calmly continued to sit in his oversized chair.

'Comrade Vodanski, as a punishment for your cowardice and as a deserter from The Red Army, your wife and daughter have been sent to a forced labour camp.'

'Deserter? I was fighting Fascists in Spain on Stalin's personal orders while you were doing weights with your pencil.'

'You are a traitor. You will be hung by the neck

before the end of the day.'

'The name of the labour camp? Now!' roared Vodanski, at the little man slouched on his chair as if it were a throne.

'You believe you can just walk in here and expect me, the new Deputy Director for Moscow's NKVD, to do your bidding?'

'Yes.' Vodanski reached across, grabbed the deputy by his black tie, lifted him out of his chair, and dragged his across the desk until his terrified face was an inch from his.

'Vorkuta! Vorkuta! They are in Vorkuta!'

'If you are lying to me about the whereabouts of my family, I will return to decorate these walls.'

Vodanski dropped the Deputy Minister for Information onto his feet, but his legs collapsed from under him. He did not wait to see him fall, as he stepped over the two guards and made his way unhurriedly down the corridor.

That morning the new Deputy Minister for Information, having reported what he overheard from his predecessor to the Security Police (NKVD), reclined in the most powerful seat in Moscow. He had thought he need fear no one again. However, twelve hours later, he was lying face down on the plush carpet of his new office and not since he was a child had he been so scared that he had defecated in his trousers.

Having learnt the location of the labour camp where he prayed his family were, Vodanski returned to his lodgings. He gathered up his belongings and hitched the first of many rides to the Siberian town of Vorkuta, over 1000 miles from

Moscow. It took nearly a month to reach the outskirts of the forced labour camp, one of many Gulags that were tasked by Moscow to mine for coal. Because of the inherent danger in the task and the extreme weather, life expectancy for its inmates was often only a year at most.

It was the middle of the night. There was no sign of any guards patrolling the perimeter, let alone the miles of barren, snow-covered wasteland that surrounded it. In the minus-twenty-degree temperatures, he was not surprised that they were content to leave the security of the area to the omnipresent yellow beams emitted from the searchlights positioned in the four guard towers. He wondered why they needed sentries at all, as no one could hope to reach the forest without being cut to pieces by the M1910 Maxim machine guns that stalked the lights. But his only hope of breaking in was the appearance of a sentry.

Having stayed awake through the night, Vodanski was relieved to see the appearance of the gulag's guards. He sat still in the woods, recording the times of each change of sentries. He recorded two shifts each of four hours. Time was short, as he had food left for only one day, but as the temperature was below minus twenty, sustenance was not his most immediate concern. He needed to break into the compound to save his family and this would require all his strength, but perfect timing. That moment had arrived. It was one hour before the guards' shift finished, and he knew that they would be tired, hungry and, therefore, not at their most diligent.

Before he rose, he thought of his wife, Nicki, and his daughter Katalina; and pondered why he only now returned to find them. It was two years since he was sent to Spain to fight; he was a soldier, and he had to go. But after he threw his commander, Major Allegro, out of the window he was then a fugitive from the Red Army. At the time, he told himself that if he had returned to the Soviet Union, he would have put them both at risk. Now he had returned. But why had he not come back sooner? Did he not love them? He knew he loved his daughter, or so he believed, though he had never seen her. Did he love his wife? They were married because that is what young people who liked each other did in his village, but he thought he loved her, or would for sure one day. Maybe deep down the thought of raising a family scared him? Perhaps he had grown to love war too much? After all this time, what if the found him so brutalised by fighting that neither would love him?

Stooping, he edged forward and fixed his eyes once more on the guards in the distance. He was here now; all that mattered was to find Nicki and Katalina. Then he would be the dutiful, loving husband and father he knew he could be.

It was time. He made his way down through the trees and worked his way behind the guards, so he was between them and the camp. He wrenched one of the wooden stakes from the warped fence out of the frozen ground with one hand.

A few minutes later, one of the sentries turned to see if there was any sign of the guards who would relieve him, only to discover a man in the snow apparently caught under a dislodged post holding up the perimeter fence.

'Please don't shoot me!' pleaded the entangled man. Both guards surrounded him and pointed their rifles at the petrified captive, curled up, covering his face with his arms.

Hauled up by his arms, the guards dragged his limp body through the virgin snow, before throwing him through the doors of the wooden hut. They eagerly rushed to inform their corporal that they had caught and returned an escaped prisoner.

Vodanski woke to discover a very familiar taste in his mouth – his blood.

'My friend, today is your lucky day as you have secured an audience with Commandant Pavlovich Kaganovich.' Vodanski remained face down on the dirty, wooden floor, listening intently while conserving his energy. 'I see you are not impressed. Maybe you know me by another name . . . The Butcher.'

Vodanski lifted his head and for the first time set his eyes on the fat, shaven-headed man sitting on a large sofa with his arms outstretched along its back support. What was striking about the man was not just his size – his skin was swollen and bulging through every gap in his uniform – but his blotched, vein-riddled face. The excess of his vices would have given his flushed appearance prominence in any company; but compared to the anaemic faces of Gevork and the guards, he looked on the verge of exploding. Only the fresh bruising on The Butcher's knuckles indicated that he did anything more than be plied with food and drink.

His bulbous pike-like lips opened, 'A few months ago, I received a communication from Moscow that certain parties in Germany would pay handsomely if you came in search of your family and were captured.' He roared even louder, exposing a full set of crooked, tobacco-stained teeth, 'I dismissed such a notion, as only a lunatic would break into a Gulag. But here you are, prostrate at my feet. I have sent a message that I have captured you and been informed that you must be kept alive until a special unit arrives from Berlin with my money, before they,' he laughed, '"sever your head and take it to their superior".' He snorted, exposing the black tar eroding his gums.

A clear, calm voice came from the motionless figure lying in the middle of the room. 'Where are my wife and daughter?'

'They are wolf shit now. We threw them somewhere out there,' said The Butcher, nodding towards the snow-framed window and out into the darkness.

'I told you! It's Vodanski! It's Vodanski!' shouted Gevork, pointing at the man on the floor.

The Butcher grinned. 'My apologies, Rat,' the name by which Gevork was more commonly known by both prisoners and guards. 'I confess I was sceptical when your message was passed to me, but I can see now that this pathetic creature is the infamous Vodanski.'

'The Hero of Kiev, look at you trussed up on the ground like a pig,' sniggered Rat, kicking the man on the floor. As the Rat's boot bounced repeatedly off his face, Vodanski rolled over. Now, with his back on the floor, he worked the handle-less knife concealed in his sleeve down into his hand. The Rat stamped on his face, as Vodanski worked the steel blade into the ropes that bound his hands behind him.

The Rat tired. He leant against the wall of the hut to catch his breath after the excursion. He went cold when he heard his victim speak in a loud, clear, unaffected voice.

'Are all prisoners searched when they first come to the

Gulag?' Bewildered, the Rat peered down at Vodanski, who spat the reservoir of blood in his mouth onto the floor beside him.

'Of course,' bellowed The Butcher.

'But do you also search those you recapture in the kill zone?' said the bruised and bloodied man on the floor as he turned his head to look at the Commandant.

'Why? Outside is a snow-covered wilderness, there are no weapons or food to be found there.' A loud laugh erupted from The Butcher, exposing his rotting teeth. 'Would you smuggle in a snowball?'

Vodanski pressed his hands flat down on the floor and lifted his right foot slightly to provide a foothold. 'But to recapture someone implies you caught them in the first place. Are you aware that your guards treated me as a captured escapee?'

The two guards standing over Vodanski remained impassive, but fear seized The Butcher as he realised what the man was saying, as did The Rat – but it was too late.

Vodanski launched himself at the guards. He lashed out with his right foot, catching the nearest guard in the ankle, sending him towards the floor and onto Vodanski's elbow, which broke the bridge of his nose. The second guard's finger froze on the trigger as Vodanski threw the blade and severing his windpipe. The Butcher desperately tried to lift his bulk up from the couch. The Rat reached the door. Vodanski retrieved the blade from the guard's neck and threw it once more to find its target – the back of the Rat's head – where it disappeared inside his skull and out through an eye-socket, pinning his head to the door.

The Butcher twisted himself to his side and was trying

to use his hands to push himself up from his seat, but someone grabbed his hand and spun him around. But he averted his face from the wide raging eyes of the man, who was no longer his prisoner.

Vodanski locked The Butcher's fingers in his powerful grasp, and flipped the wrist of the commandant's outstretched arm, forcing him down onto his left knee.

'Look at me!' yelled Vodanski. 'Look at me!' The Commandant's fingers snapped, as he cried in agony. Vodanski roared, 'Look . . . at . . . me!'

The Butcher's wrist broke. Screaming in agony, finally he stared up at the man who would kill him. Vodanski held the man's terrified gaze, as he swung his right boot up under the Commandant's chin, sending his jawbone into his brain with the impact of an axe swung into an overripe pumpkin.

Six hours later, two trucks pulled up at the gates of the camp loaded with soldiers in Red Army uniforms. Vodanski watched from the darkness of The Butcher's office – they had arrived sooner than expected. He thought the guards in the compound would have come in search of their comrades by now, but maybe they feared The Butcher as much as the inmates did, and only entered his office when ordered to.

Vodanski picked up a bottle of what he learnt to be home-brewed vodka, having bent double after taking a swig earlier. Having removed the cork, he plugged the neck with a dry rag. He doused the walls and floor with the contents of the eighteen unopened bottles he found in five boxes in a corner behind The Butcher's couch.

He could hear the crunching of the snow under the guards' boots getting louder. Vodanski opened the valve of one of the four gas cylinders by the door, which were kept in reserve for heating the room. He lit the rag protruding from the neck of the bottle with a small piece of timber he had poked into the lit stove in the centre of the room. Holding it away from him, he walked unhurriedly to the window opposite the door and opened it. Just as the wooden doorknob of the front door turned, Vodanski launched the flaming bottle into the lit stove and leapt from the half-open window, landing in the thick mass of snow. The hut exploded, scattering the body parts of the two officers on the other side of the door in all directions. In the chaos, Vodanski snuck out of the main gates as the newly arrived truckload of troops along with the camp's guards tried to smother the fire with buckets of snow.

Vodanski reached the woods and turned to look at the camp. He clutched at the dull pain running across his chest where there was no wound and wondered where the bodies of his family lay.

Chapter 5: Putting on The Ritz

August 1938, London

Jocky bounded up to Sean as Big Ben struck once. 'They thought *yer* might need help as I hear *yer* still can't wipe *yer* arse.'

'Good to know that you have found a vocation that matches your talents.'

'Machines not arseholes are my forte. Best *yer* ask *yer* next visitor, as they're sending a woman from the Admiralty. I'll wait until she arrives and woo her with my fine-tuned Glaswegian mating skills. Unless of course it's the Ice-maiden, then I'm fucked.'

'You're referring to Lieutenant Brett?'

The Scotsman ignored him and stood back to stare up at the Irishman.

'God, *yer* really are a sad, pathetic specimen. Lucky, I gave *yer* that cane before *yer* headed off to America, or *yer* would still be clutching the railings outside Bart's.'

'Would you like me to remind you what your little invention can do?' Jocky stepped back. 'Oh, and thank you by the way, it came in very useful.' Sean lifted it up to look at the small button just below the handle. When depressed, it spun the entire cylinder of the cane ninety degrees, exposing a steel blade along its length. This meant it could be drawn out sideways rather than extracted like a sword from a scabbard; extra seconds that had already saved his life. 'My angry friend, you're far more than just a pretty face ruined by years of alcohol and self-abuse.'

'Careful, *yer're nay* too *fuken* steady on *yer* legs, Bambi,' replied the smiling Scotsman.

Sean was puzzled by the reference but remembered reading somewhere that Hitler had banned the children's story of that title because its author, Felix Salten, was Jewish.

Jocky turned to look at the grand marble entrance.

'The Ritz eh, *yer* must have friends in high places.'

'Just one, but it counterbalances my association with you,' replied Sean, as both men made their way through the revolving door into the lobby of one of the grandest hotels in London.

Though it was late in the morning, many guests were scurrying across the blue-veined marbled floor as the city's theatres and restaurants were thriving.

'Well my little kilt-lifter, please don't take this the wrong way, but what the fuck are you doing here this time of night?'

'I've been assigned to look after *yer* again. As I said, some urgent arse-wiping situation nay doubt.'

'Who sent you?'

'The Commander, my boss, *nay* names. He's an old Etonian and, therefore, as cracked as a piss-pot, but a genius. *Nay* endeavour is too outrageous, *nay* challenge is impossible. He recruits the likes of me for his hare-brained intelligence schemes.'

'Where did he discover you, anyway?'

'My Da fought under the command of Winston

Churchill in the Sudan. When I decided to head to London to find work, I wrote to him and asked for his help. As soon as I stepped off the train at Kings Cross, I was handed a note inviting me to Old Admiralty House. That's when I met The Commander, who instantly spotted my talents and offered me a job as a 'technical adviser'. Naturally, when they needed a specialist to save the sorry arses of *yer* and the other Rogues in Berlin, I was the man.'

'Jake told me you drove the train out of Berlin with an engine driver's operating manual in your hand.'

'I read books, that's my real skill outside of *me* pants. I know the basics of how machines work, and I can drive anything. *Me* other passion is chemistry.'

'I thought it was women?'

'Ah, that's a different sort of chemistry and I don't need a manual for that.' Jocky was excited. 'That lump of peat between *yer* ears won't be able to comprehend this, but one day pal there will be machines where *yer* can store all sorts of information. *Yer* will be able to find the answer to any question just by typing it in. Some of these machines will even be portable; though because of having to fit in so many components *yer* will have to tow it on the back of a tank.'

'With one of those, you might be able to secure a date.'

'Yer think such a machine would find me a woman?'

'No, I was referring to sitting in the tank, as women won't be able to see or hear you. It's a long-shot, but the only one you've got.'

'*Yer* funny for a potato-picking *bastad*.' He remembered something and produced a ticket from his pocket. It was marked THE RITZ No 13 and scribbled on it, *One steel trunk*. 'I left it in the cloakroom; *yer* might need it one day; but *nay* this trip.'

Navy Lieutenant Amelia Brett entered the lobby.

'Fuck me sideways, pal, it's the ice-maiden from Berlin,' blurted the Scotsman, startling the elderly couple attempting to pay their bill.

Sean hid his smile with his hand. He enjoyed that whatever the Glaswegian thought came instantly out of his mouth.

'As I made clear to you in Berlin,' snapped the lieutenant, 'not if you were the last man on Earth.'

Without looking at either man, she retrieved a folder from her bag. 'Here are your papers for your return to Europe in two days' time. You will travel to Amsterdam where you will meet with the Polish woman.' Sean and Jocky remembered how the lieutenant refused to acknowledge Lenka by name or acknowledge her existence in the Berlin bar.

Jocky examined the identity papers. 'These are *shite*!', and to the lieutenant's horror, he tore them up. 'These wouldn't secure us entrance to Madame Tussaud's. I'll knock some out tomorrow after I do my business.'

The lieutenant regained her composure. 'I have no interest in your 'business', but I have orders for you. You are to accompany Ryan to the Netherlands.'

'Excellent, I'm up against the Nazis and His Majesty's Government assign me a mascot,' teased Sean.

He was also enjoying the discomfort they were causing the smarmy-looking man behind the reception desk.

'Away and *shite*, bog trotter,' shouted the Scotsman.

The lieutenant looked up at Sean. 'He proved himself

in Berlin; he's a base creature, but a resourceful one.'

She scowled at the Scotsman, as if he were something foul she had discovered on the heel of her shoe, before glancing at Sean's walking stick.

'And you are in no position to refuse help, Mr Ryan, no matter in what form.'

'I'm a foot away, I can hear _yer_,' said the aggrieved Scotsman. 'Well, as much as I'm enjoying swapping pleasantries with _yer_ Duchess,' said Jocky, directing an insincere smile at the lieutenant, 'and Long John Silver here, I'm off to Shepherd's Market,' which was just across the road, '_Yer_ see some women there are quite partial to a little Scottish loving.' He glanced up at the lieutenant and raised his eyebrows, smiled. 'Unless . . ?' He was met by an even frostier stare from the lieutenant. '_Nay_ harm in asking,' and with that he shrugged his shoulders and marched out of the lobby.

'A fruit and veg market open this hour of the morning?' asked Sean, turning to the lieutenant. 'Very health conscious is our little Einstein.'

Amelia ignored the remark, 'Our business is completed.'

'The Nazis were waiting for me in Budapest,' said Sean, as he waited for her reaction. The lieutenant scowled up at him but said nothing. Neither did she express surprise. Sean continued to press: 'Who knew of the mission apart from you and Winston?'

'That's confidential.'

'Not when I end up smashed to fuck it isn't.'

'If Winston hasn't told you, neither will I.'

The Irishman knew the woman's beauty belied a

resolute determination. He thought he would try another approach. 'Have dinner with me tonight?'

'I never mix business with . . .' and stopped there.

'Pleasure, and who knows, I might surprise you.' His shoulders slumped. 'Look, I leave in a few days and I have been living on hospital food for six months.' He thought it best not to mention the steak in New York, 'and it's just dinner with a poor harmless cripple.'

Amelia studied at the injured man trying to stand up with the aid of a walking stick. 'You've been in better shape, but there is nothing harmless about you. I'm not stupid. You want information.'

'And you don't.'

'I will accept your invitation, as I'm intrigued to hear how you survived.'

The lieutenant turned on the heels of her handmade stilettoes and headed off through the revolving doors and out into the traffic towards Berkeley Square. Sean watched her weave like a ballerina between the on-coming taxis. He smiled, as men often do when they encounter a beautiful woman, knowing the moment would be filed in their memory until they took their final breath.

The hotel receptionist, a thin, middle-aged man with a pinched face and a long, narrow nose, wished goodbye to an elderly couple, 'To be of service to you, has caused me immense pleasure. Any trinket that you have left me to remind me of your time here would be cherished.' They pressed a blue note into his grasping fingers, and as soon as they turned away, his smile disappeared. It reappeared as he watched the man limping across the hall towards him. As the dishevelled appearance of the man with the cane became more apparent, his welcoming smile contorted to that of someone who had to endure a very rich relative's wet dog crawling across their expensive new carpet.

'May I be of help Sir?' he asked.

As Ryan handed over the bleached white Basildon Bond envelope, he replied, 'Smiler, I'm beyond help, but you have a room for me.'

Chapter 6: Cerberus' Story

May 1919, Munich

The young Klaus Krak was not born of tragedy. Nor was he the result of abuse. He was not the product of experience. The boy, who later became infamous throughout Europe, was the result of a society that nurtured the evil within him.

'I can't eat this shit!'

'Klaus don't swear, I've told you before, only Jews swear,' said Anya Krak, admonishing her son.

'Do they all swear?' asked the boy.

'Yes, and they drink and fornicate, but this is not a conversation for the dinner table.'

The boy was inquisitive about Jews, as he had never spoken to one. 'What do Jews do?'

His father joined the table. 'Do? What they do is take advantage of our plight by lending money at rates they know the German people can't afford. They take our hard-earned money from our pockets; they smile and pretend to be civilised while they work with the Communists to destroy us. That is what they do.'

Klaus' father, Dietrich Krak, had been conscripted into the Kaiser's Army, but had never ventured on to the battlefield. He envied those who had; soldiers like Adolf Hitler, the leader of the National Socialist Party: the Nazis. Hitler had been a corporal during the Great War and had nearly died in the trenches during a gas attack (though it was rarely reported that it originated from his own side before the wind changed direction).

In 1917 the Americans had entered the war, and for the first time Germany's losses outstripped the Allies. Their Army was in retreat – but Dietrich and others still believed they were winning. Soon firebrands like Hitler had begun to articulate their thoughts and fears when he declared that Kaiser Wilhelm II's generals had been duped into 'surrendering victory to its enemies,' when they signed the Treaty of Versailles.

With the Monarchy gone, the embryonic democratic post-war Germany was delivered into the new world – Dietrich and Anya Krak were terrified of it. They feared that the new freedoms merely created a more decadent society. With its risqué cabarets that openly celebrated sexual liberation, including homosexuality, they viewed Berlin as particularly decadent. To the East, the leaders of the Russian Revolution threatened an even more terrifying prospect, Communist rule with the Soviets at its head. This was not the world in which the Kraks wished to raise their three daughters and their only son, Klaus.

Klaus' three sisters were terrified of him. Over the years, whenever he isolated one, he would cut their arms with a knife from the collection he kept in a case under his bed. When he was seven, his father had caught him slicing his elder daughter's wrists. Dietrich Krak pulled his son away from his sister. He had been holding her by her hands, watching her struggle desperately to free herself, to stop the bleeding. His father had been about to whip him with his belt, but his mother intervened as she always did. Klaus was angry; he did not like to be judged by anyone, but he learnt quickly from the experience. He focused his attentions solely on his younger sister, who had a speech impediment that made it difficult for her to communicate with others. Klaus adapted his technique and applied only his hands so as not to leave marks on her body, apart from the occasional bruising to her neck. However, his eldest sisters conspired against him, so the youngest was rarely left alone. His sadistic tendencies constrained, he turned to animals, but their eyes never registered the fear he craved.

June 1924, Munich

By the mid-twenties, many spoke openly of a society without the Jews. At the dinner table, Dietrich would quote passages from *Mein Kampf*. His favourite extracts were Hitler's pronouncements on what he called 'the Jewish Peril'. Another popular passage was that outlining how the Slavs, described as "the weak", would be made to provide space for "the strong" – the children of the Third Reich.

Klaus' father was not alone in his anti-Semitism. At the school gates Klaus heard other adults, teachers as well as parents, express similar views. There was one teacher who did not. In one of her religious education classes Fräulein Steiner said, 'We are all equal in the eyes of God.' One pupil asked if this also included Jews. Before answering, she examined the children's faces, knowing that her reply would be discussed at family dinner tables that evening. As she spoke, her stutter was more pronounced than usual. 'Yes. We are . . . all God's children and we are . . . made in his form.'

The next day, the fathers of some of her pupils remonstrated with her after school. Words turned to violence, and she was thrown to the ground and kicked repeatedly. Some men did pull back those at the front, but only to get near enough to participate in the attack. The police arrived, but soon went away, having made no arrests. Such violent incidents were becoming more frequent. The next evening, Dietrich gathered his family around him in the living room. There he read out the report of the incident from a national paper. But rather than condemning the attack, the article claimed that it was caused by a malevolent force that had infiltrated German society – the culprit being the Jew.

A month after Fräulein Steiner was beaten unconscious, the father of another pupil, Hermann Hecht, was arrested and spent the night in jail for beating up a local moneylender. He would have escaped jail, if it were not for the fact that the man he attacked was not a Jew. Klaus, the other pupils and all their teachers, now that Fräulein Steiner had been dismissed, were angry at the man's internment and raged at the indignity of the arrest. If it were not for the 'Jewish moneylender' – despite the Judge stating that the 'victim was of Aryan stock' – then to Dietrich and many others in the town, the logical conclusion was that Hecht would not be in jail.

The young Klaus rarely expressed emotion, apart from his shockingly bad language, but that had ceased since it was declared that it was a Jewish trait. However, he was becoming more resentful. At the dinner table when his father demanded that something must be done, or the Jews would always have more than them, he would grind his teeth and tremble with rage. As his hatred for Jews grew, his attitude towards his father, and even his mother, who perversely indulged his brutal treatment of his sisters and scolded them for running to her for help, altered. Klaus resented them. It was not that he no longer agreed with their views, far from it; it was because they did not act on them. It disgusted him that his father was not among the fathers who attacked the teacher and later that he was not one of those who attacked the 'local Shylock' as Hecht's father had called the moneylender. He despised his father and indeed all those who talked of the enemies of Germany but did no more than talk; to him they were just as complicit in Germany's plight as the liberal and the Jew. Klaus knew that when he had the opportunity, he would take from the Jews what he believed was his by right of birth.

Klaus bullied a younger boy, Mannheim. He, along with three other boys, would often beat and rob him as he walked home from school. It was not solely the few Reichsmarks the boy had in his pocket which made him the focus of the attacks, but his pronounced cleft palate. Klaus despised those he judged as weak, either in body or mind. His only belief, if you did not count personal ambition, was in Aryan supremacy – he did not believe in God, the family or the sanctity of life. The angry young man knew that his prejudices would change German society for the better.

The moment came when three senior officials in the National Socialist Party came to Klaus' school. Wearing brown shirts and matching shorts, the standard uniform of the *Sturmabteilung,* the SA, they marched into the Headmaster's office and ordered him to assemble all the pupils in the gymnasium. The Headmaster did so without question. The myopic, rotund party leader was helped onto the stage where he spoke of a new movement that epitomised the perfection in mind, body and spirit of German youth. He asked the assembled boys, not the girls, to volunteer to join the movement immediately.

Klaus raised his hand, but he did so with a straight arm and open palm, mirroring the salute given by the group leader and his two cohorts. He was not one of the brightest pupils, and though he had an interest in biology and chemistry, his marks were poor, but his school friends looked on him with newfound respect: the rest in awe. Many more volunteered the next day, but it was Klaus who stood out. His new status was not just because he was the first to volunteer, but because he had not thought it necessary to ask for his parents' approval. By the end of the week, the fifteen-year-old boy was given the rank of sergeant in the newly formed *Jugendbund,* the Munich arm of what later became known as the Hitler Youth. With a troop of eight other boys under his command, he was the dominant figure in the school as his position and rank meant he was affiliated with the stormtroopers of the SA.

Thomas Hecht, an older boy, whose father led the mob that had attacked the moneylender, bowed his head in respect whenever he saw Krak. Mannheim still had his food and pocket money stolen and was beaten on a more frequent basis, but it was now carried out on his orders. Even the girls in his class started paying him attention, whereas before he scared them. A month earlier he had been suspended for a week for beating a girl with his stick when she said he looked like a lizard. However, he was not interested in girls or indeed adoration from any quarter. It was total obedience he sought as he thrived on the fear that came with his new position.

Having ensured that his authority was secure, and the paperwork was in place confirming his rank, Klaus Krak could act on his prejudices. Thomas Hecht was brought before him. The anxious boy was made to sit in a chair in the gymnasium by two uniformed members of the new unit of the Hitler Youth. Sergeant Krak, in his brown uniform, sat in the larger chair that until that week had belonged to the Headmaster.

Hecht lifted his head to look at Krak for the first time since the younger boy had secured his new status. Apart from his clothes, Klaus appeared to have physically changed; dramatically so. The sergeant was tall for his age, taller than him. However, though his uniform was tailored for him, he seemed to have already outgrown it. The collar was too low for his elongated neck, and his wrists extended far beyond his sleeves. But nothing was as unnatural as the appearance of his head. The wispy, blonde hair was waxed flat against his skull, and his green eyes appeared narrower. His cranium seemed even more defined as his skin was paler, even translucent, which gave the appearance that his skull was outgrowing his skin. To the older boy it was impossible that such a change had occurred within a week, but he would swear that it had.

Klaus spoke first. 'I have information that you are a sodomite.'

'What? No! That's not true. Who has said this?'

'Do you love your father?'

'Yes, of course,' he said, turning to the other two boys from his class wearing the uniforms of the *Sturmabteilung*, the paramilitary wing of the Nazi Party, standing to attention on either side of him for support. Like expectant dogs, their eyes were trained on their master.

'Your father is a Communist,' spat Krak.

'No! No man has been braver in the fight against the Communists than–'

'No man? Not even Adolf Hitler, Hermann Göring or Joseph Goebbels?'

'No! No! I didn't mean . . . that's not what I meant . . . I–'

'Enough. In front of you is a sheet of paper for you to sign. It will prove your loyalty to your country.'

'I will sign anything. I love my country.'

'Good. It confirms that you have heard your father speak of his Communist sympathies.'

'But my Father has never said such a thing. He is not a Communist! He is a loyal follower of the National Socialist movement, he–'

'Then, if you do not sign the statement, I will submit the accusation of sodomy made against you to the SS,' he said as he pushed another note towards the terrified young man.

Hecht was sweating profusely, his fingers trembling as he picked up the paper as if it were his death warrant: in a few years' time, with a forged signature, it would be.

'But I am not a homosexual; I have a girlfriend and she is called . . .'

Krak interrupted: 'Then I hope she will sign a paper

that you have had intimate relations with her; an underage, unmarried girl.'

'We don't have sex, and even if we did, I could not ask her . . .' He tried to recover his composure. 'The allegation is a lie. A proper investigation will conclude that I am innocent and I–'

'You are right, a *proper* investigation is required, and you will be pleased to hear that I have not wasted any time.' Krak smiled, 'I have concluded the first stage of the investigation and I have found the accusation to be true. That is why I have had you brought here, as I am about to forward my findings to SA headquarters today. However, if you wish to defend yourself, I have been granted approval by my superiors for your defence to be held in a public court.'

The little composure the young man had managed to retrieve disappeared. He was on the verge of collapse. 'You ask me to condemn my father based on a lie, or face disgrace myself based on another lie–'

'Sign the document that your father is a confessed Communist or bring shame on your family and face imprisonment for your sexual perversion. As you see, I am not an unreasonable man,' he smiled, 'I am giving you a choice.'

Hecht toppled forward onto the floor. The guards standing to attention on either side of him looked to the sergeant for instruction. Krak gave no order and continued to look down at the weeping young man. Hecht lifted his head to plead.

'Why are you doing this? I have done nothing to you. Klaus, I–'

'Address me by my rank,' said the young man sitting comfortably on the newly upholstered chair.

Hecht tried again to control his fear. He lifted himself up onto his feet and stood to attention, 'Sergeant Krak, you may not know this, but–'

'I know everything,' said the uniformed man with a thin smile.

Hecht swallowed hard and again tried to control his trembling voice. 'Yesterday I enlisted in the Hitler Youth. If granted the honour of joining this unit, I will be under your command. I will obey *your* every order without question.' He wiped tears from his cheeks and stood even straighter as he spoke. 'Sergeant Krak, I am devoted to the SA. Spare me, and I will prove it!'

The young man in the larger chair was happy now, though he did not express it, on hearing the word *your*. The sergeant had secured what he required; the disgrace of the boy's father, along with him and the rest of his family. The leader of the local Hitler Youth unit never explained why he had made Hecht his first official victim, rather than Mannheim, and no one dared to ask. But the young Klaus Krak believed that when Hecht's father attacked the money lender, it raised his son's status in the school above his own. This could not be tolerated and Sergeant Krak required retribution.

The young sergeant pushed the paper he had drawn up for the boy to denounce his father across the desk, 'I will spare you.' He smiled as his green serpentine eyes narrowed. 'You see, I am a reasonable man.'

Upon leaving school, Krak joined the intelligence section of the state secret police, which was soon to become the *Geheime Staatspolizeir* ; the Gestapo. He rapidly rose through the ranks to become a Staffelführer (squadron leader). Krak quickly realised that brutal surgery would be required to cleanse the *Volk*, but that his superiors wished to keep a discrete distance from it. In return, men and women like him who would carry out the barbarous work would receive power and reward.

Fifteen years after he gave the salute in the gymnasium, Klaus Krak was promoted to the rank of major on the personal orders of Reichsführer Himmler. His superiors recognised his suitability. His innate cruelty and loyalty to the National Socialist Party were prerequisites to the role, but above all he possessed that rarity amongst Nazi ranks – a strategic mind. Cerberus also possessed the qualities that the German High Command expected from all its senior officers, the ability to innovate and develop methods to eradicate all opposition. To Himmler and Heydrich, he was the natural choice for the leader of a new elite force, the Alpha Wolves.

The Alpha Wolves were comprised not only of the most ruthless individuals selected from the SS and the Gestapo, but also from the ranks of international fascist organisations and governments with right-wing sympathies. Their task was to eliminate all opposition to the Führer and to eradicate any 'imperfections' in the Aryan nation, the Volk. His superiors empowered him to do whatever was required to achieve this, including intimidation, torture and murder. It was a responsibility that Cerberus eagerly accepted.

Chapter 7: Murder Inc.

August 1938, London

Sean Ryan wore a crisp navy suit, black Oxford brogues, and a large white silk shirt that Jocky had delivered to his room. The shirt was greatly appreciated, as it provided room for the Irishman's wounds to breathe. The purple cravat was no doubt a joke, but the chambermaid was delighted to receive such a gift as she could easily find a buyer for it on The Strand. It was good to be in clean clothes again. Apart from his black leather jacket, most of the time he wore the ill-fitting coat and trousers he had found in his hospital wardrobe. However, the toadying receptionist could not hide his disapproval when he noticed that the sleeves of the new suit were already starting to rip from the body and the bottom of his trouser legs were two inches above the man's socks.

'Did Sir, sleep well?'

Sean ignored the question. 'It was very kind of you to put me on the top floor, in the farthest corner of the hotel.'

'That side of the building is being renovated, and I thought in your condition you would not want to be disturbed by other, shall we say, more sprightly guests.'

'I will not sully your hand with money now, but I will think of some way of repaying you later,' he said, before setting off to do some research at Somerset House and later in the British Library.

On hearing the word "later" the receptionist gave a smile of an undertaker who had just been informed by a recently widowed wife that she could only afford the barest pine box for her late husband.

Sean returned to the hotel after dusk, but instead of heading up to his room, he limped into the restaurant and flopped into a chair. He ordered a double Scotch and waited.

The doors of the main restaurant were quickly pulled open by two very attentive waiters as Lieutenant Amelia Brett entered. She was wearing the very conservative naval attire of a navy jacket, skirt and tie. However, her handmade white blouse was tighter than the standard issue, which showed off the firmness of her body.

'A woman most men would die for,' greeted Sean with the broadest of exaggerated smiles.

'But not you.'

'I love life far too much.'

'No need to get up,' she said, though the Irishman gave no indication that he had any intention of doing so.

The maître d' sent the waiter over to *Mr. P. Anther & the Ice Maiden,* the names on his reservation log. Despite his considerable experience, it was unusual to see a debutante, and one in uniform at that, dining with her bodyguard. The waiter delicately placed the napkin on the lap of the most beautiful woman he had ever seen. Then, he gingerly handed the other napkin to the fearsome-looking man as if he were about to inform him that he would have to leave as he was not wearing a tie. The waiter backed away from the table without averting his eyes from the lady.

Amelia decided that she needed to take command of the conversation. She knew that over the next few hours answers would not be freely given.

'Where did you secure the cane? It's not standard hospital issue.'

'A present from our Scottish friend,' said Sean, twirling it in his hand as a majorette would a baton. 'It's standard practice in these types of negotiations that the parties take it in turn to ask questions. You've had your turn, so now it's mine. When I said that the Nazis had an informer, you were annoyed but not surprised, so tell me what you know?'

'I was neither and before you ask, I'm not divulging any information on who was involved on our side.'

Sean expected to be stonewalled, but he pressed on, nonetheless, 'The fact that you have been assigned to help us, must mean senior officers in the Admiralty want to help those fleeing their Nazi hunters. So, if there is a traitor, you must divulge everything you know or jeopardise your assignment.'

The lieutenant examined the Irishman's gaze, as she removed a John Player from a solid sterling silver cigarette case and placed it firmly between her blood-red, painted lips and lit it. After taking a deep draw, she spoke. 'All I can say is that there are those in senior positions in Government who sympathise with the National Socialist Government. They believe that Germany and Italy are our natural allies. You will find sympathisers in the aristocracy, including members of the Royal Family. Edward VIII is on personal terms with Chancellor Hitler. Some of these aristocrats are also close to Churchill.'

Amelia did not tell him anything he did not already

know, but it surprised him that she so freely cast a net of suspicion so widely.

'My turn. How did you escape from Germany?' The waiter appeared. She ordered quickly so that he would leave them to their conversation. 'Dover sole.'

'Make that two, with a bottle of house red to accompany it,' added Sean.

The lieutenant grimaced. 'A glass of white for me, Schloss Gobelsburg Riesling, providing your cellars are properly stocked.' The waiter nodded his approval before turning to the greater challenge.

'Sir, red wine with fish is not–' Sean's stern look ended the waiter's recommendation.

The naval officer gave the Irishman a look of complete disdain. 'I take it you will be able to cope if they bring your meal on a plate?'

'No problem, but I'll use my fingers if you don't mind your Highness, as cutlery makes me nervous. I might accidentally stab myself in the head.'

'Spare me your schoolboy humour and answer my question.'

'Too late, as always, your playful nature got the better of you. My turn. Did every child on the train from Berlin find a home?'

The lieutenant tightened her grip on the knife in her hand and no longer had an interest in using it to spread butter on her bread roll. 'The Germans did not check the train when it left Berlin, as fortunately the country was in a state of euphoria after taking Austria without a struggle, so all the children reached England safely.'

'That I know they reached England, but that wasn't

my question.'

'I'm just saying that their survival was due to luck rather than your revision of our plan. You have ignored every instruction sent by London.'

'An outrageous accusation. My respect for the British Secret Service knows no bounds.'

'I do not work for the British Secret Service.' The other diners looked over to see why the officer had raised her voice. 'If you did as you were told, the woman and the boy would still be alive.'

The lieutenant examined the pained face of the man opposite and was surprised that he did not respond. She continued, 'In answer to your question, over two-thirds of the children have been fostered by families in England, others in Scotland, and the rest have been taken in by families in America.'

A few days earlier, Jake had confirmed to Sean that all those sent to America had been allocated to good families, but until now neither Jocky nor indeed Churchill had been able to confirm to his satisfaction that those children who had remained in England had been found a good home.

'Back to my question. How did you escape?'

Sean took a sip of wine, 'A gamekeeper found me half dead in the forest, bound my wounds, put me in his truck and drove me to the nearest hospital.'

'That's it?'

'Yes,' he lied.

Sean remembered six months earlier, when he lay on the snow-covered slope, believing that the last image he would ever see was the swastika flying arrogantly above Himmler's

Fortress. He shivered as he remembered his body growing numb and knowing that the exposure and severe blood loss would soon result in hypothermia, then death. Lying in a foot of snow, he tried to slow his breathing so he could conserve what energy he had and not lose any more heat. He heard boots trekking up the hill behind him and that familiar greeting: 'Sean . . . is . . . it . . . you . . .?'

It was Paul, his Hungarian friend, the *agent de liaison* that London had assigned to him, but Sean could not answer. He was delirious and thought that the Nazis had murdered the young Hungarian man and he was now one of the Devil's disciples welcoming him to an afterlife that he had never believed in, until then.

'Quick, throw a blanket over his legs and I'll start binding his wounds,' shouted a woman from behind him. Sean had not heard the voice before and in his delusional state thought it was an angel who had taken him down to hell, having been mistakenly deposited at the Pearly Gates. Before he passed out, he heard the angel's voice again. 'At least he had the sense to pack frozen earth into his open wounds to stop the bleeding.'

'How did you find the families to foster the children?' asked Sean.

'I didn't. Many families responded to an appeal by the government and offered to take them in. Many were Jewish, but not all. They were vetted most vigorously by our family services people. The American had a part to play on both sides of the Atlantic, but surely I'm only telling you what you already know?'

Sean knew of Jake's contribution, but he did he

mention that he had fought alongside him a few days earlier on the other side of the Atlantic.

The lieutenant took another draw from her cigarette and suddenly tired of it, stabbed it into a heavy glass ashtray in the centre of the table. 'I guess you're testing me to see if I'm telling you the truth?'

The Irishman sat smiling at the officer.

'My turn. Why did the hospital you were brought to in Berlin not inform the authorities? Your injuries were hardly the result of natural causes unless the Brandenburg Forest has elephants and you collapsed under a herd?'

'No, the gamekeeper for some reason unbeknown to me, covered for me and told the medical staff that he found me in the road and thought that I must have been hit by a truck.'

The lieutenant ground the cigarette butt further into the ashtray.

Sean thought again of the events after he had heard the angel's voice in the snow-glazed forest. He opened his eyes and was blinded by the dazzling brightness. Had the Devil refused to take delivery and returned him to the upper level? The ceiling came into focus as pain seized his entire body; his instincts told him not to release a scream. As he tried to control his reaction, he scanned what he realised was a room. He was in a hospital bed. Inserted in his arm was a drip, no doubt containing some glucose solution, and bags of various coloured liquids were hanging from the side of the mattress; he felt more like an exhibit than a patient.

He leaned over to his left and saw a dull grey carpet bag that was open, displaying several scalpels and a bottle marked *ALKOHOL*. Either he was a prisoner, and these were the implements of a jailer, or this was a new hospital where the equipment had not yet arrived and someone had to bring in their personal medical kit. He surmised, or perhaps it was merely a hope, that it was the latter. The door opened.

'Good to see you're awake, Englander,' said the officious-looking young woman, who was in her early twenties at most. Sean's usual response would be to tell anyone who referred to him by the name of his country's natural foe to go fuck themselves. However, he decided that would be a little ungrateful in the circumstances.

'Sárika . . . he's from Ireland . . . The Englander label is a nickname that the Nazis gave him and believe me, you don't want to rile him . . . as he can be very rude . . .' said Paul, who stumbled in behind her.

'I think we will be lucky to get anything coherent from him for a while,' replied the woman, walking purposefully across the bare stone floor to her patient.

'I'm never rude, it's more that I express my opinion in a forthright manner,' said Sean, but the effort resulted in a seizure across his chest.

'Se . . . an . . . you're . . . OK!' shouted Paul.

The woman looked at the young man who joined her and shook her head dismissively. 'Paul, he has a number of broken ribs to accompany a broken collarbone, a broken leg, three broken fingers, and severe internal bleeding. He also has about a dozen metal pins, which are just about holding him together, so I wouldn't say he was "OK!"' The Irishman was barely alive when Sárika and Paul drove him to the medical school. Upon arrival she telephoned her tutors, Professors Bonhoeffer and Dohnáyi, two of the most eminent surgeons in their field for their help. Both were German, but neither had any love for the Nazis. Over a period of about three weeks they performed numerous operations on the Irishman until his internal bleeding was judged to be at an acceptable level and his bones were reconstructed to the best of their medical expertise. Bonhoeffer also donated blood, as his was the only match for the Irishman's.

Sean's heart had stopped three times on the operating table. During the first two attacks, the surgeons kick-started his heart by applying a new device, a defibrillator, which they had built as part of their research after hearing of the experiments of Dr Albert Hyman in New York. The third time, they compressed the patient's chest with their hands as the electric surges caused his stitches to burst open, splattering the surgeons and the walls behind them in blood. However, to their surprise each time the patient responded to their resuscitation techniques. Finally, when both surgeons believed they had done all they could, Bonhoeffer turned to his colleague. 'Something drives this man to live that goes well beyond our medical skills. Whatever it is, it will take an army to stop him.'

Sárika had not finished. 'Forgive me Paul, but really, do you have to keep saying OK! You've been watching too many Jimmy Cagney movies.'

'OK . . . I mean . . . sorry Sárika . . . it's just he's . . .,' and he finally had the courage to say it, '. . . my friend.'

Sárika bent her head down to peer into Sean's eyes,

113

while placing two fingers of her right hand to the left of his neck to check his pulse. Sean caught the delightful smell of some lemon-scented perfume and smiled up at his physician as she continued to turn his head to examine his eyes. 'If Paul tries to hug me, remember I killed him while under your care,' whispered Sean, forcing a smile to hide his pain.

The woman shook her head, 'Despite only being a medical student, there have been many occasions when I've had to say to patients, "You're lucky to be alive". However, in your case, not only did we find you, but this medical school was so near and my professors had the skills, time and were willing to help, that the term lucky does not do your survival justice.' She bent down to retrieve a small torch from her carpet bag to shine into each of his eyes. 'Strange though,' she said, shaking her head. 'Grey-green? I could have sworn you had blue eyes when I checked your vital signs in the forest.'

Sean tried to lift himself up on his elbows, but it was as if he were riveted to his bed. 'How many days have I been out cold?' he gasped.

'Three weeks,' replied Sárika.

'Christ!' exclaimed Sean. 'How did you find me, anyway?'

Paul stepped forward. 'Sárika came to find me at Lehrer Bahnhof . . . and we headed to Anhalter Station in search of you. As we drove in, we saw a train pull out with you on top of a carriage and . . . what looked like a motorbike wedged . . . in the back of it.'

Sárika continued the story. 'We drove along the road parallel with the track, but we lost you. A few miles later we were hailed by a man, a gamekeeper. He said he saw two men topple from a train into the woods. Your tracks were easy to follow.'

Paul continued. 'When we found you, I thought . . . you were dead. You were so broken, frozen and . . . had lost so much blood. Then, I saw your eyes, so constant, so intent, so . . . fierce. I knew then that it was not your time to . . . die. But Sean . . . what . . . did you see?'

'Did you see the Fortress and the swastika flapping above the smoke?' asked Sean, resting his head back on the pillow

'Yes, I saw . . . the chimney and . . .' His head dropped, and in a low voice added, 'Magdalena and the boy . . . you mean . . .' he buried his hands in his wild black hair. 'That's why you still alive.'

Sárika was puzzled. 'Medical science saved him, not the image of a flag.' Neither man told her she was wrong. Paul slumped onto the metal chair by the wall, letting his hands flop onto his knees.

Bewildered, Sárika turned back to the patient. 'You are still in a pretty bad way. Apart from your breaks, you have lost an awful lot of blood. But we must get you out of here.'

'Where is here?' asked Sean.

'You are in the university medical training centre in Berlin. The other students will be returning tomorrow after the summer break and it won't be long before you are discovered and the police arrive.'

Sean struggled once again to try to prop himself up. 'No problem. I need you help?'

'I'll try, but I'm training to be a surgeon, not a psychiatrist.'

115

With the aid of his right arm, he lifted himself up on his elbow. He swung his legs out from under the blanket, including his right leg, which was securely bound with two wooden splints, to rest the soles of his feet on the stone floor. He was pleased that he could feel the cold in both feet. The room began to spin. Paul and Sárika grabbed Sean and lifted him back into his bed.

Sean tried to distract himself from his pain, which was helped by the soft curves of the woman's body pressed against him, but it was her beautiful brown eyes that made him smile and drew out his mischievous nature.

'Are you Paul's woman?'

'None of your business.'

'I thought he might be homosexual,' said the Irishman, trying to move his right leg into a more comfortable angle.

'Do you have a problem if he is?' she retorted.

'No. Do you have a problem, if I don't have a problem with it?'

Sárika put her left arm around Sean to lift him back onto the pillow. 'God, Paul, you were right, when you said that your friend could start a war in a convent.'

Paul did not answer her but addressed Sean. 'Really . . . Do you think I am . . . queer?'

'My friend, that's nobody's business but your own.'

In the middle of the grand hotel's plush dining room, the lieutenant's mood was far from tempered. 'You expect me to believe that no one informed the authorities of your injuries. The German medical profession must be full of incompetents.'

'It might be worth setting up an exchange programme

with the Admiralty. My turn; where is Ursula?'

'In London.'

'Here!' he exclaimed, turning the heads of nearby diners towards him and then quickly away again. The waiter brought their order. He gave a furtive look at the man and was about to ask if they required any condiments but decided not to and reversed away from the table.

'How do you expect to stop your food from toppling onto your plate, with your mouth hanging open?' asked the lieutenant, as she delicately slipped a fork into her fish, and a small piece disappeared between her ruby lips. 'Yes, she is living with me.'

'Can you arrange for me to see her on my next visit to England?'

'Perhaps it is best you see her before you go. As we would not wish to disappoint her in case this visit is your last.'

'Once again your kind thoughts are quite overwhelming.'

Sean could not help but break into a smile at the news that the young woman, who was stricken with polio as a child, was close and he might have the opportunity to see her before he left for the continent in the morning. He returned to the battle of wits. 'Poor Ursula, don't knock all the humanity out of her. She is a sweet kid and has been through enough already.'

The lieutenant was not to be distracted from her purpose. 'I don't believe a word of what you have told me. Strangers don't risk their lives to protect others.'

'I do.'

The lieutenant looked genuinely surprised, but quickly

recovered. 'Any German doctor would be compelled to inform the police of any suspicious injuries. You could not have lain in a hospital bed with bullet and knife wounds for all those weeks without arousing suspicion . . . and a general surgeon could not have saved you, not with your injuries.'

'I'm just lucky, I guess.'

'Then answer me this. I take it that the gamekeeper didn't sit by your bed in the hospital for weeks feeding you grapes, so who transported you from the hospital to our Embassy in Berlin?'

'No one. I got a taxi.'

'A taxi?' she shouted, which again made the other guests in the restaurant look towards the woman, but only the female diners quickly turned their heads away.

'Yes, most countries have them. They are vehicles whose purpose is to deliver their passenger for a price to a pre-agreed destination, while the driver informs you, in case you've forgotten, that the world is fucked.'

The Irishman thought back to when Paul and Sárika drove him first to the British Embassy and a week later to Berlin Airport. Each time, Sean lay flat in the backseat of a borrowed Mercedes-Benz 770, as Paul's car, a Mercedes-Benz 150H (W30) was a two-seater sports car. In London, Jocky had quickly produced travel documents that were sent to the British Embassy in Berlin for Sean, which included a hospital report stating that his injuries were the result of a skiing accident. As always, Jocky's forgeries were of the finest quality and it took just two hours for Sárika and Paul to clear him through passport control. Sean was flown back to England and within 24 hours was in a bed at

St Bartholomew's Hospital, a few minutes' walk from London Bridge.

While Sárika dealt with immigration at the airport, Sean, who was lying flat across five wooden seats, spoke to Paul. 'Your girlfriend takes no shit, no wonder you can't tell your arse from your elbow half the time.'

'Girlfriend . . . Sárika . . . no . . . she's my elder sister . . . we studied at university together . . . I did languages and Sárika medicine, though her English is more fluent than . . . mine.'

Sean smiled, as he was always outsmarted by a woman he met.

Sárika returned. 'Paul, they want to ask you a couple of questions, just checks – nothing more about his condition. "Men's things", I guess, that the immigration officers couldn't ask a female medical student.' Her brother walked nervously across to the stern-looking security man at the far desk in the waiting lounge.

'Sárika, now I know that your Paul's sister, I'm sorry about your family,' said Sean.

'Amazing. Britain's most lethal and sharpest weapon, and the Nazis' greatest enemy, has finally worked out that we're siblings, has he?' Sean did not challenge her assumption that he was working for the British government, as he knew she was attempting to make light of her pain. Her head dropped. 'The Budgakovs were our first cousins, on our mother's side. Christina was her younger sister.' Sean nodded as he remembered the determined woman. 'Our mother was from a farming community, but they shared a love of horses and that is how she met our father. He is descended from the

119

Hapsburgs and the equestrian life is in our blood, except for Paul, who is hooked on horsepower. Sadly, I never made the effort to see Christina's family much, but Paul did. He blames himself for getting them involved in all this,' and she looked at Sean, 'but he doesn't blame you.'

'Have you any other family?'

'Not really. Our mother died giving birth to Paul. Our father is still alive. He is a cold man who exhibits little love for me, and none at all for my brother. He even refused to have his family name on Paul's birth certificate, so he carries our mother's surname. If that were not enough, he is a vehement fascist, much to Paul's shame. My brother loves his country and is determined to protect its freedoms, so I guess that's why he looks up to you.'

'No one will be looking up to me for a while,' said Sean, smiling as he looked up into the piercing brown eyes of the woman sitting by his stretcher.

Sárika smiled. 'My father would happily sacrifice our free will for a dictatorship. I guess that is why Paul is so unhappy. He was rudderless until you came along and gave him a purpose. For that I thank you, but having met you I also fear for him. You leave destruction in your wake, so please don't let the only decent member left of our family get killed.'

After failing to protect Magdalene and Tóth, Sean had made a vow to himself that he would never promise to protect anyone ever again. It would be a hollow gesture now. He changed the subject. 'His fast car, the expensive clothing, who pays for it all if not your father?'

'Our mother provided for us in her will. God knows how she persuaded our father to release such a healthy lump sum. She feared for our future, as farming communities do, always fretting about the next harvest. Paul inherited her anxiety.'

'You haven't.'

'I pray it's something within me and that I have not inherited any traits from my father.'

'When I reach England, I'll arrange safe passage for you and Paul.'

'I don't require your help, but please try to find him a girlfriend over there for my brother. I worry about him. He smokes and drinks far too much. He needs a strong woman to steer his path through life.'

'We all need someone.'

'Ha, you need someone to hold you back. Any other man would be in a hospital bed, convalescing too terrified to move. Instead, here you are waiting for a flight with a bottle of Irish whiskey in your pocket.'

Sean tapped the bulge in his battered leather jacket, a little going away gift from Paul. 'I'm a nervous flyer.'

'Hmm,' she scoffed. Sean looked up at the woman who had saved his life. She was strong, beautiful and resourceful; if she were ten years older, he would have tried to kiss her, though he would have needed to ask her to lift his head to do so. 'Make travel arrangements for Paul for England, but as I said, please don't worry about me. Hungary is my country; I have no wish to leave it.'

'And if the Nazis come.'

'Then I will tend the wounded.'

'If the invasion comes, they will seek you out because of Paul, as they did your cousins,' he said, nodding towards the young man being scolded at the check-in desk by an angry customs official.

'Then I pray that the war will not come, for surely after the last war our governments will not run towards the flames again.'

'By their nature flames spread, but I hope you're right. What are your plans?'

'To pass my medical studies here, then to go back home to do some further studying at the Semmelweis University, the best medical school in Hungary. There I hope to become a surgeon. Who knows, perhaps later I will meet a man who will be kind to me and we can raise a family together. That's all I want. I have no desire to travel the world, share adventures with heroes or fight Nazis. Is that too much to ask?'

'No,' and with that Sean squeezed her hand and lifted it to his lips and kissed it. 'Thank you for saving my life. I will in turn do my best to keep your brother safe.'

Two officials came over and attempted to manhandle Sean from his stretcher and carry him towards the plane until Sárika rebuked them. The two men lifted him gingerly up on his stretcher and made their way towards the plane. Just as they reached the boarding gate, Sárika ran up and placed an unvarnished wooden walking stick she had taken from the university into Sean's hands. She bent down, letting her auburn hair flick across his face as she kissed him on the lips.

'Even a sensible woman should have a brief taste of adventure,' she said, before beaming broadly.

She turned around and walked over towards the angry official who was still berating her younger sibling. As they carried him towards the steps of the Junker G.38 passenger aircraft, Sean looked at the woman admonishing her brother's tormenter. He prayed that the Nazis would not destroy her dreams.

The rest of dinner was civil, but Amelia gave up trying to coax the truth from the Irishman. Maybe it was because of the excellent wine that she relaxed and no longer reached for her glass as if it were a chess piece. Sean too had resigned himself to the fact that neither would divulge anything to the other that they did not already know. The lieutenant signalled to the waiter, who sprinted over to the cloakroom to collect her satchel. When he returned with it, he carefully pulled her chair away from the table to let the Goddess, as he described her to the head chef, rise from the table.

'It's late, I must head home. I have to be at the Admiralty early in the morning.' She stood up. 'You'd better do the same as you are booked on the midday ferry to the Hook of Holland tomorrow,' she said, picking her purse up from the white lace tablecloth.

'I'll see you to the door,' said Sean.

'Best not.' She looked at the cane resting against the table. 'It will add half an hour to my journey.' This released a loud laugh from Sean, which once again jolted the other diners to look over towards their table. Amelia looked startled. 'My apologies, it wasn't meant to be a joke; it's just my way.' For the first time, Sean saw her smile. Even her voice was softer. 'Thank you for dinner, and also for not making advances. I dread these occasions as men are always trying to entice me into bed.'

'I'm no different. You're a beautiful, intelligent

woman. In normal circumstances, I would have made some clumsy advance, but due to circumstances beyond my control,' he lifted his cane, 'I am forced to behave like a gentleman.'

Amelia held out her hand to the Irishman. 'Goodbye Ryan and try not to raze the Netherlands to the ground.'

Putting his weight on his cane, he slowly lifted himself up from the table. He tilted his head. She parted her lips just a little as he kissed her.

'I must be getting better,' said Sean.

'Until the next time, Irishman,' she said, pulling the strap of her bag over her right shoulder as she set off towards the lobby.

Sean glimpsed a young woman's face peering through one of the plain glass panels of the doors to the dining room. He stepped forward, forgetting the pain searing through his right leg, and had to adjust his gait as he hobbled over to the young woman as quickly as he could. Ursula burst through the doors, struggling to make her way as fast as she could past Amelia, until she was close enough to drop her wooden crutch and throw her arms around Sean.

Lieutenant Brett was surprised by such a public display of affection. She wondered if there was some history between them that Ursula had failed to mention. She saw that the Irishman's eyes were open as they hugged, in the way that a guardian would greet his ward.

'We thought you were dead for sure until Amy told me you were alive.'

'You better believe it, I'm here in flesh and blood. Well, maybe a little less of both.' He paused and looked over at the lieutenant's stern face and returned to Ursula. 'Amy?'

'Shush!' whispered Ursula. 'Actually, it's what I call her. You see I can't pronounce A . . . meller. I called her Amy once, and she didn't like it, so please behave.'

Sean stood back and stretched his arms out. '*Moi*, was ever a man more misunderstood?' He smiled at the young woman. 'Seriously, how are you?'

'Life is a little empty since Krakow, but I'm safe.'

He noted the sadness in her eyes and knew she was thinking of the other children, and in particular one serious little boy, called Leo. Sean smiled, as if to acknowledge that being safe was not enough.

'Have you heard from the others?' he asked.

'A few letters. Lenka continues to help organise trains to transport more children to the West, while Jake is helping with the funding, organising transportation and foster homes in America.' With urgency she asked, 'But nothing from Vodanski. Have you heard from him?'

'Yes, he's out there throwing Nazis all over the place.'

'Good,' she added with a smile. Excitedly she added, 'Golda and Hannah are living together with a family here in London. It's a place called Hampstead, and sometimes I go there for tea. Will you join me? The girls would love to see you.' She laughed. 'They tell everyone at school about the Three Musketeers who came to their rescue in the alleyway.'

'With Lenka as D'Artagnan!' but his smile faded as he remembered the death of Jewel, 'Of course, I would love to see the girls, but it will have to wait as I head for the Netherlands tomorrow.'

A solemnness descended across the young woman's

face once more. 'We never heard anything of Olen or the two children we had to leave behind in Krakow. I asked Amy to check and the reports are that the orphanage has been razed to the ground.'

Sean gently lifted her chin with his fingers and stared into her eyes. 'You have become a woman, a strong and determined one. Soon, it will be your turn to look after us battered old Musketeers.'

'Time to go. Come on Ursula,' said the lieutenant who was still puzzled by the warmth between the injured, but lethal Irishman, and the congenial, young disabled woman.

'Yes . . . A . . . Lieutenant Brett, yes, of course.'

The British officer walked ahead of Ursula out of the restaurant and towards the doors of the hotel lobby. As she did so, over her shoulder, she issued her final instruction of the evening. 'Remain in your bedroom until a car arrives to drive you to the ferry for the noon sailing.'

Sean bowed in the manner of a courtier, while he yelled back, 'I will obey your orders to the letter, your Highness. I will avoid the bathroom, piss on the carpet and curtail the urge to cartwheel down the Mall.'

The young woman hobbled after the statuesque blonde, striding across the marble floor of the lobby.

Out of earshot of Amelia, she glanced towards Sean, 'You haven't changed one bit,' she said, grinning at the man who had helped her and the other children escape over the Polish border. While waiting for the revolving door to slow down, she muttered, 'Thankfully.'

Amelia stood outside the hotel entrance, but she decided not to walk to her apartment, which was only five minutes on the other side of the road in Berkeley Square.

Instead, she walked along the pavement towards Piccadilly, taking advantage of the warmth of the summer's night. She turned to wait for the Polish girl, 'I know a place in Soho where we can have tea and cake, then you can tell me all you know about that troublesome Irishman back there.'

Sean stood by the restaurant doors and realised for the first time in recent months that he was not using a cane for support. He was recovering well, and he would need to, having read the headlines. Over the last six months Germany had escalated its military rearmament. Time was running out for free Europe.

As Sean entered his hotel room, he heard a voice from the very distance past. 'Trust *ya* to hide in a British Army Hospital. I've had to hang around this *shitehole* of a city for weeks, waiting for them to finally let *ya* out.'

'Only Ireland's very own village idiot could find London boring,' replied Ryan as he turned around to be greeted – as he expected when he recognised the voice – by a gun barrel aimed at his head.

'Hello Eoin, you psychotic lunatic.'

'Only me mates call me Eoin, to *ya* I'm Pigott. *Ya* cost me four of me best men yesterday, but this moment was worth waiting for, *ya* bastard.'

Then, one of the two younger gunmen with him brought the full force of his revolver down across the back of Ryan's head, sending him reeling across the room towards the armchair and knocking his cane from his hand. Ryan did not look at his attacker but turned to face his old enemy.

'It's very thoughtful of you to come all the way to

England, so that I can kill you. As you can see, I find travelling a bit difficult at the moment.' Ryan tipped his head towards the cane lying on the thick pile carpet a few feet away.

'Always the smart remark.'

'How can my remarks not be smart in the company of Moe, Larry and Curley.' He continued to attempt to divert the others as he lifted himself to his feet, moving towards the walking stick. 'How did The Three Stooges find me?'

'Easy when *ya* have as many enemies as *ya*. Getting *ya* to stay still long enough to kill *ya* is the *foking* problem. Can *ya* believe that even the British Secret Service came to Ireland to tell me where to find *ya*? And me, the head of the Dublin assassination arm of the Irish Republican Army. They've even paid me five hundred British pounds to do what I will happily do for *fok* all. They want *ya* dead, but they need someone else to do their dirty work for *'em*. Guess they know that *ya* working for Churchill and don't want that old bastard to know of their involvement. Have no fear though, when I eventually kill *ya*, I'll drop *'em* in the *shite*.'

Ryan was on his feet and for the first time he looked carefully at the two younger assassins. Running his hand through his hair to check the amount of blood oozing from the wound he faced his old nemesis. 'These two,' nodding to the young men standing either side of him pointing their guns at Ryan, 'they must be about eighteen, same age as us on Bloody Sunday.'

November 1920, Dublin

On the morning of 21 November 1920, Michael Collins issued his men their orders for what was to be become infamously known as Bloody Sunday. Collins, created the Irish Republican Army's assassination squad, Murder Inc. Its purpose was to kill a unit of special agents recently dispatched to Ireland. The British had sent their best, the Cairo Gang, another pseudonym derived from the name of a Dublin café where they gathered. The purpose of the crack unit of eighteen high-ranking members of the British Secret Service was simple, to infiltrate and destroy Collins' guerrilla unit.

Collins decided that this was the time to launch a pre-emptive strike, taking out the Cairo Gang in one fell swoop. Sean Ryan was eighteen, a year younger than Eoin Pigott; both of whom were members of Murder Inc, a label rightly earned due to their fearsome reputation for exacting bloody retribution on the occupying British Army and its network of informants. Collins had his own network of informants. These ranged from barmen listening in on loose talk by the counter, to cleaners searching through hotel litter bins. His network also included members of the Royal Irish Constabulary who operated from Dublin Castle. One of them was Eamon Broy, an intelligence clerk, who typed every report with an extra sheet of carbon paper in his typewriter. These carbon copies would be passed to Collins giving him a better overall view of British intelligence operations in Dublin than the British themselves as the originals often went missing. From this information, Collins extracted the names and current addresses of twenty British agents to be killed. Pigott and Ryan, the youngest members of Murder Inc, were despatched to the Gresham Hotel.

Each had a designated target.

Ryan ran up the wide wooden stairs and hurried along the corridor on the third floor to the room whose number was scribbled on the note Collins had handed to him that morning. He knocked on the door.

Major Booth opened it and was met by the barrel of a Webley VI revolver against his temple. Behind Ryan, shuffling from foot to foot, was Mick McGill, a backup shooter in case Ryan was killed or lost his nerve.

'I only ask one thing before my death,' said the major who knew by the young man's unflinching blue eyes that he had total control of the situation and possessed the nerve to kill.

'What is it?' asked Ryan.

Behind him McGill spluttered, 'Quickly, kill the *foken* bastard and we can *fok* off.'

'That you allow me to write a note to my wife?'

'I thought all you British agents did that before you went on a mission?'

'Normally, I would have, but I have only just learnt that my wife is expecting again.'

'No tricks, or I'll send your brains back to Lloyd George in an envelope,' said Ryan, as he pushed the man back into his room.

Despite McGill's pleas, Ryan nodded towards a paper and pen on the desk.

'*Foking* shoot him, it's a *foken* trick,' shouted McGill.

'Well, if he kills me, thankfully you're here,' said Ryan, calmly, and at which point McGill ran out of the room and disappeared down the corridor.

The major finished his note and left it on the table.

'Will you make sure it goes to my family?'

'Yes.'

'Do you want me to turn around? It makes no difference to me now.'

'No. I need to look into your eyes as I must live with this until the rest of my days.'

Ryan shot the major between the eyes. He slowly lowered his revolver down to his side, picked up the note paper and blew gently on the ink.

Pigott smashed his gun across Ryan's face. 'Do *ya* remember how *ya foken* landed me in the *shite* that day?'

Sean lay again on the ground with blood streaming down his face from the fresh cut over his left eye. Despite the blow, he kept to his plan to remain calm and somehow make his way to the walking stick, which was further away.

Staring at the ceiling, Ryan spoke with a steady voice, without betraying either his pain or his rage. 'I remember that after I killed the major, I heard what I thought was the high-pitched squeal of a little girl.' Ryan feigned a look of concern. 'I thought you were in trouble.'

Pigott launched his black boot into Ryan's side, making him double up in pain.

'*Foken* smart-arse to the last. They were the screams of the bitch standing in front of the man I was trying to shoot. Then *ya* burst in and stopped me from blowing the *foken* both of them away.'

Ryan had positioned himself so when he was kicked again it would roll him nearer to the cane; it worked but his anger was rising as he remembered the scene in that Dublin hotel room. 'She was an innocent young chambermaid, practically on the verge of giving birth. The Brit was using her as a shield.'

Pigott spat back, 'She was a collaborator and all those who work for the enemy deserve to *foken* die.'

'Jesus, she was cleaning his room not loading his gun you fucking maniac,' shouted Ryan.

'When *ya* rushed at me and knocked the gun out of my hand, the *foken* bastard escaped.'

'And the pregnant chambermaid lived. My only regret was that I didn't hit you fucking hard enough. But thanks for giving me a second opportunity.'

'The Big Fellah,' Collins, 'sided with *ya*, but we *foken* got him soon enough. Now, it's *ya* turn,' he yelled, aiming his revolver down at the man by his feet; a man he had waited nearly fifteen years to kill. 'Did *ya* know I've been fighting with the Fascists in Spain? Every day I prayed to the Holy Mother that I might come across *ya* out there and get a chance to put a bullet in *ya foken* head. But better late than never they say, *ya* bastard!'

Pigott kicked Ryan again, sending him across the floor so he landed on his cane.

Ryan smothered the slight click with his body, as once again the cylinder of the walking stick spun around, exposing the stainless steel blade along the shaft. The real genius of Jocky's creation was that he had designed the mechanism so that it emitted hardly a sound to alert an opponent. It was an achievement that had defeated many an armourer when attempting to muffle the metallic sound that occurs when the trigger of a weapon is engaged.

Pigott walked over to Ryan and stood beside him as he aimed his gun at the back of his head. 'Turn around *ya* bastard!' As Ryan turned to look up, he thrust the foil upwards through Pigott's pelvis and up into his heart.

Pigott's men were stunned by their leader's frozen look, an expression of shock rather than pain. With their commander's macabre figure still facing them, they opened fire. But nerves got the better of them and first three of the four bullets they fired hit Pigott in the legs. Ryan grabbed Pigott's gun as it fell, before his lifeless body toppled backwards onto the dressing table and toppled to the floor. Ryan pointed the revolver at the men, his aim as steady as it had been in that blood-splattered room in Dublin.

'Drop the guns and fuck off,' he told them.

They saw the unflinching blue eyes of the man and decided it was better to face the wrath of the IRA's high command than certain death now. Dropping their guns to the floor, the smaller man opened the door, and both men fled down the hallway.

'They must be McGill's sons,' muttered Sean, resting his head on the carpet. While steadying his breathing, he pressed his hand over the hole in his left side caused by the fourth bullet.

Sean waited a few minutes, until his pulse was a slow, regular beat, before slamming his boot under the dead man's chin. He jerked the sword back and forth until he could engage the trigger mechanism.

With the aid of the cane, he raised himself up on his feet. After cleaning the bullet hole with some iodine from the bathroom cabinet, he walked back into the main room. The bullet had thankfully gone straight through and missed his vital organs along with his bones. Stepping over Pigott's corpse to reach the large oblong mirror on the wardrobe door, he examined the fresh wound in his side. Picking up his Mother's balm, from his knapsack he applied it to his wound. Finally, after all these years he finished the bottle. He looked in the mirror. 'Ma, it was your boy's lucky day. In the last twenty-four hours, I've drunk fine brandy in the Houses of Parliament, kissed the most beautiful woman I have ever seen and even when I was hit by a bullet it went clean through.'

Sean returned to the bathroom, took some towels and tore them into strips to bandage his wound. He put on his own clothes back on: the battered leather jacket; faded navy cotton shirt; grey army trousers and military issue boots, as the suit that Jocky had supplied was splattered with blood. Sean packed everything else into a knapsack. He carried Jocky's dual-purpose gift into the bathroom and washed the steel rapier under the scalding hot water tap. Taking one last look at the room, he stepped over the corpse and made his way down the staircase to the lobby. He never used lifts – as you never knew who would be there when the doors opened.

His plan was to make his way to Charring Cross Station to catch the night train to the ferry, sleep at the port and board the first ferry to the Netherlands in the morning. Even before the latest attempt on his life, he had already decided to leave England without informing anyone. As in Berlin, survival depended on adapting every plan that originated in London.

When he reached the bottom of the staircase, Sean turned and walked up to the reception desk.

The obsequious receptionist altered his look of disdain

to a stretched smile now the man had turned around.

Sean slammed his cane down on the oak top of the front desk, causing the receptionist to drop the fountain pen that he was using to add up the tips which he never distributed amongst the other staff.

'Hello, Smiler.'

The receptionist grimaced once more at the man's familiarity to Sean's delight.

'Sir, you appear to have some blood on your walking stick,' observed the receptionist.

'Yes, recently I've undergone an operation and one or two stitches seem to have come loose.'

Ryan dropped his voice and leant forward. 'Now, that little reward I mentioned.' The man at the other side of the counter smiled as he involuntary flexed his fingers. 'Please tell the very nice chambermaid not to bother cleaning my room. You see, a niece of mine popped across the road from Shepherd Market last night and I do not wish her to be disturbed until breakfast.'

'Certainly Sir, I understand.'

'I suggest that no one enters the room apart from you, as I have left something for you by the side of the bed in recognition of your understanding.'

The receptionist smiled warmly, for when he first saw the man, he had judged him to be the type who only tipped when the service warranted it. 'To be of service to you, has caused me immense pleasure. Any trinket that you have left me to remind me of your time here would be cherished.'

'Oh Smiler, you'll never forget me.'

Chapter 8: Dutch Courage

August 1938, Amsterdam

Every movement angered the damaged nerves throughout Sean's body, but as least he could, for short stretches, finally walk without his cane. As the ferry docked in the port of the Hook of Holland, the Irishman hobbled down the gangway with his cane. On the quayside was the man who had created the unique walking stick.

'*Yer* still look like *yer've* been on a date with Sister Thekla,' laughed Jocky, looking at the evidence of Sean's injuries.

'Has the swelling gone down?'

'Oh, *yer* heard about that. All I did was ask her to have dinner with me, and she put me in an armlock and ran me into a wall and then kneed me in *ma* unmentionables. She needs to work on her bedside manner, let me tell *yer*, pal.'

'I couldn't care if she set fire to your head. But why are you here? I take it's more than to simply to make me look good. And as I took the first ferry from England, how did you arrive ahead of me?'

'The Royal Air Force got me here. If *yer* want to know how, the clues in the title.'

Despite the Scotsman's delight in his discomfort, Sean was pleased to see Jocky as the ribaldry brought a little levity into his life. God knows there had been little to smile about over the last six months.

'When *yer* reach Amsterdam,' Jocky continued, as he passed the Irishman a note and a train ticket to the city. 'Head to this address. Also, this might come in handy if *yer* get up to *yer* usual antics, but *yer* wish to attract a little less attention for once,' he said as he extracted the .32 calibre Welrod Mark 11 pistol from the inside of his jacket.

'It's heavy,' noted Sean, weighing it in his hand.

'That's because it has a built-in silencer and sounds like a punch into a cow rather than a gunshot. It's a prototype, and a few years away from securing a patent, but providing where *yer* operate where it's *nay* too public, it shouldn't draw the crowds.'

'I've heard that previous experiments with suppressors blew the gunman's hand off.'

Jocky shrugged his shoulders. 'It's *nay* my hand, pal.'

'Maybe I'll try it out on you first,' said the Irishman, to Jocky's unease. 'Who paid for the train ticket?' continued Sean.

'My boss, The Commander,' though his actual rank was lieutenant commander.

'The man in Room 39 who can't be named.'

'That's right, the Official Secrets Act.'

Sean grabbed Jocky by the lapel of his brown overcoat with his right hand. 'If you don't fucking tell me who he is, they won't even be able to identify you from your teeth after they extract them from your arse.'

'Jesus! . . . he's called–'

'Actually, I don't need to know,' said Sean. 'I was just checking to see, if after the battering they received if you had a man-sized pair. Clearly not,' as he released him, allowing the heels of Jocky's shoes to return to the pavement.

'*Yer fuking* lunatic, why does everyone think I can be thrown around like a sailor's cap in a strip bar?'

Sean placed his hand on his angry friend's shoulder. 'I am sorry. Are you coming with me to Amsterdam?'

The Scotsman was far from placated. 'Later. I've got a big-breasted Amazonian on the meter and I'm *nay* wasting serious loving time to listen to a crippled Irish prick doing the rosary.'

With that he trotted off, launching a steam of profanities in the direction of the town.

A dog tied to a lamppost leapt up at him, '*Bastad*! Everyone has it in *fer* wee Jocky today.'

'You haven't got the hang of this "friend" business, have you?' said a familiar voice from behind Sean.

He spun around so fast that he forgot he was propped up by a cane and nearly lost his footing, 'Ursula! What the hell are you doing here?'

The apprehensive young woman glanced up, 'Amy, sorry Lieutenant Brett, gave me some money to buy some "fashionable" clothing, so I waited outside the Ritz for you to come out last night. Then I followed you and bought a ticket for the ferry with the money she gave me, and I've stayed out of your way until now.'

'What do you think you're doing here?' demanded Sean. 'You can do nothing to help here,' he said as he pointed his head at the wooden crutch under her left arm.

'Oh, and you can?' flicking a steely look at his cane.

Sean shook his head, annoyed that he had not spotted her before he boarded the ferry, so he could have sent her back. However, he was pleased that she had stood up to him. She was a woman who knew her own mind, 'Come on then.'

The Irishman said nothing as they walked together towards the train. Ursula took his arm. 'I'm sorry, Sean, I want to help,' before whispering. 'Unfortunately, Lenka will blame you.'

'Of course, she will blame me, and she will be right. I should put you on the ferry back to England and throw your crutch into the sea.'

'You and the others are the only family I have,' she said, smiling up at Sean, 'and I want to be beside my family.' She pulled on his arm, 'And I will pay Amy back. I would have wasted her money anyway, as all I know about fashion, I learnt from Lenka.'

Sean laughed. He leaned down and peered into her eyes. 'I remember a young lady once warning me to be careful about what I said, as "she (Lenka) has a fierce temper".' He laughed again. 'But I do see your point about wasting the ice-maiden's money, for our dear Lenka knows as much about clothes as I do about making friends. However, your Polish guardian did teach you something far more practical.'

'What's that?'

'How to trail people and not be detected.'

With that, the young woman squeezed the tall man's arm tighter, as they entered the ticket office to buy an additional ticket for the train to Amsterdam.

Having left Amsterdam Centraal, the Irishman readied himself for when they reached the address that Jocky had given him, a boarding house situated behind the railway station. He stood to the side of the door, drew his revolver and knocked.

'Good to see you haven't lost your touch,' said Jake with Sean's gun pointing at his temple.

Jake noticed the woman who peeked out from behind Sean.

'Hello Jake,' she said, with a wide smile.

'Hi young lady, but you shouldn't be here,' and with that he bent his head and lifted her hand to kiss it. 'It's wonderful to see you.'

'Careful, remember he's a bit of a lady's man,' said Sean, as he winked at Ursula. 'And you behave Yank, as she's still under Lenka's wing.'

Jake laughed. 'I'll happily put my life on the line in pursuit of you, Ursula.'

The young woman blushed, not because of his flirting, but because she was overwhelmed to be among two of the men, she secretly referred to as her 'Uncles.'

'Lenka will go ballistic when she sees you've brought her here,' said the American, shaking his head. 'You better buy a suit of armour quickly, as we are due to meet her in Dam Square. It's a ten-minute walk from here,' as he slotted two Astra M901 semi-automatics in the holsters strapped under each arm, and pulled his brown sheepskin coat on.

'I miss Lenka, but she will be furious when she sees me,' muttered Ursula.

'That's nothing, I'm worried she'll hug me too hard when she claps eyes on me,' teased Sean.

'Oh, there's no fear of that,' laughed Jake.

The three set off to meet the leader of the Rogues.

Jake walked ahead, while Sean, who felt a new spurt of energy since meeting his friends, hung back to walk beside the young woman.

'You know I can look after myself,' whispered the woman. With a delightfully cheeky giggle, she added, 'With his blonde locks, Jake is handsome, isn't he?'

'Behave young lady; you're under my wing too,' said Sean, with a wink.

Fifteen minutes later, just before they reached Dam Square, Ursula stopped. The men turned to see what was wrong.

'Lenka is going to kill me.'

Sean peered into her pale face. 'Unlikely, as she won't have enough anger left for anyone else after she sees me.'

Jake grinned. 'He's right, she hates his fucking guts.'

Sean lifted Ursula's chin up with his fingertips and smiled. 'See, what did I tell you, come on.'

'I'll join you shortly. I just need time to summon up the nerve to meet her.'

'Don't be too long, or we will come looking for you.'

'Thank you. I just need to compose myself, then I'll join you. Promise!'

A hundred metres away on the far right-hand side of the city's main plaza, Lenka spotted Sean and Jake enter the famous square. Sean spotted her, too. It was the first time he had seen her since Lehrter Bahnhof. Even from that distance, he could see that she was as wild and beautiful as he remembered. As the men crossed the square, her face became clearer. She was as usual, riled at the sight of him.

The men aimed for the line of chairs outside the

crowded restaurant, Café Reflect. Lenka marched up to the Irishman and stared up into his eyes, as she had when they first met in Vienna.

'You look like shit. London said you only have a few scratches but look at you. You can barely fucking walk.'

'I knew I should have brought flowers.'

'Fuck off home to England, or wherever you're from.' She turned around and marched back to the table to join Jocky, who was studying a map he had unfolded on a table.

Sean turned to Jake. 'Well, that went better than I thought.'

'It did. I thought she would shoot you in the head.'

'Does she ever mention Jewel?'

Jake was surprised, as Sean had not mentioned the Australian nurse since her death in Berlin. 'No, it's still too deep and she won't let anyone in.'

'I know how that feels.'

Jake's smile reappeared. 'Strange thing though, I hear Lenka's only had a handful of men since Berlin. Maybe she's pining for someone.' The American noticed a grin appear on Sean's face. 'Personally, I think she's ill.'

Sean was still smiling as they set off to join the other two Rogues. He shook his head at the Scotsman as he eased himself down onto a seat by the table. 'That was quick. Did you ask your Amazonian for a piggy-back afterwards?'

Lenka directed her fury at Jocky. 'Can't you keep it in your trousers for once?'

Sean tapped the Scotsman's legs with his cane, 'They're shorts, not trousers.'

But, just as Jocky was about to release a fresh battery of expletives, a young woman appeared behind Lenka.

'Hi Lenka,' said the younger Polish woman.

Lenka turned and was startled to see her favourite amongst all the children she had helped to raise. She grabbed her in her arms, kissed her hard on the cheek and embraced her. It was only six months since they said goodbye, but Ursula was now two inches taller than her. Lenka stepped forward and glowered at the Irishman. 'You bastard!'

Jake nudged Jocky, 'It's just like the old days, isn't it?'

Jocky shrugged his shoulders. 'Do *yer* think she will cut his nuts off after they make love?'

'A real possibility, though Sean is wily enough to sleep with one eye open.'

'She'll rip his throat out when he blinks.'

'Getting Jewel killed wasn't enough for you, now you have to drag more innocent people into the firing line,' shouted Lenka, drawing the attention of the café's customers, wondering what was the cause of an argument so early in the day.

'She's a grown woman; she makes her own choices, as Jewel did,' retorted the Irishman.

'Hi Sean,' said the giant, ambling towards him.

'Oh Christ!' exclaimed Sean, who was stunned to turn and find Chris Kildare standing in the entrance to the café.

'Chris, I didn't mean . . .' Sean knew there was no point saying anymore as the image of the blood trickling from Jewel's mouth as she fell back into the snow returned to haunt him.

Lenka called Jake over to examine the blueprint Jocky had opened and spread across the table. Occasionally, they would glance up to observe the two men. After a few minutes, Sean spoke.

'Chris. I don't think you heard me say it on the train, but it was my fault that Jewel died.'

The sombre Scotsman nodded, but said nothing as he turned around to head back into the dining area of the café. Lenka glanced up, before returning to examine an architect's sketch of what looked like a factory.

'I forgot to ask, *yer* big lump, but how was dinner with the ice-maiden?' shouted Jocky.

Sean thought Lenka's mood could not darken any further, but the arrival of furrows across her brow made it clear it could. The two women detested each other. He thought of how men rile each other for fun, but also to mark out their boundaries and test the measure of a man. However, women like Lenka and Amelia knew immediately when another was either a friend or foe. There was no posturing, no games, when a woman sensed another was a rival for their mate, would endanger their family, undermine their status or pose an immediate threat to them. Some called it 'feminine instinct', but Sean knew that nothing will change a woman's opinion in such matters, especially as she was usually right.

'Just when I thought things couldn't get any worse, you manage to find a way, my wee friend?' said Sean, acknowledging the Scotsman's mischievous remark.

Jocky flashed a beaming smile at Lenka. 'I like explosions.'

'You'll find yourself on top of the next one,' growled Lenka.

Jocky stepped back as there was no irony in her tone.

'If you are going to look at plans, can we at least do it

145

inside,' said Sean.

'No one will notice. Hide in plain sight as the saying goes, and tourists do look at maps!' snapped Lenka.

But Sean was already making his way ahead of the others into the restaurant. He had no interest in maps, as there was someone he wanted to drink with – even if no words were exchanged.

The restaurant, with its imposing fluted columns, and the cream and gold-coloured walls was bustling with sound and colour, as darting waiters in starched white shirts pollinated each table with coffee and pastries. The tall Scotsman leaning against the bar was wearing a long, thick, grey-coloured trench coat. In front of him was a large empty Heineken glass on the brass counter amongst the drained coffee cups which only added to the air of remoteness around him. Since the death of Jewel, Chris was no longer self-conscious about how he fitted into the world.

'Another?' asked Sean, leaning against the bar.

'Line 'em up!' said Chris. He turned to Sean. 'I don't blame you for Jewel's death. She couldn't ignore the danger those two little girls were in. She would have turned back and entered that alley, whether you had been there or not.'

'You would not have allowed her to put herself in danger. We both know that,' he said as Sean hailed the bartender. 'Two beers and two chasers, barman.'

'We have Bushmills, Jameson and Glenfiddich,' replied the English-speaking barman.

The Irishman forced a smile. 'I don't care anymore. Just make them doubles.'

Chris was puzzled. 'Beyond caring; are you out to get drunk?'

Sean did not explain that it was the country of origin he was referring to and threw the contents of the glass down his throat. 'No, I'm just moving on.'

For Sean, the ornate surroundings brought back memories of the Café Griensteidl in Vienna, the last time he had seen Magdalena and Tóth alive. Lenka entered and saw the sad veil that had dropped over Sean's face – she thought it was because of Jewel until she looked at the splendour of the restaurant and was reminded of Vienna.

Chris sank his drink in one and called to the barman, 'Same again, Rudi!'

The others joined them, as a vast black cloud surrounded the square and unleashed a torrent of rain, driving the thirty or more customers and their clattering coffee cups inside the restaurant. Chris, Jake and Lenka clinked their glasses and made their familiar toast, 'Dominique.'

'Who is she again?' whispered Jocky into Sean's ear.

The Irishman shrugged his shoulders. 'I keep forgetting to ask.'

Sean added a new toast: 'Jewel,' raising his glass, and to everyone's relief so did Chris.

Lenka refused.

Then she scribbled a note and pressed it into Ursula's hand. 'Ursula, it's dangerous here, so do as I ask and go to this apartment and wait there until I return.'

The young woman nodded and headed off in the direction of the flat, following the instructions that Lenka had drawn on a napkin.

'Your place I take it?' asked Sean.

'No, your jumpy friend Paul's.'

'Paul . . . Paul Budgakov is here? Jesus Christ, has everyone descending on Amsterdam? Where's Hitler? Washing glasses out back?'

Lenka was unimpressed. 'I've gathered you all here for a reason, not because I missed your inane conversation.'

Now that the remaining Rogues were reunited, apart from Vodanski, Sean asked what had happened since he left them in Berlin. He had not discussed with the others the events following Jewel's death, but despite the pain it would cause, particularly to Chris, he needed to know. Jake ordered another round. Then, to the astonishment of the others, it was Chris who spoke. He told them of the events that followed – events he had never spoken of before. He told of what little he could remember: a fragmented picture assembled from the few pieces that had reappeared in the months that followed Jewel's death.

March 1938, Aachen

The train travelled west out of Berlin and eventually crossed the border near Aachen, Chris sat on the floor of the luggage carriage opposite Lenka, who was cradling Jewel's pale and bloodied face on her lap. When they reached the border crossing into the Netherlands, Lenka told the others that they had to bury Jewel as soon as they reached the port of the Hook of Holland. It was best to do it there, she explained, while the children were disembarking from the train and making their way to the ferry. Chris did not move, as Lenka, Jake and Vodanski dug a grave for their friend on a piece of bare earth out of sight of the children. Once they had finished, Chris raised himself up from the wooden floor of the carriage as if in a trance. He climbed down and walked over to a wooden fence and began to construct a cross from its slats. After he had constructed the marker, he slipped a picture of Jewel from his wallet and pinned it, along with a picture she used to keep of her brother, to the centre of the cross.

His memory of the journey between Berlin and his return to Scotland was like a diary, but with most of the pages removed. When he reached the port, Chris did not register when Vodanski told him it was time for him to return home to his wife and daughter. Nor did he notice when Vodanski and then Jake hugged Lenka, or when the two men turned their backs on each other without saying a word. Chris did not hear Lenka say goodbye, but later he remembered her throwing her arms around him. He had no idea why.

Chris remembered Jake's powerful grip on his arm as he led him onto the ferry, but he could recall nothing of the crossing. When the ferry docked, he stared blankly, as several little hands grabbed his fingers and shook them while tearful pale faces said goodbye.

Jake had shaken his hand when he placed him on a train to Edinburgh, but he did not register when the American asked if he wanted him to accompany him, even though he shook his head in response.

Chris spent the remaining months in Edinburgh, the city where he was born and had lived most of his life. It looked the same, yet nothing was real. People, sometimes friends he had grown up with in the orphanage, would stop him in the street. The mouths would open, but no words came out. It was as if he were isolated from them by a thick glass wall.

August 1938, Amsterdam

Chris stood silently in the bar, having finished his story. What little he had to say, took more than fifteen minutes. He had to pause repeatedly to remember what came next as this was the first time, he had talked about the events following Jewel's death. Jake would add pieces of information to help his friend when he lost his train of thought. The Scotsman would say something that was so honest, so raw, that it surprised the others.

When he reached the end of his tale, he raised his head. 'Now that I'm back among you, the world seems real again.' He shrugged, and whispered, 'As brutal as it is.'

Lenka studied Chris as he related what he could of the events that followed Berlin. He had changed more than any of them, with perhaps the exception of Ursula who had become a strong and resourceful young woman. The Scotsman retained the attributes that had led Jewel to struggle up the ladder onto the roof in Madrid, as she made the first move to being more than just his friend. For a powerful man, he was considerate and gentle, conscious of his size and power. In Spain, he was quiet and content to let the other Rogues' egos dominate: his priority was the safety of his sister Katherine and his love, Jewel. But they were dead and there was a sharper edge to him. He continued to weigh up everything before he spoke but seemed more resolute with his own opinions. In the presence of the three older male Rogues, he was an equal, still respectful, but no longer a young man in awe of them. He had crawled out from that dark abyss that opens and swallows you when you lose those you love. The Scotsman was no longer self-conscious and had no interest in what others thought of him.

Lenka said nothing as she raised her glass to Chris. Now, he was alone; no ties, no one would mourn his loss, apart from the Rogues who would toast his memory and move on. She watched the others; it was the same with Sean, Vodanski wherever he was, Jake and herself, and that – more than their strength and their readiness to fight – made them dangerous.

She asked Jake to tell them more about what happened to the children that went to America. He ordered another round of drinks and told them something of how he had found homes for several of the children and arranged their passage to the United States.

'After Chris boarded his train, I flew home to New York and got a job with the US Immigration Service. My role was to assist refugees seeking sanctuary.' Jake made no attempt to smother the anger in his voice. 'It was only then that the FBI' Federal Bureau of Investigation, 'realised that I had fought against the Fascists in Spain and tried to have me arrested for being a 'premature anti-fascist'.

'I sometimes have that problem,' said Jocky.

The others grinned, while Lenka looked like she wanted to strangle him.

Jake continued, 'However, someone in the State Department' – unbeknown to Jake it was President Franklin D. Roosevelt, following a call from Winston Churchill – 'intervened and got Hoover's men,' the FBI, 'to back off.'

Jake turned to Sean. 'Then after our battle with the

151

assassination squad in New York, you asked me to find Magdalena Ilona's husband.' Sean lifted his glass to the American. 'I began my search as soon as you and that dumb Russian bear left for England. I discovered that a Ferdinand Ilona was working in a German-owned chemical factory, here in Amsterdam. London must have heard of my inquires and a few days later I received a message,' smiling at Lenka, 'that I wasn't the only one looking for Magdalena's husband. I boarded the next flight to England, got a train to Scotland to find Chris, and here we are.'

'Are you sure it's Magdalena's husband?' asked Sean.

'We have no photo confirmation, and there is no sign of a daughter; so, no, we're not sure,' interjected Lenka. 'But, after sending messages through the usual embassy channels, I know that Vodanski arrived here yesterday morning, but I haven't seen or heard from him.'

'He was with us in New York a few weeks ago,' added Sean.

'I heard, but where did he go after you two returned to England?' asked Lenka.

'Vodanski headed to Paris. He said he has friends there.'

'Lissotte and Marilynn, the stars of Madam Jiggy-Jigs. I'll be amazed if we ever see Vodka again, pal,' added Jocky.

'He didn't spend all his time in a brothel. The Bear regularly visited the British Embassy to check if there were any messages for him,' said Jake.

'You're well informed on the Russian's movements. Why do you care?' asked Sean.

'Care is the wrong word. He's a Commie and the US state department is especially interested in one that roams the continent as freely as he does.'

'He thinks you're a US Government agent, sent to Madrid to spy on the Republican forces,' said Lenka.

Jake was furious. 'You don't believe that, after all I lost, do you?'

'No, but he distrusts you as much as you do him. You have to understand that.' She said no more and reflected that she had given Vodanski a similar speech in Madrid, but she knew that no matter what she said, nothing would quell the hatred they had for each other.

'Why are the British interested in a chemist?' asked Sean.

'You should know; isn't that why you're here?' snapped Lenka.

'I'm here because I was informed that Ferdinand Ilona and his daughter might be here. I was issued with a one-way ticket to Amsterdam and that's it. So, again, what's the Brit's involvement in this?'

'It's his work in the factory, that's why I gathered you all here.'

'That's not why I'm here,' said the Irishman straightening up.

Jocky eyed Jake. 'Here we go again.'

'Best we will go our separate ways,' added Sean. 'I you lot can blow the factory into next year's dictionary, and I'll find the girl.'

Jake interrupted the argument. 'Oh, how wonderful! The IQ of the Rogues has just dropped to single figures.'

Having spotted the others from the doorway, Vodanski made his way over to the bar. The array of customers in between moved out of his way, like gazelles scattering from a waterhole when a lion arrives to drink. Vodanski offered no welcome. He leant against the bar as if he had only just returned from popping out for a cigarette. Jocky pushed a beer over to him. '*Yer* alright big man?'

The Russian nodded.

'Where have you been?' asked Lenka.

'I've been following the man you believe is Ferdinand. It's him.'

'How do you know?'

'They were wearing plain clothes, but the escort that arrived to collect him from work last night and from his apartment this morning were the Gestapo.'

'I take it they were not in uniform, so how do you know they were Nazis?' asked Chris.

'The combination of arrogance and ignorance. The car they used was a black, shiny eight-cylinder Austro-Daimler, no expense spared and no pretence at keeping a low-profile.'

'Anything else?' asked Lenka.

'I asked about Ferdinand in the bar opposite his apartment. The barman says he is afraid of his own shadow. He speaks to no one; he never leaves his flat, except for when the black car comes to collect him each morning. One night he sneaked into the bar and got very drunk. By the end of the night, he was crying and telling everyone that the Nazis had taken his family hostage. Fortunately for him, they dismissed his comments as the ravings of a drunk.'

'Do you think he knows that his wife and son?' asked Sean, resting his arms on the bar.

'They say it's the not knowing that's the worst,' said

Chris, 'but that's no comfort to those who know,' glancing at the forlorn Irishman.

The Russian raised his glass to the others each in turn, except for the American, and drained its contents in one swift movement.

Sean observed the American and the Russian, who were clearly on their guard in each other's presence. After the battle in The Cloisters, they had waited in the roughest bar they could find in Brooklyn, for the delivery of their flight papers. Apart from Samuel, the three men carried on drinking. Vodanski toasted Sean, 'Jewel.' Jake took this as a dig at him as the 'laughing' man who killed her was thought to have been slain by the American's knife. Vodanski and Jake had each grabbed a bottle and smashed it against the bar, holding what was left of it by the neck as they faced each other. From his stretcher on the floor in the middle of the bar, Sean pointed the revolver at them and threatened to shoot if they did not stop. They did, but they still squared up to each other, until Samuel stood behind them. 'Please, don't finish what your enemies failed to do today.' Vodanski and Jake looked over at Samuel and calmed down, letting the weapons drop to the floor as the terrified barman finally exhaled.

'Well, here we are again. One big happy family,' said Jocky.

Lenka tugged the Russian's arm. 'Ursula is here.'

'It will get violent. She has to go back to England!'

'She will, but for now she is with Paul,' said Lenka

The Russian trained his eyes on the Irishman. 'He is your friend, but if he lays a hand on her, I will come after you both.'

'He won't, but believe me, Ursula is no longer the innocent little girl you knew six months ago. I would worry more about him. And by the way Vodanski, if you ever come after me, I'll be ready,' replied the Irishman.

Vodanski smiled. 'Unlike everyone who knows you, I would kill you with a heavy heart.'

'"Everyone who knows me"; that's reassuring on so many levels,' laughed Sean.

'Maybe your heart won't be so heavy when you finally turn on the rest of us,' declared Jake, stepping towards the Russian.

Vodanski the fingers on his clenched fists were white. Now, it was Lenka's turn to separate them.

'Once we learn what the Nazis are up to inside the factory, then you can kill each other.' The men continued to face each other like heavy-weight prize fighters before a major bout, but none of it was for show.

Lenka did not need anyone to tell her of the two men's fight in New York. Jewel's death had created the first tangible reason, at least to them, for their bitter hatred of each other. To the Russian, the laughing SA trooper in the alley should have been killed by Jake's knife, but he survived only to kill Jewel. Jake too blamed himself, but believed that the Russian was manipulating Jewel's death, to hold him to account. After burying Jewel, they were waiting on the platform for the train at the border, when Vodanski declared that Jewel's death was the American's fault. Both men had reached for their guns. Lenka stopped it escalating into bloodshed, only by shouting that any gunshots would alert the border guards and endanger the lives of the children. The other Rogues knew that one day one would kill the other, unless the Nazis did it first.

Ursula observed the anxious young man sitting on the bed opposite, who was repeatedly failing to coordinate his movements to light a cigarette. She leant forward, clasped his hands and lifted the match up to the thin, limp, caterpillar-shaped creation that had taken him over ten minutes to roll.

Though his cigarette was lit, the young Hungarian man did not take a draw from it, 'I'm sorry . . . it's just I become anxious when I'm in one place too long, but Lenka told me I was not to . . . move.'

'Do you always do what women tell you to do?'

'I try, but I start to become jittery and then I wander . . . usually they despair of . . . me.'

'My presence makes you even more uncomfortable,' said Ursula, sitting on the one bed in the room now with both her hands tucked under her thighs.

'It's not you . . . it's just I'm clumsy with . . . wo . . . men . . . apart from my sister.'

'Don't worry, I won't bite you,' she smiled as she liked the effect she was having on the man who was maybe two or three years older than her.

'Well Sean, you know our stories, so what happened to you after Berlin?' asked Chris, as he leant his big frame against the bar, so he was between Vodanski and Jake.

Sean studied the man, and though he was pleased to hear that he bore him no malice, he was sad that the man's innocence and hope had been replaced by the solemnness of someone who had suffered the loss of those he loved. Ten minutes later Sean finished his story. He left out the fight on the train and the details of his escape, telling them what he believed to be true about the fate of Magdalena and the boy. Lenka, Chris, Jake, Jocky and Vodanski stood in silence, trying to absorb the horror of what they had just heard.

Chris spoke, 'Sean, you can't be sure they are dead. You haven't been inside the Fortress.'

'Sticking a chimney onto a castle; do you think that the Nazis built it to bake bread? The Nazis also have a specially adapted train that ferries prisoners to the Fortress. If their prisoners were Roosevelt or Stalin, I might understand it. Maybe it's a factory run by slave labour, but why go to all that trouble to capture a young woman and a little boy and deliver them to such a place? If they have unique skills or knowledge, then I failed to discover them.'

Lenka looked away and closed her eyes briefly. Both Vodanski and Jake were similarly deep in thought. Chris spoke: 'Sean, I'm sorry, but how can this be? This is the Twentieth Century, for Christ's sake.'

'If Magdalena and Tóth walked in the door, no man would be happier than I to be proven wrong.'

Jocky's ashen face scanned the dour faces at the bar. 'Intelligence has heard some terrible things about what the Krauts are up to, but nothing like this. A specially constructed incinerator to burn innocent men, women and children; I canna see any reason for it. The Nazis execute prisoners every day, and there's no sign that they are running out of bullets and rope from what I hear.'

Sean raised his head, 'A few years ago, in Norway, I came across a German owned factory where they were modifying vehicles so that gas from the exhaust entered the body of the vehicle.'

'For use in an abattoir?' asked Chris.

'If it was simply for animals, why carry out such research in one of the most uninhabitable places in Europe?' Lenka and Jocky glanced at each other. 'Look, there is no need for any of you to believe me, but we know the Nazis have developed clinics where parents hand over their disabled children to be "treated".' Jocky and Lenka knew this to be true. 'Part of their doctrine is the eradication of what they term sub-humans. They believe that the Jews are legitimate targets too as we all witnessed in Berlin. They have assembled a special unit of fucking psychos to carry out their programme.'

'If *yer* didn't blow all the evidence to *shite* when *yer* touched it, we might believe *yer*,' said Jocky.

Sean scanned the sceptical faces around him and finally, exasperated, he raised his hands. 'Ah, fuck it; believe what you like. As I said, you can all go and infiltrate, blow up, whatever you plan to do with the factory and I'll find Magdalena's daughter.' He turned to Lenka, who was deep in thought. 'Lenka.' She did not acknowledge him. 'Lenka!' he repeated. She lifted her head. 'Lenka, with your network, do you have any information on the girl's whereabouts in the city?'

Lenka pulled herself away from her thoughts. 'No. But, if she is not with her father, the Germans must have her nearby to produce her if he doesn't do as he's told.'

'Poor bastard, first they keep his wife and son as hostages and now his daughter,' said Chris.

Sean decided that there was nothing else to discuss or explain, so he moved on to the one subject they could all agree on. He shouted over to the barman, 'Same again.'

The new barman, who had replaced the English-speaking one, was bemused.

The Irishman looked at Jocky: 'Do you know any other languages, apart from the "blue" variety?'

'What's the *fuken* point, even the English don't understand me when I speak English.'

'I'll try French; so, what are you drinking, Valentino?' asked Sean.

'Just a coffee and a wee biscuit for me,' given him an exaggerated big beaming smile. 'What do *yer* think, *yer* daft Irish *bastad*?'

Sean turned to the bartender, but continued in English, 'Heinekens and whiskey chasers for everyone, and a coffee and a small biscuit for my little angry friend here.'

The Glaswegian launched another tirade of profanities at the Irishman. The bartender returned with beers, taking his direction from the empty glasses on the bar. Soon, the Rogues were drowning the horrors of what they had heard in alcohol. After an hour, they even began to laugh at the continuing repartee between Jocky and Sean, apart from Lenka. She remembered the only other time they had been together in a bar. Jewel had been laughing with them.

Chris could easily have joined in with the banter, but preferred to remain silent on the side-lines. He smiled occasionally even if he did not laugh. Then, to the surprise of the others, Lenka put her arms around the big Scot and rested her head on his right arm. The other four men looked at them and recognised that look, it was the look of those united in grief.

Lenka detached herself from Chris. She had concluded

that if Sean was going to remain in Amsterdam, it was best he was part of the operation rather than causing mayhem on his own. She rolled out the diagram on a table, this time out of sight, around the corner from the bar and told them of her plan to enter the factory. Ten minutes later, she had finished. Sean expressed his opinion on the revised plan intended to include him.

'Bollocks!'

'Bollocks! Is that all you have to say?' asked Lenka, starring up at the ornate ceiling.

'I'm sure I'll have more to say, if you press me.'

'You never were one of us; you think your way is the only way.'

'I do now. One minute, I'm told I am a liability, the next I'm the designated bodyguard to our little mascot here when entering the factory?'

'Look Paddy, we Scots built the steam-engine while *yer* lot were digging for spuds to put on *yer* breakfast plate,' huffed Jocky.

'Jocky, you're here to blow the factory up, or worse, regale the Nazis about your love life and drive them to suicide. But, I'm here to help a man and his daughter escape. I've fought in one war, and that was enough.'

'I was wondering why someone like you hadn't got involved in fighting the Fascists in Spain,' said Jake.

The Irishman turned angrily on the American. 'If you want to fight in other people's wars, then that is your choice. The war I fought was to free my people.'

'Quite right, *yer* tell '*em*' Paddy,' said Jocky, who did not understand why the other Rogues had fought in other countries' wars when their own survival did not depend on it.

'Was your war worth fighting for?' asked Jake.

Sean knew Jake was sincere. 'I regret that I had to kill good people. When the Nazis stretch out across Europe, I'll be at the front alongside you but not before.'

'London believes the Germans have moved the manufacture of parts for new gas-fired burners to Amsterdam,' said Lenka, calmly.

The other Rogues were stunned. Lenka decided she had no choice but to tell them of the communique she had received explaining the importance of the factory.

'What we have learnt is that the Nazis are designing and building new huge industrial incinerators, similar no doubt to the one you believe has been installed in Himmler's Fortress,' nodding towards Sean.

'New in what sense?' asked Chris.

'Ones that can be installed on existing facilities. It's quicker than having to build one entirely from scratch.'

'For what purpose?' asked Chris.

'That's what we need to find out, but we believe the answer lies in that factory.'

'You knew what I was saying was true,' snapped Sean. 'But said nothing, and then you accuse me of not working as a team?'

'We knew what the Nazis were planning to do, but until you told me of the Fortress, I had no idea that they had already built one. Look, we still have no proof, but together we may find it inside the factory. Are you with us, or pissing off to do your own thing as usual? I don't care either way, but if you are with us you do as I tell you.'

Chris interjected, which again surprised the others.

'Why would the Nazis have such an operation in Amsterdam?'

'The Dutch are experts in gas extraction; the Germans believe that gas is more efficient than coal. Whatever they build, no matter how big can be loaded onto a barge and ferried down the Rhine,' said Jocky.

'Wouldn't the Nazis be better off bringing the experts to Germany and building it on their own territory?' suggested Sean, before realising he had answered his own question. 'They think this will soon be their territory.'

'You see now that we must smuggle Jocky in to discover if it's true. He will know what to look for,' said Lenka.

'That's really your objective? To secure proof of these Nazi devices?' asked Sean.

'Maybe more; if I have a chance, I may apply a little Scottish mischief,' said Jocky with a smile.

'Not if I'm to be part of this; it's in and out, no sabotage and no explosions,' said Sean.

'I'm with the bog-trotter; I may get hurt if there's fireworks, pa. Err . . . Lenka.'

Lenka ignored them, 'London contacted me on the radio last week and put me in contact with a man who works at the factory with Ferdinand; his name is Józef. He left a message earlier that he would meet us here.' She saw a man wearing a long shabby coat standing nervously by the door to the restaurant. 'He's here,' she said, waving him over. The tall, gangly man managed to steady his trembling hand long enough to set his frayed hat on the hat stand by the entrance.

'Hello Józef,' said Lenka.

'It is good to see you again Lenka,' replied the tall man who joined them at the bar. 'And these are your friends, the *kindly gentlemen* you spoke of?' he said looking at the threatening looking troop around him.

The Rogues looked at the man with a combination of suspicion and amusement at his choice of words.

'Lenka any other surprises coming our way?' scoffed Sean. 'Have you posted our whereabouts on notes in local phone booths?'

'If I told you someone was coming, you'd only ponder on how many ways you could kill them if I did,' replied Lenka.

Józef withdrew his hand from Sean's, as he looked back towards the door.

'Don't worry, these idiots really are my friends,' said Lenka.

Chris grasped Józef's hand and shook it.

'I'm relieved to hear it; I wouldn't want any of you as an enemy,' said Józef, who smiled briefly, though his hand was still trembling when the enormous Scotsman released it.

'*Yer* right there, pal. It's *nay* for show, trust me they're all nutjobs,' said Jocky, who lifted his elbow up to prop it on the bar alongside Vodanski's.

Józef drew a deep breath. 'I'm sorry that I could not be here earlier. Also, I must apologise for the history lesson I am about to give, but I believe it will help if you have some understanding about my country. I will be brief.'

'*Yer* better be, pal, this is Amsterdam and I've some entertaining to do and–' Lenka kicked Jocky, who promptly released a few expletives.

She kicked him harder and this time he got the message. The violence did little to calm Józef's anxiety, but the woman bade him continue. He drew another deep breath.

'Unlike everywhere else in seventeenth-century Europe, Jewish settlers in the Netherlands did not have to live in ghettos or wear a mark that declared they were Jews. Today, we have a socialist government and Jewish people have more opportunities than most to find work. In turn, we play an active role to help benefit the community. But that is changing. Some now fear that because of their liberal approach to the Jews, the Nazis will invade.'

'They will invade whatever happens; it's the nature of the beast,' said Sean.

Józef shook his head. 'Yesterday I saw a sign in a café window which read, VOOR JODEN VERBODEN (No Jews Allowed).' He swallowed once more, attempting to calm his nerves. 'But most Dutch people do not think that way and want to remain neutral as we did during the Great War.'

'So, you're telling us that the Dutch are no friends of the Nazis,' said Chris.

'Yes, but we mistrust the British as much as we do the Germans. Many hate the British even more because of the Boer War and distrust those who are outspoken English critics of the Nazis, men like Winston Churchill, who fought in *that* war.'

'I see Winston's not popular here either. The man may outdo me in the "pissing off everyone department",' observed Sean. 'What do you know of what is being developed in the factory?'

'Well, we know that gas-tankers have recently delivered supplies there.'

'Businesses need fuel,' said Chris.

'I saw the paperwork for one of the consignments and it was marked *CONFIDENTIAL: WESTERBORK EXPERIMENT.*' The others in the little room looked blankly at each other. Józef continued: 'Westerbork is a transit camp just outside Amsterdam, near Amersfoort, which was recently set up on the orders of the Dutch authorities. It is an internment centre for the influx of Jewish and Roma immigrants forced to flee from Germany and Austria. The Germans believe them to be *Untermenschen*, a term that expresses their belief that both groups, along with Eastern Europeans, are racially inferior. Rumours are that the Germans are trying to make a deal to bring the camp under their control, but the Dutch Government has refused their request.'

'Rumours based on?'

'Ferdinand received a note, and it referred to the camp as a *Judendurchgangslager*, which is the term the Nazis use for concentration camps.'

'Do these things really exist?' asked Chris.

'Yes, the British built the first ones during the Boer war. Perhaps you begin to understand our mistrust of your country.' Józef looked down at his watch. 'Maybe Ferdinand and I are a little paranoid, but with recent events we are so glad you have come to help us discover the Nazis' intentions. We have seen that they have influence with some government officials. Ferdinand's guards,' he said as he glanced at Lenka, 'have been issued with documents by those officials with right-wing sympathies to operate in the

166

city, providing security for the factory, as long as they keep a low profile. Józef looked anxiously at his watch. 'I am sorry, I must go now to make sure that my daughter, Isobel, is collected from school. Then I will join you in a couple of hours when we will meet Ferdinand.' The man acknowledged each of the Rogues with a slight smile, a nod of his head, a handshake and repeated, 'Thank you for helping us, *gentlemen*.' He made his way towards the door, but Lenka grabbed his arm 'Where will we meet you and Ferdinand?'

'My apologies, my mind is not what it was. Please forgive me once again. Ferdinand will meet you in the Café Karpershoek a few kilometres from here as you walk towards the train station. He is too afraid to come here, as it is too public.'

Lenka waited until the man had left the restaurant. 'When he said to see his daughter, he was telling the truth. A Catholic family have taken his daughter in and will raise her as their own, as Józef fears the Germans will march in soon and send her to places like Westerbork. I met him last night. He confided to me that every weekday afternoon he waits across the street from his daughter's school to make sure her new family collects her. But he stays out of sight so as not to jeopardise her new life. Dutch families are taking in Jewish children and raising them as Catholics or Protestants, so the Nazis sympathisers won't detect them. Their governments may refuse to believe, but many good people know the war is coming.'

Chris looked across at the raindrops angrily battering the windows. 'See the hat stand; even the thundering rain did not remind the poor man to collect his hat.'

Ursula and Paul were in the bar on the ground floor of the building where he rented a room.

'We are out of the apartment, you have a glass of wine and a cigarette in your hand, so why are you still nervous?'

'Yes . . . I'm sorry. . . but I'm useless at conversation and the only woman I know is Sárika . . . my sister.'

'What of your mother?'

'She died . . . in . . . childbirth.' Ursula did not press him, but something told her that it was his rather than his sister's birth, as his stutter grew worse. Nevertheless, he confirmed it: '. . . My father says it was my fault . . . He didn't love my . . . mama, you know . . . but he was right, I did cause the death of my mama–'

Ursula clasped his free hand in hers which startled him, causing him to spill his wine over his trousers. He did not appear to notice as he made no move to wipe the stain away until the young woman handed him a napkin. For the next few minutes, he rubbed at the wine stain as he continued to look in every direction except in Ursula's. He refilled his glass and emptied it with one gulp and looked at the woman sitting beside him still holding his hand. 'You are . . . nice . . .' he said, he stopped. 'Sorry, I'm . . . an idiot . . . I–'

'Is that it? Nice?'

'Ah . . . yes . . . I mean no . . . no . . . I don't mean that you are not . . . nice, in fact you . . .' he was transfixed by her hazel coloured eyes, 'are beautiful,' gazing at his bitten fingernails.

Ursula laughed 'I think that is enough for now, we don't want to wear you out do we, but thank you.' She squeezed his hand tighter.

'I just meant that . . . it wasn't all I had to say . . .'

'It's fine. Take your time, just take a breath, sit back and focus on what you want to say. We are young; we have plenty of time.' With that she placed her hand over his heart and pushed him gently back into his seat.

Paul smiled and sat quietly, as he composed what he was going to say. Ursula sat upright and smiled encouragingly at him. He began again and spoke slowly. 'I meant to say . . . that you are so nice, but . . . that it is strange that you have formed a bond with . . . Sean.'

'Ah so that's what's troubling you. Now, you've said it, was that so hard?'

'Yes . . . it . . . was.'

'Of course, I like Sean. In a short time, we have experienced much together.'

The young man's head dropped.

'Hey,' as she lifted the empty wine glass from his other hand and set it down on the battered wooden table, placed his other hand in hers and leant towards him. 'Not in that way; he and Lenka are more like my . . . parents . . . I mean that in a good way though, not like mine who abandoned me.'

Paul could not hide his delight and excitedly started talking again, 'Good . . . you and Sean are not lovers . . . Sorry, I should not have said lovers . . . very good . . . excellent . . . no, I don't mean being abandoned is good. . . I . . . I . . . I have a chance!'

'Remember, relax, deep breaths.' She sat upright. 'No wait, continue, I like this.'

A thin man, clearly nervous – more so than his friend Józef

– entered Café Karpershoek. Many locals said it was the oldest bar in the city. The shelves were lined with mementoes of ships from when the Dutch had one of the world's largest trading fleets. Józef had re-joined the Rogues, who were sitting at a table by the bar. Chris unobtrusively returned the frayed hat to Józef under the table.

Józef saw his friend and beckoned him over. The thin man approached the intimidating-looking group with even greater hesitancy in his step.

'Good evening. . . I am Ferdinand.'

Sean stood up and pulled out a chair for the man to sit down. It had been a while since he had encountered anyone more anxious than Paul.

'You are the one whom they call The Englander, the man sent to help Magdalena and my son, Tóth, escape. Please, tell me, where are they?'

The Irishman could not hide the pain he felt when he looked at the man who was scanning his face desperately in search of hope. The man had been through so much, needed to know the truth. The Irishman pressed his hands on the man's sloping shoulders to gently push him onto a chair. Now that the man was seated, Sean told him what he knew, or thought he knew of his family, and watched as the man crumbled before him.

He spared the man the details of what Magdalena told him of her torture, but he ended his account of the events with, 'I am sorry, but I believe your wife and son are dead.'

The man's head wilted into his hands, he wailed loudly as his body rocked back and forth. Ferdinand believed that his wife and son were dead, but to hear it spoken was impossible for him to bear. He collapsed towards the floor, but Sean and Jake grabbed him in time and with Vodanski's help they lifted him back up onto his chair. Jake or Vodanski could have easily lifted Ferdinand up onto the chair on their own, but with his recent injuries the sudden movement caused Sean immense pain; not that he would let the others know.

Sean held the man upright and spoke firmly, 'You have a daughter. We are here to help you both escape to England if that is what you want.'

The Hungarian man was still in shock, as tears rolled down his pallid face like raindrops on a corpse. Józef put his arm around his friend.

Finally, Ferdinand answered, though it was barely audible, 'Yes.'

'To save your daughter, you must be strong and put all other thoughts and emotions to one side, at least for now.' It was not Sean that spoke these words, but Jake. He surprised himself. Jake the adventurer; Jake the ladies' man; the elusive Jake, the man who made it clear that he would never become close to anyone. But, during their short time together, Dominique had changed him; she had turned the selfish adventurer into a caring and decent man. Having observed the tormented man before them, Jake decided to join forces with the Irishman. His objective was no longer that of Lenka's, to discover whatever the Germans were doing at the factory, but to make it his personal responsibility to help Ferdinand and his daughter escape.

'Do you know where they are keeping your daughter?' asked Sean.

'They have told me nothing, only that I must continue

my work in the factory. If not, I will never see her again.' He closed his eyes as he spoke. 'Once a week, they let me talk to her on the telephone, but I have not seen my little girl since they took her from our room six months ago.'

'Does the operator put you through? Is it an international call?' The man shook his head in response to Sean's question.

'I am sure that your daughter is alive and not far from here,' said Sean. Trying to reassure the man, he added, 'I'm telling you what you already know, but as she is their leverage over you; no harm will come to her as long as you work in the factory. In the meantime, I will find her.'

'I'm with you,' said Jake.

Sean did not say it, but he thought the Germans would keep the girl alive knowing the man's precarious state of mind. Rather than refusing to cooperate, he was more likely to kill himself if he believed all his family were dead.

'Do you know where the headquarters are of your Nazi escort?' asked Sean.

Ferdinand tried to control himself as he spoke. 'No.'

'Tell me the guards' schedule.'

'They sit in the Austro-Daimler that is always parked across from my building unless they use it to drop me off at the gates of the factory or collect me. They never speak to me.'

Vodanski was tempted to ask how he escaped that night he got drunk in the bar across the road from his building but he decided not to. It was probably the time when he first realised that his wife and son may be dead.

Ferdinand scrutinised the faces around the table. 'The Germans know you're here. The leader of the Gestapo unit based here is Captain Vile Kruger. I've never met him, but one morning my driver had to make a telephone call. As he did so, I looked at a file he had left in the car and I can now see that the photos it contained were of all of you. The driver caught me and later that night they beat me. Afterwards, I was given a message from Kruger that if I encountered any of you, I should report it to my escort immediately, or my family will face the consequences.' He squinted at Sean and Jocky. 'You two were not in the photographs.'

Vodanski turned to Lenka. 'After the fall of the Republic, Franco's Government must have handed over all the files they held on us to the Nazis.'

'Makes sense; I wasn't in Spain, neither was my friend here,' said Sean, pointing to Jocky.

'But, they know you're here too, as the file contained sketches of both of you,' said Ferdinand.

'Ah, *shite*!' cursed Jocky, making no attempt to lower his voice.

Sean said nothing. Ferdinand continued, 'but looking at you both, the sketches are not that good they look like normal people.' The man did not see what was funny, but Lenka appeared to smile.

Jocky was a little relieved but, as with Sean, his thoughts turned once again to the spy within their ranks.

'How do you get in and out of the factory?' asked Lenka.

'Seven days a week, I am collected each morning at six o'clock and taken to the factory. Each evening, I am picked up at seven o'clock. I am taken back to my apartment where I am ordered to stay until they arrive to collect me again the next morning.

'How did you get here tonight?' asked Vodanski.

'I find it difficult to sleep and sometimes I weaken for a drink to steady my nerves. There is a rickety, disused, metal staircase at the back of the building and I used this to creep out at night.'

'Do the guards ever enter the factory with you?' continued Lenka.

'No, they remain outside. Mostly they sit in the square outside and drink coffee all day until they collect me. It provides them with a clear view of the main gates, the only way in and out of the building, as behind it, is a canal.'

'Your specialist field is gas production?' asked Lenka.

'No, water.'

'Water! That's their special research project? Why the interest in water?' asked Jocky.

'I and several other chemists are researching the molecular structure of water, in particular we are attempting to break down the structure of the atom. A German chemist, Otto Hahn, is working on a project to split the atom. As part of their research they are experimenting with what they call "heavy water" which contains hydrogen atoms that are twice the size of normal atoms.'

Chris was intrigued. 'What is so important about hydrogen? It's not as if it's a rare element.'

'It's to release the isotopes in its atoms to create a new source of energy.'

'How do you produce this heavy water?'

'You can produce small amounts through electrolysis, distillation and other chemical processes.'

Sean looked at Jocky. 'Does this mean anything to

you?'

'Yep, we believe the septic tanks,' he replied, as he gave Jake a quick glance. 'Sorry pal, I mean Yanks, are looking at how to harness the power of atomic elements. But it's all pie in the sky from what I hear. I know the Norwegians built a plant four years ago to produce it commercially. We haven't been able to prove it as the Norwegians are very secretive. We have *nay* idea where it is, and aerial photographs of the potential areas have turned up sweet Fanny Adams.'

'Who is this Fanny Adams?' asked Józef.

'It's slang for "*fuk* all" pal.'

Lenka kicked him harder, while clamping her hand over his mouth to smother his response this time.

Sean winked at his friend, now released from Lenka's hold. He was still swearing but had enough sense to muffle the phrase 'mad bitch'.

'Try the fjords, near Tinn. The Norsk Hydro plant a few miles from the rubble of another facility once owned by a German company,' said Sean. 'The Nazis built it to spy on the Norwegians, but it was also used to conduct experiments on genetics.'

'Ah, the factory with the adapted trucks *yer* mentioned. Seriously Paddy, is there a country that *yer* haven't ripped it a new arsehole?' said Jocky, grimacing as he rubbing his badly bruised leg.

Lenka wanted to return to the discussion on London's plan to enter the factory, but the man who had just joined them stood up to leave.

'Please, I must return before they discover I am here, but you must find my daughter and help her escape.'

Lenka spoke first: 'We will, but we need you to make copies of all the designs you can get access to by tomorrow.'

'Yes, but I can't smuggle them out, if I'm caught what of my daughter?'

'Leave them in your desk in case they search you when you leave at the end of the day. We will do the rest.' Jocky opened a copy of the original draftsman's design for the factory and passed a pencil to the man. Lenka asked him to mark where his office was as well as the workshops. Lenka continued: 'Once inside, if we discover they are manufacturing a new type of weapon Jocky can use his expertise to make it inoperable without attracting the suspicion of the Gestapo or the Dutch authorities. After that, we will head to your apartment, overpower your Gestapo escort and make them tell us where your daughter is.'

'The Gestapo will not give up information, quickly,' said Ferdinand.

'They will,' said Vodanski.

Lenka and the others looked at the Russian's impassive face and realised that extracting the information would not be a problem.

She continued. 'We will free your daughter and take you both to England.'

'Excellent plan,' replied Sean, which perturbed Lenka. He turned to Ferdinand: 'Make the copies first thing.'

'It's best then, as the other members of the staff will arrive around nine.'

'Do you have a photo of your daughter?' asked Sean.

'Only this one,' said Ferdinand, as he lifted the gold

pendant and chain from around his neck.

He opened it revealing a small picture of what was once a family of four.

'I'll give this back to you, when I return your daughter,' said Sean. He stared at it for a while remembering how Magdalena had touched his face and asked that no matter what happened to her, he must protect Tóth. For the first time, it occurred to Sean that it was not Lenka who had brought them all together – it was Ferdinand. He looked at the dishevelled man. 'I'll find your daughter, I promise.'

Lenka glared at Sean; she disliked his repeated use of 'I'.

Ferdinand lifted his head. 'Promise me that if you find my daughter that you will leave without me, if collecting me means it will endanger her. Please, you must promise me this.'

'I promise,' replied Sean, breaking the oath he made to himself in England once again.

Then Sean asked the question that Magdalena had evaded. 'Why did you leave Hungary taking only your daughter, leaving your wife and son behind?' Ferdinand wept once more, but Józef answered for him while tightening his arm around his friend's shoulders.

'My employers demanded that he go to Amsterdam, but Hungarian immigration officials would only provide Ferdinand and Magdalena with a visa for one child. By keeping the other under the watch of fellow fascists in Hungary, it ensured that my friend did as he was instructed. When Magdalena heard that one of their children had to stay behind, she refused to leave. It was decided to leave

Lens with her mother, but when they told the boy, he refused to leave his little sister behind. Ferdinand tells me that Tóth *was . . .*' he stopped himself and looked at his friend, 'is a very determined little boy.'

The Irishman did not respond, but the anguish on his face was evident.

Ferdinand trembled as he spoke. 'You know Magdalena was a teacher and taught deaf children?' Sean nodded. Trembling, the man's voice grew louder. 'You wish to protect my feelings by not saying it, but I know that they took Magdalena's eyes. She lost not only her sight but her contact with the children too. Can you imagine what that did to her? In one cruel act, she was no longer able to communicate with the children she loved and cared for, and this meant that they could no longer engage with the world.'

'Was there no one else who could help the children?'

'No, after her torture her colleagues were told to leave and fled to nearby schools. You cannot blame them. That's the other terrible cruelty of all this; the Nazis make examples of people to send as a warning to others.' He broke down once more. Eventually, he composed himself and raised his head. 'Did she tell you that she wrote to me a few days before she reached Budapest?' Sean shook his head. 'She wrote that she would bring Tóth to me, but as she was blind and disfigured that she would understand if I didn't want her anymore and would leave.' He cried out, 'But of course I wanted her! I loved her! I loved them both!' and the man was raging and shouting at Sean, 'and you . . . you think I abandoned them!'

'I need to know everything. What happened when they took your daughter?'

178

The other Rogues were angry as Sean continued to press now-hysterical man. Vodanski stepped forward. 'Stop this!'

Sean rose and stepped towards the Russian, 'Because of me, this man lost his wife and his son. Now I need to know everything so that he does not lose his daughter. Have you got a fucking problem with that?' The other customers, mainly merchant seaman, looked over to the group the raised voices emanated from but decided it was prudent not to interfere.

Vodanski placed his weight on his left foot to prepare to launch himself at the Irishman. Jake straightened up. 'Sean that's enough. The man is a wreck, if you continue you will break him.'

Sean positioned himself, so he was equidistant between the two men, focusing his crystal-clear blue eyes in preparation to counter whoever was first to attack. Lenka slipped a knife from her belt. Jocky edged himself away into the side-room at the end of the bar.

Then without a word, Chris walked between the men and grasped Ferdinand, who was completely unaware of what was happening, by the arms and bent down to speak to him.

'Please, we need you to be strong. We want only one thing, to reunite you with your daughter.'

The man looked up at the gentle, softly spoken Scotsman and quickly regained his composure. 'I understand. Please, ask me anything. You are right. Lens is all that matters.'

The three men standing in a triangle, turned to look at Chris. The man was that rare combination of ferocious fighter and peacemaker. With a few words, he had extinguished their anger. Perhaps after all he had suffered, Chris' had returned the *conscience* that Lenka believed had lost since Jewel's death. Perhaps that is why the Rogues so readily turned on each other since Berlin.

Sean spoke softly to the man, 'I'm sorry, but I need to ask you about the man who tortured your wife. I must ask you, as I did not press your wife on this' – which he regretted – 'as I did not want her to have to revisit the horror of her time with him. But from what she told me, the man took an almost personal interest in her. I believe that anything that may help us find him, may help us find your daughter.'

'He is not a man, but a beast. They call him Cerberus!' yelled Ferdinand, his body shaking as if it were in a seizure. Sean eyes narrowed. 'The name is frequently mentioned by the guards. They make no attempt to hide his name. They speak it with an air of pride, even with awe!'

Lenka slipped her knife back into her boot, as each of the three men standing wondered who would have been the first to feel her blade.

She spoke. 'He appears in German communiqués, particularly in those limited to the German High Command. He is the leader of the Alpha Wolves, the special elite units we encountered. His real name is Major Klaus Krak. He has as many pseudonyms as you do Ryan: "Himmler's Scalpel"; "Heydrich's Hammer"; "Hitler's Beast", but all have the same prefix – "Cerberus".'

Jake leant back against the bar, 'His name is known to the US State Department too, but we thought it was a generic code word for the leaders of a number of cover units operating in every country in Europe and recently even the United States.'

'Why?' asked Chris.

'The name is linked with almost every major assassination and scandal involving European governments, their armies, their police and even opposition parties and groups, ranging from Jewish organisations to the Jehovah's Witnesses in the last two years. We thought it impossible that one person could be behind over a hundred similar incidents.'

'Did you learn anything else?' asked Lenka.

'A year ago, an American agent in Berlin tried too.'

'Did he get a description of the man,' asked Sean.

'No. A few days later, there was a report of a terrible odour from under the floors of the American Ambassador's residence in Berlin. When someone went to check out the rat-infested sewers, they found the gnawed remains of the agent wedged into the main overflow pipe leading into the house.'

Having decided it was safe to return to the table, Jocky contributed what he knew. 'The Commander,' he always mentioned his boss in Room 39 in Admiralty House with pride, 'is obsessed by him. He says, "his claw marks" are on every covert Nazi operation in Europe. He keeps sending dossiers up to government officials marked, "Cerberus – The Alpha Wolves". But there's no concrete proof linking the Nazis to the latest politician, Jew, homosexual or opponent of fascism to die in a tragic accident or resign, only to kill themselves when a scandal breaks.'

Ferdinand gathered his thoughts and spoke calmly. 'Now you know the identity of the man, does it help you?'

'I honestly don't know,' replied Sean.

'But what of you Englander? I asked Józef to check the library to learn more about you.' His friend looked awkwardly at the Irishman. 'The Englander is referred to in the international press from Bolivia to China, but there is never a photo. Some reports say that you take on impossible odds, even armies.' Ferdinand clasped his hands and started to rock back and forth again as he wept. 'Yet you sit there and tell me that you failed to protect my wife and son.' Sean said nothing, as Józef helped his friend up from the chair and together they walked listlessly towards the doorway. They disappeared into the pouring rain. Neither man wore a hat.

'Poor bastards,' whispered Vodanski, turning back to the others. 'None of you has children. You fight; but worry about no one but yourselves. To produce a family is life's greatest pleasure, but in war the threat to your family becomes your greatest fear.'

The others looked at each other and knew it to be true, but no one said anything, even Jake appeared to nod. Lenka pondered on what Ferdinand had said earlier.

'No surprise that bastard Franco passed everything he has on us to the Nazis, but how the hell have they circulated our photos to every outpost across Europe?'

'This is the Twentieth Century, the dawn of technology, *yer* crazy bit . . .' Jocky stopped when he was met by the cautionary expressions of the men and the cold stare of the woman. He recovered quickly. 'You were all in Spain, so I'm surprised this is news. A great man, Pau Abadi Pera (Sabadell) an inventor from Catalonia, designed and built a device for transmitting images and documents by radio and wire about ten years ago. By transforming dots into electrical impulses, it is possible to transmit, receive and reconstruct a photographic image.' He reclined but shot forward again when he realised it was a stool. Recovering his composure, he continued, '*Yer* see, I'm *nay* just a pretty face.'

'Not even that,' said Sean, though he was as impressed as the others.

Sean pushed his beer glass to one side. 'Change of plan. I must find Ferdinand's daughter before you enter the factory.

'Why?' asked Vodanski.

'If they rumble you, they'll kill the girl.'

Lenka countered, 'I know you think I'm a heartless bitch.' None of the others said anything. She carried on unperturbed: 'The factory is the priority; if you are caught trying to find the girl, the Nazis will seal off the factory with her father inside it. Once we have the designs, we will search for the girl.'

'I apologise for repeating myself, but bollocks. I will do what I have to do, and you are not going to stop me.'

'Oh, I'll stop you Ryan,' drawing the knife once more from her boot.

Jocky sighed. 'And there was I, thinking that we would leave fewer dead fascists behind this time.'

'Don't bank on it,' said Sean, as he turned to Lenka. 'Drop that knife back into your high heels, or you'll never sit comfortably on that beautiful arse of yours again.'

Lenka whisked the knife up and brought it down on the table leaving it embedded in the pine table an inch in front of Sean's hand.

Chris pushed his arm between them. 'There are enough of us to save the girl and stop whatever the Nazis are planning, so can you two calm down?'

'No worries, Chris, the lady was just making her point,' added Sean.

'I was just making a point, was I?'

'Your body didn't lean forward, and your eyes telegraphed your intentions.'

'Next time, I'll keep them shut, stab widely and hope for the best,' replied Lenka.

She emptied her glass and ordered another round. It took some time to attract the attention of the terrified manager who was pretending to be in a conversation with an incoherent drunk at the end of the bar.

Sean returned to his revision of London's plan. 'Your strategy is based on securing intelligence, not on saving a little girl. I will find his daughter, while the rest of you break into the factory.'

'And if you don't find her, then what?' asked Vodanski.

'You, Chris, Lenka and Jocky carry out the plan as agreed with London. Afterwards, you can still try to extract her whereabouts from his guards, free her, and make your way to England.'

'As always, you're holding something back,' said Lenka.

'Why do you care? All I'm saying is that you continue with your original plan, while I search for the girl.'

'You were part of the plan.'

'"Were" being the operative word. That was before you saw my injuries, and as you said yourself, I'm a "liability".'

'You always were,' said Lenka.

Jake interjected. 'Sean, you may be able to walk without a cane, but even the Glaswegian here is in a healthier state than you and has more of a chance of finding the girl.' Jocky glowered up at the American but as Jake was nearly twice his size, and as he was within range of one of his powerful arms and considering how pumped up everyone was, he decided to let it pass. 'I'll happily search for the girl.'

'No. Jake,' replied Sean. 'You heard they have photos of all of you. You won't get within a hundred feet of the girl before they kill her. Thanks for offering to help, but you will be the *liability*, my friend. That leaves Jocky and me, as the Nazis only have a couple of poor drawings of us. If it's not going to be me, then it will have to be Jocky. That means you have no technical expert to execute your plan.'

'What? Me! Me, go looking for Nazis?' shuttered Jocky.

Lenka was furious. 'I don't trust you one fucking bit Ryan. Leave you to your own devices – no chance. Okay, I agree. One of us searches for the girl while the rest of us head to the factory, but that could be any of us. We still have the element of surprise.'

Sean was in no mood to compromise. 'Take the Nazis by surprise? Are you joking? They know every fucking move we make. Let's settle this now. You're in charge of the operation, so you have to go into the factory. Jake and Vodanski we know for sure are known to the Nazis' assassins, as they have already tried to kill them, so they must be back-up. Chris does not know the city,' and at that point Sean turned to the big Scotsman, 'I guess you've never been to Amsterdam before and believe me with all its canals it's a maze. You will be lost in five minutes. Trust me.' Chris nodded. 'That leaves Jocky, who knows Amsterdam like the *palm* of his hand, and me.'

'Very funny, Paddy,' responded the Scotsman flipping his hands up, 'he means the back of my hand,' continued the very frequent visitor to the city's red-light district.

'No I don't.' Sean returned to his plan. 'Look, I understand now that your mission depends on securing the designs within the factory. But, I'm in the worst shape, so of all of you I'm the most expendable. If I fail, it doesn't affect your mission.'

Jocky spoke and did so, in a reverent tone, 'I have to agree, the Holy Mother is right.'

Lenka looked like she was about to kill him. Jocky recognised the look and quickly clarified his outburst. '*Nay*, I mean about finding the little girl. If it's a choice of me or this mad Irish *bastad* here, he has my vote.'

To Jocky's surprise, first Sean, Jake, Chris and finally Vodanski started to laugh. Lenka gave the men a stony-faced look, particularly the Irishman, who when he laughed, did so heartily and easily. Sean caught her look and maybe it was the drink, maybe it was just wishful thinking, but he was sure that there was a hint of a smile. He looked at Lenka again. Yes, it was the drink.

In a little bar, a half a mile away, Paul was abruptly pulled backwards off the wooden chair by the largest of a group of men sitting at the table behind him.

'Fuck off queer boy,' yelled the man in his ear. 'Your

lady has a beautiful mouth that needs to be put to good use.' The man, one of eight very drunken Dutch soldiers, clapped his hand around Paul's mouth and squeezed it. 'Come on pretty boy, say goodbye to your girlfriend before you go.'

'Leave him alone, you ugly pig,' screamed Ursula, as two of the man's drinking party leapt forward and restrained her.

Another seized her wooden crutch.

Paul continued to struggle, desperately trying to pull the man's hand from his face but the soldier was too powerful.

'Come on, homo, just say something before you leave your crippled bitch with us tonight,' he said, as a mixture of saliva and beer dripped onto Paul's face.

Lenka was the first to come through the door, followed by Chris, Jake, Jocky, Vodanski and Sean.

Paul strained his eyes to look at them. Then, he turned back to look up at the man who was pinning him down onto a table.

The drunken man and his friends ignored the unusual assortment of new customers entering the bar and released his grip a little. He dropped his left ear over the young man's mouth. 'What is it pretty boy, what are you're trying to say?'

The Hungarian, whose face was blood red, was finally able to speak. 'You . . . are . . . fur . . . ucked!'

Chapter 9: Jocky's Story

July 1918, Glasgow

Mrs MacPherson loved her wee son, Jocky. She would scold him, but never beat him when he got into trouble – his eldest sister, Maureen, was happy to do that when their mother did not give him what he deserved. When it came to mischief, he was leagues ahead of the other children in the tenement block. One day, Mrs MacPherson had to deal with two separate visits from the 'polis' to interview her about Little Jocky's activities, while both sets of officers squeezed together on the sofa. Even when she tried to scold him, his cherub smile and his honest replies, 'I'm doing it for *yer* and the bairns, Ma!' usually drew a smile from one of the most formidable women in Glasgow's tough Gorbals district. Rather than a clip around the ear, she would prepare tea. If he was lucky, his Ma would add one of the scones she made when there was enough milk that week to accompany the cuddle, she gave him.

His 'Da', Jamie, was a professional soldier who had fought under the command of Winston Churchill of the 21st Lancers in the Sudan. His Da was a quiet man and, unusually for a man on the housing estate, when he was at home would join his wife, Janet, in doing the washing up, cleaning and attending to his children.

Little Jocky, he was small for his age, had a cheeky side to him and this caused much of the laughter that came from the one-bedroom tenement. Jocky and the younger twins, Michael and Dougal, would play up to attract Da's attention, as his leave only brought him home for two short weeks a year – but what wonderful weeks they were. Da would give Jocky's mother and sister gifts of chocolate or lace. Little Jocky and the boys would be presented with carvings that his Da had whittled from one of the wooden stakes in the trench: a model of a car or a plane of some sort – but never an animal.

Jocky remembered that when the time came to return to his regiment, before he would fasten the buttons on his tunic and lift his large backpack over his shoulder, his Da would drop to his knees and sweep them all up in his arms. Da would kiss each of them in turn as he told them he loved them and that they must be good to Ma. Only once they had each nodded that they would, did he release them, giving each another kiss on the cheek. His Da would carry out the final part of his ritual before he left, which caused his sister considerable embarrassment but made Jocky as well as his mother giggle, as he would seize Ma in a passionate embrace while placing his hand on her backside giving it a big squeeze.

'Yer Da is dead,' said his mother, having called all her children together around the kitchen table. Jamie MacPherson fought in the Great War, during which he asked to be transferred to the 6th Battalion of Royal Scots Fusiliers when he heard that Winston was made its commander. His regiment suffered terrible losses at the Battle of Ypres 1914, and he was killed a few miles from the town in the last days of the war.

When their mother broke the news of their father's death, Maureen burst into tears and ran into her arms. The twins, aged four, were not sure what to say, or how to react as they tried to comprehend what death meant and were wondering when they would see Da in heaven. But Jocky understood that he must do everything he could to help his ma to look after the bairns.

'Ma, I'll get a job. Little Jocky will make sure his kin never go hungry.'

His mother was determined to be strong in front of the children and not cry as she had done all night, but on hearing her Little Jocky's words she wept openly.

'Ah, my lovely wee man, what will *yer* do, *yer* are just a wee bairn *yerself*,' said his mother as she dabbed his tears with her already wet tea towel.

'I'm nearly eight Ma and as the man of the house I will provide for *yer* all.' He gathered the twins up in his arms, but though he tried, they were not long enough to stretch around his sister. Dragging the stool over to the kitchen door, he climbed up on it to reach for his father's ceremonial regimental Tam-o'-Shanter headdress and placed it on his head. His mother was about to laugh and had to press the soaking tea-towel over her mouth. Maureen looked at her little brother in his multi-coloured shorts and a cap the size of a dinner-plate on his head and said he looked like a 'diseased mushroom'. Little Jocky ignored her and walked out the door with purpose and confidence in his stride, but as soon as he was out of sight of his Ma and the others, he lifted the little carving of a bi-plane from the pocket of his shorts and finally allowed the tears to stream down his face.

Jocky had grown up in the company of women, and it was female companionship he preferred at school. When asked by a teacher if he wanted to join the Boy Scouts, he replied that it was the Girl Guides, or nothing at all – but he made it clear that he would not wear a skirt. Rumours followed and his mother was worried, as being suspected of being a homosexual in Glasgow could reduce one's life expectancy. Her fears were quickly dispelled on the day she was summoned to his school by the Headmaster.

'Mrs MacPherson, *yer* boy was discovered this morning hiding in the girls' showers.'

'Thank the Lord!'

'*Wat?*'

'Not that I would not love my wee Jocky any less if he were a Jessie, it's just I don't want to see him locked up in the Big *Hoouse*,' Barlinnie Jail, Glasgow's largest prison, '*fer* it.'

'This is *nay* a laughing matter, Mrs MacPherson.'

'I'm not saying it is *yer* honour' (she had a habit of using the term to address anyone in authority). 'He's a wee boy. Has he ever touched, or forced himself on any girl?'

'*Nay!*'

'Well then, they are all a wee bit curious at that age.'

'I'd say more than curious Mrs MacPherson. We found him under the shower grate in the floor.' Jocky's Mother's eyebrows drew up at the edges, like theatre curtains at the start of a play. The headmaster continued. 'The wee *bastad* nearly drowned.'

Apart from women, Jocky's other passions were machines and chemistry. Like most boys, he loved pulling things apart: the sleepy clock on the mantelpiece that lost time, his mother's washing mangle, and soon the engine of Maureen's boyfriend's four-seater Rover 12. When Maureen's beau discovered the engine on the floor, he set off in pursuit of Little Jocky, who threw the starter motor into the river Clyde. Maureen's boyfriend was far from happy at having to continue courting Jocky's sister by taking her for long walks and having to do his fumbling under cold, windswept bridges. Eventually even his irritation with Little Jocky subsided, as his future brother-in-law became an excellent mechanic.

This should not have been a surprise, for Little Jocky did not just like pulling things apart; he also liked putting them back together, sometimes making adaptions that improved the operation of the device. After one of his 'tamperings', the clock on the mantelpiece no longer lost an hour each day.

His love of chemistry involved him spending large amounts of time mixing and heating various substances he stole from the school's science laboratory. On one occasion, fumes forced his neighbours out onto the outside landings when an experiment with a container of sulphur went terribly wrong.

The smallest boy in any class would usually be bullied, and Little Jocky was – but not regularly. Any verbal abuse was quickly quelled with one of his acerbic responses, and his ready humour meant he was well-liked by the rest of the boys, but even more importantly to him by most of the girls. Gowan, a boy in the next year up took exception to Little Jocky, resenting his popularity especially with Janice, a girl he liked but who did not reciprocate his feelings. The older boy made it clear to Jocky that if he ever spoke to her again, he would 'cave *yer* head in'.

The next day, after festering with rage all night, Gowan rushed to grab Little Jocky's lapels and head butt him – his dome shaped forehead was infamous throughout the school for breaking noses (nine to date). But it was Gowan who ended up screaming with pain as he lifted his hands to find them coated in blood due to several small but deep lacerations. Jocky, who had sewn twelve scalpel blades into the inside of his lapels, ran off as fast as he could to dispose of the evidence.

Little Jocky used his new skills not just to defend himself, but to make money. He could start cars when the owner claimed to have 'mislaid their keys' usually along with the documents of ownership. Unpicking door locks was another lucrative task, as the deal was twenty percent of the sale value of the contents found inside. Some locks could be more difficult to open, but – by the time he left school – he was also an expert in using just the right amount of explosive when his mobile tool kit was not enough. By this time, his skills were already finely tuned through an enthusiasm for reading engineering manuals, and a passion for Sherlock Holmes novels – from these came a yearning to go to London.

August, Glasgow 1926

Jocky's mother was not pleased when a neighbour told her that her eldest son had secured his first job, after he was thrown out of school, as a 'runner' collecting the rent for Charlie 'Spam' Fritter who ran several brothels in the city.

His expulsion was linked to his new role, as he was caught breaking into a chemist with six-hundred prophylactics stuffed in two shopping bags for the *who'ers*. He was still wearing his school uniform.

'Jocky, do *yer* have any morals? Have I been such a terrible mother that *yer* freely consort with *who'ers*?'

'*Yer* a wonderful ma. I love *yer*, but all I do is collect the money and run errands. I'm not a pimp, Ma.'

'But *yer* take money from the girls?'

'Not for *meself* Ma. The girls call me to collect money and deliver it to Spam. They don't want to risk having money in the house, so when it is known that Jocky is a regular caller, robbers don't trouble 'em.'

'So *yer* see *yer* occupation as performing a public service?' his Mother asked incredulously.

'More a *pubic* service,' and with that his sister grabbed a wooden-spoon. For once Mrs MacPherson let Maureen have free rein on Jocky's backside as she carried on knitting while shaking her head, 'Oh dear. My wee Jocky, what will become of *yer*?'

'*Yer* wanted to see me, Spam?' said Jocky, entering his boss' office.

Mollies Bar, better known as The Chib, was one of the roughest pubs in the Gorbals. The surface of its long bar matched that of its twenty tables as the varnish was gone, due to the regular clattering of glasses descending on them with undue haste.

Claire, the barmaid, shouted over, 'Heavy, Jocky?'

'I doubt it, as I have been entertaining most of the afternoon.'

'Dirty *bastad*, I meant *yer* drink,' she replied, laughing as she poured a pint of bitter.

'*Yer* entertaining is what I want to talk to *yer* about. Park *yer* arse wee man,' said Spam, offering him the chair opposite.

Jocky grabbed his pint and sat down in front of the corpulent, radish faced man with a blue-veined, bulbous nose.

'*Yer* alright big man?' asked Jocky, of the man who was a martyr to cheap whisky.

Spam was only an inch taller than Jocky, but he weighed over twenty stone. Despite his wealth, his trousers were held up by a piece of twine. It was clear to see why Spam never strayed far from The Chib: his legs were splayed wide apart due to the size of his thighs and though he was sitting on one of the pub's wooden chairs, there was no visual evidence of it from the front. The man who was only in his early thirties resembled a sack of overflowing red potatoes waiting for collection.

'*Yer've* been taking liberties with my ladies.'

'Spam *yer* said that if the ladies offered it, I could have a freebie every now and then.'

'They must love *yer* as *yer're* keeping some of them busy three times a day; customers are queuing up.'

There was an element of truth to this, for if the prostitutes did not love him, they were certainly pleased to see him and made him welcome. They also trusted him, though he was a man.

When it came to clients getting heavy with the girls, Jocky left that to the pimps as he hated violence. However, when a pimp was not around to sort things out or did not bother to do anything even when he was, Jocky found his own way of dealing with an abusive client. Christine, at fifty-eight, one of the oldest of the working girls, was robbed by Tommy 'Rook', a regular visitor to Glasgow's brothels who was well known for his liking to inflict pain. Many of the older women, now that their looks were no longer hidden by extra layers of make-up, would put up with far more violence than the younger girls. The following day, the Rook discovered that someone had removed the money that he had stolen and hidden under the back seat of his car. In his fury, he started ripping out the dashboard and did not notice the three police cars that had surrounded him. They had received a tip-off that the twenty revolvers stolen from the Police Station the night before were in the boot of his car. To the Rook's bewilderment, that was where they found them. The Rook was given a cage in The Big *Hoouse* for the next eight years.

Jocky had enemies; Spam's pimps. However, his humour and quick wit, plus the fact that he was one of Spam's favourites, saved him a beating – usually. When one of Spam's girls was not making enough money, she would find a few pounds in her purse. This would occur just after the runner had left and just before her pimp was about to administer 'the treatment'. Though the pimps got their money, they did not like it when anyone interfered in their business.

'Are *yer* alright, Sandra?' shouted Jocky as he pushed open the door of one of Spam's flats. Sandra was one of the new girls, and a very popular one as she was blonde, very innocent for her age and elfin in appearance, which attracted the 'paedos.' She was sixteen and had a baby to feed and clothe.

'He's taken all *me* money Jocky. How will I feed the bairn?'

Jocky looked towards the side room and walked in to discover a baby asleep under a beautifully knitted shawl. He returned to the weeping young woman. 'Who took it? I'll have Spam get one of his boys after '*em*!'

'It *was* one of Spam's boys, Connor Wallace.'

'That psycho *bastad*.' Connor was the most vicious of Glasgow's pimps, but unfortunately for Jocky, the man was not partial to his humour.

'Darling, here's some money and I'll try to talk to him,' Jocky said as he pressed the full roll of notes he had in his pocket into her hand. He placed his hand gently on her chin and turned her face a little to expose the bruising above her hairline – despite his enjoyment when he administered 'the treatment', Connor still had to think of the customers.

Four hours later, Jocky entered The Chib with the day's takings for Spam. His boss was nowhere to be seen. Jocky turned around and collided with Connor.

'Yer wee *shite*, what *yer* doing here?' demanded the pimp, clamping his huge hand on the top of Jocky's head and tightened his hold.

'Looking for Spam?' as the man squeezed his fingernails into Jocky's head.

'*Yer* interfering wee *shite*. *Yer* saved that little pixie 'the treatment', but I'll give it *yer* instead."

Jocky urinated into his trousers, but he summoned the courage to stand up to the man who was twice his height and just as broad. 'Just don't hit her big man!'

Connor launched him backwards into the packed bar. He split open the back of his head when he landed on the brass foot rail that ran along the base of the bar. A few customers moved forward to help his – until Connor appeared.

'Leave the wee *shite* be, or I'll *fuken wallap yer*!' There were some big powerful men in the bar: ship-builders, construction workers, even two off-duty policemen, many of whom were friends of Jocky, but no one dared cross Connor, 'the Skullcracker'.

Before he lost consciousness as the huge man bent down and began to pummel his face with his fists, he muttered, 'Big man, I'll pay her rent, just leave her enough for the bairn.'

A few weeks after receiving 'the treatment', Jocky was out of hospital and back working as a runner. He was also once again providing a service offering access to cars and on one occasion even to an owner who had locked himself out. Once again, he helped gangs liberate savings – never their own – from banks and of course it was not long before he was 'entertaining' again after his barren spell. A few weeks later he received a summons from Spam to The Chib.

'Ah wee man, I could nay bring *yer* grapes to hospital, *ack*, *yer* know how it is.'

'*Nay* trouble Spam. It's great to be back, big man.'

'Connor gave *yer* a good going over, but *yer* shouldn't interfere with business.'

'Sorry, big man.'

'Conner was arrested this morning.'

'Ah dear, that's terrible, I had my issues with the man

but I'm sorry to hear that Spam.'

'It's a big loss, a brutal *bastad* as *yer* well know, but he was very handy when Kinnock,' a rival gang lord from the west side of the city, 'and his gang tried to take over my plots last year. He was the one who cut that *bastad's* ears off, *yer* know.' Jocky swallowed hard and feigned a smile as the gangster continued. 'The *polis* got a tip-off, and they found the sacks from four bank jobs that took place in the last month, all empty mind apart from the bank's cheque stubs. Funny that, as *yers* only been out of hospital for a month.' Jocky's mouth was so dry that he had nothing to swallow.

Sam's slug-like lips sucked the whiskey from the clipped half-pint glass. '*Yer* knew the Rook, didn't *yer*? Same type of thing happened to him. Cana *yer* believe it, both caught red handed. I hope they don't share the same cell, as I hear the Rook likes to fiddle with people when they're asleep. Connor will shove his head so far up his own arse, he'll spend the rest of his life walking around like a crab.'

Spam's luminous red face looked like it had suffered a power surge. 'Me new gal's gone too, Sandra, along with her bairn. The girls think she came into money. They think Connor gave her some of his money from the raid; funny though, I didn't think he liked women, let alone the *who'ers*.'

'Life's full of surprises, Spam,' smiled Jocky, relieved to hear that this was the story circulating around the Gorbals. 'Is that why *yer* wanted to see me, Spam?'

'Nay, yer dirty *bastad*. Because of yer freebies, I'm nay broke. I may be the first *bastading* pimp in history to be declared bankrupt.'

Chapter 10: The Factory

August 1938, Amsterdam

If any of the Rogues had a hangover the next morning you would not have known it, or that in the final bar they had visited they had left eight Dutch soldiers in urgent need of medical attention. The largest of the troops was in a critical condition after being put head first through a glass case containing a stuffed albatross.

After only a couple of hours sleep, Ryan was the first to leave the boarding house. Thirty minutes later he was standing in a shaded area of the courtyard outside the factory as he waited for the Gestapo to arrive. The factory had a small, freshly painted wooden plaque by the entrance marked *Magyarmite-Chemicals*. The building took up one side of the three-storey rectangular structure that framed the plaza.

The black Austro-Daimler drew up outside the enormous, newly installed iron doors of the German-owned business. Ferdinand emerged from the car with two escorts, but the chemist entered the red brick building alone. Once inside, the reinforced doors were locked behind him. The two escorts strode across the courtyard and ambled up the stairs of a boarded up nondescript grey building.

Ryan made his way towards the other door at the far end of the building that the Gestapo agents had disappeared into. When he reached the door, he began to 'jimmy' the lock with a knife. At first the lock's rusted mechanism refused to give until he smashed his elbow against the handle of the blade. Inside, there was no sign of anyone on the first, or second floors. He continued his way up the staircase, gripping the Welrod in his right hand.

On the third floor, he peeked through a small side window into a large spacious room. Inside, the two plainclothes Gestapo agents were helping themselves to coffee from a metal pot on a bare table. Ryan watched as they walked across the room to sit down on two serviceable, sold wooden chairs opposite a tall and imposing woman who was sitting behind a desk.

While the men kept a rigid posture, the woman adopted a more relaxed position – showing who was clearly in charge: the one they called Kruger. The three Nazis were approximately six-foot, powerfully built and precise in their movements. Kruger had the same cropped haircut as the men, very different to the Nazis female stereotype, accentuating the homely and mothering qualities of Aryan women. She reminded Ryan of automatons off a production line in Fritz Lang's 1927 dystopian science fiction film, *Metropolis*. As with the lead character, the destructive robot Maria, the woman's breasts were merely an adornment to the design with no other evidence of the other attributes of her sex. There was no sign of a little girl.

The Irishman pressed his hand down on the brass doorknob of the door that led to the room. It was locked. Professionals never relax. The Irishman stood back, gripped his gun in his hand and smashed his left shoulder into the door. It exploded into the room with such force that it brought most of the door frame with it. The two escorts spun around, drawing their Lugers as they did. Though their reflexes were fast, Ryan had already taken aim with his magazine-fed weapon and the dull 'thud, thud' of the suppressor released a bullet into the chest of each man – 'the incapacity shot'. He pulled back on the trigger as the muffled 'thud, thud' sent two more bullets into their foreheads – 'the kill shot'. Kruger dived to the floor while grabbing a Luger from the open drawer of the desk and was now in a firing position, aiming the barrel of her pistol at Ryan. But he released a fifth 'thud' that hit the trigger of her weapon, removing most of her left hand, including three of her fingers. The impact launched the Luger into the air, and it only came to a stop when it clattered off the wall below the window ledge a few metres away.

'No fucking around. Where's the girl?' Ryan examined her reaction, hoping she would understand English. He did not have to wait long.

'Why should I tell . . .' Ryan shot her in the right kneecap, one of the most painful of wounds, but which, if treated soon, was not life-threatening. The grimacing woman seized her right knee as the Irishman aimed the Welrod at her left.

Kruger stared at Ryan, refusing to acknowledge her pain or incapacity. 'You are early Englander. We did not expect you and the other Jew-lovers until tonight.'

'Well, you know how it is,' replied Ryan, ignoring the woman's inaccurate nom de guerre for him. The Irishman pushed his boot down on the chest of the first man he had shot looking for life signs and trained his gun between his eyes in case there were. 'In these chaotic times, one must be flexible,' he said as he pressed the heel of his boot into the wound of the second man, again aiming the gun at what remained of his skull.

Ryan noted that Kruger never once took her eyes off him, even when gritting her teeth when she examined her wound: she had an incredible pain threshold that matched his own. As with the other Alpha Wolves he had encountered, she was a well-trained professional. He knew that without the element of surprise it would have been him on the ground. Ryan pulled the trigger of his pistol back.

'In the loft above,' shouted Kruger.

He knew she had not confessed through fear, as there was no reverberation in her voice. She had calculated, as he would have done, that it would give her precious time if she sent her opponent in search of his goal.

Ryan kept his weapon on the woman writhing in agony on the floor as he limped over to the ladder leaning against the wall in the far corner of the room. He propped it against the edge of the hatch leading to the roof, keeping the gun on the woman. He lifted himself up onto each rung of the ladder, never once letting the weapon stray from the woman. He lifted the hatch slowly. It was completely dark inside, lacking even a window. Striking a match against the border of the hatch, in the far corner he saw a little girl huddled in the corner peering out from under a tattered blanket.

'Cerberus will cut your fucking heart out,' screamed Kruger from below.

Ryan bent down to stare at the leader of the European section of the Alpha Wolves, before emptying one chamber of his pistol into her forehead. He straightened himself up and peered back into the loft to look across at the blonde-haired girl. The photo her father had given him was still in his pocket, but he did not need it to know that it was her as she had the high cheekbones of her mother.

'I've come to take you to your father.'

She sat up, 'Papa, sent you,' she said in a voice that surprised her as it was so long since the angry lady below had allowed her to speak.

'Yes, your Papa sent me,' said Sean, smiling.

The girl crawled along the dirty floor. When she reached Sean, he lifted her up with his right arm, as he needed his left to secure his hold on the ladder. It sent a surge of pain through his shoulder and down his spine. With the girl secure, he tucked her head inside his open leather jacket, so she could not see the carnage below. Tentatively, he descended back down the ladder. As Ryan walked towards the door, again making sure that the girl was facing away from the three bodies on the floor, he noticed that the left leg of the European leader of the Alpha Wolves twitched. Once outside the room, he set the little girl down and asked her to wait as he had to quickly 'clean' the room. The girl nervously, but obediently, nodded. Ryan stepped back into the room and emptied the last chamber into the horrified open mouth of Kruger, who had rolled onto her side. Limping from one corpse to the next, he removed any papers and placing them inside his jacket to examine later.

Ryan stepped back into the hall and gently lifted the frightened little girl's hand. After being kept in complete darkness for six months, the light from the windows terrified her.

'The men will come again,' she spluttered, too scared to move. Sean took the gold chain from the inside pocket of his leather jacket and opened it to reveal the photo of her family. 'Papa's pendant,' cried Lens, squeezing Sean's hand.

The Irishman carefully picked up the girl with both arms and made his way slowly down the staircase.

In the town square nearby, a church bell rang nine times. Lenka and the others, apart from Jocky, had assembled a few minutes earlier in Krupp's Café opposite the entrance to the arch that led to the plaza and the factory. Jake, Paul and Vodanski stayed at the bar, while Lenka, Chris and Ursula took a table by the window, so they could take it in turns to watch the factory until they made their move after the workers had left for the day. They were not prepared for Sean's appearance in the café's doorway holding a blonde-haired girl in his arms.

Lenka leapt up and rushed at Sean. But when she saw how exhausted and frightened the little girl was, she suppressed the rage in her voice. 'First the factory and then we go and find the girl. That is what we agreed.'

Jocky entered the café after spending the night 'on urgent business' as he referred to it. He laughed heartily when he saw Lenka once again venting her fury at Sean, as he shook the hands of his two friends at the bar.

'It's nine in the morning; even the potato-picker couldn't have added any Nazis to his score sheet yet?' His jovial disposition was met by a cold, indifferent look from Jake and Vodanski, shrugs from Chris and Ursula, finally a look of embarrassment from Paul. His high spirits evaporated. 'Ah, *shite*!' Only then did the Irishman swing the girl into view. He grinned and twiddled his fingers in an Oliver Hardy manner at the girl. 'Perhaps this time it was worth the Paddy *fuking* everything up.'

The little girl frowned. 'Naughty man, mind your language, please.'

Jocky bowed his head. 'Sorry Goldilocks, I did *na* realise *yer* spoke English. Jocky is very ashamed of himself.' The girl giggled.

'We're supposed to be a fu . . .' growled Lenka, as Lens stared at her, 'a team.'

'I never said I was in a team!' snapped Sean, as he lowered the girl down onto the floor. The Irishman raised himself up slowly; the pins in leg stabbing at him as always. 'Why do you think we are called Rogues? We don't join teams. We respect no authority and trust no one. There's no collective term for Rogues?'

'A "mayhem" of Rogues?' suggested Jocky.

Sean and Lenka ignored him. Jake laughed, and the others smiled.

Chris rose, 'For now, the threat posed by the Nazis forces us together and is greater than our instinct to fight alone. If we met in any other circumstances, we would probably kill each other. Look at us. Even now we are at each other's throats. What's done is done.'

Sean bent down on one knee. 'The big man is right. I'm sorry that I raised my voice, Lens. Don't be scared, as the angry woman and her ugly male friends are here to make sure that no one will ever take you away from your Papa again.'

The little girl looked around, as Vodanski, Chris and Jake playfully pulled grotesque faces. She looked at Lenka and Ursula, and back to Sean. 'They are not all ugly; the ladies are very beautiful, even the angry one.'

Ursula grasped Lenka's hand and whispered, 'The girl is safe; that's the main thing.'

'No, it fucking well isn't,' growled Lenka.

Sean laughed. 'Well young lady, this beautiful lady, the pleasant one,' he said as he looked past the scowling Lenka at Ursula, 'will take you to your father. Then, you will be given food, a bath, some fresh clothes and a warm, comfortable bed in that order.'

Ursula placed her wooden crutch against a table and bent down to the girl. 'I'm Ursula. I will take you to my friend's flat where your Papa will join us later this morning.'

Taking the girl's hand, she nodded towards Lenka, whose clenched fists signalled that she would return to the argument with Sean once they had gone. Lens smiled again as only a child could after such an ordeal, but she gasped and stepped back when Vodanski walked towards her. The Russian smiled as he offered the child a bar of chocolate he took from the counter. The little girl was hungry, but her mouth was open, still transfixed by the size of the man.

Only when the Russian crouched down and said, 'My name is Vodanski, please eat this,' did she bite into the chocolate bar.

Lenka embraced Ursula and whispered, 'This afternoon, find a café near the entrance to the station and look out for us.' Ursula kissed the woman who had raised her on the cheek and turned to leave with the girl. Jake handed Ursula her crutch. He smiled as he looked down at the little girl who was again transfixed by this new world of giants. Paul ran to open the door, but missed the handle with his hand. Chris leaned across, pushed the lever down and opened it. Lens looked up at the men. Everyone seemed so much bigger since she last entered the outside world. Perhaps it was because the only person she had seen was the nasty woman who had to bend down under the rafters to bring her bread and water, only then to scold her.

The little girl had never bitten into a 'grown ups' chocolate bar before. She had finished half of it before she realised that she was standing outside on the street. She pulled her hand away from Ursula's and ran to the window to wave to the tall, pale gentleman who had freed her from her prison. The smaller woman was standing in front of him and yelling, but to her delight the man turned to give her a wink and smile. Lens wished he was not in so much pain. She clutched the hand of the young woman beside her tightly, before offering her the last block of her chocolate.

Inside the café, Lenka continued berating Sean.

'You don't trust anyone, do you? You fucked us over again, even though we all agreed to meet here after the factory opened. It was you who said, "Best not to arrive too soon, in case the Nazis spot us when they deliver Ferdinand to the factory".' Vodanski and Jake observed the argument but said nothing as the cafe owner deposited two coffees on the bar. However, knowing that the plan to break into the factory would have to be expedited, each checked their coat to ensure that their weapons were where they had placed them this morning. 'You do exactly what you like. Nothing has changed since Berlin.'

'Your mission was to enter the factory; mine was to find the girl.'

'I take it the Gestapo are out of the way?' asked Lenka,

slumping onto the chair closest to the window facing the street. Sean nodded once. 'Brilliant, so they won't be reporting in. You bastard!' cursed Lenka.

Sean shrugged his shoulders. 'If we're going in, we have to do it now.'

'We don't have any fucking choice, do we?' she spat back. 'If you don't get killed before the end of today, I swear I'll happily do it.'

'Perhaps we could squeeze in a light supper first?' said Sean, with an exaggerated grin.

Jocky held his head in his hands, 'Night time, when no one was around, that was the *fuking* plan. Not to march in there in daylight, *yer* thick *fuken* Paddy.'

Chris looked at Sean. 'Maybe it's time to get you that "press agent"?' Sean smiled, remembering Chris' remark when they met the remarkable Otto Weidt and hid in his factory in Berlin.

Sean sat down as Jake poured him some red wine from the bottle that Paul had ordered. 'I would have helped you this morning if you'd let me know. But, Lenka's right, you really don't trust any of us, do you Sean?' said Jake.

The Irishman smiled but said nothing.

Paul's expression did not alter as he sat uneasily at the table with the coffee he had not ordered and cigarette untouched in his hand.

Sean spread out the identity papers he had taken from the three bodies on the table in front of Jocky.

'The photographic documents are of no use, as even you, my angry friend, cannot work miracles in what little time is available.'

'A bullet-hole in the mug-shot of one in his papers,

and blood all over the others puts paid to that idea, yer *bastadering* Paddy,' sighed Jocky.

Sean produced three other official documents. 'But these letters, I think, bear the official stamp of the Dutch Government. But are they authentic?'

Jocky lifted them up, but his hands were trembling so much that he could barely read the print. He pressed them into Paul's hands to steady them, which made it impossible. Sean held the documents up for him, but though he could scan the papers, looking at the Irishman only added to his anger so that his thick Scots brogue was unintelligible. Chris placed a double whisky in front of his countryman, who downed the contents in one gulp. He calmed down and his voice slowed as he retrieved the papers from Sean. 'They're authentic; these are official stamps, but I've no idea what they say.'

Sean looked to Paul, 'You're the linguistics expert, any thoughts?'

The anxious young man leant forward, forgetting that his untouched glass of wine was still in his hand. Jake grabbed it just before he splashed his drink over the papers, before unleashing a stream of profanities at the young Hungarian. Paul looked anxiously at the others.

Sean turned to his friend, 'If Ursula were here, she would make sure "her man" was given time to pull his thoughts together.'

Paul smiled and drew a deep breath before collecting the papers from Sean's hands and applied himself to the text.

'Dutch is not one of my languages, but it has Germanic influences.' After scanning the note, he made his assessment. 'I believe the first line reads, "By order of the Ministry of Interior", and is followed by "The person in possession of this paper is granted unhindered access to this establishment" and that's it.'

'It doesn't name any individuals, or state where it can be used, so it's a "to whom it may concern" letter to provide access to any government affiliated building?' said Sean.

'I believe so, but unless you know someone who speaks Dutch that you can trust, you won't know for sure until you hand it over at the gate.'

'Ah *shite*!' repeated Jocky as he put his head in his hands once more.

Chris placed his hand on his friend's shoulder to comfort him, as he could not think of anything to say. But his fellow countryman could. 'We're *fuked*.'

Looking across at Paul, Sean said, 'You've done all you can here, best you go and help Ursula.'

The Hungarian looked hesitantly at the others as he rose and walked uneasily out of the restaurant into the glare of the morning sun.

'Not so much wine today, my friend,' said Chris as he walked past.

Paul replied, as Vodanski and Jake looked unsmilingly at him, 'I understand; I have responsibilities now.'

Lenka declared, 'Okay, that's me, Jocky and one other.'

Before Vodanski, Jake or Chris could speak, Sean interjected, 'I got you into this and with my cane they will be less suspicious.' He looked at the other three men. 'If we fail, you have the fire power to take the direct route. Deal?'

The men all nodded, but Lenka added, 'I wasn't

joking; if you fuck us over again, I'll kill you.'

Thirty minutes later, Lenka, Jocky and Ryan had negotiated their way past the suspicious Dutch security guard who answered the sound of the steel door knocker. The guard made a telephone call immediately afterwards to the official whose signature was on the Government documents. The man at the other end of the line, who sat in the Dutch parliamentary office, was apoplectic. The clandestine deal with Berlin was now public.

It was mid-morning and those gathering around desks and workbenches were too busy pushing rulers and marking large sheets of paper with pencils to notice the three visitors making their way along the corridors. Jocky followed the map in his hands and within minutes of entering the building led the others into Ferdinand's office. Ferdinand nearly collapsed with shock when he saw them. 'You can't'– but Lenka held her hand up.

'We had to come now. The Irishman has found your daughter, and she is safe.'

The man collapsed onto knees, clenching his hands and sobbing uncontrollably. Jocky helped him to his feet as Lenka went to the desk and searched for any copies that the man might have made that morning. Ryan stayed by the door.

The distraught man lifted his face to Jocky, who was struggling to raise him off his knees. 'Dear God, thank you, thank you, thank you all!'

Lenka took Ferdinand's arm and directed Jocky to the diagrams she had piled up on a chair.

'Are these all the copies?' asked Jocky, as the man

nodded. The Scotsman flipped through the papers. 'Good!'

Lenka seized Ferdinand arms and shook him. 'Get out of here, use any excuse, an illness, an urgent call, anything, and then head to the Krupp Café on the other side of the archway. There, you will find Chris and he will take you to Paul's flat. Your daughter is there. It's not far. Now go.'

Ferdinand wiped his tears away with his hands. He continued to cry as he made his way to the door. He turned the handle and gave a brief smile to Sean. 'Thank you, Englander,' he said as he closed the door behind him.

'Fuck it, even when people thank me, they insult me,' Sean huffed. For the first time since he entered the café this morning and discovered that Sean had turned everything upside down, Jocky laughed.

Lenka looked at both men dismissively. 'Children!'

Jocky sat behind the desk, transfixed by the largest of the blueprints while the other two waited by the door. He looked up. 'Get me to the workshop.'

'Have your balls just dropped?' asked Sean. 'You're getting very courageous all of a sudden.'

'Time for a little bit of that Scottish mischief I mentioned. Anyway, you promised to keep me alive, bog-trotter.'

'I don't think I did.'

'Grow up the two of you. Why the workshop?' asked Lenka.

'This is a design for a new type of gas cylinder pump. It's piss easy to screw up; a few little lines added by Jocky and when they flick the switch, it will be as much use as a chocolate dildo.'

'You lost me with the technical jargon, but if you're

214

not going to blow the place up, I'm sold,' said Sean.

'I'll take the remaining copies and meet you in the café.' Lenka rolled them up, put them in a satchel and hooked it over her shoulder. 'I'll organise a diversion on the way out,' she continued as if it were standard practice in these situations and walked out the door without looking at the men.

Jocky lost his nerve. 'If we're challenged *yer* can't speak Dutch, can *yer* Paddy?'

'Well, you can't speak English, so go for the middle ground and pull faces!'

The two men waited in a side office, but they did not have to wait long, as the screeching of fire alarms sent everyone into a mad frenzy, out into the corridors towards the stairs.

'Lenka's great, isn't she pal?'

'I wouldn't know, I haven't had a chance to analysis her as she's been too busy telling me to get fucked.'

'That's what I mean.'

As people frantically ran down the main stairwell and into the courtyard, no one paid any attention to the two men walking in the other direction towards the main workshop. Inside the largest room in the building were twenty or more workbenches. On each was an array of tools ranging from sledge-hammers to the smallest of screw-drivers, all meticulously arranged as if preparing for the most macabre of surgeries. Jocky found the table with the components that matched those on the blue-copy paper he had unfurled in his hands. He placed it on the table, weighing each corner down with some washers, and began to adjust several assorted components with a screwdriver.

215

Each time he made a physical change to a piece of machinery, he diligently amended the blueprint.

As he worked, Jocky made comments, not for Sean's benefit, but to help his thought process as he imagined every facet of the machine's design. The Irishman was fascinated by how the Scotsman tackled his task, even to argue with himself as he worked: 'the Death Skull markings on the canisters, *nay* breeds confidence'; 'an interesting *wee* valve on this gas-condenser,' 'Hmm! Two inlet pipes? Tricky *bastads*!'

Jocky pondered, before applying a little white spirit that he always kept in his camel-coloured duffle coat to the blueprint. Once done, he waited for the mixture to dry. Delicately he began to add new figures to the paper, with a blue graphic artist's pen, another thing he carried along with a cigarette case containing a wide assortment of coloured cartridges.

'This should put the tiger amongst the Alpha Wolves,' he said, as he made a quick copy of something in pencil.

Delicately, he added some additional lines and figures to a section of the master drawing. Finally, he stood back, wearing the contented smile of an artist pleased with his finished work.

'What have you devised, my little pocket Einstein?' asked Sean.

'I've added what on the surface appears to be a third inlet pipe, but when operational it becomes an outlet pipe.'

'Brilliant! . . . Why?'

'Well, there are two pipes that mix the contents of the canisters together. But I have amended the valve where they join so instead of pumping the mixture forward it diverts it back along the new third pipe I've added.'

'Then what?'

Jocky looked pensively at the blue-graphic again before walking over to the largest of the mechanical components and altering the dimensions of the part that intrigued him most of all – the inlet valve. After ten minutes, he released the broadest of smiles.

'And?'

'I've widened the outlet valve at the junction of the two original pipes so it can't open forwards. I've also reduced the thickness of the cap on the third pipe going in the other direction so it's as thin as foil.'

'What will that do?'

'When the gas pressure builds up the head of the cap sealing the third pipe will burst before the junction valve opens.'

'And?'

'It will send the toxic gas back into the operator's chamber. If the gas they are experimenting with is flammable and it hits a naked flame–'

'They go up with it?'

'Exactly. The Nazis could beat us into space.' Sean looked puzzled. 'Put it down to The Commander's outlandish imagination, pal,' said Jocky. 'He thinks they have experts that could one day land men on the moon.'

'Could it be part of a propulsion device rather than a pump?'

'*Nay*, for a start the casing is too thin. It's not made for combustion.'

Sean was once again impressed with the man that he dismissed as a hedonist. 'But, won't they spot your amendment?'

'There's a good chance they will, but the design I have altered is marked *original*, while the others are marked *prototype*. I think what we have on the table is what has been signed off by the designers, and this pump is being assembled to be shipped off sharpish to be attached to whatever vehicle they have in readiness.' Jocky was in deep thought. 'I'd stake my reputation that they can only properly test this when all the components are together.' Sean's eyebrows rose. 'I mean my *professional* reputation, *yer sarky* Irish *bastad*.'

'What kind of vehicle do you think they intend to attach it to?'

'Could be anything; the designs don't stipulate what, but it's something big. Too big for a truck, if *yer* thinking of that pile of rubble *yer* left in Norway. Perhaps it's not meant for a vehicle at all, pal. Maybe they intend to fix it to something in Himmler's Fortress, something that's meant to feed *yer* furnace?'

'You hide your genius well,' said Sean, but he wasn't smiling.

'Are we taking a little reward here?'

'If it works, my friend, when this is over, I'm going to rob a bank and put all the money I can grab into your hand and hold your trousers as you run amok from door to door in the red-light district.'

The Scotsman walked back over to Sean. 'Then it's time to take *yer* up on *yer* offer as my work is done; now let's get the *fuk* out of here.'

The clatter of gun shots erupted below them.

'*Shite*!' shouted Jocky, 'the Krauts have found us.'

As the door burst open, Ryan aimed the Welrod, but it was Lenka with her revolver drawn. 'The Dutch police are outside, I guess the papers tipped someone off.'

'Why the gunshots?'

'To keep their heads down. Quick, this way, the back stairs,' she shouted as she disappeared. The two men did not argue and followed.

At the base of the stairs Lenka burst through the doors to find Jake and Vodanski waiting, each in a boat with an Elto outboard four-cylinder two-cycle motor on the stern. Jake shouted over his shoulder, 'We found them moored behind the police station a couple of hundred metres back.'

'*Bastad*! It's a canal!' cried Jocky. 'I canna swim!'

'Jesus, just get in,' barked Sean, as he lifted him by his collar with his left hand and dropped him into the nearest boat, the one with Jake at the helm. Ryan followed, seizing the Thompson M1921 submachine gun lying on the back seat.

Lenka hollered as she leapt into Vodanski's boat, 'Get going, we'll hang back in case anyone tries to join us.'

The four Alpha Wolves amongst the factory workers did not follow the workforce when the fire alarm went off. Instead, they had made their way up from the basement and scrambled out on to the small dock at the back of the factory. As the speedboats sped off, the men unveiled their assortment of weaponry – Lugers and the latest MP 38 semi-automatic machine guns – from under their lab coats. But before they had a chance to open fire on the two speeding boats, two of them fell into the water as the bullets from Chris' semi-automatic pumped into them from behind. The other two fell in quick succession to his knife.

The first of three turbo speedboats smashed through the boarded-up arch of the bridge opposite the factory. Chris dived into the waters, as all three vessels directed their firepower at the dock. Bullets pounded into the timbers, disintegrating the little quay and reducing it to flotsam in seconds.

The three larger, more powerful vessels bore down on the two smaller, slower boats.

'A trap, did you fucking know, Sean?' shouted Jake.

'*Yer*, like I knew these fuckers were going to come out of nowhere,' said Ryan, opening his machine gun on the lead boat, but he had expected an ambush.

Jocky grabbed the other Thompson M1921 beside Jake. Ryan was taking careful aim and picking off any of their pursuers that came into view with a single burst of fire. Beside him, Jocky frenziedly directed fire on the boats bearing down on them.

'Take in the trajectory and aim just above them,' shouted Ryan. 'I didn't think killing was your thing.'

'Killing isn't but stopping these *bastads* from killing me is.'

'Semantics, Jocky,' shouted Jake over his shoulder as he weaved the vessel the vessel around a bend to avoid another spray of machine gun fire.

'Semantics! I thought they were Nazis?' yelled Scotsman.

'Are you any good with a gun?' shouted Jake.

'It's a machine, isn't it?' he said, but after engaging the trigger, the greatest risk he posed was to any stray bird passing above.

'Jocky, for Christ's sake, aim *just* above their heads,' shouted Ryan.

The Scotsman continued to squeeze down on the trigger with his weapon still vertical while keeping his eyes closed.

'Genius my arse,' muttered Ryan.

Vodanski's boat was a more disciplined affair. He remained fixed on the water ahead, as Lenka released concentrated bursts of machine gun fire to hole their pursuers below the water-line to slow them down. But, having entered a wide stretch of the waterway, the first of the larger boats had a clear line of fire at their vessel. The windscreen shattered as the Russian spun the steering wheel sharply anti-clockwise, sending the boat under a bridge to the left. His execution was perfect, as was the idea, as the arch of the bridge was too small to allow the boat behind under it but it did not halt the pursuit. Rather than slow down or turn away, the larger boat smashed through the wooden bridge as if it were made of balsa.

'What the hell are those things?' shouted Ryan as the second speedboat gained on them.

'*Kriegsmarine* S-7s, the German navy's "Stuka dive bombers of the Sea",' bellowed Jocky. 'Some do over forty knots I'm told, ten more than this *bastad*,' shouted Jocky who was barely audible above the sound of the engine. 'They're torpedo carriers, but I've never heard of one being used on an inland waterway before.'

'Torpedo!' shouted Ryan, as the first of them skimmed past to the left of the boat.

It thundered into a barge fully loaded with barrels of gasoline, causing it to explode. The barge quickly sank into the grasping fingers of the flames.

To their right behind the close-knit sentries of stretched, terraced houses they heard an explosion followed by the sight of flames leaping excitedly towards the gathering rain clouds. Another explosion erupted to their right on the canal bank, drenching Jake's boat. With the gunfire and numerous explosions, it was hard to discern what was going on. Ryan knew it was not another torpedo from the vessels behind them, but a rocket-grenade from somewhere beyond one of the bridges to the left of them. Busting forth from under a raised drawbridge, the speedboat that had disappeared in pursuit of Lenka and Vodanski reappeared. Ryan looked back at the black smoke rising from where the explosion had erupted moments earlier, fearing that the returning S-7 had caught its quarry.

Then Ryan and Jake saw where the rocket-grenades were coming from. The 8-cm *granatwerfer* 34 heavy grenade launcher and the two men manning it were now visible on the boat that had re-joined the pursuit. Jake opened the throttle fully, as he powered the little boat through the city's narrow canals to evade the barrage of explosions. The three S-7s pounded on relentlessly, scraping against the stone walls while continuing to launch rocket grenades and bursts of fire from the mounted MG34 submachine guns fixed on the bows. Moored cargo vessels exploded to the left and right of the speeding vessels, as they were hit in the cross-fire.

On the road that ran alongside the river bank to their left, the familiar black, shiny eight-cylinder Austro-Daimler shot into view.

'*Shite*!' cried Jock. 'Can it get any *fuken* worse?'

The driver of the car produced a stream of gun-fire in the direction of the canal, sending Jocky diving onto the floor. But to Jake and Ryan's amazement, the automatic blasts of bullets were aimed at the larger vessels behind them. It was Chris, and he was opening fire with one of the submachine guns he commandeered when he pulled himself back up onto what little was left of the dock.

'He's not the kid I met in Berlin,' yelled Ryan.

Jake laughed loudly. 'When someone starts stealing cars from the Gestapo, then you know they're Major League.'

Jocky peeked over the side to look and when he saw Chris, shouted, 'Trust the Scots to save the day.'

The crew of the S-7 with the rocket-launcher rotated it towards the black car. But the resulting explosions landed aimlessly on the shore, launching parked cars and cobblestones randomly into the air. At the same time, its intended target roared towards the bridge ahead, but rather than veering to cross it, it smashed through the wooden rails and shot into the air. Chris threw himself out of the driver's door, before the car landed dead centre onto the rocket-grenade launcher mounted on the S-7. The powerful Scotsman disappeared below the icy waters once more, just as the fuel tanks of the boat and the car collided, engulfing the vehicle, the S-7 and the bridge it was passing under, in one massive explosion. Windows of the buildings on either side of the canal roared, sending shards of glass into the street.

'*Fuk* my old boots. One minute he takes out four gunmen, the next he's driving a car into a torpedo-boat,' yelled Jocky.

'Chris certainly is a different man from the one we met in Berlin. Resourceful, but one with a death wish,' shouted Jake.

'To survive what we do, you need a death wish. We all have it,' said Ryan. A terrified Jocky looked at him, 'Well, apart from you, my friend.'

The leading S-7 was smashing down onto the stern of the smaller boat, as bullets rained down, puncturing its wooden shell. Jock had, by now, rolled himself as tightly as he could under the small wooden seat on one side, but Ryan continued to return fire, desperately trying to pin their attackers down.

The second of the smaller speedboats reappeared from under a bridge about one hundred metres ahead. It launched itself into the air from a landing ramp and landed alongside one of the S-7s. Lenka aimed her submachine gun at its most vulnerable point. She pulled back on the trigger, only releasing it once she had emptied the entire chamber into the diesel tank. The explosion that followed was so powerful that Vodanski was only just able to fling the smaller boat under the cover of a stone arch before flaming debris rained down on it.

The Russian turned the engine off as the little boat bobbed in the waters, trapped under the bridge. Lenka unsheathed her knife from her boot, but all she could see was a torso bobbing amongst the carnage; there was no sign of the rest of the crew. At that point, whatever was in the barrels in a boat tied up by the riverbank opposite launched a ball of flame into the dark morning sky. Liquid spewed forth, covering the surface of the river, but did not reach the tiny wooden vessel. Lenka could not see them, but she could hear the screams of the men who dared to raise themselves above the waters into the carpet of blue and yellow flame.

'Jocky, take the wheel,' cried Jake, as for the first time he saw that one of their attackers had blind-sided Ryan and was lifting the MG-34 from its secured stand and could train the eight-hundred rounds per minute weapon down on them.

A torrent of bullets peppering the smaller boat caused Ryan to throw himself backwards onto the deck, but he continued to return fire from the floor. Jocky edged his way over to reach the wheel, despite the bullets splintering the wood panels around him. The American dived to the floor and grabbed the submachine gun that the Scotsman had abandoned.

'Stick to women and engines and I'll take care of the killing,' shouted Jake.

The American's aim was precise. The impact of his bullets blasted both marksmen out of the boat and into the water. In the commotion, the other snipers on the larger boat looked to see what was happening, which gave Ryan a chance to leap up, bringing the last of the gunmen into his sights. Bullets sprayed through the matt black, unmarked clothing of both men, sending their bodies into electrified convulsions before falling lifeless to the floor.

Having no weapons, the pilot of the speeding S-7 slammed his larger vessel up against the smaller one to crush it against the solid stone walls of the riverbank to their left.

To Ryan and Jake's surprise, Jocky removed his hand from the throttle, leaving the S-7 to shoot past. The larger vessel turned its bulk full circle as it entered a wider section of the canal. The pilot of the S-7 pressed the throttle forward, unleashing the full power of its turbo-engine towards them. Jocky opened the throttle once more, just as Ryan and Jake attempted to grab him and leap into the water before the S-7 rammed them. Jocky spun the boat, shaking off Ryan's hand from his collar as he powered the vessel towards a bridge to their right. The bridge was similar to the one that the other S-7 had demolished earlier, except it was a drawbridge with a heavy iron winching frame erected on top of its wooden frame. The smaller boat bounced off something just below the water line, sending Ryan and Jake flying backwards. Ryan and Jake tried to scramble up on their knees to return fire. To their astonishment, just before the larger boat crashed down on top of them, the S-7 was lifted high into the air and into the wood and metal frame above. As Jocky powered their boat out the other side of the bridge, Ryan and Jake looked on in disbelief at the flaming drawbridge and the explosions going off as the tanks of the S-7 and those of the boats moored around it exploded.

'I'm fucked it I know what just happened,' said Jake.

'You and me both,' said Ryan.

Jocky moored the boat by the side of the bank. He cut the engine, turned to his friends, lifted his arms up and slapped the men on the base of their backs. 'I noticed there was a solid wall just visible above the surface that was laid across the water below the bridge on either side. Some bridges have them to stop boats going under bridges where the foundations are eroding.' The three watched as the bridge crumbled and disappeared into the water. Jocky continued, '*Yer* probably didn't notice with all *yer* mindless gunfire, but we bounced over it, as I calculated we would. But that big *bastad*,' he nodded towards the debris of the torpedo launcher, 'has a far heavier and deeper hull. I knew that when it bounced off the barrier, it would send it up upwards. The wooden support frame would disintegrate but not that big *bastading* lump of iron above it.'

Ryan looked at Jake. 'What would we do without this little bundle of testosterone here?'

'Carry on scraping *yer* knuckles along the ground, *yer* pair of Neanderthals.' Jake and Ryan exchanged a look of resignation and smiled.

The Scotsman did not try to hide the wide grin on his face, as he restarted the motor-engine and spun the steering-wheel to turn the boat around and head back down the canal in search of the others. Ten minutes later, they had reached the point where they last saw their friends. The fire was still raging, including under the arch where Vodanski had steered the boat to avoid the blue flames, which were still feeding from the gasoline on the water. When they saw that the little boat under the stone arch was on fire, Ryan and Jake quickly removed their coats and shoes. They were about to dive in to a patch of water yet without flames dancing on top, when they heard a familiar woman's cry from the river bank.

'Arseholes! We're here!' shouted the naked woman on the bank, as Vodanski and Chris sat grinning beside her, wringing water out of their shirts and trousers.

'I don't know why I bother,' said Sean.

The three men watched from the boat as Lenka bent down to return to beating her soaking canvas trousers against the river bank.

Jocky looked up at Sean and said with a cheeky grin. 'I do.'

Paul and Ursula were at a café table opposite Amsterdam Centraal when they saw the Rogues, now clothed, making their way across the street to the entrance of the station. No one paid them any attention, as all was chaos: people were running in all directions and the deafening sound of police cars and ambulances drowned out the explosions still erupting across various parts of the city.

'Thank God you are all alive,' said Ursula, rising with the aid of her wooden crutch. She grabbed Lenka's right arm. 'When we heard the explosions and the gun-fire across the city, we feared the worse.'

'You should have taken the first train out when you did,' replied Lenka.

'I could never leave you if I thought you were in danger.'

Lenka held her so she could look into her eyes. 'I'm sorry I get so angry, it's just I worry about you. I've lost too many of those I love. I can't afford to let anything happen to you.' Ursula tightened her embrace. Paul walked over to the Irishman and seized his hand to shake it.

'What is it? Do I owe you money, or something?' asked Sean.

'No, of course not,' he replied, not realising that the man was joking. 'It's good to see . . . you.'

Sean looked at Ursula and winked. 'What have you done to this boy? I preferred it when he was terrified of me.'

'Nothing, I just made him realise that he is very special.'

Paul blushed.

Sean adopted a serious tone. 'Be careful young lady, he's a heartbreaker. Women wail and pine for him in cities and haystacks across Europe.'

'No! Ursula, it's not true. I have no women anywhere,' said Paul.

Lenka looked slyly at the Irishman, frowned and shook her head, betraying a little smile as she did so.

'Sean, you are a terror, stop teasing him,' said Ursula as she grabbed Paul's hand and pulled him towards her.

The Irishman raised his hands. 'Fair enough! But don't come crying to me when a milkmaid comes banging on your door, with a baby feeding on her breast holding a glass of wine in one hand and a cigarette in the other.' Paul protested, but he stopped when Sean slapped him on the back, and said, 'Slut!'

'Paul and I are taking Ferdinand and Lens back to London on the next train. Are any of you coming with us?' asked Ursula.

'Best we all split up as the Dutch police will be checking papers and will be looking for groups of foreigners,' said Lenka.

Ursula walked over to Vodanski and threw her arm around his waist. She looked up at him and whispered, 'I'm sorry that you have lost those you love, but we are your family now.'

The Russian smiled, cupping her face in his huge hands and kissing her on the forehead.

Keeping his eyes on the young woman, he delivered a

message to the attentive man standing beside her. 'Take care of this lady, or I will rip your heart out through your arsehole.'

The young Hungarian swallowed hard and to the amazement of the others, but to the younger Polish woman's delight replied, 'I will because I love her, not because you threaten me.'

Vodanski looked sternly at the young man and released a smile. 'Good answer.'

Ursula turned to Jake and wrapped herself around him too. 'Any chance of you and Vodanski calling a truce?'

'Sorry, who?' said Jake, smiling as he returned her embrace. He bent right down to kiss her on the cheek. 'Stay safe, you're the only good one of us left.'

Next, it was Sean's turn to receive a tight embrace. When she released him, he said, 'I will see you in London in a few days.' He retrieved the envelope that contained the hundred pounds that Churchill had given him and tucked it into the inside pocket of her coat. 'Find a place of your own, stay out of sight and don't contact anyone.' He cradled her face in his hands. 'And I mean anyone.' He handed her his cane. 'Take this and if you're ever in trouble, click here,' he said, pointing to the small button below the head, 'and don't think twice about using it.'

Ursula nodded. 'How will you find us?' Sean just smiled and so did she: she knew he would.

'Young lady, my turn,' said Jocky who stepped forward with his arms outstretched.

'Alright, but remember I have a cane in my hand, and my three uncles and my boyfriend are watching you.'

'I'll risk it,' said Jocky as he lifted her hand to his lips to kiss it.

But Ursula threw her arms around him, before pulling back to look at him. 'I meant four uncles.'

Jocky was delighted and did a mock little jig, which brought smiles to everyone, except Lenka. As Ursula and Paul headed off to join Ferdinand and Lens on the train, Jocky clapped his hands together loudly. 'Well, I have some urgent business. I canna say it's been fun, so *fuk* the lot of *yer, yer* mad *bastads*.'

'We have blown up half the city, so the police will be looking for anyone suspicious,' said Jake as he looked at his friend who was coated in ash and reeked of gasoline.

'I don't think they will be looking where I'm going, and I have many friends here. Let's not forget, everyone loves Jocky.'

Lenka scowled at him.

Sean walked over and peered down at his friend. 'Just watch yourself, the Germans have spies everywhere and some wear suspenders, or in your case dildos, the non-chocolate variety.'

'*Yer* a funny *bastad*, Paddy.'

'I'm just saying, beer and an argument in Paris on Friday, that's if your legs are not too weak "after *yer* business" to climb the steps of the train,' said Sean.

'Make it after the weekend. I have a lot of business to attend to here, as it's been a very stressful few days. But try not to blow it up before I get there. Why Paris anyway, big man?'

'It's a big city, so as good a place as any to stay low for a while until I can figure out what the fuck all this is about.' Sean and Jocky eyed each other and knew that the other was thinking about the ambush at the factory, and was wondering who amongst them was the spy.

Lenka sighed. 'I'm heading there too, as the Nazis will be staking out the British Embassy here.'

Jocky looked at the other men. 'I take it you will each go your own way now.' Vodanski nodded. 'Chris?'

'Edinburgh, it's my home though I don't know anyone there anymore.'

Jake added, 'You are lucky my friend that you can call it home. The rest of us are all fugitives in our own countries.'

Vodanski did not bridle at the American's comment, as he knew it to be true.

Jocky gave Lenka a smile, held his arms out wide, bent his head to one side and fluttered his eyelashes at her. 'What do you say darling, a little squeeze for Jocky?'

'Fuck off, you depraved sex maniac.'

'Depraved is a trifle harsh,' said Jocky.

'Quite right, I think we can all agree on sexually inadequate,' added Sean.

Jocky ignored him. 'I take it that's a no then,' as he looked at Lenka, dropping his arms while his body sagged like a punctured barrage balloon.

'Just how stupid are you? The place is swarming with police, and the Nazis and their informers will be tearing the city apart to find us, and you're off to a brothel.'

'Not just the one,' said Jockey, with a knowing glance. 'Admit it, you'll miss me,' he whispered, and smiled.

'Well, maybe I will, but like all men your brain disengages when you get an itch in your pants.'

'*Yer* right gorgeous, but how else would you control

us?' said Jocky.

Lenka's mouth fell open, as she looked at the grins on the other men's faces, as each either shrugged his shoulders or gave a slight nod. Jocky took advantage of her surprise and jumped forward to plant a kiss on her cheek. Then, before she could hit him, he threw his bag over his shoulder and walked off towards the seediest part of town.

Jake turned to Sean and Chris. 'What tune is he whistling?' The men looked at each other blankly.

Lenka's face lost its rage, and she smiled as if she forgot the others were there. 'I think our horny little friend is whistling, "Thanks for the Memories".'

Chapter 11: Lenka's Story

October 1921, Kraków

Little *'Charakterny'* – meaning feisty in Polish – Lenka Haberman was one of the smallest children in the orphanage for her age; twelve. But she was known more for her temper and her fearlessness than her size. From an early age, she had made it her task to protect all the children, even the older ones, from the adults. When one of the staff was in a temper and about to hit one of them, she would corral the others behind her. If they approached further, she would yell the most shocking abuse and was not afraid to scratch or bite.

Years earlier she had already worked out that although the men and women who ran the orphanage were good people, some had a weakness for money and food. This went some way to explaining why the children's rations were meagre, as the staff took much of the food to sell or for their own children who were also hungry. This long-term practice had stopped recently when the thieves, known to Lenka, got home and unpacked their bags. They discovered that stones had replaced the food they had taken, along with what they had purchased legitimately, before leaving the orphanage.

But, in the case of two of the orderlies, the

Krzeptowski brothers, the abuse went far beyond this. 'Fucking,' she heard it was called. At night, they would select one of the children, steal them out of their dormitory and molest them in the barn at the rear of the house.

The assaults were not as frequent as they were during the Great War. Over those years, many of the medical staff had gone to the front to fight or nurse the wounded. Those that stayed behind included the two orderlies, and a third man, The Doctor, would often visit at night to perform operations on the girls. There was another doctor, a qualified one who lived in the nearest village to the orphanage, which was located on the outskirts of Kraków. Dr Kossel was a kindly but frail old man, who had a horse and trap, which meant he was only a twenty-minute ride away if needed. However, not once had he been summoned to the orphanage during the four years of the war.

For his nocturnal services, the brothers allowed The Doctor to have his choice of any of the orphans until morning – speed was his paramount objective when performing his tasks – and it was always the youngest boy he chose. Little Charakterny was one of those who had what she learnt years later was called an 'abortion'. As with the others, it took place on the kitchen table. The loss of blood nearly killed her. During the war, eight girls had died on the table. It was also the last time she cried, as the tears ran through the fingers of her abuser's sweaty hand as it pressed her face onto the table top.

Even though she was a child, she knew who was at fault, and refused to listen to her abusers' whispers that she brought it on herself – then the 'fuckers' would win as she impressed on the other children, regularly. Whenever she saw either man, she would fix her eyes on him until he left the room. The elder and meeker of the brothers felt intimidated and avoided her, turning his attentions elsewhere when the girl with the cold, calculating stare was not around. The younger brother, though, enjoyed hurting her even more. That was until the morning he entered the dormitory to find Lenka pointing a blunderbuss at his genitals.

'Bang! Bang!' shouted the girl.

He was relieved to see that the weapon had been decommissioned as the trigger was missing. But for some reason he could not explain, he went cold when he saw grey powder from a box of cartridges heaped up in the centre of a cloth beside her. He backed out of the room. Now, he believed his brother that the girl was possessed.

Little Charakterny seized every opportunity to tell the nurses and every visitor what the Krzeptowski brothers were doing. Her pleas were ignored, mainly out of fear of the brothers, known for their violence when they were children growing up in the town. One new nurse was furious when Lenka told her and turned on the girl.

'What a horrid, cruel, devil child you are to make such terrible accusations.'

Every night when she was alone in her bed in the dorm, Little Charakterny was a frightened little girl. Memories of the pain, the pungent smells and the calloused hands that held her tiny wrists and muffled her cries, tormented her. But, as daylight began to creep over the blankets to rouse the thirty, or so, girls and boys who shared the dormitory, she would dismiss her fears as self-pity – no one was a tougher judge of the small girl than herself. By the time she ran down to help prepare breakfast, her confidence and resolve to defend the other children and one day punish her abusers had returned. If there was one thing that everyone who knew her agreed on – Little Charakterny was a survivor.

As a young woman, if men craved sex with her, she would use it if it meant food for the others or warmth for herself on a cold night. But, her most common reason for sex, usually with the most dangerous male but one who was not threatening to her, was to use her lover as an unofficial bodyguard. It allowed her to sleep, as a night of undisturbed sleep was rare unless she was exhausted. Only many years later, in her early twenties, did Lenka enjoy sex. Until then it was synonymous with violence and never consensual, or a device to protect herself or those close to her.

When Little Charakterny was not watching over the other children, she was either reading or writing letters. Academically, she was viewed as unworthy of further education beyond that the children received in the village school. Her teacher wrote on one report that she was *tepy* (thick), though she was good at languages, French and particularly English, along with mathematics. But she had shown little aptitude for the core subjects of cookery and bible-class. Her letters though were a source of pride for those staff at the orphanage who loved and cared for the children – and the subject of fear for those who did not.

Clara, who ran the institution as least in name, was in her eighties, deaf, and as diagnosed by Dr Kossel twenty years earlier, senile. She would collect the responses to Lenka's letters and have them framed and put on the wall of her shambles of an office – though she had no idea who Lenka was. Soon she had so little space left, that she had taken the clock and even her grandfather's old blunderbuss down from the wall to make room for them. Among the examples on display were letters signed by The President of the United States, Woodrow Wilson; the British Prime Minister, David Lloyd George; two from the French Prime Minister, Georges Clemenceau; and one from the new Polish Prime Minister, Ignacy Daszyński. There was also a letter accompanying several book donations from British Secretary of State for War, Winston Churchill.

There were no replies from the Premier of the Soviet Union, Vladimir Lenin, or Emperor Taishō of Japan, but these did not disappoint Little Charakterny, as much as the one returned marked 'Not at this address'. Unlike all the other letters that asked for financial support for the orphanage or donations of paper and crayons, this was the only one she sent that was a personal request for help. It was addressed to Mr Sherlock Holmes, Private Detective, at number 221b Baker Street. Enclosed was a letter commissioning him – payment was a drawing of the orphanage's kitten Molly – to find Nicholas, her teddy bear.

During the bitterly cold Polish winter of 1920, around the time of Lenka's eleventh birthday, an extraordinary thing happened. The Krzeptowski brothers woke up in the room they shared to find a note in crayon by the pillow of each of their beds. Each note had written in crayon, 'DEAD TO CHILD FUKER.' Soon everyone who worked in the orphanage knew of the notes, but discussed them only in whispers. Neither of the men went near the children for a week until one was seen touching one of the girls. That night the elder of the brothers was lifted out of his bed by an explosion, and when the dust had died down, the younger brother discovered his brother's torso.

Dr Kossel examined the powdery remains in the shattered glass on the floor. He dabbed his finger into the flakes and placed a little on his tongue. He did the same with the darker powder that lay under the wax on what was left of the man's chest. Dr Kossel revealed his prognosis to Clara. He deduced that sleeping powder had been slipped into the dead man's drink, so his mouth could be filled with gunpowder. Then a candle was stuffed into his mouth and lit. 'The rest, as they say, 'was history', along with his head and the headboard,' said Dr Kossel.

Clara was shocked and spluttered, 'Who are you?'

A police officer was sent from Kraków to investigate. Little Charakterny opened the door to the police sergeant, the tallest and largest man she had ever seen. She led him to the room where the torso was. 'Thank you, young lady, but best you wait here. It will not be nice in there,' warned the policeman.

'The pig with no head won't hurt us anymore, but his brother will.'

The sergeant bent down on one knee. He looked at the girl and seemed to read her face. He nodded. 'I have heard such stories. That will stop. I promise you.'

Little Charakterny was astonished that the huge man believed her. Her mouth lay open as she watched the police officer straighten up.

Inside the room were some of the staff and the dead man's brother who was lying in bed crying. He was not mourning the loss of his brother, with whom he disliked sharing the children with, but was afraid for his own life. The sergeant stood above the man. He tapped the headrest with his truncheon and smiled. 'If you touch another child,' he said, 'I will return to find your head detached from your body and wedged in this.'

The surviving brother was petrified, but the attraction of finally having all the children to himself overcame his initial urge to flee. He also convinced himself that he was 'smarter' than his brother, so no one would get near enough to drug him. However, the staff were terrified of another explosion that might lead to the burning down of the orphanage with them in it. They agreed amongst themselves to monitor his every move.

A month later, the surviving brother was caught trying to undress a girl in the barn at the back of the house. He was discovered because for the first time one of victims screamed, knowing that at last there was someone out there who would help her. Six women, two nurses, three kitchen staff and a cleaner, decided it was time to deal with the paedophile. They dragged him a kilometer away from the building, stripped him, beat him and left him in the snow to die. An hour later, incredibly, the man was still alive and had crawled back to the house, only to find that the front door was locked. Someone had secured the bolt at the base of the door, but for some reason not the one at the top. The naked man made his way around to the windows, all protected by iron bars, until he reached that of Clara's office. He banged his fists on the metal frame and screamed. But the old woman, who had a cup upside down in her lap, refused to stir from her deep sleep. There was no sign of anyone else in the house.

Overcome by exhaustion and crazed with the bitter cold, he staggered back to the front of the building and wait on the doorstep. There he wrapped his arms around his naked body, in the belief that someone would soon enter the kitchen and he would terrorise them into letting him in. A few minutes later, a small bottle of brandy from Clara's secret stash was pushed through the letterbox and bounced off his head.

The following morning, the man's corpse was discovered frozen to the front door. Naturally, everyone inside the orphanage and later in the nearby towns believed that the onset of hypothermia had killed him – they were correct, but there was far more to it. Again, the sergeant was sent by his superiors to investigate.

As the sergeant emerged from his car, he was met by an inquisitive, but skittish little dog who had picked up the dead man's scent a few minutes after the Sun's rays stroked his skin. When the sergeant saw who the dead man was, he smiled. One nurse rushed out of the house, wracked with remorse. She fell to her knees in the virgin snow and confessed that several of them had chased the man from the house after finding him with a girl. The only reaction from the sergeant was to kick the man to ensure he was dead. The fixed wide eyes and frozen, open-mouthed expression of horror confirmed that he was. The sergeant retrieved out his notebook and made a record that there were no suspicious circumstances. With the investigation officially concluded, the police officer went inside, having been offered refreshment. He found the reheated contents of the coffee pot on the stove surprisingly relaxing and fell asleep.

If the sergeant had brushed away the shroud of snow and looked closer, he would have discovered an empty bottle clenched in the man's frozen hand. If he had sent the container to the forensic science laboratory in Kraków, he might have learnt that it contained crystals of sleeping powder. This might explain why in his final moments the man had not screamed out for help, not that anyone would have heard as the coffee pot on the stove used by the staff, was similarly laced with the powder. With this information, the police might have launched further inquiries and interviewed the staff – though not Lenka; she was only a child, after all.

Instead, when the undertaker arrived in a horse and cart, the sergeant ordered him to throw the body into the back. The supervisor denied knowledge of the man – Clara's intention was not to avoid the expense of a funeral, but rather that she genuinely had no idea who anyone was. As the costs of burial would now have to be met by the state, the funeral director unceremoniously wrenched the naked body from the entrance, leaving most of one side of his face and the skin from his shoulder frozen to the wooden doorframe. The hungry dog looked forlornly at the undertaker who dumped the body into a wheelbarrow and wheeled it towards the cart.

The sergeant trudged over and slammed his leather boot down on the frozen lump of the man's cheek. It landed on the step. As the undertaker signalled his horse to set off, the sergeant glanced over towards the disappointed mongrel. The sergeant kicked the only remaining evidence left of the man off the step towards the dog who happily devoured it. The animal slept well that afternoon.

In the weeks that followed, there was some good news. Little Charakterny's nightmares had subsided, and she was no longer pestering the nurses for sleeping powders.

The staff at the orphanage remained anxious, but once everyone was sure that the abuse had stopped, daily activity within the orphanage returned to normal. Meanwhile, Little Charakterny carried on drawing pictures with her crayons, which somehow, she never ran out of, even securing enough to furnish the other children. No one knew where she secured her supplies, but everyone knew that somehow the little girl would always find a way.

January 1937, Kraków

'Doctor, do you remember me? It's Lenka, I have something for you.'

'Ah, Little Charakterny! Come in. Come in,' said The Doctor. 'It has been too long. What have I done to deserve this pleasure?'

'I have to go abroad for a while, so I want to make sure that all the children will be safe before I go.' She was on her way to take the night train, the first stage of her journey to Madrid.

'Of course! Of course! I will be happy to look in on them in the evening,' said the stooped, bespectacled old man as he surreptitiously raised his liver-spotted hand to lift the revolver from the shelf by the door.

The weapon had rested there, ever since the morning he heard of the last of the brothers was found dead by the entrance to the orphanage. He was determined to be ready for when that "lethal little bitch" came for him.

Lenka said nothing, as she entered the man's tiny shack, a man who had never attended a medical institute, nor read a medical book – or any book, as he could not read. She shut the door behind her, having already drawn the knife from her boot.

Chapter 12: *"A Fellow of Infinite Jest"*

August 1938, Amsterdam

Cerberus insisted that wherever he performed his interrogations, the room was cleared of anything that might distract his victim. The subject's focus was to remain on him. The only furniture would be items that Rerck had been ordered to carry from the train.

The Gestapo officer sat in his usual chair, carved from Bavarian oak; on the ends of its wooden arms were iron plates depicting the embossed faces of crazed wolves. Its oval-shaped backrest had a padded velvet cushion studded into it, as did the seat. Jocky sat on a reinforced steel chair, with his hands bound behind him with Cerberus' specially designed steel-mesh reinforced leather straps tied around his wrists. There were two tables in the room. One was a functional table of basic design, three-foot high, with four sturdy legs. On top of it lay a closed suitcase and a large teak box. The black leather case had spots of gloss around the handle and the sides were dull and marked, as you would expect, as it had to be scrubbed clean after each interrogation. In the middle of the room was a small oval table, again made from Bavarian oak, and resting on it was a tool-bag made of red cloth, embroidered with gold thread.

The major sat with a cigarette in his right hand and his right foot stretched out straight. Jocky was naked apart from his underpants, stained yellow by a combination of sweat and urine. Rerck landed a restrained punch to the back of his head.

'Jesus!' yelled his victim. '*Yer* mad *bastads*. *Yer* didn't have to kill the ladies.'

'Ah yes! The white and black whores who were entertaining you when we arrived. How very egalitarian, as well as greedy, of you,' commented the major.

'They had names, Tracy and Trinny.'

'You have as much interest in their real names, as I do. Spare me any pretence that they were more than objects to you.'

'They were. I bought champagne, and we had gone for dinner, *yer* fuc . . .'

Rerck slapped his cupped hand against the side of the man's head terminating his protest along with his hearing in his left ear. When Jocky tried to release a further stream of expletives, the bodyguard locked his jaw in his gargantuan hand.

'Has the Irishman told you about me?' asked Cerberus.

Rerck released his grip. Jocky was trying to control the stream of blood flowing from his mouth.

'Nay, the *bastad* never mentions his boyfriends.'

'The English stiff upper lip: a stupid, non-thinking, clichéd response. Please, spare me the name, rank and number routine.'

'I'm Scottish, and I'm scared shitless.'

'I have warned you that I detest bad language.'

'Then let me go *yer fuked* up praying mantis.'

Cerberus nodded to his bodyguard who hit Jocky with the flat of his hand breaking his nose. He placed his hand over the man's face to smother his screams.

The major turned to the hot plate on the table beside him and warmed one of his souvenirs, a fork from his school days. He had used it to stab another boy in the throat. The boy had volunteered to join one of the Hitler Youth units in Munich and found himself under the command of Sergeant Klaus Krak. His stab wound resulted from his refusal to hand over a silver watch, an heirloom given to him by his grandfather, when Sergeant Krak demanded it.

Cerberus indicated to Rerck to remove his hand. Jocky spat more blood onto his chest as he gulped for breath.

'I'll tell *yer* everything *yer* want to know. I'm no hero, anyone will tell *yer*.'

'One has. However, you are missing the point. You see, I already know everything,'

Rerck opened the teak case on the table to unveil a gramophone. 'Wagner, I bet *yer bastad*! Any chance *yer* smashing in my good ear?'

'I have no interest in music, but we should at least make an effort to drown out your screams.' On the smaller table beside him, Cerberus removed the gold-coloured ribbon and began to unfold the bright red cloth. Removing several items, he laid them carefully on the table next to the gramophone. He grinned as one would when touching mementoes that revived memories of loved ones, as he stroked various sizes of pliers, hammers, tongs, knives of varied sharpness and the most abundant of the tools, gouging spikes. 'This is my mobile kit. I prefer to work in my specially adapted interrogation room on my train, but as so often has been the case over the last two years, I have had to carry out my work in the "field".' He turned to the hot-plate. 'Excellent, it is ready. Now we can begin.'

Jocky could feel that his heart pounding, as if knocking at his rib-cage desperate to escape.

'According to my source, you are a gifted technician, so you will appreciate that tools are only as good as the hand that applies them. Once due to a weak power supply, I had to use a spoon. I could have used a fork, but I wanted to retain the woman's eyes and store them in aspic. Unfortunately, such a blunt instrument only caused each eye to burst under my efforts. However, I am sure I will have many more opportunities and as you can see, I have had a box specially made.' He produced a small oblong box made from walnut with an open-winged eagle holding a swastika in its claws. Cerberus opened it, exposing its purple silk lining and a glass case that fitted snugly inside containing a transparent gel. 'But do not be alarmed. We are not primitive animals, but men of science. Rerck, please show our guest.'

The colossus of a bodyguard lifted the red-tipped prongs from the heated electrical hot-plate and raised them up to the man's eyes. Jocky passed out.

Rerck shook him violently until he regained consciousness. The Scotsman panicked at the thought of the blistering fork approaching and was too terrified to open his eyes. He passed out.

The bodyguard slipped a heavy-duty industrial steel chain through a large iron hook screwed into the main wooden support beam above. When Jocky opened his eyes, they were drawn to the case that lay on the table, and he failed to notice what the man behind was preparing to do.

Rerck wrapped the lower end of the heavy metal chain around the Scotsman's bound wrists.

'What the *fuk*,' shouted Jocky, aware that something was happening behind him.

The bodyguard moved around the chair to face the man screaming at him. Rerck waited for the order. When his commander instructed him, he delivered another blow with the flat of his shovel-sized hand, again into Jocky's face. It was enough to knock his front teeth out. The Scotsman's curses turned to shrieks. Rerck cupped his hand over the man's face, smothering the man's screams once more.

The major leaned forward. 'My skills are wasted on someone who passes out at the merest thought of pain. Hence, I have decided to put these implements aside and instead I will leave you in the capable hands of Rerck.'

Rerck walked over to the leather case and lifted out a hessian sack.

'Let the music begin,' commanded the major.

Rerck placed the gramophone needle onto the rim of a recording of the composer's last completed opera "Parsifal", before returning to the man tied to the steel metal chair.

'*Fuk yer*,' shouted Jocky, tears racing down his cheeks as the bodyguard produced a gas mask from the sack and forced it over the struggling man's head. Jocky panicked as he gasped for air. Rerck winched him, along with the chair he was tied to, towards to the beam. He came to a halt when he was two feet from the ground. Jocky's screams were contained by the apparatus over his face, but his bulging blood-red eyes betrayed the pain ripping through him like a butcher's knife.

Cerberus lifted his cup from the saucer, but before he took his first sip, he spoke calmly as if he were a doctor explaining to the patient the details of the surgery he was to undergo. 'Today, I want to try something different that reflects your character. You are a crude, base individual, but as I have said, one interested in mechanics.' He watched the bound man continue to struggle futilely. Cerberus remembered a butterfly he had once watched as a child. It struggled desperately to free itself from the cocoon it had outgrown – only to perish in the attempt.

'I understand how uncomfortable you must be, but that will be nothing compared to when the weight on your shoulders rips them from your sockets' (this had already happened). 'Now, we reach the part of the exercise that I have been eagerly looking forward to.'

The only sign of emotion evident in the man were the pulsing blue veins pressing against the skin on either side of his temples.

The man in the chair no longer struggled, having blacked out. A primeval survival instinct roused him from his unconscious state as he sensed death approaching. Panic and pain seized him but were sealed in silence behind the two glass sockets of the mask. Jocky's body fell limp as he saw the instrument that would soon tear out his heart and every other organ of his body.

Rerck led the massive, black and grey creature into the room. It was shackled by a heavy-duty steel chain attached to a restraining collar around its neck. The blood-veined eyes of the salivating beast were fixed on its fettered prey.

Jocky kicked out frantically as Rerck let the chain slip from his gun-barrel sized fingers.

The wolf leapt through the air, locking its steel-like jaws into Jocky's throat when he landed. Soon, blood and entrails began to spray the walls. The makeshift leash whipped and slashed the floor, creating a frenzied pattern of crimson strokes, like the brush of an artist seized by madness.

The bodyguard wrapped a tooth-marked leather sheet reinforced steel-mesh around his right-arm as the creature always turned on him after it had finished with its tethered prey.

Four hours later, Sean and Lenka burst into the room in the building next to the German Embassy. Neither said anything but just stood and stared at their friend's carcass hanging from the ceiling. Unbeknown to them, Rerck had removed the steel chair by hacking away at the cadaver with a meat cleaver before rehanging their friend from the ceiling.

Sean stepped forward, grabbed the bloody stumps of Jocky's thighs in his arms and lifted him. Lenka climbed up on Sean's back and lifted the chain holding the body off the hook in the beam. The Irishman did not make a sound, even though the combined weight antagonised the steel-pins in his leg and shoulder, and caused the bullet wound to reopen above his left hip.

Slowly he lowered Jocky's body down on to the blood-stained floor. Lenka removed the knife from her boot. With great difficulty, she cut through the leather bands that secured the only parts of his body that had not had the flesh ripped from them: his wrists.

'Do you think he told them anything?'

'Everything he knew. You may not have liked him, and though he was not a brave man, he never claimed to be anything other than who he was.'

'Well, we are fortunate that there was nothing to tell.'

'He knew where we were heading.'

Lenka nodded once. 'Are you sure it's Jocky?'

'Yes,' as he held what was left of his friend in his arms.

'You know that if I didn't care for him, I wouldn't have suggested that we go to the red-light district to find him and drag him back with us,' said Lenka.

It was a friend of the dead prostitutes who told them that a huge German man manhandle their friend into the building annexed to the German Embassy.

'Jesus Christ! How can you smile, when you are covered in the blood of one of our own?'

Sean shrugged as he held his dead man. 'I just thought that our friend here would have at least given his torturers a shit load of abuse.' Sean lifted back the rubber mask from Jocky's head, the front of which had been torn away, along with his face. 'Maybe that's why they had to strap this on him.' The skull came away from the body. Sean caught it. Then, like a scene from *Hamlet*, he held it up in his hand.

'Alas, dear Jocky, your enemies knew your vices far too well.'

Sean placed his forehead against the skull and closed his eyes. He spun around to glare at Lenka. 'Fuck 'em! I'm tired of trying to outrun these Nazi bastards.'

'I'm held together by ship rivets, so my days of

running are over, anyway. They will track me down soon enough wherever I go. Best you head to London.'

'I've never listened to a damn thing you've ever said, and I'm not going to start now. And you?'

'Paris, as I said, they'll be waiting for us there. Best not disappoint them.'

'There is no place of safety left for either of us anymore.' Lenka looked first at the skull, before turning to Sean. 'Paris, it is as I have a friend who might help us.'

'Can he create miracles?'

Lenka looked at Sean and smiled. 'No, but he claims to know someone who can.'

Chapter 13: The Angel of Saint-Gervais

September 1938, Paris

'Lenka! Lenka! How wonderful to see you and in my Church too,' exclaimed the thin, but jovial priest. 'Young lady, have you finally sought the forgiveness of the Lord?'

'Not today, Father Fabien, but I have brought you an even blacker soul to save.'

'Thank you Lenka,' said Sean. 'Introductions can be so awkward.'

The priest placed his hands on the woman's shoulders, which was easy as he was about her height. Then, he remembered something, as he extracted a little black book from his cassock. He skimmed through a few pages until he found one that pleased him. 'Tomorrow is Sunday and I have a fitting pray for a lost sheep. You must come to Mass Lenka and I will grant you absolution.'

'You'll need more than a day, Father,' added Sean. Lenka looked up at him with her familiar look of disapproval. Sean bent down to whisper in her ear, 'A priest, I thought all your friends were rogues and dysfunctional reprobates.'

'He's the exception.'

'How many times have I warned you about talking to normal men?' Sean was pleased to see her break into a rare smile before she addressed the priest.

'Father, we seek the sanctuary of your Church.'

Sean caught sight of the vast array of magnificent bells to his left hanging above the mezzanine of the Church erected in the transept. 'Jesus, there must be thirty of the buggers up there.'

'Have you run out of enemies that you now have to pick a fight with God in his own House with your blasphemy?' said Father Fabien.

'Sorry, Father. I'm Sean, by the way.'

'An Irishman, then it is likely you are a Catholic and one of God's flock.' Before Sean could answer, the priest let out a deep sigh. 'However, with your arrogance and lack of humility, I would guess not.'

'Am I that easy to read?'

'Sadly yes, you are one of those whose only belief is in themselves.'

Sean had argued with many priests over the years, not because he was an atheist or opposed the Church, but he found its ministers were very quick to judge.

'If there is a God, then he is not a merciful one. I have seen too many children die in pain, to believe that the suffering of the innocents is an essential requirement of some divine plan.'

'We are all tested to see if our faith is strong enough to lift us above hatred and bitterness.'

'Then I too have failed the test, but as I said, we need your help,' interrupted Lenka.

The priest smiled, clasping his hands. 'My child, I can never accept that you and your friend are not God's children; my beliefs are based on helping all those who ask for help and forgiving those who repent. In the meantime, I will take solace from the parable of "The Prodigal Son" that one day both of you may recover your faith in God.'

'Thank you, Father,' said Lenka. 'And now I have to find the British Embassy, which I'm told is in Rue du Faubourg St Honoré.'

The priest walked over to a side room and called to the altar boy. 'Phillipe, would you accompany this lady and take her to where she needs to go?'

'Of course, Father, but I will take my bicycle as I need to be home in time for supper,' said the boy.

The priest nodded.

'Father, I have one more request. I need to ensure that this arrogant man stays out of trouble until I secure his passage to England. Don't worry about his comfort.' She smiled at Sean. He returned the gesture. 'Just somewhere he can sleep so you can keep an eye on him.'

'Yes, we can find somewhere towards the heavens,' replied the priest.

Sean looked up. 'Not too close or I may blister.' At the end of the mezzanine beneath the magnificent cluster of bells was a ladder that led up to one of the two towers on either side of the transept, which bordered the bell-tower at the back of the building. To the right of it, in the apex of the Church, were six similar bells that sounded the hour.

The priest nodded. Lenka turned around and without a glance at Sean, pulled open a small door that was cut into one of the large beech entrance doors and disappeared into the sunlit cobbled street. The priest smiled at the Irishman. 'Not one for small talk is our Lenka.'

'How did you meet?'

'We only met last year, when she brought me letters

from some priests in Spain who were persecuted by the Communists.'

Sean knew that the Catholic Church was aligned with Franco's Fascists: Lenka was full of surprises.

'Why bring them to you, Father?'

'I volunteered to be the contact between the clergy in Spain and the Vatican.'

'I didn't mean to offend your beliefs, Father.'

'Your atheistic beliefs can keep their own company in Cassandra's room,' he replied as he pointed up to the bell tower above the altar.

'Cassandra, who . . .' Sean said, before he saw a tall woman appear from a side door to the right of the altar. Apart from her height, she was striking in appearance, having short red hair and sparkling, bright green eyes, but her skin was as pale as those at death's door. The woman stood in silence, poised by the door like a ballerina awaiting her cue from the side of the stage. As Sean looked closer, he noticed that she was memorable in another way; stress lines were etched into her face like hairline fissures in sculptured marble statues of the saints that surrounded them.

Sean smiled and was about to say something in greeting, but the priest stayed his arm. 'Please do not approach her or try to engage with her. Believe me, it is best.'

The priest sat down in a pew with a look of resignation, like a man about to tell a story for the hundredth time. Sean joined him, in the hope that it might put the woman at ease.

'This exquisite Church of Saint-Gervais was my

second parish as a young priest, just after the Great War. This church reflects the pain and delight of its followers. In the vaults, are a collection of instruments bequeathed by French musicians who provided so much pleasure here over the centuries. While above us, the repairs you see remind us of the sad loss of over 100 lives when a German shell landed here in 1918.' The priest smiled as he looked over at the hesitant woman. 'Nine months after that terrible attack, a German priest guided this poor young woman to my Church.' He turned to Sean. 'I say guided as she refused to let him help her up the stairs.'

The woman stood by the altar, with an air of sanctification reflecting that of the iconic statues that adorned the alcoves in the walls.

'A kindly German priest, Father Lobenhoffer, had discovered the girl in a house on the Belgian border. It was a staging post for German troops. He made the treacherous journey to bring her here. However, he could tell me nothing more about her. But though she carries no visible scars, I cannot imagine what the poor girl went through at the hands of the soldiers.'

'Why did he bring her here?'

'We were novice priests together at the seminary in the grounds of the Church of Saint-Sulpice before the outbreak of war.'

'And you have learnt nothing else about her?'

'No, and she has never spoken a word to me.' He shook his head and sighed. 'All she had that day was a rag doll, and a broken set of a child's rosary beads in her hand. They may have been hers or those of someone else; we do not know.'

Sean looked at the woman and smiled. She looked through him.

'She has lived here ever since. Yes, people talk, but I don't care. This is a house of sanctuary. I believe no one has ever had greater need of it.'

'How do you know her name?'

'I don't. But a week after her arrival she closed all the shutters on the Church windows even though it was a sunny day. It was as if she were expecting a hurricane to hit. I humoured her, but when she returned to her room, I reopened all the shutters. After I left the Church for the day and returned to the manse, she set about closing all the shutters once more. That night a ferocious storm hit the city. If she hadn't covered the windows that night, we would have lost most, maybe all, of the beautiful stained-glass windows you see around you. Do you know the mythology of Cassandra?'

'Wasn't she the Prophetess of Doom?'

'A misnomer. According to Greek mythology, she was a soothsayer, but one who had spurned the God Apollo's advances. In his rage, he punished her by casting a curse that no one would ever believe her prophesies ever again. I and my congregation will never doubt her again.'

'She fears men?' asked Sean, as she looked anxiously at him.

'Yes, but some more than others. A few years later The Bishop of Berlin, Konrad von Preysing, a good and brave man and no friend of the Nazis, visited our Church. But when she overheard him talking, Cassandra froze. We walked over to her together. She was as still as the surrounding statues. It was as if her mind had abandoned its host in search of sanctuary. I told the Bishop what I knew of her, and he fell to his knees in tears and prayed for forgiveness on behalf of his countrymen. However, she did not move until the Bishop decided he should depart for the sake of her well-being. The same thing happens whenever she hears a male German accent.'

'I have no need of the lady's room,' and with that Sean raised himself up and walked over to the statue of the Madonna and Child. Around its base, he noticed a small broken string of beads. Unbeknown to Sean, these were all Cassandra had left of her former life as she had lost her rag doll some years earlier.

'Cassandra exerts herself too much when she rings the bells and no fastening can withstand her exertions.'

Sean smiled first at the beads and then at the woman eyeing him nervously. He swept up all the baubles into his cupped hand and walked towards the woman, who backed away into the shadows. Sean whispered, 'I have some strong twine in my bag, and I would like to string these together for you. That is, if you have no objection?' She stared at him but said nothing. He drew back and turned to the priest. 'Right, Father, can you direct me to an area of floor, so the potential prodigal son can lay his head down for the night?'

The priest chuckled as he led the Irishman towards the wooden staircase and up to the wooden floor where the bells hung above in silence.

Sean looked up. 'Seriously, you must have more bells than Notre Dame?'

'You were conservative in your original estimate. Apart from our own, there are forty-two bells in total. When the

Great War began, they were brought here from churches on the outskirts of Paris as the German advanced. It was to save them from the pounding of the heavy artillery, and even worse, being forged into munitions. What you see here are those from churches that were destroyed. Ten others were returned after the war, hence the ropes dangling freely down from the hooks you can see in the rafters. The others remain here for the purpose, God forbid,' as he made the sign of the cross across his chest, 'of warning the citizens of Paris if we are ever invaded again. Fortunately, they have never been sounded.'

Sean turned to the priest. 'Do you have Quasimodo on standby?'

'We have Cassandra.'

'One woman? But each one must weigh a ton.'

'You are a doubting Thomas. Our local carpenter, André, developed an intricate pulley system, and he is adamant that Cassandra can wake the black beasts if needed.'

'Is that the man up there busying himself with a chainsaw?'

'Yes, up in the transept André is laying a new floor on the mezzanine, as you can see.'

'And hear,' added Sean, and he was not referring to the noise of the chainsaw, but the gruff man's frequent shouts of '*Merde!*'

'I have told André not to curse but, like you, he has no respect for the House of God.' The priest added, a little deflated, 'He has the honesty you would expect from a native of the countryside, particularly when drawing attention to my many faults. He told me never to attempt to peal the bells myself as I am old and meek, and I would be swinging impotently up there for years like a eunuch in a . . . well let's say a place of ill-repute.' Sean laughed, which did not improve the priest's mood. The priest walked away shaking his head and mumbling, 'He once told me that I only got ordained because I heard that the likes of me would one day inherit the Earth.'

The Irishman picked up his knapsack and made his way up the steep staircase and across the mezzanine.

'Bonjour André,' said Sean, who was astonished to see that the carpenter was operating a two-man gasoline-powered chainsaw by himself.

'*Anglais . . . merde!*' said the huge bear of a man as the teeth of a large Dolmar chainsaw attacked the thick plank of beech trapped over a gap in the floor with his knee.

'Yes, I'm fine. How kind of you to ask,' replied the Irishman, as he stepped on the ladder and climbed toward the tower.

Sean was sitting down on the blanket he had spread over the stone floor of the tower. He looked out of the glassless window at the wisps of clouds that trailed the far larger and darker clouds on the horizon. Taking the last of the thick thread from his mother's small medicine bag that he carried with him, he completed his task. The medical kit was the only item the British had allowed him and his sister to take from the house before they razed it to the ground. The destruction of their home was an attempt to ensure it did not become a monument to British oppression following the murder of his family. In this aim it failed as many families placed pieces of rubble on their mantelpieces, so they would not forget.

In the medical bag were a bottle of sterilising iodine, bandages and an assortment of darning needles, which, along with the strong thread he had used to apply to his wounds, had saved his life on many occasions. He examined the coloured baubles, which were unusual for rosary beads, and a small crucifix still attached to the broken string. The cross was made of copper while the beads were lead crystal, the same as worn by Hannah with her silver Star of David. When he was recovering in St Bartholomew's hospital, to the surprise of the medical staff, he had asked to see a rabbi. His purpose was to understand more about Judaism. The rabbi explained that the lead crystals of Hannah's Star were known as 'Jewish glass'. Once he had finished threading all the beads, he tied a firm knot in the two ends of twine and pulled it hard to test it. He was satisfied that like the stitches that had held his wounds together over the years, only a sharp blade would separate Cassandra's keepsake now.

The doves in the rafters took flight towards the window. Sean looked up and noticed several nests overhanging the beams. One appeared to contain something bound in cloth. He flipped an empty wooden crate on its side and stood on it. Sean stretched up on tiptoe to peer inside the abandoned crown of twigs and saw the remnants of a rag doll. The Irishman delicately lifted it out. He jumped down, retrieved a needle and twine from the threadbare bag, and began to sew up the numerous holes where the brittle straw poked through.

Half an hour later, Sean climbed down the ladder to the platform below the bells and made his way across the newly repaired floor and down the staircase to the nave. At the base of the statue of the Madonna and Child he placed the necklace, along with the unattached crucifix beside it. The Church bells rang out. He lifted his head. Though he could not see her, he knew it was Cassandra informing the city that it was midnight. The Irishman made his way back up the staircase, across the mezzanine and up the ladder into the tower.

He wrapped the blanket around him, as the clouds that had sneaked up upon the city erupted in the distance above Sacré-Coeur, making the air cold and damp. It was at times like this that the steel pins in his leg and shoulder and the fissures in his spine reminded him of their presence. His pain, however, was nothing to that in the soft voice of a woman that he listened to over the next few hours repeatedly counting in German, '*Eins, Zwei, Drei, Vier, Fünf.* . .' occasionally interrupted by sobbing.

Sean could not sleep. He walked lightly towards the window that faced out onto the Seine. The doves had settled down to sleep on the window seat by some seed that Cassandra must have left for them. The birds flew off when he clicked his fingers. Scooping most of the seed up in his hands, he climbed down the ladder once more and walked across the platform with the giant sleeping bells suspended high above him and made his way down the staircase. He knelt on one knee, and under the watchful gaze of the inquisitive birds above, sprinkled the seed along the inside of the Church's gigantic entrance doors. When he had finished, he turned around to find Cassandra standing a few feet behind him.

He smiled and whispered, 'I thought we might need a

burglar alarm. In case the Naz . . .' he caught the fear in her eyes. 'It's just that we may have visitors before morning. You might want to stay somewhere else tonight, perhaps go to Father Fabien's manse, as it might be too dangerous to remain here.' Then, as an afterthought, he placed his hand inside his faded blue cotton shirt and produced the rag doll. 'Please, take this with you. It needed a few stitches, and it certainly needs a good wash,' as he passed the dolly to her.

The woman nervously retrieved it from his outstretched hand. She pressed it to her face and looked at him before turning back towards the spiral stairs that led up to the bell tower.

Ten minutes later, Sean lay on the blanket in the tower, staring out of the arch window. Four times the bells chimed, and each time he heard the woman counting in German.

The clouds parted as if inviting the moon to introduce itself. It was silver, and as unblemished in its nakedness as the night little Leo was killed. How could he not have heard the little boy's footsteps as he made his way down from The Sleepy Armadillo? Why hadn't he stayed back to stand guard at the entrance of the alleyway until Jewel and the others were safely in the car? Could he not have reacted faster and sidestepped his advancing opponent when he threw himself on him, propelling them both from the top of the train? If he had, could he have saved Magdalena and Tóth? Then there were the nightmares: the recurring image of the swastika unfurled by the thermals above the Fortress, before the faces of the young woman and her son appeared. They were asking him something and waiting desperately for him to give them an answer, but he could not hear their

268

questions. As they faded away the swastika reappeared, fluttering proudly, high above the Fortress' chimney stack.

Each night, these and many other images would flick past his eyes like grotesque sleeves in a photo album – but he never knew where it would fall open and torment him as he slept. But tonight, he had no intention of sleeping. He heard the doves take flight below.

Ryan leapt to his feet. His body electrified by the surge of adrenaline. For the first time in months, he felt no pain, as his limbs were no longer shackled by damaged nerves and torn muscles. He was already clothed and quickly slipped on his battered black jacket. Then, he opened his bag and armed himself with the Welrod pistol, the Thompson M1921 and the American Ka-Bar hunting knife that Jake had given him at Amsterdam Centraal.

Edging his way to the ladder with the Welrod in his right hand, he pulled the door gently open with his left. He peered down from the darkness of the tower into the nave. The first of the plain-clothed men with submachine guns was stealthily making his way across the stone floor of the atrium. Seven, eight, then nine armed men spanned out across the nave and along the pews, but he could hear others scurried in the shadows. He sensed a figure behind him. He spun around and aimed his gun at the silhouette, before Cassandra came into view. She approached wearing a long white cotton nightdress and a black cloak draped over her shoulders.

He said softly, but firmly, 'Stay here.' She ignored him and unwrapped the white cotton handkerchief in her hand, unveiling the bracelet of beads he had repaired. To his surprise, she lifted his hand, placed the beads in his palm, and folded his fingers over them and whispered. 'Thank you, but I have no faith . . .'

She said nothing more, nor made any gesture as she made her way out of the concealed side door that led to the bell tower. Now that the mystical vision had gone, Sean looked again at the bracelet to convince himself that he was not dreaming.

Ryan placed the small bracelet in his inside pocket and returned to survey the intruders below. To his left, he watched as Cassandra entered the bell tower and made her way to a rope wrapped around a hook on the wall. She unwrapped it. For the first time, the rope attached to the elaborate mechanism started to slide up and down. The ranks of magnificent bronze domes began their march as if some magical spell had been cast. At first, they rocked back and forth, out of step like soldiers who lacked drill practice. Gradually, the army of bells exaggerated each step, swinging high up towards the rafters. Suddenly, as if overwhelmed by their own brilliance, the iron marchers began to applaud as the clappers inside clattered against their metallic shells.

The Welrod was useless at that range, so Ryan turned to the Thompson. The assassins below were pointing their *Maschinenpistole-40* submachine guns upwards, trying to discover who had decreed the marching of the bells. As Cassandra was not a visible target, Ryan bided his time until he calculated that the fifteen men below were the entire squad of assassins sent to kill him. Satisfied that it was, he unleashed the five-hundred plus rounds per minute at the man down to his right, nearest to the entrance. Having cut off their retreat, he threw a stream of gunfire from right to left in a zigzagging motion. The assassins scattered, throwing themselves in all directions. Eight were fatally hit, blasting them backwards into the pews. The other seven, some wounded, managed to dive onto the floor and edge their way to any cover they could find by the walls. Ryan edged his way down the ladder. The first of the *Stielhandgranate-24* grenades landed on the partially reconstructed wooden floor below him. He tried to scramble back up as the first of the explosions ripped most of the mezzanine floor apart. As the ladder toppled onto the stone floor below, he threw himself backwards towards one of the abandoned ropes dangling from the metal hooks above.

Ryan caught the rope with his weaker right arm, while grasping the Thompson in the other. Taking advantage of his panoramic view from above, he emptied the magazine at the intruders darting in between the stone columns in the direction of the staircase.

The men scrambled once again to find a makeshift shield, as The Englander, the name given to them two hours earlier by Captain Maurras, the leader of the Alpha Wolves' operation in France, resumed his attack. Maurras and his men were caught in a hail of bullets. Pews and statues disintegrated as bodies juddered under the firestorm. Four assassins lay lifeless to the floor. The most experienced and ruthless of the three remaining, selected by Major Klaus Krak, was not one of them.

Ryan swung between the frenzy of bells as bullets ricocheted around him. He leapt towards another rope in a desperate attempt to escape. The Irishman caught it, but the men below were making their way up the stairs, providing each other with covering fire. He expected nothing less from well-drilled, professional killers. By the time they reached the mezzanine they were low on ammunition and had to resort to their Luger semi-automatic pistols. The Irishman released his redundant Thompson. It clattered onto the stone floor. He drew the Welrod from his leather belt. The three men below took cover behind the neglected wooden pulpit to their left to reload.

He swung back and forth. When Ryan reached the apex of his pendulum, he was motionless in the air for a brief second: it was enough to release two rounds, dead centre, into the front panel of the wooden pulpit. Swinging back down, he judged that he must have hit one man as the other two leapt out to run in opposite directions. The man to his left was running along the edge of the frame that held the few planks of the mezzanine structure. The other man, powerfully built but incredibly agile, raced to his right and disappeared behind a partition.

Maurras had reached the ladder behind the wooden partition that he had seen from the bullet-ridden pulpit and began to scale it. He was pleased to see that it led to a raised platform that was on the same level as the tower where The Englander had been. Once there, he would have the advantage of height, aiming his weapon down towards his target. As he climbed, he heard two bullets hit a stack of bricks propped up near the top of the ladder. He flung himself to the side of the ladder as the bricks toppled towards him, knocking his gun from his hand. Cursing, he saw his weapon bounce off the carpenter's open tool box and plunge through one of the huge holes in the wooden structure before crashing down onto the stone floor of the aisle.

As the bricks fell, Ryan grabbed another rope and swung towards the remaining assassin, who was still working his way along the frame of the mezzanine. The man had stopped and had him in the sights of his Luger. Ryan was upon him. Before the assassin pulled the trigger, the swinging man caught him perfectly, smashing the heels and soles of his boots into his chest. The assassin flew backwards along the wooden platform, his bulging eyes focused on his killer. He fired one round. Ryan heard the glass shatter behind him, as one small panel of red glass disappeared from one of the magnificent stained-glass windows. The assassin toppled from the platform. His scream was accompanied by a frantic flapping of arms and legs, before he landed head first onto the polished marble slab.

Chattering teeth of the chainsaw caused Ryan to spin round, but not before it tore into his back. Desperately trying to hang on, he tried to focus on what had happened. He saw his attacker. It was the man who he thought had been crushed under the falling bricks. Now he was swinging on the rope with the gnashing teeth of the frenzied saw, hungry to rip more flesh from his body. Ryan aimed the Welrod and released two rounds. Each 'thud' confirmed they had found their target. Though his attacker had two bloody holes in his chest, Ryan was amazed to see that the man not only retained his grip on the rope but was still coming towards him with the two-man chainsaw gripped firmly in one hand. Ryan tried to raise his feet to meet his attacker, but it was too late. The hungry metal teeth tore into his right arm and his pistol slipped from his hand.

The two men grappled frantically with each other, hanging from the ropes amongst the thundering bells. The assassin did not try to halt the blood spurting from his body; instead he pressed the manic teeth of the rotating chain into his target. As the teeth ripped through his leather jacket, Ryan flipped the length of rope below him up into his free hand with his foot and bound it around the man's neck. The man's eyes bulged as he realised what The Englander was trying to do. He made a grab at the rope around his neck, but as he did so, Ryan seized the chainsaw by the handle. It was so heavy that the Irishman could barely hold it, but he used the momentum of his swing to make one almighty effort to launch the hysterical teeth up into the rope holding Maurras.

The metal teeth slashed clean through the rope, before the chainsaw flew through the air and plummeted to the floor. As Maurras watched the rope above him slacken, he threw himself on Ryan, but the impact on his wounds sent skewers of pain through him. He lost his grip. The leader of the assault team did not fall far as the rope around his neck brought him to an abrupt stop, snapping his skull from his spinal cord.

Ryan hung onto the rope, pressing his forehead against it. The Irishman carried out the ritual that he adopted after every battle. He regulated his breathing, to reduce his heartbeat and reduce the adrenaline pumping through his body. This would release more oxygen back into the blood and replenishing his energy in time for the next fight. As his breathing slowed, he braced himself as adrenaline is a powerful anesthetic. His latest wound, the four-inch opening in his right arm, started to throb. As the pain from the wounds across his arm and back increased, he knew from experience that his injuries were superficial. Tentatively, he worked his way down the rope. He lowered himself onto the fractured wooden platform and collapsed onto his knees. Blood spiraled from his mouth, as stared down at the body of broken body Maurras encircled by a dark crimson pool of blood. A fatally wounded man had supported himself with one hand, while attacking him with a two-man chainsaw swinging in the other – what manner of creature were they fighting? But what of the woman who had distracted his attackers and given him the opportunity to take advantage of their confusion?

Ryan rose, but his concentration was not helped by the madness induced by the bells that continued to toil around him. Then he saw her. Exhausted, covered in blood and with no idea how he would get down, he managed to nod and smile. She released the rope and though some distance away, he could see her face. Cassandra did not return his smile, but she seemed tranquil, as if at peace. A machine gun roared. Blood flew up and splattered her cheeks as her chest exploded.

The Irishman watched the woman topple forwards. Her expression did not change, reflecting neither pain nor shock or even bewilderment as to why she had to die now. As she fell, her arms stretched out and her body turned slowly in the air before she landed on her back in front of the altar. Ryan turned towards the submachine gunfire and saw her murderer appear from behind the redundant pulpit on the mezzanine floor. Her killer, whose left thigh was soaked in blood, glared at Ryan as he threw his empty weapon down the staircase.

Despite Ryan's bullet ripping away a chunk of the man's thigh, he sprinted across the platform and launched himself at one of the ropes. Ryan kept hold of the rope with his left arm and waited. The man swung his body back and forth until he managed to throw himself forward onto the rope that was the nearest to the Irishman. The teeth marks on the back of Ryan's right arm were not so deep as to stop him withdrawing the knife from his jacket.

Cassandra's killer was only a few feet away, having gathered momentum with his pendulum swing. The last of the French Alpha Wolves was a foot away. He slashed out with his SS combat knife as he swung up past Ryan. The Irishman was ready and parried the blade away with his knife, before slashing it across his assailant's stomach.

The man screamed, but as he reached the highest point of his climb, he realised that when he dropped back down, The Englander would be waiting. In desperation, he threw his hand up to catch one of the bell hooks screwed into the rafter above. He succeeded, but in doing so impaled his hand on the spike. Screaming, he attempted to focus on alternating his other hand between supporting his weight and stemming the flow of blood and entrails cascading from his stomach. As he did so, the rope slipped from his hand.

Ryan jumped onto one of the few wooden planks left of the mezzanine. He ran down the staircase, paying no heed to the screams from the man hanging from the roof.

Sean crouched down next to Cassandra, splayed out on the bloodied steps at the base of the altar. Her once clear green eyes, now broken by burst blood vessels, flickered. The Irishman lifted one section of her cloak that was not soaked in blood and dipped it into the holy water seeping from the bullet-riddled font. He dabbed her face lightly. With each light wipe of the cloth, her face became clearer, but thin lines of blood set in the hairline fissures in her skin.

She touched his cheek lightly with her fingertips. He bent closer, gathering her limp body up in his arms, pressing her to him. Cassandra squeezed him tightly and buried her face into his chest. He heard that familiar sobbing. Then the crying and the pealing of the bells above stopped, and her arms fell back onto the cold, unforgiving floor.

Chapter 14: The Conciergerie

September 1938, Paris

The bells across Paris pealed five times, but not those above Sean, as he closed the smaller door cut into the imposing doors behind him. Father Fabien appeared from the darkness as he ran up the steps of Saint-Gervais with Phillipe beside him. Cassandra's final warning had been heard, as terrified Parisians darted across cobblestone boulevards to ask others if the Germans had returned.

'Father, do not let the boy enter,' said Sean.

'What has happened? And . . . Oh, my Lord! There is a section missing from the stained-glass window,' said the priest.

'Actually, Father, you'd better not go in either.'

The priest heard the cries coming from inside the church, 'My Lord! Is that someone screaming?'

'It's nothing; he'll be down in a minute.'

'I've just heard. Lenka . . .' he gasped once more, 'she's been taken.' He slumped on the steps and rested his hands on his knees as he had run from his house when he had heard the explosions.

'Who's taken her?' demanded Sean.

The boy answered for the breathless priest. 'After I had left her outside the British Embassy I was about to ride home, but I looked back just as a big man walked up to her and punched her in the face, knocking her to the ground. Then, he threw her into the back of a car and drove off.'

'Do you know where he took her?'

'I cycled after him. I'm a good rider and as he was caught in the evening traffic. I was able to follow him. I saw him drive into the Conciergerie. I went home and told my parents, but they said it was late and I should leave it to them to tell Father Fabien in the morning. But I snuck out of my bedroom window as soon as I could.'

'It was a former palace . . .' shuttered the priest, 'then a prison, but they shut it down a few years ago. It's on . . . Île de la Cité.'

Sean placed his hand on the priest's shoulder. The crumpled clergyman peered up, fearing what the man was about to say. 'I am sorry Father, but if there is a heaven then Cassandra has finally found peace.'

Cerberus took a sip of Earl Grey from his bone china cup. 'Marie Antoinette was a prisoner here and so also was,' as he shook his head, 'Robespierre. Its history of bringing even the most powerful to their knees attracted me to this place.'

'If you want a history lesson, let's talk about 1918,' said Lenka, spitting out blood, and a broken molar onto her blood-stained blouse.

Rerck hit the woman once more across her face with the back of his powerful lead like hand, breaking the skin under her right eye. Cerberus was pleased, as his personal tutoring of his bodyguard was going well. Rerck had killed the first prisoner in his charge too quickly with a similar blow, but he was learning to control his awesome strength.

However, his bodyguard had a tendency to think for himself and act without orders. The Wehrmacht wished to encourage innovation in its ranks, but Cerberus did not - he demanded absolute, unquestioning obedience.

'Lenka – for though you refuse to acknowledge it I know this is your name. Firstly though, please accept my apologies. Rerck has had little sleep as he had to clean up the mess after we dealt with your friend in Amsterdam. However, there is no excuse for expressing uncontrolled emotion at such times. We are professionals, and you have my personal assurance that from this moment on you will be struck only upon my command.' Rerck stood to attention with a short, abrupt nod of his head to his superior, acknowledging his rebuke. 'The last twenty-four-hours have been particularly busy for us. However, with the death of one of your Scottish friends and now that The Englander has been dealt with, I can promise you that from now on you will have our undivided attention.'

Lenka lifted her head. 'You've killed him?'

'Captain Maurras is one of my best. He and his men have never failed me. The Englander was dead as soon as I learnt that your priest had granted him sanctuary.'

'You would attack a church?'

'A church, a mosque, a synagogue – what are these to us? These self-proclaimed sacred institutions will be razed to the ground if any offer protection to enemies of The Third Reich.'

Cerberus signalled to one of the Alpha Wolves guarding the door, 'I am ready for breakfast: two boiled eggs and two thin slices of pork sausage.' He turned back to Lenka. 'The Jew won't be eating.'

'I was telling your Scottish friend before he left us, that due to expediency I have devised a mobile interrogation facility.' He lifted his arm to direct her towards the display of implements opened out on the red cloth edged with gold thread. 'It is such a terrible shame that one must resort to these basics as I have had a specially constructed carriage on my train furnished for my guests. But pragmatism is called for. I cannot risk transporting you there; you and your friends have proven to be, how shall I put it —unruly passengers. Let me take advantage of this rare opportunity to tell you about it while we wait for my breakfast to be prepared.'

'Fuck yourself!'

Rerck looked at his commander for instructions, but the major stayed his command, as he was not sure that his Polish prisoner would survive a further blow.

'Your Scottish friend was very crude and expressed similar profanities. That was reprehensible, but for a woman to do so, even though you are a Jew, is totally unacceptable.' Lenka continued to strain the leather straps that bound her wrists behind the steel chair. This pleased the major, for despite her brutal interrogation she was far stronger than he had thought her to be. 'My living quarters have been furnished to the highest standards by the finest of German craftsman; but I will not waste time discussing what you will never see or would not appreciate if you did. Instead, let me tell you of the connecting carriage: my detention carriage. It has been built to my specifications and is based on my many years of experience carrying out interrogations. I would go as far as to call it a monument to the art of persuasion. My commander, Obergruppenführer

Reinhard Heydrich, calls it my Carriage of Truth, and I hear my guards call it the Carriage of Horrors. But such flights of fancy are far too melodramatic for me.'

'What do they you call you?' coughing up blood. 'A "monument to grotesque art", you fucking moron?'

'Rerck,' commanded the major, showing his open palm. The bodyguard obeyed and slapped the woman across the side of her face, sending two more molars and a stream of blood across the floor.

'The carriage has eight isolation cells for my guests on the left and a walkway on the right side for my guards. Each cell has six hundred square centimetres of floor space and is one metre high. No occupant can stand fully upright, or crouch, let alone lie down. Each cell has four wire-mesh protected light-bulbs on each side; sleep is impossible. There is a small drain in one corner, but no toilet facilities.' He smiled. 'Animals do not mind their own waste . . . do you? All the wooden walls, floors and ceilings are sealed. There is no ventilation except for one hole in the roof that is a centimetre wide. Usually, I leave my guests to their own devices for three to four days without food or water, and then we turn on a sprinkler above to wash the prisoner for a few hours in icy cold water. Naturally, once released they could not be more cooperative. I find that psychological measures are more effective than physical ones, as men, women and, as I have learnt recently children, become consumed more by the fears they envisage than by those they have experienced. However, if they do not freely provide me with the information I require, I will question them in a far more forceful manner.'

Cerberus continued to speak as if he were giving a lecture. 'Not all my work is on foreign soil, as on occasion my skills are required back in Germany. Let me explain. We have a unique power in German-occupied territories called the *Schutzhaft* – in English it is called "protective custody", which means we have the power to imprison people without judicial proceedings. But we are not brutes, as a prisoner must sign his own *Schutzhaftbefehl*. This is an order declaring that the person has requested imprisonment. Occasionally, when a prisoner does not know what is in their own interest, with the use of my instruments, I ensure that they do.'

'You pass laws simply to meet your own sick ends. Legitimise it anyway you like, but I know' she began to choke, 'You're . . . all sick . . . fuck . . . ing . . . bastards.'

'Rerck!' shouted Cerberus, and the big man hit the woman across the face, opening another wound across her right eyebrow. 'Now you understand my disappointment, as you will never have the pleasure of taking advantage of my facilities. If it's any consolation I expect that hundreds, perhaps over the decades thousands of our enemies, along with your friends, will.' He sneered. 'Have you heard that our troops have marched unopposed into the Sudetenland?' Lenka was surprised to hear that the Nazis had occupied the German-speaking area in the north of Czechoslovakia, but she refused to give the man any pleasure by betraying it. 'The rest of the country will follow shortly. We let the Western democracies puff and bluster before all goes quiet again, as we did with Austria. Of course, they may decide to take some form of military action.' He edged forward. 'Tell me, Lenka, with your contacts in Britain and France, do you think they will?' Then, for the first time, Rerck and the other six Alpha Wolves in the room heard their commander laugh out loud.

Lenka had controlled her reaction to the news, but she could not hide her shock at what the man said next. 'The two trains loaded with Jewish children you helped organise in Berlin and Vienna are now under my control.' He grinned on seeing the pain on her face. 'Oh, yes, I am aware of your role and that of the American in this. However, I believe that neither of you has told the other Rogues the full story.' Cerberus tutted. 'How sad it must be to live in a world with so little trust.'

She lifted her head to plead for the children, though it took all her energy to do so. 'But why, the children are only a burden to you?' She straightened up, but grasped as one of her broken ribs was pressing against her lung.

'But they are not a burden. They are an enticement.'

She swallowed hard. 'An enticement?'

'Good, you have adopted a more civil tone. If you continue our conversation in such a manner, I will pretend that you are human, and not one of those feral creatures you call Rogues.' He lifted the bone china cup to his mouth as he looked at her bloody and battered face. He shouted across to his bodyguard, 'This is tepid. I will require a fresh pot,' as he returned the cup and saucer to the silver tray on the small oval table beside him. One of the three guards by door headed off towards the kitchen. 'Yes, the children are an enticement. They will lure your Rogues out into the open, for they will try to save them: it is the nature of the beasts. That is, unless you tell me where your friends are now. Then I will release the children as they will be no longer of use to me.'

'I don't know where they are, but you are such a soulless bastard that you will do whatever you want with the children even if I did know and told you.' The effort of speaking pressed her broken rib deeper into her, forcing her to throw up what little contents she had in her stomach onto her semi-naked body.

Cerberus' smile disappeared as he nodded to Rerck, who wrenched the woman's head by her hair and swung his rock of a fist into her stomach again. She had nothing to throw up but blood.

Ryan reloaded the Welrod and edged his way under the main arches of the grand Gothic hall that welcomed visitors into The Conciergerie. All around him lay building materials used for the renovation to what the Ministry of the Interior called its 'former glory'. The period they wished to restore it to was not when it was a grand Royal Palace, but the years that immediately followed the French Revolution when it was a prison – a time known as The Terror.

There was a knock on the sturdy wooden but steel-reinforced door of the first of the restored prison cells. The guard, who had just returned with the major's breakfast, opened the door and was killed instantly by the ball-peen hammer embedded in his skull.

'Morning,' said Ryan as he stepped quickly over the body and entered the room pointing his silencer at the five men.

'The Englander,' said Cerberus. He expressed no emotion, nor was there any inflection in his voice.

'Call me The Englander again and this will end in tears,' countered Ryan, as he assessed the weaponry, position, physical abilities and therefore the threat posed by each of the men.

The other men, bar one, were wearing the black uniform of the Gestapo, but on the top right-hand jacket pocket was a silver-plated wolf's head and hanging from their leather belts was a black, thick metal plate. Each jacket had a chevron on the right sleeve. Ryan had read extensively from books on the Nazis in St Bartholomew's small but adequate library and knew that this indicated that they had excelled in at least one area of recognised proficiency within the SS. In the centre of the room stood a bald, thick-set man who was stripped to the waist. His face, neck and chest were splattered in blood. In one hand, he held a scalpel caked in blood and pieces of flesh, and in the other a bendable copper pipe with another blade attached to the end by a coarse wire. He was the only one who was smiling.

In the centre of the room was a tall, skeletal man sitting on a chair wearing the uniform of a major in the Gestapo. But it was difficult to secure a proper view of the officer, as a goliath of a man quickly stepped in front of him, blocking Ryan's line of sight and therefore his line of fire. The two Alpha Wolves guards standing behind the major each had their hands poised on their MP40s, waiting for the order to use them: an action that Cerberus knew, in such a confined space, might inadvertently kill him.

There was no sign of Lenka. Then, the half-naked man moved aside to reveal her limp, bloodied body. Ryan tried to control his rage as he looked at the multitude of open wounds. Her hands were tied, along with her ankles, which were bound wide apart to the metal legs. She looked close to death. She was bleeding heavily from her mouth; her eyes were dark and sunken. On the floor lay her finger and several toenails. Worst of all was the blood covering her thighs, flowing from her vagina. The surrounding cuts that he could see matched the bloody blades in the half-naked man's hands.

Lenka looked up at him through her cut and swollen eyes and through her equally bruised and bloodied lips she muttered, 'Kill . . . every . . . fucking . . . one . . . of . . . them.'

The Irishman looked at the men and assessed the odds of granting her wish. He could not kill them all and free Lenka. Having released two, maybe three rounds from his pistol, at such close quarters the others would immediately be upon him. To have any chance of escaping with Lenka, he needed to distract everyone in the room. It was their only hope.

The giant, the half-naked torturer and the armed guards were all focused on their commander. It was clear to Ryan that if he could undermine the officer's authority, his men would be rendered ineffectual as least for a few crucial seconds. It would be no easy task. What Ryan did not know was that the officer did not derive his power simply from his rank, but from the knowledge of all those in uniform that he reported directly to Heydrich. This meant that he carried the supreme and unquestionable authority of the Führer.

From the major's reaction in those few brief seconds, Ryan knew he was a man who required total control over

288

everything. His cold demeanour suggested that he was not one to give that up by letting his emotions take over.

Cerberus wiped the blood from the pliers he had used to extract Lenka's nails with another of his favourite souvenirs: a white linen handkerchief.

'Kill me, and my men will shoot the Jew whore.'

'That will give me time to put a bullet in each one of them.'

As Ryan made his way slowly over to Lenka, Rerck drew his Luger from his holster to add to the two machine guns already trained on Ryan.

'I'm in no rush to die. Take her,' declared the major, while doing the opposite by indicating to the bare-chested man with the nod of a head to stand in front of the door.

Ryan kept his glacial blue eyes and pistol aimed at the officer who wiping the blood from his long, pale fingers. Kneeling beside Lenka, he slipped off his battered black leather jacket, while moving the gun to his other hand. He draped it around her shoulders and began to cut the bindings around her wrists with his knife. As he did so, he pivoted the barrel of the Welrod at the major's face, for despite his bodyguard's immense size, the Irishman could still see the lower half of the man through the giant's legs. Then, he delicately slipped Lenka's canvas trousers back up her legs and gently eased them over the damage that he could see to her pelvis. Lenka swallowed and nodded, to confirm that she was willing to be lifted. Ryan did so while retaining his silencer aimed at the major. He had never wanted to kill anyone as much as he wanted to now.

'Your concern for the Jewess will be your downfall. You are from that rare breed of men, who refuse to let physical pain stop you. Only death will serve that purpose. However, you can be hurt by witnessing the pain of those close to you.' Cerberus lifted the cup and was about to take a sip when he remembered it was cold. 'How forgetful of me.'

Ryan caught his first proper look at the officer's face. A smile appeared on what looked like a skull, as his skin was so tightly stretched over his face it was translucent. The bodyguard adjusted his stance, and the major disappeared once more from view. 'But know this, Englander: I will hurt you and hurt you as you have never suffered before.'

Cerberus waved the guards forward, to make it clear that Ryan and the woman would not be allowed to escape. The major continued. 'If this was Germany neither of you would leave this cell alive, but we can't embarrass our contacts within the French Government.'

'Friends in low places,' replied Ryan, as he continued to edge his way to the door.

Lenka draped her arms around Sean's neck, but her hold was weak. She whispered, 'Cover my face . . . don't give them the pleasure of seeing my pain.'

The Irishman's jaw clenched as he grasped the woman tightly to his chest. He turned to confront the bare-chested man blocking the door. Ryan had achieved his first objective, and that was by not making any threatening movements or gestures; her captors had allowed him to free her from the chair. But he still had no idea how to undermine the officer's authority. The four men under his command were like Pavlov's dogs, waiting to react to the slightest gesture. But the next few words uttered from behind the giant identified the weakness Ryan had been desperately seeking in the man.

'Before he exhaled his last breath, your Scottish friend asked me to deliver a message to you. He said, that if I should ever meet you, I should tell you that you should treat me with the same respect as he would if he had been granted an audience with the Pope.' Ryan understood and smiled. 'I must say I am flattered. Before you go, let me introduce you to Rerck; he is of pure Aryan stock and is Grossmann's replacement.'

'Grossmann? Was one of your army of psychiatrists?'

'He was my bodyguard. You killed him when you both toppled from my train.'

'Doesn't ring a bell. Was he the one who had to strap you into your straitjacket when the Führer walked into the room so you didn't masturbate yourself to death?'

Cerberus could barely think now; for the first time in his life he was blatantly the object of ridicule of someone he could not silence. It was intolerable, and it took all his control to not leap from his chair to silence the Irishman. A thin wisp of blonde hair slipped from the wax mooring it to his scalp. The unusual warmth rising from his head weakened its adhesive quality.

'Grossmann was the man you killed in the Brandenburg Forest,' hissed the major.

'Ah, another one of your toy soldiers,' replied Ryan, stepping towards the door. As he did so, he was looking over at the inscrutable face of Grossmann's more dangerous replacement. 'I see that good staff really are hard to find, so you have to make do with this living brain-donor here.'

'If you are trying to be funny, your childish humour lost on me; and more so on Rerck, as he does not speak English. However, I admire the British, as our countries have much in common, so I am fluent in the language. He shook his head. 'However, you possess none of those qualities that exemplify the superiority of our cultures. Our meeting is a terrible disappointment as you are sadly only a brutal thug. I expected so much more from you.'

'You don't have that much in that rodent-shaped head of yours either; you got the wrong country for a start.' Ryan was pleased to see that not only was the major rattled, but the men were looking more at their commander than at Lenka and himself. 'Well, I've noticed one thing about you psycho bastards; you have polite euphemisms for murder, torture, rape, enslavement and war. I guess that's what you call culture. You would probably use terms such as deliverance from choice, cleansing of the Volk or some such bollocks! To me you're just another fucking dysfunctional psychopath with a superiority complex.'

Cerberus reclined in the black leather armchair, but the blue veins on either side of his temples betrayed his fury. 'Have you heard that our army has marched into the Sudetenland? And what does your government do?'

'I told you, you prick, it's not my government.'

The blue veins swelled. 'The British Prime Minister has already acquiesced to our demands and signed a treaty with the Führer.' He smiled. 'Did you hear that Chamberlain has declared it "peace for our time"?' His grin disappeared as he looked at the Irishman and the Polish woman. 'Even if I were to allow you to leave this room, soon you will have nowhere to go as your free world is shrinking. Both of you will be consigned to the history books: ones that we will eventually burn. Hostile governments will capitulate in the face of our military superiority while their people will embrace us in return for sparing their lives.'

'A dysfunctional psychopath, see what did I tell you!' replied Ryan, taking another step towards the door.

The blue veins were pulling at the man's eyelids. 'But what do you, your Jew whore, and those other misfits do? You turn to violence like the barbarians that you are. Together you have killed more of my Alpha Wolves than the armies of the lands we have taken.'

'Misfits! Don't be making enemies of us now,' said Ryan, now only a few feet from the door handle; providing he could pass Lenka's torturer and his scalpel.

'Tell me, Englander, why do you help those people? My informant tells me that you are not ordered to do so; it is not for country and nor is it for reward. You have no link to the Jews. Nor can a man of your physicality have any truck with sub-humans, for surely, a man who kills so readily must appreciate that it is the nature of the beast that we eliminate the weak from the herd.'

'No, you're right, it's far more normal to burn someone's eyes out with a spoon, you fucking lunatic.'

'Your language is crude. I expect that from a savage.' Ryan noted that though he appeared visibly calm, anger had entered his voice. 'Do you know the etymology of the name Cerberus?'

'Yes, I looked it up. It derives from the Latin, meaning sexually inadequate lunatic.' The veins throbbing on the Nazi's temples turned a darker blue. 'Now, you're German.

Whereas the Führer, that one-bollocked Looney Tune, is Austrian. I bet he knows some great "Knock! Knock!" jokes? He'd be the life and soul of any party. Of course, at the end of the night, they'd have to return him to his padded cell with you and the rest of the straitjacketed fruitcakes trying to climb the walls with their teeth.'

The major's fury was increasingly evident, as thinner veins burrowed under his eyes. 'Mark my words, Englander, when we next meet, I will slowly skin you for the Jew-loving pig you are. I will set aside some special time for you the day you fall under my hand. It will be soon and when it comes, I will flay your body.' He pointed to the case on the table and the red cloth where his scalpels and pliers had been neatly unpacked and arranged by Rerck. 'However, I will keep you from the point of death while I start to rip the skin from another part of your body.'

'You appear to have plenty of time on your hands, so obviously you don't have a large social calendar, you fucking pointy-headed lizard. But I guess you've got to get your rocks off somehow.'

Cerberus was apoplectic. The worm-like veins turned purple as they pressed frantically against the diaphanous membrane of his forehead. His men, including Rerck, were transfixed for they had rarely seen their commander express emotion and now he was consumed by rage.

'Englander, I will position a mirror, so you will see yourself transformed by my hand into the most hideous creature the world has ever seen. I promise you that I will make it my life's ambition to make sure that you don't die in the process.'

'Really, is that your ambition in life? Not, end poverty,

deliver peace on earth, open up a sanctuary for injured bunny rabbits? Well, one thing is for sure; you're one windy bastard. Know this, that when we next meet, there'll be no fucking around when I get hold of you. It will be Night, Night Vienna!'

Cerberus' voice returned to a monotone level, as if the demon that had possessed his body had taken flight. 'It was foolish of me to lower myself to your depths. Your goading has distracted us and brought you and the whore to the door, but you will go no further.' A smirk drew itself once more across his face, which seemed to frighten the dark purple worms away from the surface. 'It is time that I introduced you to Lanska. He is part of the Alpha Wolves latest intake,' as he pointed towards the semi-naked man whose trousers covered his aroused state.

'Some months ago, my men executed a leading Latvian politician and his family, only after which, did they encounter the man's bodyguards. Lanska was the leader, and aware that his men were no match for us, so he volunteered to join us rather than be killed. To prove his worth, he sliced the throats of his eight comrades one by one with a scalpel.' Cerberus stared at the injured woman. 'As you can see, he excels in its use. This unusual method of execution was brought to my attention when I also discovered that he likes to inflict pain through the private regions of both men and women. Personally, I do not like to look at let alone touch such grotesque body parts – and certainly not those of a Jew. So you see, we complement one another. He is my tool to carry out my experiments in sterilisation – you only have to look done at your woman to judge the quality of his work.'

Now, it was Ryan who was about to lose control. He wanted to grab the scalpel from Lanska's hand and plunge it into the bullet-headed man's skull. He only managed to fight the impulse by pressing her cold face against his through his open shirt. He needed to wait just a few more seconds until he was one step closer to the door – for Lenka's sake.

'Lanska is an example of how we are prepared to absorb those into the Reich from the East, providing they willingly submit to our authority and do our bidding.' The Latvian released a toothless grin. 'Are you aware that members of the SS can be of any religion – apart from Jewish, obviously?'

Ryan ignored him and turned to face Lanska. The major saw the slash and the blood across the back of the Rogue's battle-scarred leather jacket.

'I'm pleased to see that Captain Maurras and his men left their mark on you.'

The Irishman did not answer as he was within arm's reach of the door handle. The man who had experimented on Lenka under his commander's instructions did not try to hide his erection. 'You enjoy your work, don't you?' snarled Ryan.

The semi-naked man smiled and lifted his penis out of his shorts. He waved it at them, before spitting towards Lenka's face. The Irishman swung her to his left to avoid the phlegm, but as he did so, he launched his right steel-capped boot into the Latvian's groin. The man fell to his knees and then onto his side, holding his blood-stained crotch. Ryan saw that he was still clenching the scalpel in his hand. He slammed his boot down on the tip of the handle, sending it into the man's shattered pelvis. The remaining guards were just about to open fire, but Cerberus held his hand up, suddenly aware of the steel plate on the door directly behind the Irishman was. In those few seconds, not once did the barrel of the Irishman's gun move away from the firing line to the Gestapo officer; pinning Rerck to the spot.

Ryan looked at the men to see if any of them would come to the aid of the screaming Latvian on the floor, but their interest was only in the Irishman. He pressed the handle down with his elbow and kicked back with the heel of his boot to fling it open. Before he backed out, he bent down to gather up Lenka's clothing from the dustbin by the door, using the hand of the arm that held her. He still had the silencer trained on Cerberus. Rerck continued to move to block Ryan from taking a clear shot at his commander.

Leaping back into the vast gothic hall, he opened up his weapon. He heard a scream, but he had no idea how much damage he had done. He spun round and slammed the heavy door shut with his boot. With the barrel of his pistol, he rammed the heavy bolt across to secure it. Lenka grimaced as he did so, crunched up in his arms.

'Sorry,' said Sean, pressing his face against hers as if to absorb her pain.

'You still have no idea how to treat a lady,' she whispered.

As Sean carried her slight frame through the hall, he noticed under the soft light that her wounds seemed to cover her entire body. Ryan looked around for anything that he could double-back with to blow up the cell. Machine gun fire pummelled the steel door behind them, reminded him that Lenka's safety was paramount.

He stuffed her clothes into an empty sack by a workbench. Sean lifted her head up and stared into her ashen face. 'The door has steel panels across it, so it might take them a while. Anyway, best that we get out of here. You will have to make do with my jacket until we are far away from here. Then I'll put your clothes on.'

'That's your . . . excuse,' she murmured.

'Behave,' as he kissed her damp hair, detecting signs of a fever.

Sean knew he needed to get her to a hospital quickly. But as if she had read his mind, she spoke very faintly. 'No hospital; that is where they will look first. Just get us to a telephone,' as she handed him a number on a note from the pocket of her short black leather trench coat that was peeking out of the open sack.

'Lenka, you'll be dead before morning if I don't get you to a doctor.'

'Ask for François Marcel, he is my friend Bridgette's husband. Tell him to bring his father, he is a doctor, to "God's waiting room". He will understand.'

'Lenka, why don't I just ask for Bridgette and she can organise . . ?'

She looked up into his warm grey-green eyes. 'She is mute. Now trust me for once and do as you're told.'

Sean nodded reluctantly. Lenka's voice was fainter as she told him where to take her. He pressed her closer, while ripping a curtain from a window with his free hand in one mighty wrench. Sean wrapped it around her shivering body and gently lifted her up. She did not look up, and he feared she had drifted into a coma. Then he heard her mumble,

'You and your bullshit. I would have just got on with garrotting the fucking lot of 'em.'

Outside the grey, imposing former prison, he squinted up at the clock on one of the medieval towers across the street. It was nearly dawn, but it might as well have been midnight as black clouds once more crowded together across the sky and driving rain swept through the desolate Parisian boulevards. With each day there were fewer Rogues, he thought. Jocky was dead, and he did not know if Lenka would survive the night. He held his head up to let the rain pummel his face. There was no sign of a break in the clouds. Sean tucked the leather jacket around the face, and shoulders of the sleeping woman cradled in his arms. He walked as silently as he could across the deserted bridge of Pont Saint-Michel, so as not to wake her.

Chapter 15: Kristallnacht

September 1938, Paris

Sean stood with the injured Lenka cradled in his arms on the edge of the little park at the junction of Avenue du Général Leclerc and Rue Froidevaux. He looked apprehensively at the grey stone building and peered at the deathly pale face of the woman covered in a mix of light rain, sweat and blood. He too was exhausted, having carried her through the backstreets for two hours until they reached the Montparnasse neighbourhood in the south of the city.

'Jesus, this is grim. You wouldn't want to be seen dead here.'

'You'd be surprised,' replied Lenka in a pained, low voice. 'There is no safer place. Very few people know what it is, while those that do fear to enter it.'

He laid her down on the only patch of dry grass he could find under a thick clump of ferns. Having done so, he was about to make his way to the imposing door that led to the vaults twenty metres below, when Lenka produced a long iron key sewn into the collar of her shirt.

'This is where you stayed last night?' She gave a slight nod of her head. 'It looks like the entrance to Hades. What is it?'

'You should read more. It's an ossuary. Beneath us

were once stone quarries.' Talking was exhausting, but she was determined to show Sean that despite her state, her brain was intact, and she refused to be viewed as a victim. 'Two hundred years ago, the cemeteries of the city were full. The authorities deemed them a health hazard, so they made space by digging up all the bodies and transporting them here.'

Sean looked again at the entrance and saw the faded script etched into the stone plaque above the oak door that had been relocated from one of the larger cemeteries.

Cimetière des Saints Innocents.
Fermé 1780.

'Ah, I understand now; we couldn't be in a safer place, as neither of us is permitted to die here.'

He forced a grin as he looked at her, but she did not return it. The Irishman stared down at her wet, limp body and wished he had something with which to dry her. But the relentless rain had drenched the clothing he had commandeered after breaking into a dress shop as they had made their way through the backstreets. Lenka shivered as she clung tighter to his battered leather jacket draped over her shoulders. Her fever had begun.

'For once, can you just do as I ask and take me down the stairwell to the tombs and leave me with my things? Then go to London. You know what you must do.'

'I can't leave you in this godforsaken hole.'

His anger rose as he looked at her blood-soaked canvas trousers, now the jacket had slipped from her and landed in the clingy mud.

'Everywhere we go,' as she tried to keep eyes open, 'is godforsaken. Now shut up and take me down into the catacombs.'

'Christ, I might as well be talking to a mule!'

'They don't have my level of stubbornness. I must have passed out. Did you make the call to Bridgette's house?'

'François said they would be here within the hour as he had to collect his father.' François was Bridgette's husband, a shy, but well-respected young man who was an administrator in the Museé du Louvre. It was he who, four years earlier, had opened the letter sent by Lenka. It was sent on behalf of a mute young woman, Bridgette Marceau, who, it stated, was fascinated by antiquities (she wasn't) and who was soon to leave the orphanage in Krakow and was seeking employment.

'I trust Bridgette and François with my life.'

'You are.'

'She is the curator here.'

Sean looked across at the rain-blackened rust on the lock of the door that led down to the crypt. 'She must be rushed off her feet?'

Lightning announced its arrival, drawing its jagged signature across the sky. Its seething companion, thunder, launched a roar seconds later.

'Look, I don't care if François' father is the best doctor in Paris; I can't leave you here. There has to be somewhere else we can go?' She lifted her hand a little to silence him. 'Bollocks! Last night, you weren't half dead. You need comfort and warmth, not a derelict crypt covered in mould and damp.'

303

Sean watched the stream of water that had formed on what was once a cobblestone path disappear under the forbidding door.

'That's if it's not flooded.'

'Just look upon it as a reconnaissance mission. It might be useful one day if the Germans occupy France again. For now, Bridgette will take good care of me.'

'Lenka, if your injuries don't kill you, infection will.'

Only then did she notice that her hand was inside Sean's open shirt and she had his chest hair in her clenched fist. She released her grip and lifted her cold fingers gingerly up and placed them on his lips.

'Promise me one thing, that when you reach London, you will not tell Ursula that I'm wounded. She will only come here to look after me, putting her life needlessly at risk. I can survive what the Nazis have done to me, but not her death.'

Sean gritted his teeth and acquiesced with a nod. Lenka looked up at the concern carved into every crevice of the Irishman's face and gently placed her hand on his cheek and smiled.

'Now take me down the steps into hell's waiting room.' She pressed her hand harder against the Irishman's cheek and forced a smile. 'Then fuck off!'

November 1938, Berlin

In his austere study in the new Reich Chancery, the Führer repeatedly paced up and down, slapping his hands together with delight. Jubilant at the news of attacks on Jews throughout Germany, he exchanged pleasantries with Hess,

Goebbels, Göring and Himmler. Hermann Göring was as enthused as his leader, as he kept lifting himself up and down on his heels and tapping his white baton into his hand. Goebbels nodded repeatedly, elated at his success in the national media in projecting the victims of their latest atrocity as the culprits. Himmler laughed openly, as he always did when the Führer was pleased. Only Hess remained stoic, almost disappearing into the decor between the dispassionate iron eagles mounted on either side of him.

This was the first time they had gathered since the events of *Kristallnacht,* the Night of Broken Glass, two days earlier. That night, over one hundred Jews were murdered, shops were ransacked, and synagogues attacked with sledgehammers. The murders were reported by the International Press and along with the governments of Western democracies, most charged Chancellor Hitler and the Nazis as the perpetrators. It was a significant development, and delighted Hitler and his Reichsführers, as they no longer needed to conceal their persecution of the Jews (though subterfuge was still required to disguise the means) – as the world united in doing nothing.

December 1938, London

'The words were hardly out of his mouth before the Nazi atrocities upon the Jewish population resounded throughout the civilised world.'

Winston Churchill's speech to the League of Nations Union on 9 December 1938, referring to the Munich Peace Treaty

The day after his speech, Churchill returned to his parliamentary office. As he walked across the Central Lobby, he was accosted by several members of parliament and not just those who sat on the Government benches. They accused him of 'acting like a spoilt child' for remonstrating against the Munich Agreement. Churchill listened to their angry tirades. He enjoyed a robust argument and had come up with a suitable response, but as it was late, and he had more important matters to occupy his time. He decided it was more expedient to tell them to 'Bugger off!'

He sat in his chambers and looked forlornly at the fire, cradling a balloon of brandy in his hand. He had been sitting alone for three hours, when there was a knock on the door. 'Come in Kathleen.'

Kathleen Hill had been Churchill's confidential secretary since he and his wife had first moved into Chartwell. She, like many of those close to him, was devoted to him. This was a considerable help as he often worked late into the night and expected his dictations to be taken down whatever the situation. At Chartwell, she once had to follow him up a ladder to take a note while he was bricklaying.

'Winston, I have been asked to pass you a message from the Foreign Office. They have just heard that—'

'Is it good news? I pray so, as I am starved of it,' barely lifting his eyes to look at her.

'Yes, I believe it is Sir. Our Embassies in Berlin and Vienna have informed us that one of the trains carrying the children that were embargoed by the Germans has been granted permission to leave.'

'Thank God!' said Churchill, slapping his hands on the chair's leather arms and releasing a loud, unfettered sigh.

'Further messages received from our Embassies in Amsterdam and Paris report that it is heading to Channel ports. The Government has ordered ferries to be arranged to transport the children to England.'

'Do we know why the *Narzees* intend to released it? I would find it hard to believe that suddenly they have been imbued with humanity.' His personal secretary shook her head.

'Well, bugger why for now. This is welcome news, but we must exert all our political pressure to free the other train.' Kathleen was used to what she called 'his colourful language'. She closed the door behind her and stood there for a while, pleased that she could finally impart some cheering news to Winston as these were dark days indeed for the 'old man'.

November 1938, Paris, a week after Kristallnacht

The walls of the train carriage standing at the Gare du Nord train station were hidden behind shelves stacked high with bulging files. At the same time in Frankfurt, two further carriages were being adapted to be attached to the train when it next returned to Berlin to accommodate the growing number of documents. Cerberus had initiated a filing system with each document containing information on anyone considered by the Nazis as a threat. The categories were many and were broken down by country: COMMUNIST PARTY MEMBERS; JEWISH LEADERS/BUSINESSMEN; ROMA [PROMINENT];

307

JEHOVAH'S WITNESSES; RESISTANCE GROUPS [NATIONAL & LOCAL]; SEXUAL DEVIANTS [HOMOSEXUAL/ CHILDREN / FETISH / JEWISH SPOUSE]; GOVERNMENTS [DEMOCRATIC] (covering the twenty most powerful countries); GOVERNMENTS [AXIS] (including Japan, Italy and Spain), and DOCTORS, TEACHERS and RELIGIOUS LEADERS (split Christian, Hindu and Muslim).

Cerberus stood on one side of a large table made of Bavarian oak, while nine German officers, all holding the rank of captain, stood to attention around the other three sides. Though they were aware that the major had recently been wounded, nothing prepared the officers for the sight of their disfigured commander when they entered the carriage. With a third of the left-side of his face blown away, his doctors were amazed that he had survived his horrific injuries. Indeed, the surgeons who had rebuilt his skull were even more surprised when their patient ordered them to administer only a limited amount of anaesthetic, so he was conscious when they sawed fragments away from his jaw-bone. Throughout the six-hour operation he never once lost consciousness, keeping his bulging blood-shot eyes fixed on theirs.

Though he had been operated upon by the finest surgeons in Berlin, he was as frightening a sight as any of Dante's Furies. What remained of the skin on the left-side of his face had to be stretched across and sewn up to the remaining skin and muscle on the right-hand side of his face. This meant that when he spoke the skin was pulled down from under both eyes giving the appearance of a body in the initial stages of an autopsy. Saliva continually oozed from his corrupted mouth as it could no longer form a seal – The Englander's bullet had found its man. To reach its target, the bullet had removed most of Rerck's penis and left his testicles as redundant as a cylinder of an empty gun.

His officers stood to attention by the table and paid no heed to the bloodied body at the far end of the carriage. 'You have performed your tasks adequately, but you will suspend all operations. From this moment, you have but one objective,' announced Cerberus, as drool slipping out of the corners of his mouth. The captains of the Alpha Wolves assassination squads were diligently examining the five dossiers that Rerck had laid across the desk. Cerberus continued. 'These three are your targets. The Jew whore and The Englander are already marked for death.' As he spoke, he continued to daub the spittle from his thin, crooked lips with a white linen handkerchief.

The captains present led the Alpha Wolves operations in America, France, Russia, Africa, China, Europe, South-East Asia (including Japan), Italy and Spain. Only the head of operations covering Britain and the Republic of Ireland was absent.

'Now, you may speak.'

Touvier, the new leader of the French section, was the first to do so.

'The Rogues have been the one thorn in our side, but they have no support behind them. I ask with the greatest of respect, is there a need to suspend operations and divert all our resources to kill them?'

'Your mission is to kill them, along with their associates, and to erase all evidence of their existence. Stories are spreading of the Rogues' battles in Spain and our encounters with them. One day they may become a symbol to those who challenge our supremacy.'

Touvier saw an opportunity to impress his commander. 'Major, I wish to volunteer my unit for the task of exterminating them, leaving the other squadrons to carry on their essential work.'

'Your ambition is admirable,' Cerberus said with clear disdain. 'But you risk the same fate as your predecessor, Maurras, who underestimated the danger posed by the Rogues.' He looked at Ferranti. 'As did your former leader, Calvera,' and finally he looked at the equally dead eyes of Tak, captain of the European section, 'and Krüger.'

The major continued to move his eyes clockwise around the large oval oak table. 'The Rogues have gained a legendary status that far outweighs their abilities. Their small victories threaten to bring renewed hope to those who refuse to bend to our will.' The major addressed Tak. 'Do you remember the letter in the hand of the girl you shot after your men burnt down the school on the Czech border?' The head of wider European operations on the continent shook his head, as he could not remember the letter or indeed the girl.

Cerberus once again wiped the froth building up on his twisted lips with the moist handkerchief.

'The envelope was addressed to "Lenka: Nazi Killer". If we discovered a child had written a note to Santa Claus to ask for a toy, we would tear it up and punish the child for its stupidity. That note was challenge levelled at The Third Reich.'

If the officers thought that the major was overreacting or was indeed right to fear a scribbled note from a

310

murdered eight-year-old girl, none of them expressed it. Neither did they acknowledge the trails of saliva dotted across the folders.

'Are you aware of *The Art of War* written by the Chinese general and strategist Sun Tzu?' asked Cerberus.

The officers shook their heads. Cerberus smiled – not that it was possible for an on-looker to discern it – at their ignorance of the military genius.

'Tzu explains the concept of "rapid dominance": to destroy his enemy's willingness to fight through a number of small but selective surgical strikes. These attacks are not for military gain, but to secure a psychological advantage. This is the concept of Blitzkrieg (lightning war) and why our victory in Spain was absolute.'

He stared at the stuffed files on the surrounding shelves. 'Once the Rogues are eliminated, through the information we have accumulated in these files we can return to our mission to release the full force of the Alpha Wolves and eliminate our enemies in one fell swoop.'

The officers nodded without expression as they stared at the bulging lever arch files that decked all the wooden panelled walls of the carriage.

'These files contain the means to rip the eyes from our enemies.' Cerberus smiled at the thought; he had a fascination with eyes as they betrayed what a person was thinking.

'You may have wondered why I released one of the trains loaded with Jewish children?' No one acknowledged that they had. 'Following *Kristallnacht,* we have learnt that the British Government and others are offering financial assistance to support the transportation of these children by train to the West. Kristallnacht has resulted in some sympathy for the Jews, but Goebbels now wishes to undermine any,' he fumbled for the words, 'humanitarian efforts. To fracture this new opposition coalition, the Führer will issue worthless invitations to Western governments to attend peace talks, sending a signal to the world that we are,' he smiled, as he recalled Heydrich quoting Goebbels words, '"reasonable people". The leaders of these countries will be only too willing to convince themselves once again that our ambitions need not concern them. While they busy themselves with peace delegations and drawing up treaties, those who oppose us, like Winston Churchill, will once again find themselves isolated. I have therefore issued the order to release the Vienna train. In the meantime, we will focus all our resources on hunting down the last of the Rogues.'

The major was pleased to see that Rerck had refreshed the pot of tea and brought a fresh handkerchief. The mountain of a bodyguard stood to attention next to the tortured body of a young woman at the rear of the carriage. There was no indication from either his stance or his expression that he had been castrated by Ryan's bullet. The bullet continued on ricocheting off one of the steel plates on the end of the arm of Cerberus' chair, before removing a large section of the major's face.

The major sat admiring the eighteenth-century Mandarin china from a ransacked Hapsburg Palace in Vienna, a gift from Reichsführer Heinrich Himmler. Then, his demeanour changed as the hoods over his eyes tightened. Unbeknown to his officers, the abrupt change in strategy had another influence. Heydrich, the Reichsführer's deputy, had stated his displeasure at the recent failures in New York, Siberia, and Amsterdam. He had summoned Cerberus and made it clear that if the leaders of these unit had survived, he would have had them executed. Cerberus informed his commander that he would have carried out the task personally. However, the major failed to inform his mentor of the recent events in Paris; an operation he had led – his survival now depended on the eradication of the Rogues.

Cerberus lifted the china cup to his corrupted mouth, and before he took a sip he asked. 'Has London gone according to plan?'

'British communication lines are silent, but the leader of our British operations has confirmed that their mission is proceeding exactly to your instructions,' replied Tak.

'Good, now the others will head to their leader, Lenka. Then we will finally have what is left of the Rogues all together.'

Cerberus took another sip of Earl Grey. Most of it dripped from his disfigured lips onto the white handkerchief he held underneath. 'Is everything in position in Paris?'

Touvier added, 'Yes, the Jew whore believes she is undetected in the depths of the Catacombs.'

The major lifted the teacup but stopped. He turned to the woman tied to a steel chair beside his bodyguard, wearing only her thick cotton bra and panties. She had been a "guest" in one of his rooms in the next carriage for the last ten days. Without looking at his captains, he waved them away, giving only a cursory arm gesture in response to their salute.

Minutes later, with a cup and saucer delicately cradled in his hands, Cerberus reclined into a black leather armchair opposite the semi-conscious woman.

'You are indeed privileged that I have brought you here. It is standard practice that Rerck 'evacuates' all guests prior to crossing any borders. However, I have made an exception in your case, even having you brought to my quarters, as I have spent a very pleasant few hours in your company. These are precious moments as I can only speak freely in front of those whose obedience to me is absolute,' nodding towards Rerck, 'and those like you who will never leave this carriage alive and will perish with my secrets. Power is knowledge, it is said, and it is a rare adage as it is true. That is why I have not made copies of the files you see around us. If there were, my influence would be diminished.'

Rerck noted that the major was amused. Though he could no longer register a smile, his commander's right eye would open wider when he was pleased, as the damaged jaw muscle on that side of his face would contract, pulling on the nerves above.

'But from a professional perspective I must say I am disappointed that our engagement has yielded nothing of importance,' continued Cerberus.

He placed his cup and saucer and the fresh handkerchief that Rerck had handed him on the small table. Slowly he picked up a pair of thin black leather gloves and very deliberately pulled them over each skeletal finger.

'You see, I am an expert at extracting information, therefore, I can only assume that you know nothing.' He glanced at her severed tongue that lay beside the cut-throat razor on the table. 'Forgive my little joke,' he smiled, as he turned back to look at the young woman, 'and they say we Germans have no sense of humour.'

Cerberus raised his arm slowly and grabbed the woman's long auburn hair to lift her head. Though near death, her body still shuddered when she saw his face. With his left hand, he lifted the gleaming ivory-handled blade. With his right hand, he pivoted his victim's head at various angles to examine the haemorrhaging vestige where her tongue once was, along with the multitude of abrasions and deep lacerations that covered her face.

Leaning forward, he looked past the swollen, dark blue circles that framed her tear-drained brown eyes. Holding her head up higher by her damp hair, Cerberus dug the silver blade of the cut-throat razor into her skin below her left ear. He drew the naked blade slowly across her smooth, flawlessly white throat. He had cupped his hand over her mouth, but there was no need as death came as a relief.

The major reclined, absorbed by the sight of the woman's body convulsing before she finally fell still. Cerberus nodded contentedly. 'Did you really think I would not find the person who saved The Englander's life?'

The eradication of all those associated with the Rogues had begun – but Sean was never to learn that Sárika had not been allowed to live her dreams.

Chapter 16: The London Affair

November 1938, London

Unrelenting rain had lashed London's streets for over a week. Lieutenant Amelia Brett stood under an umbrella outside the main entrance to Liverpool Street Station. She was in full Naval uniform, a navy-blue double-breasted jacket, tie and matching skirt, white three-cornered hat and well-polished black leather shoes. Her rank was defined by the two yellow bands with a diamond, the laurel leaves on her hat, and the distinctive lace strips above her cuffs. But her crisp white blouse was not the standard starched variety but was handmade of the finest silk, as were her stockings.

Amelia put a great deal of time into her appearance and, as was usually the case, not a man passed her by without taking a sly look over their shoulder or a woman tightening her grip on her companion's arm.

The lieutenant walked up the darkened steps and determinedly made her way across the slippery stone concourse. She stopped when she reached the barrier to platform 13. The lieutenant adopted a firm stance, with her chin up and her hands grasped behind her. She was ready for her next encounter with the man who in the corridors of Old Admiralty House had a new nickname to add to the list – Churchill's Rogue.

The tall, rugged and instantly imposing figure of Sean

Ryan stepped down onto the platform. The lieutenant noticed that he was walking quickly, with purpose in his stride and for once he did not look like he needed medical attention. However, on closer inspection his black and increasingly battered leather jacket had a few more stitches, and one new patch had been sewn right across its back. A few feet away, she saw the grazes across the back of his right hand that held his one item of luggage, a knapsack.

'Winston asked me to collect you from the station. My car is outside, so follow me. It's raining hard, so when we reach it jump in the back along with your *luggage*.'

'My, you have acquired a sense of humour while I was away. They must have summoned the best surgeons in the world to complete that delicate operation.'

The lieutenant ignored his remark. 'You should get rid of that jacket; you look like a tramp.'

'Once again, your kind words are quite overwhelming.'

She looked straight ahead as they marched in silence across the station concourse. They glanced up at the angry sky, before stepping out into the deluge. The lieutenant did not offer the Irishman cover under her umbrella – nor did he expect it.

The lieutenant skipped down the steps, as the rain found a new ally in the strong wind. Sean shouted as he walked unhurriedly behind her. 'A new car. Just for my benefit. You shouldn't have!'

Sean was impressed by the grand and stylishly sculptured vehicle.

'It's a 4.5 litre Bentley. A 3.5 couldn't cope with the additional weight of the modifications I require.'

'You've replaced the drop-head roof with a metal one.'

318

'For my ski rack, as you can see. Skiing is my passion.'

'I never associated you with one,' he said, noting the heavy iron frame secured to the roof that ruined its stately design, rather like a monarch wearing a backpack during their coronation.

She persisted, unperturbed by his remark. 'I also had a Daimler semi-automatic transmission box installed.'

'Incredible!' he added, with an insincere and profoundly exaggerated smile. He leant towards her, adopting a feigned look of bewilderment 'Does that mean it can fly?'

The lieutenant contrived a smile of her own this time. 'It's a pre-determined gear change activated via the foot pedal rather than manually interchanging the clutch, so quickening the gear changes.'

'Fascinating. I'd certainly be impressed if I just read that in a novel,' he said, dismissively.

He threw his knapsack in the back of the car and got into the front passenger seat.

'Still as impertinent as ever,' noted the lieutenant as she got into the driver's seat and pressed the recently added ignition switch to kick the engine into life.

'Why change perfection, I say.'

The lieutenant stared at Sean and for the first time dropped her reserved demeanour. 'I was sorry to hear of the death of your Scottish friend. Do you think it was him who told them that you and "that woman"' (she refused to acknowledge Lenka by her name) were in Paris?'

'I'm sure he told them everything he knew, with a few descriptive comments thrown in.'

His thoughts turned to the task ahead as he gazed out

the window at St. Paul's Cathedral.

Twenty minutes later, the red Bentley drove past Whitehall and pulled to a stop outside the grey, officious building known as Old Admiralty House. A sentry raced down to open the car door as he saluted the lieutenant. Amelia discarded the umbrella, though it was still raining heavily, and with her legs pressed together, she emerged from the vehicle. Standing upright, she walked the way her tutors had instructed her when she was a debutante in a college for young ladies on the Kings Road.

When she reached the bottom of the steps, she shouted at Sean without looking at him, 'Walk this way.'

Despite her skirt being extra tight after having been taken in by four inches, she briskly made her way towards the steps of the building.

'If I walked that way, I'd be in The Guards,' remarked Sean to the sentry.

The soldier looked sternly ahead, not even stealing a glance towards the woman as she disappeared into the mouth of the building. To Sean's surprise, the trooper smiled and replied, 'I've already applied.'

Sean laughed. In his dealings with the English – when they were not trying to kill him – he had noticed that beneath the stunted emotional surface lay a thick stratum of acerbity fractured by rich seams of dry wit.

The Irishman joined the lieutenant who was waiting impatiently in the hall, and together they made their way up the grand staircase. When they reached the landing on the sixth floor, the lieutenant stopped below a painting of Lord Nelson. Pointing to the corridor on Sean's left, she said,

'Carry on walking along the corridor until you reach Room 39. He is waiting for you.'

Sean wanted to wipe the rain from her cheeks. 'Thanks for the ride.'

'It will only ever be a car,' she replied, turning on her heels.

A tall, smartly dressed, arrogant looking young man came out of a side room. He promptly dropped the bulging file he had under his arm as the lieutenant strode past. Sean smiled as he looked down as the man scrabbling around on his knees to collect his papers, while straining his neck to catch another glimpse of the woman before she disappeared down the staircase. The Irishman strode down the hall until he reached the last door. Having checked the room number, he pressed down on the brass door handle. As he entered, he received what he regarded as the most welcoming of greetings.

'Drink?'

'Anything in a large glass, as long as it's not that Alka-Seltzer.'

'It's a sad indictment of the modern world that young men fail to appreciate the finer things in life. Champagne imports a feeling of exhilaration as the nerves are braced, the imagination is agreeably stirred, and the wits become nimble.' He handed four fingers of fine Hine brandy to the Irishman. 'However, that leaves more Alka-Seltzer for me.' Churchill adjusted the watch chain draped across his black waistcoat, as he sat down in one of the armchairs positioned either side of the fireplace. 'Are you up to date with events with Herr Hitler and his cronies?'

'Afraid not. My day job trying to stop the Nazis

mounting my head on a pole outside the Reichstag is a full-time occupation.'

Before taking a sip from his glass, Churchill glared at Sean sitting opposite. 'If my head is ever to join yours, I hope they mount it a respectful distance from such a philistine.'

'Condemnation indeed, that even when someone contemplates their demise their first concern is that they're a respectable distance from my sorry carcass.'

Sean gulped two-thirds of the contents of his glass.

Churchill smiled. 'If that is to be our fate, I will quote the last words of the French revolutionary Danton. He told his executioner to hold his head up to the crowd, declaring that it was worth looking at.' He chuckled, 'They say that the poor fellow was apparently renowned for possessing the ugliest face in Paris.'

Sean raised his glass. 'To Danton,' draining the container.

Churchill's mood was sombre. 'It is a bleak picture. When the *Narzees* marched into Austria unopposed, a further six armoured divisions came under their control. Having pushed on into the Sudetenland, it freed up further German battalions no longer required on the border with Czechoslovakia. They also acquired the Skoda armaments factories. Soon, they will occupy the rest of Czechoslovakia and turn their attention to Poland and after that France.'

The Statesman's face was grey and mournful. '*Narzism* is a monstrous tyranny, never surpassed in the dark, lamentable catalogue of human suffering,' pronounced Churchill leaning forward in his chair. 'And what do we do? Nothing! Instead of snatching his victuals from the table,

322

the German dictator has been content to have them served to him course by course.' Sean had never seen Churchill as angry as he was now.

'However, virtue will conquer such villainy,' proclaimed the Statesman as he reclined into the armchair. 'But it will not be soon.' Churchill met the Irishman's steely gaze. 'Have you seen the newsreel of our prime minister disembarking a plane at Heston Aerodrome waving that worthless document signed by Herr Hitler proudly in the air?' He did not wait for a response. 'A shameful document that reneges on our responsibility to respect the borders of our Czechoslovakian allies. He declares it, "Peace for our time!" What rot!' as he looked towards the unlit coals in the hearth. 'Herr Hitler in turn has said that the Sudetenland was "the last problem to be solved".' Churchill released a grunt. 'You might as well try to sit down with a crocodile and try to reason with it that it should live solely on vegetables.'

The politician was in full flow, deriding the agreement as he had been all week whenever the speaker of the House of Commons had granted him the floor. 'Western democracies have abandoned the Czechs, but this is only the beginning of the reckoning. This is only the first sip, the first foretaste of a bitter cup which will be proffered to us year by year unless by a supreme recovery of moral health and martial vigour, we arise and take our stand for freedom.' He grunted again. 'Did you hear that Chamberlain had declared that Chancellor Hitler is, "a man who can be relied upon"?'

'Due to other pressing engagements, I have not been to the flicks or listened to the radio for a while.' Sean lifted the decanter from the side table to refill their glasses. 'You're still a lone voice, I know that much.'

'Sadly true, my voice is drowned out by appeasers. They call me a warmonger, but I am not. I am too aware of its horrors, but this is a battle that will happen whether we like it or not. When it does, we must fight it with every fibre in our body or die in the attempt.'

'From my encounters with the Nazis, I have seen no evidence that they have an interest in peace.'

'The *Narzees* are a beast of war, dependent on perpetual conflict, otherwise sensible men and women might question their actions and then common sense may prevail.' Churchill took a sip of brandy. His mood grew sombre once more. 'I was sorry to learn of Jocky's death. His father and I were good friends.'

'You're the second person to say that today. I will acknowledge your condolences in the manner he would have wished.' He raised his glass and drained it. The Statesman did the same.

Churchill scanned the walls of the room that he used for meetings whenever he paid a visit to his old ministry. He particularly admired the portrait of the Duke of Wellington, the Iron Duke, as it captured his determination and forbearance. 'This is Jocky's commander's office, you know.'

'Lieutenant commander.'

Churchill smiled, as there was no plaque on the door and no evidence of the occupant's rank that he could see in the office. 'Quite so. An interesting chap, fascinated by espionage and involved in all sorts of skulduggery. The fellow conjures up even more hare-brained schemes than I.'

He continued his conversation with the Iron Duke's fellow countryman. 'And what of the Polish woman, Lenka?'

'She's injured,' Sean said nothing further as he refilled his glass. The Statesman registered the man's clipped response and how he slammed the stopper into the decanter. It was clear that the woman's injuries were severe, and that the Irishman was worried.

'Will you return to the continent?'

'I take the first ferry in the morning.'

'You will try to free the children on the train in Vienna?'

'Yes, but I haven't worked out how.'

'So, why return to England?'

'I have some money, but I need papers and any contacts you have in Berlin and Vienna.'

'Lieutenant Brett will furnish you with money, documents and embassy officials in both cities.' Churchill swirled the contents of his glass in his hand. 'Is this the real reason you returned?'

Sean looked at the man but said nothing as he took a large mouthful from his drink.

'I will not tolerate blood on our streets,' announced Churchill, slamming his fist down onto the arm of the chair.

'As with the war when it comes, neither of us wants it but it won't be our decision where the Nazis will launch their attack.'

Churchill nodded and took a sip from his tumbler. 'When your former boss, Michael Collins, and I worked to secure peace between our two countries, I had hoped we would fight bigger battles together.'

'As I said, I'm not up to date with world events.

Enlighten me.'

'Your Prime Minister De Valera has managed to push Chamberlain into respecting Ireland's neutrality and signed an agreement that Irish ports in the South will no longer be available for our ships.' Churchill looked at the man. 'I digress, but I hope you will not suffer the same fate as Collins and that you will not leave the battlefield prematurely.'

'I'm in no rush to die, but we each fight in our own way in the time we have. As for where the Nazis will launch their next strike, I have as much knowledge of that as I do the timing of my death or its location.'

'You talk of death freely; you do not fear it?'

'I've seen so much of it; the novelties wore off.'

Churchill smiled and nodded before slapping his knee with his hand. 'I will do all I can to help you to steal the Jewish children from the grasp of the fascist claw. Meanwhile, I will continue to try to rouse parliament from its slumber and pray that we have time to build our defences.'

'Have your scientists analysed the plans that we stole from the factory in Amsterdam?'

'Our experts confirm that the *Narzees* are designing a mobile device, but they believe it is some elaborate air pump. As for the horrors that the *Narzees* are perpetrating across Europe, I believe you, but without irrefutable evidence no one will believe me.'

Their business concluded, both men decided it was time to end their meeting as neither had the patience for the niceties of polite conversation. Sean rose, and though he was in far better shape than when they last met, the muscles in his right shoulder were torn and with every movement they tightened on him like an invisible reprimanding steel hand.

Sean smiled as he stared out of the window and glimpsed the Changing of the Guard taking place on Horse Guards Parade. Across the road from it some school children were chasing a family of mallards across the grass in St James's Park.

'I wonder if we will ever meet in more peaceful times?' he whispered, without expecting an answer.

'Sadly, I fear you will never find peace,' replied Churchill, 'but I do sincerely hope that we shall meet again.'

The Irishman said nothing as he held out his hand to the Statesman for the first time. Churchill broke into a huge smile as he accepted the man's hand and shook it firmly. Sean did not turn around before he closed the door made of the finest of British oak behind him. His look may have betrayed his thoughts as he knew – as indeed did the Statesman – that they would never meet again.

Churchill was back in his parliamentary chambers thirty minutes later, after a brisk walk down Whitehall, with his cane swinging in an exaggerated motion like a pendulum on a ship's clock caught in a hurricane. Kathleen was standing attentively by the desk, notebook in hand. Churchill looked out at the view across the river, a scene he found calming, but this time it did not seem to register.

The Statesman had his back to Kathleen, but she knew that his mood was grave, it had been all week. The world had again set its face against him, but she had seen that even when he was at his most depressed – when the 'black dog' appeared – he remained unbowed. The Statesman turned around. 'There is no need to write this down.'

She knew that her employer was about to scatter his thoughts freely. He often did this to help him structure his arguments before he asked her to scribe them.

'I have just been informed that the *Narzees* may release the train holding the children in Vienna. However, I fear this is merely a prelude to war as the march of the fascists will not cease. The Americans refuse to intervene despite Roosevelt's tacit support. Neither will Stalin, as he would happily watch Germany and ourselves tear each other to pieces. If our French allies are not able to withstand the Wehrmacht's advance, we will be isolated. When that time comes, Great Britain and Germany will be like two lions corralled together, with us the weaker. Even worse, we continue to have our back to the beast, which will only entice it to attack. We need more time to prepare our forces. Our army has fewer weapons, our navy has fewer ships, and our air force has fewer planes. Meanwhile, innocent families try to flee their persecutors and are hunted down like game.' He retrieved a cigar from the mahogany box on his desk and lowered the lid.

'Sir, may I be impertinent?'

'By asking if you can be, you clearly have no intention of being so.'

'Sir, is there no hope of averting war?'

'No, the *Narzees* made clear their intentions when they invaded Austria and Czechoslovakia.' Kathleen noted that even in the House he chose to pronounce it '*Narzees*', as if the word had such a repugnant taste that he needed to spit out. 'It does not negate the threat of war because we choose to ignore it.'

'Sir, can the actions of mavericks such as the Irishman make any difference?'

'Your question is framed around a conclusion that you have already reached. But your implication is correct. The Rogues can make no difference in the grand scheme of things. However, that is not Ryan's purpose. He does not seek confrontation or to stymie the Nazi war machine.' He noted her quizzical look. 'I firmly believe this; despite the casualties he has inflicted on the *Narzees*. All that matters to him is to protect the children. If I thought the Irishman was waging some covert war against the *Narzees*, I would severe all contact with him. However, an unintentional consequence of his endeavours and that of the other Rogues has been to expose the unwarranted overreaction of the *Narzees*. They have diverted a considerable amount of their resources to hunt down the Rogues.' The recent events in Amsterdam and Paris have dispelled any doubts he held about the Nazis involvement in New York. 'It is an intriguing development. It shows a fracture in the invincible facade that the Third Reich has so far presented to the world.'

'Forgive me, Sir, but is it a weakness that the Nazis turn more of their weapons on those who would fight back?'

'Yes. Now we know that if you poke the beast, it will abandon its original goal and, in its rage, will turn on the implement rather than the hand holding it. It will involve sacrifice, on our part, but we can now see that the *Narzees'* direction of travel can be diverted. To do so, we must prod it in its most sensitive area.'

'Where is that, Sir?'

'Pride. Their belief in Aryan supremacy and that it gives them the God-given right to dominate all others. Therefore, any opposition, no matter how small, will draw down the full firepower of the *Narzees* far beyond the threat posed. The *Narzees* have shown us that they are prepared to sacrifice everything, perhaps one day even Germany and its people, to save face.' He smiled. 'As for your question, these mavericks as you call them,' he preferred the mischievous connotations that came with the term 'Rogues', 'may make a difference.' Through the mayhem they cause, they may delay the *Narzees*' preparations for the war. Even if it is only by a day, it may save thousands of lives.'

'Thousands, Sir?'

'When the gathering storm unleashes its fury, it will cast an even greater swathe of destruction than the Great War.'

'Sir,' she hesitated but felt compelled to ask, 'when the Nazis attack, can we win?'

'The battle is not to win the war, but to survive it. We are a great, but we are a small nation and we cannot beat them alone. All we can do is stand fast against the Wehrmacht until the Soviet Union and hopefully one day the United States step forward and stand alongside us.'

'Do you think the Irishman and the others will survive?'

Churchill lifted his head to look at the river, but he did not search for succour as there was none to be found. 'No, the odds against them are insurmountable.' He drew on his cigar and blew the resultant smoke out of the open window.

He watched it as it was swept up by the wind, only to be overwhelmed by the rain. 'But no one knows that better than they.'

Sean emerged into the downpour to find the lieutenant standing beneath her umbrella, holding the back door of the Bentley open.

'I hope you haven't been upsetting the old man. Word has it that some members of the Cabinet are pressing him to retire.'

'There's more chance of you bursting into tears at the end of *Gone with the Wind*.'

To the lieutenant's consternation, Sean opened the driver's door and leapt in behind the wheel.

'You can't drive this vehicle,' she snapped.

'Don't worry; I'm sure I'll get it going somehow.' He pressed the ignition button and the rattle of the engine caused the curious pigeons pacing up and down in pools of water to fly off. 'See, easy!' he shouted out as he wound down the window and released the handbrake. 'You're staying then?'

The lieutenant leapt into the back of the immaculate vehicle as Sean drove off. The Irishman looked in the rear-view mirror at the stern-faced woman.

'Where to ma'am, The Ritz?'

'No, they're still cleaning up the mess after the last time you were there. Head straight to Berkeley Square, as I have a house there. You can have Ursula's room, but please be kind enough to leave me with a roof over my head in the morning.'

'Don't ask me to make promises I can't keep.' Sean

pulled out into Whitehall and drove up towards Piccadilly.

'It will be good to see Ursula again,' he looked at the cold eyes fixed on him in the rear-view mirror.

'I hardly see her; she's moved into a flat in Notting Hill with that bundle of nerves, you know.'

'They're young. Weren't you ever reckless at their age?' He smiled as he caught her imperturbable look in the passenger mirror.

'My apologies Ma'am, what was I thinking?'

Sean smiled, as she was also more beautiful now that she was annoyed, as it brought colour to her creamy white cheeks.

Ryan pulled the car into the side of the road on the slope leading up towards Piccadilly.

'You've stopped at The Ritz!' said the lieutenant.

'Jocky left a case for me in the cloakroom,' he said, waving the receipt at her.

The lieutenant snatched the ticket stub from his hand. 'Best I collect it, for as soon as you set foot in the lobby, I fear the staff will try to flee through the windows.'

A half-hour later, Sean deposited the brown leather case that Jocky had left him on the dressing table. He opened it. Inside it was a Walther semi-automatic P38 pistol (surprising, as it was of German manufacture and the latest issue specially commissioned by the Wehrmacht); a Webley MK VI revolver; a British Army throwing knife; and a Sten Mark 11 submachine gun with a 32-round magazine. There was a tag tied to the trigger of the automatic. It read:

'The bullets fly out like ravens from a bell tower, but as with all things, it has a weakness — is sensitive to dirt and jams. Make sure you point the barrel away from you, you thick as pig-shit excuse for a Paddy. Jocky.'

Sean meticulously cleaned each weapon. Once he was content, he reassembled the guns, tested the firing mechanisms and handling of each. Aware of the Walther's tendency to jam, the Webley was his preferred revolver. He also liked its double rather than triple action mechanism. This meant that after each discharge the cylinder automatically rotated to the next round, so there was no need to manually cock the trigger — a safety measure in other guns. Sean loaded it and placed it on the bed.

'Why do you have to bring those into the bedroom? Are you afraid I might disturb you during the night and that you won't be able to fight me off?'

The Irishman looked at the woman standing in the doorway, wearing only a fresh white cotton towel that barely reached around her. It just covered her breasts and was a stretch to wrap around her hips. Sean walked over to her. She gave him that familiar look that bordered between disinterest and patronising. 'I thought you despised me?' he replied.

'That indicates some effort on my part, I would prefer disinterest?' She spun around and walked barefoot towards her bedroom. The sway in her movement as if she were on a catwalk and the enticing bareness of her smooth. Sean rested his head against the doorframe. He released an unintended sigh as she slammed the bedroom door behind her. With a wry smile, Sean returned to Jocky's arsenal.

Sean was not tortured by the fractures in his bones that night. Nor by the nightmares – always accompanied by the unfurled swastika flapping arrogantly above the Fortress – that followed when sleep overcame him. Instead, he lay on the bed looking vacantly up at the two-hundred-year-old cream and gold painted ceiling rose. His thoughts were of how to release the children on the embargoed train in Vienna. But the problem remained. Without the Rogues, even if he freed the train, in his condition it would never reach the Austrian border.

An hour later, Sean raised the revolver he had placed on his bare stomach, to train it at whoever was about to enter. In the doorway stood Amelia, naked, resting her arm against the wooden door frame.

'Will one gun be enough to keep me at bay?' She walked towards him without a further word being exchanged between them that night.

Amelia spread her legs above him and slid down slowly as he slipped easily inside her. He looked up at her firm body. Her porcelain skin did not have a blemish, not a birthmark or mole. Sean remembered the naked alabaster angel that fascinated him as a boy, when he was dragged to church on a Sunday morning. He never listened to the Gospel, the hymns or the gossip that made its way along the pews, but was transfixed by the curves of the statue and the frozen look of piety on its face. Only the blackness of Amelia's pubic hair made her real and confirmed that she was deceitful in one sense; she was not a natural blonde. In contrast, his body was hard, rough and scarred. They were like different species mating. Amelia began to move, finding a rhythm as she lifted her face up and closed her eyes. She drew deeper breaths as she lifted her body up and then pressed down deeper on the shaft inside her. The woman appeared so rapt by the sensations building in her body that she did not notice the glacial blue eyes staring up at her.

Ursula pulled on Paul's hand, but he protested, 'The traffic light is still red.'

'It's dawn and there are no cars anywhere. Quick, let's catch Sean before he disappears again.'

Ursula coaxed Paul to drive across Piccadilly. He steered the little Morris Minor (he could no longer see the point in having his Mercedes-Benz 150 sports roadster shipped over from the Netherlands) into Curzon Street. He drove past the deceptive red brick frontage of Leconfield House and went round the bend in the road leading into Berkeley Square. To his surprise, Ursula seized his arm. 'I was wrong!'

She directed Paul to pull the vehicle into the kerbside and turn off the engine. To the right of them, at the end of the road, were parked four black Wolseley automobiles, the latest edition, the 18. Each of the vehicles contained three men, all wearing homburgs and in various coloured trench coats, which was not surprising as the dark clouds above had formed a tight seal over the city. Their eyes were fixed on the red Bentley parked six hundred yards ahead. Paul noticed nothing as he was trying to hold Ursula's hand while searching for his cigarettes. Ahead of them Ursula saw Sean leave 'Amy's' home, with her following closely behind. She heard the engines of all four cars at the end of the street awaken together. With the aid of her wooden crutch Ursula quickly raised herself out of the car, leaving

Sean's cane on the back seat. She turned to see the four black cars racing full speed along the road. A passenger in the first car leaned out of the window holding a submachine gun.

'Run! Sean, run!' she cried at the top of her voice towards the square which startled Paul. His cigarettes flew into the air.

The driver of the first car had heard her cry out and steered his vehicle up onto the pavement.

Paul saw the car speeding towards Ursula. He dived across the front seat and fell out of the passenger door. As he struggled to raise himself, Ursula pushed him backwards off the pavement. Paul landed on his back on the cobblestone road in front of the stationary Morris Minor. He glimpsed Ursula's frightened face staring at him before the car hit her. In seconds, both she and the black Wolseley were gone. He tried to comprehend what had happened as he lifted himself back up onto his feet. In front of him on the pavement, her wooden crutch lay shattered. The other three Wolseleys sped past and continued into the Square.

Paul saw Ursula's motionless body lying on the road thirty yards ahead of him at the corner of the Square. The car that hit her reversed back to pull up beside her. She did not move, but as he ran towards her, he heard a groan. Before Paul reached her, a man emerged out of the parked car. He walked towards Ursula, who lay at an unnatural angle in a circle of blood gushing from the back of her head and drew his pistol.

Ursula turned her head to look up at the man pointing a gun at her. But before he was about to fire, Paul's anxious face eclipsed the man and the weapon. Pressing his forehead against hers, he wrapped his arms around her face. She heard the four shots. Blood began to flow freely down onto her face, as Paul slowly released his hold. Ursula followed Paul's bloodied face slip as slipped onto her shoulder. The gunman reappeared and again aimed the barrel of a Luger at her. She gently reached her hand up behind her man's blood-soaked, matted hair and lifted her head to kiss a small, unblemished patch on his forehead. She looked up at the impassive face of the man above her, before he emptied the last two chambers of his Luger.

As Sean walked towards the red Bentley parked outside the lieutenant's house, his attention was drawn to the crescendo of engines breaking the silence of dawn. He shouted, 'Get back in.'

He heard a loud, dull thud. He spun around to see in the distance a woman dragged along on the bonnet of a black Wolseley until she was unceremoniously thrown off onto the road as the car sped into the Square. The car came to an abrupt halt, only to reverse back towards the woman. He recognised Paul as he ran; then realised who the woman was. Three black cars sped passed the woman and were heading towards Ryan at maximum speed, obscuring the scene playing out behind them, but he did not need to see what he already knew.

Ryan held his pistol steady and aimed between the cold, dark brown eyes of the driver of the lead vehicle and released the first of five shots. The windscreen exploded along with the back of the driver's head. The car shot across the pavement and came to an instant halt when it hit a police phone box. The passenger behind the driver died instantly, but the other passenger leapt out and crouched behind the front passenger door, opening fire as he did so. It offered inadequate cover. Ryan pumped the last bullet to the left of the middle of the car door, but dead centre of the man's sternum having been framed by the two black brogues visible below. The man behind the redundant shield fell back, having received a bullet through his right eye that punctured a hole the size of a saucer in the back of his skull.

Behind him, Ryan heard Amelia run from the house towards the Bentley, yelling 'Jump into the car!'

She launched herself into the driver's.

Sean stood in the middle of the street and calmly reloaded his weapon as if he were on a shooting range. As he spun the chamber, he focused on the two Wolseleys shooting past the wreckage of the other car. Ryan lifted his revolver as he adopted a firing position. The passengers dangling out of either car released a loud clattering of machine gunfire that forced Ryan to throw himself backwards onto the pavement.

'Ryan, for God's sake just get in the car!' screamed Amelia.

This time he edged his way towards the Bentley, whilst emptying the chamber of his revolver into the charging vehicles. All six bullets hit metal, but not flesh. As he reached the back wing of the red Bentley, he reloaded his gun once more. The drivers of the Wolseleys read the situation and knew that the gunman would target them rather than the engine or the tyres. Without exchanging signals, the drivers expertly synchronised the spinning of their vehicles at right angles to form a black metal wall across the road. The occupants got out and began opening fire. Considering that the assassins had not assumed a stationary position before firing their pistols, their aim was exceptionally good. Ryan knew that his current position was no longer defendable.

Ryan stretched his arm across to the handle of the boot, rotated it, and pulled out the case that Jocky had left for him. He had been impressed with his late friend's selection of weaponry. Ryan rested the case on the ground behind the cover of the Bentley, as he released a few shots at the two cars with enough accuracy to remove a side window from each. That would delay any advance for a minute or so, giving him time to select his weapon. He instinctively slipped the knife up his sleeve and lifted out the Sten-gun – his aim, maximum destruction.

The first spray of bullets to puncture the Bentley missed the fuel tank by inches.

The lieutenant screamed again at Ryan, 'There's too many, get in!' Ryan threw the leather case onto the front passenger seat and to Amelia's amazement he climbed up onto the roof.

'What the hell are you doing up–'

'Just drive and pass me up the weapons from the case when I shout for them,' replied Ryan in a steady voice that belied the mayhem around them.

The six gunmen behind the makeshift barricade stood up and sprayed the Bentley with automatic gunfire. Amelia put the car into gear and shot forward. The back window exploded.

With machine guns blazing, the three black Wolseleys flew out of Berkeley Square after the Bentley, like ravens in pursuit of an exotic bird. As the vehicles raced through the back streets of Mayfair, pedestrians dived to the ground while shop windows exploded above, showering them with glass. Ryan lay down flat on the roof rack and opened up his weapon on the first of the Wolseleys gaining on them. A hail of machine gun fire from the Sten-gun cut through the first of the black cars, fracturing the radiator and exploding the windscreen along with the chest of the driver behind it. It veered into a London plane tree and was engulfed in flames as its passengers burst through its back doors. Their respite was short lived, as the fuel tank had cracked open and the ground they landed on was bathed in petrol. It ignited within seconds.

The other two Wolseleys were gaining. A line of gunfire was released from the weapons behind, puncturing holes into three sides of the once beautiful red car.

With its magazine empty, Ryan threw the redundant Sten into the air. It bounced off the bonnet and cracked the windscreen of the nearest Wolseley. He pulled himself across, so he could lower his head towards the driver's window. 'The Walther,' he shouted down to the lieutenant.

Seconds later, Amelia's hand appeared from the open driver's window, and raised the gun. The speed of the Bentley did not slow as she passed up the weapon. As the Irishman grabbed the gun, he saw that her hand and the handle of the gun were smeared in blood. Wiping the blood off on his thick, navy cotton shirt, he thought of Ursula. 'Bastards!' he roared at the car about to ram them.

What he did next stunned cowed onlookers – already frightened by the sound of screeching tyres and gunfire. Through the streets of the West End, Ryan stood on top of the speeding car, with his feet wedged firmly in the roof rack. No longer hindered by having to use one hand to hold the roof rack to secure himself onto the car, he took careful aim at the two Wolseleys as they continued to levy machine gunfire. A bullet ricocheted off his cheekbone, whipping a strip of crimson across his eyes. He looked again at the blood on the handle of the gun, and despite his blurred vision, his aim was never truer. With both hands steadying his aim, he released four rounds that punched through the broken windscreen and disappeared into the shocked face of the driver. The head of the man behind the steering wheel disintegrated, but he had already slammed on the brakes. The car shuddered to a halt causing the spine of one assassin, who had been hanging half-way out of the passenger window, to snap. Such was the man's strength and resilience that his broken back did not kill him; although the wheels of the London omnibus passing in the opposite direction he fell under did.

The other man was jettisoned straight through the windscreen, and a few seconds later came to a halt when his head collided with a set of railings. The impact ripping his ears off. With his training and extraordinarily high level of fitness, the man might have survived his injuries, except that having hit the fence at over thirty miles per hour his head was hanging limply out the other side of the buckled railings a foot from his neck.

The remaining Wolseley raced up alongside the Bentley, as both vehicles shot across Marble Arch and raced into Baker Street. Ryan had a clear shot at the driver and pulled the trigger. The gun jammed. Ryan pulled the trigger once more, but to no effect. He threw the Walther at the windscreen of the Wolseley. This time his weapon ricocheted ineffectually off the windscreen.

Ryan swung down towards the other vehicle and grabbed the man taking aim, by his necktie. With one almighty wrench, he lifted him out of the passenger window, this despite the efforts of the driver who was pulling him back into the vehicle by his belt. Both men were shocked at the strength of the man on the roof of the other car. They were again surprised when he released the tie of the man – the man who had murdered Ursula and Paul – bridging the gap between the speeding cars, dropping him under the back wheels of the Wolseley. The Irishman withdrew the knife from his boot and threw it as hard as he could at the driver peering at him through the open window. It caught him in the side of his neck. The man threw his hands up to the handle, as he frantically tried to extract it. The assassin behind him threw himself over the driver's seat in a desperate attempt to take control of the wheel. Before he could do so, the car flipped into the air and bounced along the road like a discarded beer can until it exploded, sending metal fragments along with limbs in all directions.

Ryan pulled himself back onto the roof rack, just as a gunmetal grey supercharged Duesenberg SJ Riviera Phaeton shot straight out from a side road ramming into the side of the Bentley. The Irishman flew backwards through the air until he landed on the pavement by the side of Regents Park. He heard the familiar, sickening dull thud of the back of his skull hitting stone; it was the kerbstone that bordered the gravel pavement. Ryan knew his survival depended on remaining conscious. He forced himself to roll over onto his left side. As he did so, he watched the blood that flowed from his head wound disappear between the chipped stones.

The Irishman thought he must have passed out as he opened his eyes to see his battered reflection in the red pool of blood that had formed. Ryan turned his head gradually to his left and on the other side of the road he saw a man standing astride Amelia. She fixed her green eyes on her lover from the night before and gave him a pained look of submission. She opened her mouth, but nothing came out. Her blonde hair had a broad red streak through it. The man astride her placed his foot on her chest, as he raised the Luger towards her head. She lifted her right arm up to cover her face. The man fired one shot as blood erupted over his cream trousers. Ryan stared at the man who turned and strode towards him. He tried to move but was unable. The Irishman turned his head once more to look at Amelia. She was motionless, her face coated with blood-matted hair.

The sound of heavy steps stopped as black, blood-splattered shoes appeared in front of Ryan's face. One of shoes rose, before coming to rest on his forehead. Slowly, it rotated his head until it was facing upwards.

He recognised the man raising the Luger. The Irishman could barely focus on the barrel of the gun pointing at him as he drifted into unconsciousness. Then, like the shutter closing on a camera lens, all was dark. Ryan never heard the gunshot.

Next, the final novel in
The Rogues Trilogy,

The

Darkest

Hour

NOVELS BY JOHN RIGHTEN
ALL AVAILABLE ON AMAZON

The Rogues Trilogy: *Churchill's Rogue; The Gathering Storm* & *The Darkest Hour*

....

The Lochran Trilogy: *Churchill's Assassin; The Last Rogue* & *The Alpha Wolves*

....

The Lenka Trilogy: *Heartbreak; Resilience* & *Reflection*

....

The Englander

....

The Benevolence of Rogues

....

The 'Pane' of Rejection

I hope you enjoyed my novel. Reviews are always welcome on Amazon. If you have posted a review, I have limited edition sets of postcards of The Rogues Trilogy, The Lochran Trilogy and The Lenka Trilogy covers, plus *The Benevolence of Rogues* and *The 'Pane' of Rejection*, which, stocks permitting, are available free of charge including p&p. If you would like a set, please send me a personal message via Facebook, Twitter or Instagram with the name of the novel you reviewed, so that I know which set to send, your name/pseudonym and postal address/ PO box no.

"An author writes in isolation – it has to be. But when they receive a kindly review it brightens their world."   John Righten

What the critics said . . .

The Rogues Trilogy

Churchill's Rogue – The Rogues Trilogy Part 1
December 1937. Winston Churchill asks a former adversary, Sean Ryan, for his help to save a woman and her son. Ryan agrees to help, but on his own terms. They, and other refugees, are being hunted by a specially formed SS unit, the Alpha Wolves. They are led by Major Krak, a psychopath, known by his enemies – he has no friends – as Cerberus.
Ryan encounters a formidable woman, Lenka, and other Rogues who have their own personal reasons for helping those trying to escape their Nazi pursuers. The Rogues were born of struggle, each forged in the flames of the

Irish or Spanish Civil Wars, the Great Depression or the Russian Revolution. We learn how each fought, suffered or lost those they loved.

Despite their bitter rivalries, the Rogues join forces in a desperate race to save as many families as they can. But for each of the Rogues the struggle comes at a terribly high price. Meanwhile, Churchill stands alone, ridiculed by governments desperate to appease the evil stealing towards them.

Thus, begins the story, leading up to the outbreak of war, of the men and women who dare to challenge the Nazis. Churchill's Rogue is the first in a rousing trilogy, followed by *The Gathering Storm* and *The Darkest Hour*, which chronicle the bloody encounters between the Rogues and Cerberus' executioners.

Churchill's Rogue review

"This is British author John Righten's debut novel following the first instalment of his non-fiction autobiography *The Benevolence of Rogues* which brought to the fore some of the real life 'Rogues' he's met during a multi-faceted life spent in some very dangerous places. John isn't someone who has just had an exciting, precariously balanced life; he also has a talent for transferring such existences to the page. Anyone doubting this should certainly read *Churchill's Rogue* – and hold onto your seats!

Churchill's involvement is interesting as, in an era when the UK and US were dithering as to whether the Nazis should be fought or be expeditiously befriended, the future Prime Minister was a lone voice of almost prophetic warning.

Although there are other factual characters appearing (e.g. Himmler and the Fuhrer himself) the most compelling are the fictionalised. Sean Ryan is almost a 1930s Irish Jack Reacher and yet, as much as I love Lee Child's work (and I do love it!), John Righten adds rugged, scream-curdling realism and a pace that would render Jack Reacher an asthmatic wreck.

Speaking of scream-curdling brings us to the most wonderful baddie in the Earl Grey drinking Cerberus. His real name – Major Krak - may give rise to a smirk or two but we don't laugh for long. He enjoys torture and, to give him credit, he's certainly got an imagination for it.

Indeed, earlier I described the novel as 'bloody' and for a good reason; it's definitely not a story for the delicate. However, the intensity of violence isn't for gratification. It reminds us that in the real world shootings and explosions don't just produce a tidy red dot on victims' bodies; death can be a messy business!

The other thing we notice is that this is doesn't suffer from that usual first in series malady, set-up-lull. As we follow the pasts and presents of Australian, Russian, American and British Rogues we back-track them through other conflicts like the Spanish Civil War and the Russian Revolution. The more we come to know them, the more we can't help loving them while also realising why it's best not to get close to anyone in this line of work. We're at the mercy of an author who will kill at will (in literary terms) but having started on the emotional

roller coaster, I don't want the series to end. Bring on *The Gathering Storm* – I'm braced and more than ready!"
The Bookbag (UK)

....

The Lochran Trilogy

Churchill's Assassin – The Lochran Trilogy Part 1
New Year's Eve 1964 and a young Irishman, Lochran Ryan, is being transported by Special Branch to a secret rendezvous with Sir Winston Churchill. Just as he arrives, a sniper tries to kill the statesman. But why kill a man who the world knows is gravely ill? This is the first of many questions that Lochran tries to answer. His quest for the truth takes him from New York, to London and Moscow, where he encounters the most ruthless criminal gangs, including Delafury – a one-man crime organisation – who warns Lochran that a new force is rising that will change the world.

Churchill's Assassin review
"A riveting political thriller. Due the strength of characterization and plotting, the story reels you in immediately. Although Ryan and Churchill make for strange bedfellows, the concept nevertheless works brilliantly. *Churchill's Assassin* is a fine mixture of historical detail, thrilling action, and detailed characterization, making for a riveting spin on one of the world's greatest statesman that will have readers eager to pick up the next

book in the series."
Editor, *Self-Publishing Review* (US)

The Last Rogue – The Lochran Trilogy Part 2
January 1965. After the brutal murder in the orphanage and the bomb attack in London, the young Irishman, Lochran Ryan, is thrown in jail. Now Lenka, the last of the Rogues, must try and discover who was behind the attempt to assassinate her old friend, the dying Sir Winston Churchill – and why?
Meanwhile, crime bosses from around the world assign their best assassins to eliminate Lochran, the one man who has discovered their closely guarded secret.

The Last Rogue review
"John Righten ratchets up the tension quotient tenfold in *The Last Rogue*. Thanks to the novel's strong characterization, steadfast narrative, and solid emphasis on historical relevance, Righten makes his story an irresistible read. The novel can easily be enjoyed as a standalone, but historical political thriller fans will most certainly want to start from the beginning of this dynamic series."
Editor, *Self-Publishing Review* (US)

….

The Lenka Trilogy

Heartbreak – The Lenka Trilogy Part 1

1990. Lenka Brett, a smart but unworldly young Irish teacher, volunteers to deliver medical aid when the world learns of the horrifying plight of children in Romanian orphanages. An English naval officer, Captain Simon Trevelyan, volunteers to be her co-driver. Together, they join a convoy of humanitarian aid drivers known as the Rogues, the last hope for those in areas where official charities cannot enter. Lenka falls in love with one of the drivers, but when the Rogues become the target of mercenaries, tragedy follows and she discovers her lover is not who he appeared to be.

Heartbreak reviews
"Righten's novel is a revealing and emotionally charged account of the political volatility in Romania, where orphanages overflowed with traumatized and abandoned children in the aftermath of dictator Ceausescu's genocidal reign and Bosnia, torn apart by war and hate. As the title of the book suggests, images of such human frailty and suffering indeed cause immense heartbreak, yet Righten effectively uses camaraderie, humour, and bantering dialogue between his characters to lighten the effects of what might otherwise have been a fairly daunting read. There's also plenty of action and several good twists to make the novel work at the pace of a thriller.

Righten's protagonist, Lenka, is compelling from the start. Having inherited many of her dead parents' sensibilities, including a heart condition and a formidable sense of resolve, she's formidable without being menacing, forthright and above all, loyal to those she loves. At times veering towards being overly heroic, she's nevertheless easy to root for - quick on her feet and using her intelligence to outwit her adversaries, rather than resorting to overt violence. Viscount Arbuthnot "Foxy" Foxborough, on the other hand, is the perfect foil for Lenka's serious demeanor. Flagrantly irreverent and always ready with a witty retort, he adds just the right amount of sass and pompousness to an otherwise very serious story.

Heartbreak is both thrilling and poignant, and a strong start to The Lenka Trilogy, with a surprise ending that will have readers asking for more."
Self-Publishing Review (US)

Heartbreak is a work of action and adventure fiction penned by author John Righten and forms the first novel in The Lenka Trilogy. Written for mature audiences due to some moderate references and language, this exciting and enjoyable novel takes place in the year 1990. Taking the form of a recent historical thriller, we follow central character Lenka Brett as she embarks on a mission to give foreign aid to orphanages in Romania. With the assistance of a motley crew of former officers, alcoholics and general lunatics, the humanitarian quest begins, but there are even more dangers than one could imagine as the group is targeted by mercenaries with totally ulterior motives.

Bucharest comes alive in this thrilling work as author John Righten paints a poignant picture of tense political

aftermath, terrible poverty, and a fraught atmosphere that only the bravest souls dare navigate. Lenka is an instantly likable character despite her initial naivety and overconfidence and, throughout the novel, the narration enables us to see right into her heart and connect with her motivations for wanting to help. The more she gets sucked into the dangers of the world, the more formidable and stronger she becomes, adapting intelligently to situations but also remaining vulnerable to tragedy, like anyone else. I particularly enjoyed the inclusion of Foxy, whose witty repertoire lightened even some of the darkest, most grim moments of the tale. *Heartbreak* is a harrowing but also hopeful story that sets up a powerful trilogy: a highly recommended read.
Readers' Favorite (US)

"There are certain periods of history that often feel too close for writers to establish the right perspective, but author John Righten digs into one such recent era with *Heartbreak*, the first installment of The Lenka Trilogy. The 1990s might not have the same distant ring as the 1960s or 1930s - the subject of Righten's two other well-received historical trilogies - but the author's personal experience in critical areas of Romania, Bosnia, and South America during the 1990s provide him with unique insight and a confident pen, making this book a solid start to what portends to be a strong series.
Drawing on those all-too-real experiences, *Heartbreak* is an intense dive into the war-torn hearts of both Bosnia and Romania, seen through the eyes of a teacher

delivering aid to orphanages in desperate need of assistance. Volunteering for such a dangerous task, one that takes main characters Simon and Lenka face to face with tragedy and horror, demands a very special kind of person, and these characters certainly make the cut. Fiercely independent but loyal, confident, cautious and occasionally bristling, the dynamics between this pair make the dialogue in the novel sing, and bring the story to life.

These characters on a mission that few others would undertake, but there is also a relationship developing between them - one of mutual respect and trust, and perhaps something more. Violence and heartache are not strange bedfellows, and Righten manages to weave emotions beautifully well in these pages. The personal reflections for both that are revealed through the narration give the characters real depth, and encourage readers to engage in their lived experience, their shock, and their impassioned responses. Whether Simon is learning about AIDS being spread amongst orphanages as a result of unclean supplies, or encountering places of supposed refuge running out of food or building supplies, readers are brought to the frontlines of a humanitarian crisis.

Some authors stumble and overly romanticize horrific situations, but Righten has a strong clarity of memory, and at times it is difficult to tell where the author ends and the man begins. Such authentic and gripping writing about modern history is uncommon, and *Heartbreak* provides a genuinely powerful experience for readers, particularly those who are unfamiliar with Eastern European conflicts of the 1990s. There is factual history woven brilliantly throughout this novel, demonstrating both a dedication to the truth and a rare gift for storytelling.

This book is an impressively researched and powerfully depicted tale from an author who can write equally well about fictional characters and historical events. While John Righten proved his storytelling mettle in his previous historical series, The Lenka Trilogy is shaping up to be something far more personal, and for that reason it his most powerful writing yet."

The Independent Review of Books (US)

Resilience, The Lenka Trilogy Part 2 review

Resilience is a work of fiction in the action, adventure, and recent history sub-genres, and was penned by author John Righten. Forming the second novel of The Lenka Trilogy, the work does contain the use of some explicit language and is more suited to mature audiences. We revisit our heroine Lenka in 1992, where she sets her sights on her next mission to provide aid in war-torn Bosnia. Her interpersonal drama continues as secrets are unveiled about a former lover, whilst the brewing conflict spills over and threatens to quite literally explode onto a global scale, with Lenka and her delivery missions right at the center of the storm.

Author John Righten continues The Lenka Trilogy with style and flair, developing the protagonist as our young Irish girl once again finds herself in deep danger and put to the test. One of the things which I really enjoyed about the work was the inclusion of so many other essential characters who aid in her missions, which gives a good sense of how these operations work during wartime. The dialogue too was excellent for conveying the realistic experiences of the piece, and for establishing the time and cultural setting of the work. In terms of the plot, the novel eases us in gently and provides a good catch up from book one, which then rockets towards a very exciting story with plenty of new twists and turns to enjoy. Overall, I would definitely recommend *Resilience* to fans of the existing series and action/adventure stories set in real conflicts.

Readers' Favorite (US) 5-Star Award

....

The Benevolence of Rogues

The Benevolence of Rogues reviews

"Aid worker's missions find unlikely support from prison forgers, gangsters' henchmen and sympathetic police… John Righten has been in the wrong place at the right time since the 1980s. Then, he was in Romania, delivering medical supplies to orphans suffering from Aids. Subsequently he was in Bosnia in the 90s, sneaking in medical supplies and in South America – Brazil, Chile, and Peru – during the 2000s. Righten is now back and has put together his experiences in his autobiography, *The Benevolence of Rogues*."

Hampstead & Highgate Express (UK)

"This is not a memoir for the straight-laced, politically correct or faint of heart: massive quantities of alcohol are consumed, many teeth are knocked out and sarcasm is in generous supply."

Kirkus Independent (US)

Printed in Great Britain
by Amazon

70642710R00210